John
THE BAPTIZER

ALSO BY BROOKS HANSEN

The Brotherhood of Joseph: A Father's Memoir of Infertility and Adoption in the 21st Century

The Monsters of St. Helena

Perlman's Ordeal

Caesar's Antlers

The Chess Garden

Boone

JOHN
THE BAPTIZER

≋ A NOVEL ≋

Brooks Hansen

W. W. NORTON & COMPANY
New York   London

For information about permission to reproduce selections from
this book, write to Permissions, W. W. Norton & Company, Inc.,
500 Fifth Avenue, New York, NY 10110

For information about special discounts for bulk purchases, please contact
W. W. Norton Special Sales at specialsales@wwnorton.com or 800-233-4830

Manufacturing by Courier Westford
Book design by Helene Berinsky
Maps by Adrian Kitzinger
Production manager: Anna Oler

Library of Congress Cataloging-in-Publication Data

Hansen, Brooks, 1965–
John the baptizer : a novel / Brooks Hansen. — 1st ed.
p. cm.
Includes bibliographical references.
ISBN 978-0-393-06947-1 (hardcover)
1. John, the Baptist, Saint—Fiction. 2. Christian saints—Fiction.
I. Title.
PS3558.A5126J65 2009
813'.54—dc22

2009006674

W. W. Norton & Company, Inc.
500 Fifth Avenue, New York, N.Y. 10110
www.wwnorton.com

W. W. Norton & Company Ltd.
Castle House, 75/76 Wells Street, London W1T 3QT

1 2 3 4 5 6 7 8 9 0

To Elizabeth, Theo, and Ada

If I prove myself a student of Yahya-Yuhana, his name will be forever written in my book; If I do not prove myself, then my name will be blotted from his.

—Jesus to John,
from the Mandaean Sidra d Yahya
(Book of John)

Contents

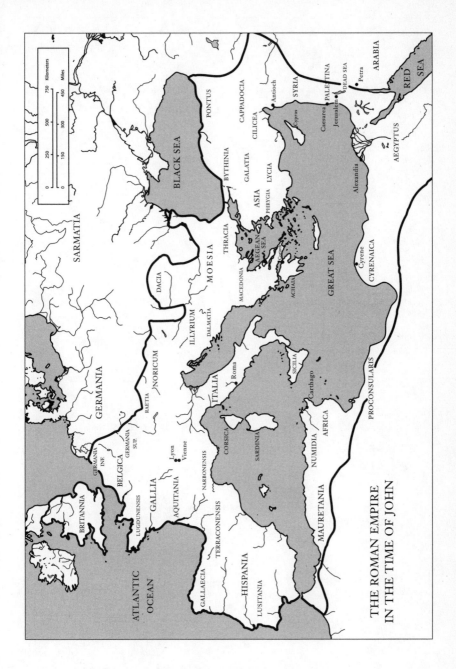

The Roman Empire during the Time of John

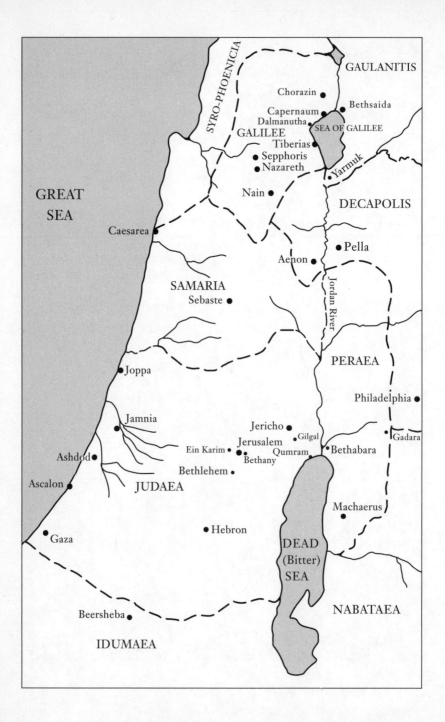

Palestine during the Time of John

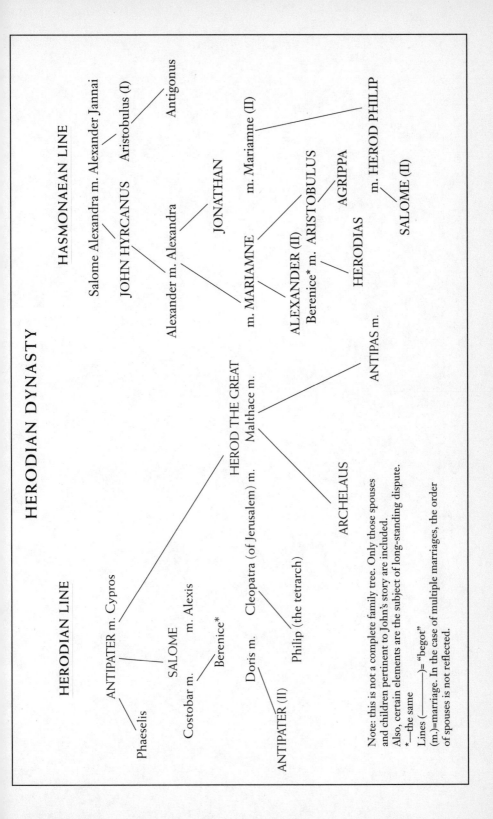

HERODIAN DYNASTY

HERODIAN LINE

HASMONAEAN LINE

Note: this is not a complete family tree. Only those spouses and children pertinent to John's story are included. Also, certain elements are the subject of long-standing dispute.
* —the same
Lines (———)= "begot"
(m.)=marriage. In the case of multiple marriages, the order of spouses is not reflected.

JOHN
THE BAPTIZER

Prologue

JOHN HAD BEEN IN PRISON FOR SIX MONTHS WHEN THE GUARDS came down for him that final time.

And when his head was presented at the banquet hall, after all the guests had seen it and offered their remarks—"how empty," "how dumb" (a "mug," the sultan of Palmyra snickered)—the tetrarch's wife, Herodias, instructed that the servants be sure to bury it separate from the body, the fear being that if the head and the body were buried together, there stood the chance that they might couple again, might recombine and seek some kind of revenge.

"We wouldn't want that." Her eye slid beneath its kohl black stripe, over in the general direction of her husband, Antipas, who was already pale and trembling.

John's disciples came for the remains the following day. They took what they were given, the body alone, and carted it off—some say all the way to Damascus. As for the head, Herodias directed only that it be buried in an "unclean place," and there at Machaerus. The whiff of the prophet's death she did not mind apparently, only the prospect of his return intact.

But ever since that night, the severed head of John the Baptist has haunted Judaea and the surrounding regions, appearing and disappearing in various mountain caves, in tombs and ossuaries on both

sides of the Jordan, from Petra to Harran and all the way to the Phoenician coast. Everywhere the people heard John's voice, worshippers
and excavators and collectors have hid the relic safely here, while others hid it safely there, often at the very same time, their claims conve-
nient to the find.

"The marks upon the tongue, observe—from when the tetrarch's
wife removed the needles from her hair and stabbed him there, to
silence him for good."

Where no such marks were found, no such story was told.

According to another version, there was one member of Herod's
court, a follower of Jesus named Joanna, who was so distraught at the
thought of the holy man's head being discarded that way, she went to
the place the servants had buried it, a makeshift pen where boar were
being kept for a hunt the following day. With her own bare hands she
dug it up from the muck and the urine and the excrement. She set it
in an earthen crater meant for wine and secreted it away along the
northern road, the King's Road, that snaked its way along the eastern
coast of the Bitter Sea, up to where it met the Jordan.

At dawn, just beyond the northern tip of the coastline, she washed
it in a little stream that fed the river from the east, the wadi Abara.
Witnessed only by a bank of thirsty willow trees and the swallows
that made nest there, she gathered up her dress between her legs and
waded out to the middle. It took two hands to push the vessel down,
the waters turning circles around her, sliding over the rim and in. She
did not presume to touch the head, just let the water gush in and sur-
round it, and seep inside the hair and cavities, and lift out all the matted filth and worms and parasites that had been packed down on it.

Slowly the face appeared: the skin a milky blue beneath the undulating surface; the famous wild mane, hair billowing like black silk; the
eyes, wide set and deep, resting beneath smooth lids; the brow, without furrow; the mouth, broad and relaxed; the tongue, which once
had loosed such fire upon the throngs of Israel, now at peace. The
disembodied countenance of near-perfect serenity.

But was this the face of John, Joanna wondered, or of death? She had no way of knowing. She had never seen the man in life.

Among those who know his name, few have ever questioned that John was sent by God. Even the Muhammadans attest that John was the purest of men and therefore great before the Lord. All agree that the truth was revealed to him in the desert and that he came into Judaea to testify so that others might believe through him. They say that he bore witness to the corruption of the day, and the worldliness to which man had fallen prey, but also to the light that he had seen.

Most agree about this light as well, that it was the same that had been revealed to David and to Moses before him, and to Enoch and to Zoroaster and to Adam before them. It was the light that shines in the darkness, the spring of life that flows from the mind of God and that the darkness cannot swallow. On this, people of many different faiths and creeds will still agree.

But where exactly did John see this light? And by what window was it to enter into the world? This is where they differ.

To those sitting on the near side of the river, the answer is simple: John saw the light in Jesus. At Bethabara and then again at Aenon, near Salim, he pointed and he said, "This is the one I have been speaking of. When I said there is one coming after me who was before me, this is he, the chosen one, the lamb of God." John himself was not the light. John performed no miracles. He was a voice calling out into the night, an early cock's crow, attesting to the day at hand. This, they say, is who John was, and this is why—as Jesus himself once said to his disciples—all prophecy was severed with the head of John the Baptist, because John bore witness to him, who was the fulfillment of all prophecy. Whoever denies this, denies John.

But there are two sides to the river, and on the far bank they shake their heads when they hear this. They raise their fingers, no. "Who so believes *defies* John. He listens, but he does not hear. He claims to know, but he was not there."

And they will offer their own accounts of what took place in Jerusalem and Bethabara, and what was seen and heard at Aenon and many other places as well, including Machaerus, where John was kept for those last six months. They will speak of what the jailers heard, the ones who brought him bread and water. Like those outside the prison walls, they too believed John was a prophet, but he did not speak to them of a Lamb, or the Kingdom now at hand. He did not speak to them at all. He prayed, and what he prayed for, according to the only ones who heard him in his final days, was his own forgiveness.

Part One

THE FORERUNNERS

≋1≋

Zechariah

ZECHARIAH WAS A PRIEST AT THE TEMPLE. LIKE HIS FATHER AND his grandfather before him, he made the pilgrimage from Hebron to Jerusalem four times a year, sometimes five: once each for the three great feasts and then again with his order, the course of Abijah, to perform their weeklong turn of service at the Temple.

From Sabbath eve to Sabbath eve, he and all his brethren would perform the various rites and sacrifices that the Lord God Jehovah first asked of Moses' brother Aaron, father of the priestly line. They would conduct the cleansings, the blessings, and the offerings, precisely as they had been described in Torah and then refined and elaborated down through the generations. And though Abijah was but one of twenty-four different priestly orders that came and served in rotation, the Temple elders often remarked the exceptional care with which they went about their observances. Younger priests and novices were brought in to watch Abijah serve, to see how immaculate they kept their garments; how evenly and noiselessly they moved from station to station; how, in perfect unison, they spoke each required prayer and all with the same inflection; how they raked the coals of the sacrificial fire; how they set aside the blackened flesh and delivered the ashes below; even how they washed their hands and feet at the laver, right hand to right foot, left hand to left.

"No time is idle," the elders would say. "No gesture is without ordinance."

Zechariah knew each and every one. He had been taught them, and studied them, and honored them without fault or hesitation: which wood to choose and how to scatter it; how to apply the blood to the stone of the altar; how to choose the lamb and bring it water and bind its legs, first the front and then the back.

"And see how each performs as every other," the elders would observe, for Zechariah and his brethren aspired to this as well, to be no different; to be like vessels, like the chalices and timbrels and salvers they took from the treasury each morning and used for their purpose, then cleaned and polished and returned to their places each night when the day of service was complete.

The novices made note, and none ever ventured to ask why this order in particular should be so consummate. The example of their fathers, it was supposed. And their fathers' fathers. Tradition. What mattered most was their abiding purpose, which was the same as held for every priest of every order, and every son and daughter of Abraham for that matter: to demonstrate their loyalty and their obedience to the Lord God Jehovah, so that He would look down and recognize them and bless them to be fruitful and to multiply, to give birth to nations and reign in the land of Canaan, for the Lord had promised them this, to be friend to their friend and enemy to their enemy, to deliver them from the hand of their oppressors and show them mercy and redeem them, so they might serve Him without fear, in holiness and righteousness all their days.

As for himself, young Zechariah wanted only to pass down, to bestow the privilege of service to a son and see that his son, like him and like his father before him, should love the Lord with all his heart, with all his soul and all his might. Zechariah looked to the day that he would teach his son these very words and talk of them when they sat in their home and when they walked along the way.

This was his most ardent prayer.

≋2≋

Herod the Great

THE KING OF ISRAEL AT THIS TIME WAS HEROD THE GREAT. IT was Herod who, at thirty-three, had finally managed to wrest the Jewish crown from the last infighting heirs of the Hasmonaean dynasty, which had ruled over the land for the previous one hundred years.

But Herod's rise was, in the eyes of many, an apostasy. He had only come to power with the explicit backing of Rome. He bore no Jewish blood. He was no one's rightful heir. There was no law that recognized him, other than Caesar's. There was no will that appointed him, other than his own, of course—and the Lord's, but only if one believed the story he liked to tell his courtiers.

"But it is the truth," he would say, as they leaned in solicitously to hear again. "It happened down there on Tyropaean Way, as this was the quickest route from where my family lived to the home of my tutor.

"Every morning I would pass beneath an old stone bridge, you know the one—beside the cheesemakers—where for a time, I noticed that a strange Essene had seen fit to sit and take the shade.

"I knew he was an Essene, of course, from his tunic, and so although I did bid him good morning from time to time, I made sure to give him a wide berth, as my father had warned me of their kind."

The courtiers all chuckled. The Essenes were actually a most respected sect. They lived out in the wilderness for the most part, in pacifist communes where they did nothing but work, eat, sleep, and pray. They ate no meat, they had no possessions and no families, and in these respects were thought by many to be the "purest" of Jews. Yet for these same reasons—because they guarded their knowledge, rejected the Temple and the calendar, because they did not pass down their faith by blood but rather drafted their membership from the street—the Essenes were also deemed to be somewhat strange and threatening. The courtiers could well understand young Herod's apprehension.

"One morning, however," the king continued, "I could not help but note in passing that this man stepped farther out, bowed farther down, and called me 'Sire.'

"Being of sensitive age, I assumed that he was making fun and so continued on my way. But the following day there he was again, and once again I could clearly hear him say 'sire' as I passed.

"This time I stopped. 'Why do you call me this?'

"'Why? Because,' he said, 'you will be king of all the Jews someday.'"

The courtiers stood back, as if hearing this for the very first time.

"This did not seem possible," the king continued. "I said, 'You must have me mistaken. I come from a common family.'"

And here they clucked their tongues: not true. Herod's family was hardly "common." His father had been governor of Idumaea, his mother was Nabataean royalty. And yet as foreigners—that is, Jews by conquest—no son of theirs would ever be allowed to set his foot inside the Temple, much less serve as its High Priest. And the High Priest *was* the king. The king was the High Priest—at least back then.

"But do you know what he did? This man whom I had never met, never *spoken to* before that day?" Herod would look from face to face, as if anyone there would dare steal his line. "He raised up his hand and *struck* me! He swatted me on the rear, so hard I fell to my knees."

The courtiers gasped, while Herod laughed. "'But you will be king,' he said to me, 'as God has found you worthy!' He said to me not only would I be king—as he had seen it—but that my reign would be a long and fruitful one, is that not so?"

And here the king would turn to him, the man himself, the "strange Essene" who had spanked him lo those twenty-odd ago. Often as not he was standing right there, in the same white tunic typical of the sect. Menahem was his name.

"Did you not say this," Herod would ask, "that my kingdom would be the envy of all men, that I would be a just and pious ruler, and that history would remember me?"

All the court would turn and wait for Menahem's answer, as if it were in doubt, as if it would remotely affect the consensus in the room that the story was a fiction, conceived to lend the sheen of prophecy to a crown that otherwise lacked all legitimacy.

Menahem would allow a quiet nod. Everything His Majesty had said was true, and this *was* true. The story was in no way a fabrication.

The king had simply failed to tell the end.

3

Elizabeth

ZECHARIAH'S WIFE WAS NAMED ELIZABETH, AND SHE WAS BORN to the line of Aaron as well. Like her husband, Elizabeth was faithful to the Book. She gave at the Temple, laid her coins in the trumpets, remembered the Sabbath, and obeyed the commandments without murmur or complaint, always praising and giving thanks to the Lord God of Abraham.

Like her husband, she yearned for a child, but as yet she had not given him one, even after years together, and even though Torah commanded that a man take a wife and beget and multiply like the sands of the sea. She prayed, and prayed again, that the Lord would hear her prayer and bless her womb as He had blessed the womb of Sarah. But moon after moon she bled, and leaf turned to leaf, and still it did not please the Lord to lift her affliction. She felt only pain inside—when she saw the swelling wombs of her cousins, and her pain was doubled that she could not rejoice with them and share in their happiness, but she felt too empty. And when the wives of other priests bore sons who could follow after their fathers in service, Elizabeth saw the faint remove in her husband's eye, the tremble in his hand when he blessed them, and she ached inside. And she ached at the silence of their home and at their table.

Often she went off to the hills alone, but her sorrows only followed her. She went up to the streams where her weeping would not be heard. "Woe is me," she would grieve.

Why was I begot?
What cruel womb would bring me forth
to be accursed before mankind
and all my brothers and sisters?

To what should I be likened?
Where else is my kin?
Not the birds in the sky.
The birds of the sky will multiply
and flock before the Lord.

Nor yet the lowly beasts that graze and bray,
for beasts abound in droves and drifts
and sing thy praises in their way.

Woe is me. Why am I?
Nothing is my kin.
Not the cold dead earth, which crumbles in my hand,
for even it will warm someday
and bring forth fruit in season.

The river offers me no company.
Its waters run and gush with fish inside.
The river's flow observes the tide
and shines in celebration of the Lord.

Woe is me. Why am I?
For woe was I begot,
to be accursed and shunned,
that others might observe
and offer thanks that they are not.

One of the elder priests of Hebron, Ruben, observed the young couple's sorrow. He went to them to offer counsel.

"You should not doubt that the Lord has heard your prayers. The Lord hears all, and He has answered, but you must hear His answer and take heed.

"To you, Elizabeth, I commend the words of Isaiah. 'Sing, O barren,' he has said, 'for more are the children of the desolate than of the married wife.'

"To you, Zechariah, I say much the same, and more. Many a brother have I observed exchange his love of God for the love of his own children and then withdraw from service. But you, having no other charge but to serve and attend unto the Lord, may do so more devoutly than before.

"And if you still desire sons and daughters, then consider the case of your own house. You were not sons of Aaron until the sons of Aaron took you in and treated you as theirs."

This was true. The original course of Abijah was still living somewhere near Babylon, having been among the noble families that chose to remain there even after the captivity was ended. Zechariah's line was adopted into the priesthood only to take their place and to preserve the integrity of David's calendar. That is why they went about their service so mindfully and precisely—as if to compensate in deed for whatever they might lack in blood rite. (That was also why Zechariah had married Elizabeth and why his father had married his mother: so that their sons could be assured and reassured of Aaron's lineage.)

"And so I say to you as well," Ruben continued, "expand thy tent, and drive thy stakes deeper. Think of all the great teachers and patriarchs, all the princes and sages and scribes who took no wife and begot no sons, yet in their wisdom each had sons, and their sons became prophets in Jerusalem."

Zechariah heard what the old priest said. Soon after, he and Elizabeth moved from Hebron to the little village of Ophel in the Kidron Valley to be nearer to the Holy City and the Temple. King Herod had recently decreed that, in light of the damage done during his own siege and the prior siege of Pompey, the people's house should be restored—and not just restored but rebuilt entirely, stone by stone. Yet as only priests were allowed near the Temple, priests were now required to serve as carpenters and masons as well. Zechariah offered his hands, to drag the marble and cut new cedar; to dress logs into beams, and stones into ashlar blocks; to raise pillars, pilasters, and parapets, to join trusses and fit pipes, all for the greater glory of the Lord.

He did more than that, as there were many daily tasks a priest could perform, aside from with his order. A priest must bruise the incense. A priest must count the lots. A priest was required to keep the wine, to bake the bread, and to tend the nests of fowls. A priest must dig the wells, repair the gates, likewise all the veils and vestments. A priest must bless the firstborn sons and favored ones, take the shekels from their mothers (or doves from those without the money). A priest must lay his hands on them and commend them to the protection of the Lord.

A willing priest had many ways to serve, then. Zechariah performed them all, and if he suffered doing so, he gave no sign, not even as he looked upon his brothers and cousins when they came for their turn, how they taught their sons, and showed them the ways and spoke to them in their homes, while his own house remained as quiet as a tomb.

Less fell to Elizabeth, in respect and use. A wife could serve her husband, and she did. A wife could grind the corn at Pentecost or weave silk for the veil (though she herself demurred from approaching the Holy Places, on account of her known barrenness). She could expand her tent. There were children who served at the Temple, who lived above the hollowed caves on Olivet. She could go and pick the hyssop with them and show them how to tie the stems and teach them to be pure. She filled her days, but Elizabeth was not as able as her husband to abide in service. Her service was not so well esteemed.

⋛4⋚

Mary

IT HAPPENED THAT FOR A TIME ZECHARIAH AND ELIZABETH WERE given to care for one child especially, the daughter of Elizabeth's aunt Anne, who was the sister of her mother, Esmeria.

Like Elizabeth's, Anne's womb had been shut for years, and it was thought that she was barren as well. But one spring she arrived at the Temple with her husband, Joachim, and they had brought a daughter with them, a girl named Mary, who was just three.

Elizabeth was overjoyed for her aunt, knowing the hardship she had endured, the loneliness and the sorrow, and the reproach that followed from her prior state. Assuming her aunt and uncle had brought the child to be blessed, she and Zechariah held a feast for them in celebration. And when Elizabeth held the girl, she forgot the pang that quickened in her, to have been abandoned in her fruitlessness. She saw how the roses gathered in Mary's cheeks and how sleep lay pure and peaceful on her brow.

But she also saw that Anne was pale with sorrow. When they were alone again, she asked her why.

Anne confided, "Throughout the years when Joachim and I were childless, I prayed to the Lord that if He would look upon me and lift my affliction, then I would return His gift to Him and offer the child to serve Him.

"We did not forget this vow when Mary was born. We made a sanctuary for her, where nothing unclean would ever enter in, and we made sure that she was cared for by only the most chaste of maidens.

"We did not forget the vow when she turned one. We thought to bring her to the Temple then, but I could not part with her. The same was true when she turned two. I could not let her go. But now the child is three, and I can no longer account for her purity alone or forget my vow . . ." And she left off there, weeping.

Elizabeth understood now. Her aunt had not brought Mary merely to be blessed. She was offering her to serve at the Temple and to be raised there.

Elizabeth tried consoling her. She told her aunt that neither she nor her husband, Joachim, should fear being wholly parted from the girl, that they could come see her as often as she wished, and that when they were not there, they could trust that Mary would never feel alone or without kin, as she, Elizabeth, would care for her and see that she was kept pure and devout, in honor of her mother's vow.

After Anne and Joachim had left, Zechariah arranged a place for Mary among the children who lived above the hollows, and Elizabeth kept her word, caring especially for the girl when her mother was not there. She taught Mary how to pray and how to read and to weave. And she made certain that nothing impure—no ferment, no foul beast, and nothing dead—ever came near her.

When Anne and Joachim came to be with Mary during the feasts, they could see the care Elizabeth had taken. At the Feast of the Tabernacles, when the Temple was aglow with a thousand lights, they watched Mary climb the steps to be nearer the lanterns that the maidens carried.

"Look how she delights," Elizabeth exclaimed. They stood back and watched her dance, and they remarked how she did not once look back at them.

As soon as Mary was old enough, she was chosen to serve. When the pilgrims who had been defiled by death came to the Temple to be purified, it was to the children that they presented themselves. One such child was Mary, and here again she proved how well she had been chosen and prepared. Even the first time she descended to the city, sitting high atop the bull the priests had brought, the people bowed before her. They fell silent at the Pool of Siloam when she paused to fill her cup. They knelt before her at the Beautiful Gate and then again within the Court of Israel. Elizabeth saw the glow in her husband's eye as he took Mary's hand and helped her down from the great beast. He led her to the kneeling pilgrims and walked behind her, watching closely and with pride as she dipped the hyssop into the water and the heifer's ash and, with a gentle flick, swept away the stain of death.

That night Elizabeth took her dowry and her jewels out into the hills again and knelt beside the stream. There she poured her soul out before the Lord, and just as her aunt Anne had done, she made a vow. "O Almighty God," she prayed, "if Thou will only look upon your servant's misery and remember me and give to me a son that I may give to Zechariah, then I avow that we will keep him pure and render him back unto Thy service all the days of his life."

To bind her word, she spilled all her jewels into the water, and she prayed this same prayer every night thereafter.

That glint that she had seen in her husband's eye was no mere reflection. Zechariah loved Mary, and he too counted it a blessing that he should have a hand in raising such a child. Once, when the priests were near completing their work on Herod's Temple, Zechariah hid her inside the folds of his robe and sneaked her in to see.

When some of the other priests were told, they reproached him for bringing a child into the sacred space. Zechariah answered back. "Is it that you fear corrupting the Temple? You should fear corrupting the child," he said, as already he had begun to question whether it was fitting that the people's house should be so gilded and adorned. Had they been less devout in the desert when their tabernacle was a tent?

Sometime later, after their work had moved on to the outer courts, Zechariah was delivering fresh oil to the Holy Place. He was passing through the sanctuary when he saw a shadow in the corner, of some-one small.

"Mary, what are you doing here?"

He could see she was eating something. He went to her. He took her wrist. "What is this in your hand?"

She showed him it was a crust of the shewbread, meant for the Holy Place.

"Where did you get this?"

"It was given me," she replied, "by the woman."

Zechariah did not press. He had heard her speak of her imaginary friends. "You should not enter in this place alone. You should not take what isn't yours."

The girl could see he was disturbed. She took his hand. "All is well, Old Father. Surely the Lord gives to whom he pleases without measure."

That night Zechariah knelt alone and prayed: "O Lord, who hears and knows all things, knows my bones are weak and that my hair is hoary with age, but knows as well that I have never once forgotten thee, or wavered in my prayer.

"O Lord, who hears and knows all things, knows well how I fear for my own house and how it is abandoned by its own children. I only pray, then, do not cut me off! Do not sever me from mine. If my wife cannot give me a son, then grant me one from Thee, who knows best and art the best of all endowers. Grant me a true son, and I shall make him heir to me and to the house of Jacob. Only make him, Lord, one in whom Thou art well pleased."

These were their two prayers, the husband's and the wife's, which they spoke every night, but separately. Neither ever doubted they were heard or that the Lord had answered in his way. No child was born to them, nor did they take in another after Mary, either girl or boy. In time their hopes all died. Their home fell silent. They ate in silence. They slept in silence, a wall between them.

⅀5⅀

Mariamne

OF ALL HIS WIVES, AND HEROD HAD NINE, THE ONE HE LOVED the most was Mariamne. She was also by far the highest born, a purebred Hasmonaean, which was part of the reason he had married her: to cleanse the line, to make it so their children could reunite the crown and the Temple once again, which was paramount.

But Mariamne was also very proud, very worldly and beautiful, with a complexion as pure as it was pale and hair that shone like burnished cedar. Her carriage was open and unflinching, her figure a marvel of proportion and balance. Perhaps most alluring of all, she utterly despised him.

"Scum. Murdering coward." She said this to his face. "Get away. The smell of you makes me gag."

This enmity began early in the marriage, not long after Herod, as a gesture of goodwill, appointed Mariamne's younger brother, Jonathan, as his first High Priest (seeing as he himself could not serve). Everyone had thought this an inspired idea, as Jonathan was another stunning specimen of nobility. Those present said that when he was first presented at the Feast of the Tabernacles, the sacred vestments rode upon his frame as if the Lord had been his tailor. The gilded frontlet shone with the sun's renewed approval. Many priests, as they watched him ascend the ramp of the great stone altar, burst into tears, they were so moved by the sight.

"Because they knew," said Mariamne. "They could see with their own eyes what a true king looks like."

Herod didn't deny it. It was indeed a pity that Jonathan should have met with his accident so soon after the festival, drowning in a swimming pool in Jericho. Mariamne blamed Herod. Herod understood.

He tried to make it up to her. He consented to allow her mother, Alexandra, to come live at the palace with them. He divorced his first wife, Doris, a commoner from Jerusalem, and forbade their son from even entering the city except during religious festivals—all this for the sake of his sons by Mariamne, to let them know they needn't fear any challenger for his affection or his crown. He sent the two boys off to be raised in Rome, to enjoy the friendship of the emperor's family and be educated by the renowned Jew Pollio. They lived like princes, and why not? Herod had been king when they were born, and their mother's blood was as blue as the beautiful Sea of Galilee.

"Not like the bilge that runs in your veins," she would seethe. "And your sister's. 'Princess.' A bunch of Philistines is what you are, and you . . . a petty tyrant, who rides another man's train to power, then cuts his throat for glancing back."

This was reference to another sore subject, her maternal grandfather, John Hyrcanus, the last of the legitimate Hasmonaean kings and the one whom Herod's father had used so deftly for his own advancement.

Hyrcanus had been living in Parthia at the time of Mariamne's wedding to Herod, enjoying his twilight years in the safe embrace of his most loyal supporters. They had pleaded with him not to return to Judaea—for safety's sake—but the marriage of his granddaughter to the new king proved too tempting; to see the diadem upon her head, to set foot again on the land of his people, home of the covenant.

"He should have known," she rued. "The way you think—like a thug. He was too innocent, too trusting."

Maybe so. Hyrcanus had been in Jerusalem for two days when Herod heard rumors that he was plotting to take back the crown (despite the fact that Hyrcanus too was now unfit to serve in the Temple, having been disfigured by his own nephew, who literally chewed the ears from his head before sending him to Parthia). Herod played it safe, charging Hyrcanus with conspiracy and then having him executed.

"And not because he wanted anything." Mariamne fumed. "The crown was no concern of his, but because you knew in truth that it belonged to him."

Again Herod did what he could to distract her from her rage, mostly by expanding and enhancing the kingdom of his heirs, her sons. He brought the region of Samaria back into the fold, as well as Jericho and Gaza and much of the Phoenician coast. And everywhere he ruled he built. There was the new Temple, of course, which included the reconstruction of the entire mount, as it turned out. A new headquarters for the Sanhedrin. The palace. The tower of Antonia. And whole new cities and fortresses. He set to work on Herodium and Machaerus and Julia and Caesarea, which he envisioned someday competing with Petra and Alexandria as a trading center. He even hired Roman engineers to build a brand-new harbor called Sebastos (Greek for Augustus), with ingeniously devised underwater "wings" to control the turbulence of the water.

Mariamne was not impressed.

"You could build an ivory bridge from here to the moon, you'd still be swine."

If Herod's love was such that he could look past his wife's abuse, neither his mother nor his sister was so moved. They resented Mariamne's high chin, her foul mouth, the way she sniffed in their direction. And they had no cities they could build or ports to design, so instead they repaid her insults in kind, with slander and calumny.

Herod could see this in retrospect, how they'd deliberately told lies and sown seeds of doubt and distrust in him.

"But you cannot say you don't provoke, my dear," he later explained, or tried to, standing pathetically outside her chamber door. "They are sensitive about the meanness of their birth. And I only wish you'd see that if they succeed in stoking my jealousy, what else is that but the measure of my passion and my devotedness?"

He waited for an answer—a shift, a snort, a sniffle. Anything.

"With other wives, what would I care? Let them lie with donkeys. But you, my jewel, I confess it, the thought of another man's so much as breathing the air that your precious lungs have discarded—it makes me fitful. Do you not see? Please, please forgive me."

The incident that had him feeling so contrite traced back to a letter written by Mariamne's mother, Alexandra. She had never quite recovered from the drowning of her son, Jonathan, and made a private appeal to the Egyptian queen, Cleopatra, whose sway with Rome (and Mark Antony) was well known.

Cleopatra had been coveting Judaea for some time and therefore lent a sympathetic ear to Alexandra's complaint. She pressed Mark Antony to hold Herod accountable, telling him it was not right, it was not acceptable, that a man like Herod, who was king only because Mark Antony had named him one, should be allowed to commit such crimes against people who were in fact of true and royal blood.

Mark Antony was eventually persuaded—enough at least that on his next visit to Laodicea, he summoned Herod to come and account for himself.

Herod, though still unaware of his mother-in-law's complaint, nonetheless detected the scent of Egyptian perfume, which was cause enough for concern. He knew of Cleopatra's longing for his kingdom and of the role she'd played in the deaths of Ptolemy's son, Lysanias, and the Arab Malchus.

Sensing his anxiety, Herod's sister, Salome, chose this moment to prey on his jealousies. She went to him, claiming knowledge that Mariamne had recently sent some sort of obscene picture of herself to Mark Antony. Salome called her a "harlot," and "false," exposing herself like that to a man like that, who everyone knew could not control himself.

Herod refused to believe it at first. Outside his beloved's chamber, he reminded her of this. "I denied it. I told my sister to be careful what she said, that you were far too virtuous and modest for such a thing, but my sister has a way, as you know, of insinuating.

"And it isn't that I believed her—I did not—but I'll admit a jealous heart beats inside this chest, and given the state I was in, not knowing what was to come of me, how could I be sure? I did what I did, and is what I did so awful? For again, I did not *believe* my sister's lie. I only acted in the event that it *might* be true, which one has to do, after all. . . ."

What he had done was go to his sister's husband, Joseph, a good man, who understood duty and the bonds of blood. Herod had already tapped Joseph to oversee affairs of state while he was away, but in addition to this, he asked if Joseph would be kind enough to look after Mariamne, keep an eye on her.

Joseph said he would. He said it would be an honor, so Herod went a step farther and confided his even more earnest and private desire. He confessed to fearing that he might not be returning from Laodicea—alive, at any rate—and that his fate had already been determined in Mark Antony's mind. But faced with the prospect of death, he said his love for the queen had been revealed to him more clearly than ever; was so burning, in fact, that he could not bear the idea that she would know another after him. So he asked Joseph—in the event that he did not survive this trip—if he would take Mariamne's life.

Joseph balked, as any good man would, so Herod put it more simply: that just as he could not bear the thought of life without Mariamne, neither could he bear the thought of death without her—that is, to be parted from her in any way.

Joseph understood this better and agreed to do as Herod asked, out of his sympathy for the obviously powerful feelings at play, but also his faith that the king was not the sort of man who walked headlong into deadly traps. In either case, with Joseph's word his bond, Herod gathered up the gifts and his best arguments and left for Laodicea.

The tragedy of the affair was how well Herod had chosen his man. Joseph assumed his duties, first as Herod's proxy in government but also as private minder of Mariamne. That meant spending a great deal of time with Mariamne's mother as well. The two women were nearly inseparable, their favorite pastime being to stoke and provoke each other's complaints. They did not curb themselves in the presence of the brother-in-law. On the contrary, they made a show of their misery and hatred for Herod.

"Bloodthirsty coward."

"Smelly mongrel."

Joseph did his best to hold his tongue, but when their complaints turned into outright feminine raillery, he was moved to step forward and defend his king. He chastened Mariamne in particular, telling her that she should not be so quick to question her husband's affection. "The king staggers beneath his passion, truly, so much he cannot endure the thought of life without you. Or death."

The women laughed. They called him too naive, and so again— and only in the king's defense—Joseph divulged to Mariamne what Herod had asked of him in private—that is, if he would deliver her to him in death. He told her this as proof of Herod's love.

Mariamne failed to appreciate the romance. She was furious, her mother too. Not that either of them feared Joseph or considered him remotely capable of carrying out Herod's order. Clearly they did not, for it was at this same time the rumor began to circulate that Herod was dead, that Mark Antony had tortured him first, then executed him. Mariamne was very pleased, but rather than flee Joseph—the man assigned to kill her in precisely this event—she went straight to him and pleaded with him to come with her and her mother. She said they could take haven among one of the Roman battalions and then go present their case to Mark Antony, who would only have to look at Mariamne to recognize the righteousness of her claim and set her on the throne directly, alone.

Her confidence was never tested. A thick bundle of letters presently arrived on Joseph's desk, all from Laodicea and all clearly written in Herod's hand. Far from dead, the king sounded in very high spirits. As it turned out, Mark Antony had agreed with him that to keep interfering in his affairs undermined the authority of the Roman Senate's own decision in crowning him. "A king who must answer for his action to another government is no king at all," Herod wrote. "Those who have given him his authority must stand by their decision and permit him to make use of it."

The end result of the trip had been entirely to the good. Cleopatra had been quieted—Antony had decided to give her Celesyria instead of Judaea—and Herod felt more assured of Rome's support than ever. "Mark Antony and I are friends," he wrote. "I sit with him at hearings. I take lunch with him and enjoy all sorts of other favors from him." He said they even planned to go to Parthia together, after which Herod would be returning to Jerusalem.

Mariamne's plan to flee to the Romans was clearly off.

But not forgotten. As soon as Herod arrived back in Jerusalem, his mother and sister descended on him. Eagerly they told him what Mariamne and her mother had been up to, how they'd planned to take advantage of his death. Worse, Salome took him aside and told him that Mariamne and Joseph had grown much too close to each other while Herod was away, that the two had engaged in intimate and criminal conversation. "A shameless harlot," Salome called her.

"And I did not believe her," Herod subsequently pleaded, still standing at Maramne's door, still begging to be let in. "I did not, as you well know. You know because I came to you directly."

He did. He had found her in this very chamber, preparing for bed. He had been in a state of great agitation, of course, but as usual her beauty disarmed him. Looking at her reflection in the glass, he had been amazed. She was more lovely than his memory would allow.

Still, he asked her, was it true? Had she been intimate with Joseph?

She scoffed. She told him no, don't be ridiculous. She said all the things one would expect an innocent woman to say, that such accusations were false and absurd, the rotten fruit of jealousy and spite.

She used her beauty too. She let him come near enough to feel her warmth, and such is the nature of passion that if it cannot expend itself one way—jealous fury, say—it finds another. He was overwhelmed by longing. He fell to his knees and started begging for her forgiveness. He began making love to her and promising he would never doubt her again. "If my right hand should suspect you, I'll cut it off that day, but I cannot lose you. I cannot bear life without you, as you are the only woman I have ever truly loved."

This—the last phrase in particular—was more than she could stomach. She wrestled him off. "And a fine way of showing it"—she covered herself—"telling your own brother-in-law to kill me."

At this, Herod stopped stone cold.

"That's right," she said. "He told me your plan, how if any harm should come to you, then I should pay with *my* life"—she sniffed—"as tribute to your love."

"Joseph said this to you?"

"Yes, Joseph, who you know as well as I is too good a man to lie."

Herod stood, stunned. "Then it *is* true. Is that his smell on you?"

Mariamne waved her hand dismissively, but Herod was already turning red in front of her, and trembling.

"Why else would he tell you this," he sputtered, "unless he had debauched you in my absence? He would never have divulged what I confided in him unless there had been intimacy. I can smell him."

The logic was not strong, but the emotion behind it overwhelming. To save her from what he might do, Herod left the room. He stalked out into the hall. He started howling and tearing at his hair. Like a wounded bear, he staggered against the pillars, saying things that he should not have. He was stark raving. His mind was a blur, a blank.

"But I do regret it, and I confess, Joseph did not deserve his fate. I beg forgiveness of my Lord—and you, my wife—for such an order if I gave it." He waited, still standing there outside her chamber again, his arms filled with lilies, her favorite. "It is a terrible thing, but I will not beg forgiveness for the cause, or seek some remedy for how you, the very thought of you, does fill my heart to overflowing, flood the banks. But it has been how many days now? Three? And not a word. You must speak to me."

He peeked in. She did not move. She neither welcomed him nor stopped him.

"If I could return, I would," he said, inching closer. "I'd beg his mercy as I beg yours, and he would give it too. Pray, take heed of Joseph and his goodness and the devotion he knew I felt for you, and speak to me. Return my kisses . . . for I shall take them in any case."

She stayed silent behind the veil of her bed.

He set the flowers down beside the rest—the calamus and balsam and marjoram.

She was unmoved.

Still, he could see the round of her hip, the alabaster sheen of her pure skin.

"You must speak to me soon. If you keep this silence, I shall make of it consent. I shall take what's mine if I hear no objection."

He waited. Nothing.

"I have given you all. And more. I would give you everything if you would take me. Speak to me. And if you do not speak to me, I will take, I will."

Still silence.

"And I have told you what silence betokens. That you have forgiven me. That you *will* have me."

Once more he waited, praying for no answer. And his prayer was answered. His heart leaped.

"Oh, thank you! Bless you." He threw aside the veil and fell on her, weeping. "Forgive me."

He flung back her cover. He pulled up her gown. He spread her legs. "And bless you, my dear. I promise. Never, never again will I doubt—"

He kissed her—her hair, her cool, round forehead, her clear, perfect cheek. He kissed her lips. The coldness he could ignore. She had not spoken. She had not eaten in days, she had been so upset.

"You are too good, too good." He pressed against her, rising now. He opened his mouth on hers, hungrily.

But then he stopped, for he could not ignore the taste or the dry bristle of her tongue—like a cat's—and he remembered now. Yes, that was no dream.

As before, Herod staggered off in search of fruit and the strongest ferment he could find, anything to help him forget what he had done: strangling her to death with his own bare hands just before ordering the arrest of Joseph.

And he would succeed, in fact, at forgetting. At least according to the guards, he violated Mariamne's corpse twice more before finally acknowledging what had taken place and allowing her body—moldering by then—to be taken away and suitably entombed.

⪻6⪼

Dreams and Visions

THE DREAMS BEGAN SEVERAL WEEKS BEFORE THE EIGHTH TURN of service, though none of the afflicted priests could say exactly when, as it was the recurrence of the dream that finally brought it to the attention of their waking minds, that and the fact that so many of them were apparently suffering it.

The elements were all more or less the same, as was the sequence. It began with the nighttime sky and the skein of heavenly stars all shining down on Jerusalem and the hills surrounding. One of the stars would suddenly burst loose, pull free from its place and fly down like an arrow, landing inside the walls of the city. The sound would follow—a rumbling and a groaning, "as if the heavens and the earth were grinding out of season," said Ezar. A freezing cold would then descend on the hills. A frost swept across the vineyards, seizing on the children living there.

"In mine," said Ashabel, "the children were in their beds."

"The children *are* in their beds," Zerai agreed.

Smoke would begin to rise from within the Temple—not from the altar, but as if the Temple itself were on fire. As the trail rose up and up, the sky would crack. The hills would shudder and heave, and there would be the star again, down low, but divided now, like little flames, floating above the woman.

"Old Father's wife," said Zerai.

"Yes, they hover over her like a hummingbird—"

"Like a butterfly."

"I saw three," Ezar put in, "but not around the wife. I saw them glowing in Old Father's chest."

Yes, the others agreed it was like that too, their eyes growing wider and wider.

Zechariah was aware of none of this. His own dreams had been relatively undisturbed—that is, until the second morning of the order's turn of service. Sometime before dawn he was awakened in his bed by two of the brethren.

"Old Father," they said, "come with us."

They led him down into a room nearby the baths, the Chamber of the Hearth, where at least a dozen others were waiting, most of them from the order and all with the same troubled countenance.

Simeon, who was then head of the order, went to him and knelt. "Old Father, you must leave the Holy City, you and your wife."

Zechariah looked around at them, confused. "What is the meaning of this?" He wiped the sleep from his eye. "Why have you called me here at this hour?"

"Old Father," said Simeon, "the priests have been having dreams."

"Not dreams," said Ezar. "Visions."

"Visions of portent," said Gureon.

And they proceeded to tell him—of the falling star and of the fire, of the heaving hills and the frost that froze the children in their beds. They told him of the lights that seemed to hover over him and his wife.

Zechariah could see the fear and wonder in their eyes, but he was still confused.

"Since when have priests paid heed of dreams?" he asked.

"But I tell you," Zerai insisted. "It was not a dream. It was a vision, a vision that has been foretold."

"I've heard others speaking of it," Gureon put in, "in the baths. Anan the Elder claims having seen it too. Even Eleazar."

They nodded, all impressed. Eleazar was the new High Priest, appointed only months before.

"You must trust us, Old Father," said Simeon. "If they were only dreams, we would not be here. We would not have sought the meaning . . ."

At this, one of the younger brothers, Tab-Yumin, stood up and presented Zechariah with a parchment.

"From Lilyukh," he said, "the hermit."

Zechariah was still uncertain, wondering if he himself was dreaming, but he took the page over to the lamp and read what was written there.

It said:

> *Woe unto you, ye priests.*
> *Woe unto ye rabbis.*
> *A child from the heavens will be planted, for*
> *Elizabeth shall bear a son.*
> *This child shall be born in Israel, and given Old*
> *Father.*
> *But woe unto ye teachers, and woe unto ye pupils.*
> *Woe to Mistress Torah, for he shall be called*
> *prophet.*
> *And his name shall be Yohannan.*

Zechariah made no show of his reaction until he had finished reading. Then he looked at them. "What game is this? Have you gathered here to mock an old man?"

"We are not mocking," said Zerai. "We are warning you, for your sake and for ours, you must leave Jerusalem."

"Because of this?" He waved the parchment like a rag. "Because of what a wild man has written down?"

"Because we all have seen," said Simeon, now pleading. "Even Eleazar, as Zerai says."

"Eleazar." Zechariah scoffed. "You say this name as if it merits respect—"

"Old Father—"

"—as if the High Priest's office were anything but Herod's closet now, where he can try on this robe and then that—"

"Old Father, take care what you say."

"I take great care of what I say! I say if you are having nightmares, if you are having visions of portent, you need look no further than this Temple to understand the cause. Or at the new High Priest. His mother was a wanton—"

"Old Father!"

"A wanton was she! From far below his father's house, as anyone of age will tell you. And he would have divorced her if he could have spared the hundred staters, but he abandoned her instead!"

"Old Father, you should not speak this way."

"And yet you speak this way to me." He turned to Tab-Yumin, his eyes afire. "Tell me! Has a day passed that I have not looked to Moses? Has a night gone by that I have forgotten my prayer? Yea, has there been an hour I have not honored Torah?"

No, they all shook their heads.

"Then why should I abide this insult, where you take me from my bed and bring me here and speak these lies about me?"

"They are not lies," said Ezar. "And they are not insults. They are good news: a child, planted from heavens—"

" 'A star out of Jacob!' " said Gureon, quoting prophecy. " 'A saber shall rise out of Israel—' "

"Silence!" Zechariah cried." And how dare you torment me with this?" He turned on him, who was father of seven. "I say to you my wife will not bear a son to me. Not now or ever!"

The priests stood back. Old Father had flown into a rage before them. His eyes were filled with tears.

"Show me where the dead are raised that my wife should carry life? Where are the blind given back their sight? Where do the lame walk that my wife should bear me a son?"

"Old Father, take hold of yourself," said Ashabel, who had known him longest. "Sit, be calm and think. Have you forgotten Abraham and Sarah? How late were they in their years, yet they were blessed with sons."

"And what of Elkanah and Hannah?" said Simeon. "Why, if there were no visions in Judaea, then all that Moses said would be a lie, and all the prophets after him."

Old Father turned to him, his eyes still red. "And you would follow such a prophet if he came? You lie to yourself as you lie to me. You say that I must leave because you dream. And what of you? If it were true, if such a one were to come, would you lay down your miter? Would Eleazar remove his frontlet and bow down and drink from his cup?

"Do not wake me with your nightmares. I say to you, neither through me nor anyone shall my wife bear to me a son."

He cast their parchment into the fire, yet even as he turned to go, there were some among them who claimed to see the lights still floating around him, the same as in the dream—like hovering flames, or hummingbirds, or butterflies.

⋛7⋚

The Lilith

OFTEN WHEN ZECHARIAH WAS CALLED TO SERVE AT THE TEMple Elizabeth would travel south to Hebron, as she still had family there.

On this occasion, her traveling party had stopped midday, the second day of the journey south. Most had taken shade to sleep through the heat, but Elizabeth had gone out with her maidservant, Battai, to gather myrtle leaves as a gift for when they arrived.

They were both kneeling in the sedge when they heard a voice calling out to them.

Battai was the first to remark. "My lady, what can this child want, and why is it alone?"

"What child are you speaking of?" asked Elizabeth.

"There beneath the locust tree, calling out to us."

Elizabeth looked again. "How long have we been walking, Battai? Are you awake? There is a woman there. Tall and lean. Her arms are like a mantis's."

Battai shook her head. "It is a child," she said, but when they looked again, there was neither a child nor a woman. There was no one nor any voice calling, only the wind sweeping through the leaves and sedge.

Together they searched awhile, as both were certain of what they'd seen, but in time they gave up and returned to the camp, where the others were just now awakening. When Battai told them what had happened, they shrugged. The day was hot. Heat makes people see things.

When the week was done and her visit at Hebron was through, Elizabeth and her party came back along the same road. They stopped again near to where the locust trees grew, though it was nightfall this time. Elizabeth waited until the others were fast asleep and then returned to the place, just herself. There was no moon, but the stars were brilliant, and this time, alone, she saw neither a child nor a woman out beneath the locust tree, but a wild goat standing there, an ibex, looking back at her with large black eyes and long, notched horns.

It turned and started away. Elizabeth followed it through into the desert and deep into the night, until at length she came upon the coast of the sea and a much more verdant place, bursting with fern and flower, all draped across steep rocks, and surrounding pools and springs. Many of the same goats were there, springing from shelf to shelf as light as beetles. They also had large, unblinking eyes, telling her that she should look down to the shore now.

There was the woman, waist deep in the water, beckoning her to come. Elizabeth descended along the rock. She crossed the sand and entered the water to where the woman was standing. The woman handed her a bowl of water.

Elizabeth knew the sea was bitter, but the woman tilted the bowl, and Elizabeth drank. This water was pure and sweet. And when she had finished it, she lay down flat—again at the bidding of the woman. The surface bore her up like a leaf. Elizabeth looked up at the stars, which all seemed to be looking back down at her, and as she floated there, she began to hear a strange sound, a kind of song coming from on high. It was as if the lights were calling out to one another like birds on distant branches.

"Are these the stars I hear?" she asked.

The wild goats on the rocks replied, "They call out every night. They call out to one another all across the heavens. It is the sound of them praying."

She listened again and it was more clear now, how each one had taken voice and was singing.

How glorious, she thought.

"Did you not know that all things pray?" the goats replied. "Always and everywhere? Only those who are asleep cannot hear, but the pure of heart, they can hear, and they pray with them."

The sound was like a choir now, and as Elizabeth lay there, weightless and unseen, it did not seem possible that anyone could not hear this. Each voice was so clear to her, and yet she understood it was the sound they made together that sang the true name of the Lord.

She lay all night and listened until the first light of dawn. The stars and their hymn slowly faded, replaced by the song of the birds in the trees, the swallows, inviting her back. The woman was gone as well, but Elizabeth could feel how she had been opened, how the water of the sea had healed her, and the water of the bowl had filled her and was still filling her with life, and that it was taking root within her even now.

⥥8⥤

Gabriel

No more was said about the visions the priests had been having or of the hermit's prophecy. The dreams all stopped, and Zechariah did not speak of what had taken place down in the Chamber of the Hearth.

The evening of the Sabbath, the final day of their turn, the brothers all gathered one last time in the Hall of Hewn Stones to choose who among them would offer the incense for the evening service. For all the other duties of service, the morning lots sufficed. Those who'd dressed the altars at dawn would dress them again at dusk. Those who had trimmed the lamps before would trim them again. Those who had offered the first lamb now would offer the last.

The lighting of the incense was different. Signal of the people's prayer, this was the rite to which all the rest, including the sacrifice of the lamb, had been a preparation. As such, the Law prescribed that no priest should know the privilege twice in his life, even on the same day.

So the brethren gathered in the glow of the low descending sun, peering in through the window and reflecting off the polished stones so brilliantly it was as if they had walked inside a giant shell. They formed a circle around the captain of the Temple, just as they had done all week, and just as he had done, the captain counted lots, calling out a number, to which the priests replied by holding up their fingers—either one, two, or three. The captain then tallied them aloud, rounding the circle, hand by hand.

To those who had been down in the Chamber of the Hearth three nights before, it came as no surprise that the final count should land upon the index finger of Old Father.

The captain asked him if he had ever performed the service before. Old Father shook his head no. In all his years of service and all the duties he had performed time and time again, he had never once been chosen to light the incense.

As it was the Sabbath, there was a multitude of worshipers waiting outside, as well as more priests and Levites than usual. All watched with heightened expectation as Old Father slowly ascended the Temple steps, trailed by his assistants, Jaozar and Gamla. Once atop, he took up the hammer and struck the magrephah. A low gong shimmered through the court, cleansing the ears and stilling the minds of all who'd come, while Jaozar and Gamla now turned and made their way first into the sanctuary and then into the Holy Place, to collect the salvers and the bowls.

As they emerged again, the worshipers below withdrew into the outer court. There they knelt together, bowing their heads and extending their arms in front of them, as now a nearly perfect silence descended upon the Temple, all but for the muted shuffle of Old Father's sandals entering the Holy Place, for the first time in his entire life, alone.

The air inside swirled and spiraled around him, adrift with the pungence of cedarwood and cypress, soaked with incense. There were no other doors; a high set of horizontal windows provided what light there was, they and the lamps of the seven-branched candlestick, hovering to the right, flickering in welcome.

He had been here countless times before, of course, to prepare the altars and exchange the bread. He knew the colors and the light, the scent as well as every ornament around him: the wainscoting along the walls, half cedar, half gold; the molded figurations that adorned them, acanthus leaves and lulav. To his left was the Table of the Shewbread, with the pile of salt between two columns of bread; straight ahead, the veil, the light too dim and sifted to make out much of a difference among the blue, the purple, and scarlet. The Altar of the Incense stood chest high before it, though its resplendence too was muted by the dying light and the heavy air, the golden front made visible only by wavering reflection of the candlelight, that and the orange smolder of the coals.

The incense was there, piled on a plate to the side of the altar, and there beside the plate was a silver palette knife.

He knew what he should do, by Law and by instinct, as if the very ethers of the space had somehow preserved the mind and memory of every priest who had ever entered here, and ever would, and made it so that he had only to breathe and the knowledge seemed to subsume him.

He took up the palette knife; he felt the weight. He sank it half-way into the pile and, with a turn of the wrist, cast a first heap onto the coals. A cloud instantly arose, obscuring the holy veil and just as quickly filling his nose and lungs with the thick perfume of galbanum. He cast a second heap; a second flurry billowed up before his welling eyes. He closed them. He raised his hands and readied himself to speak the prescribed prayer: "True it is thou art Jehovah—"

And yet his voice did not come.

He lifted his hands higher. He opened his mouth, but once again his tongue flagged helplessly.

There was someone else in the room, or something. He could feel it as surely as if two hands had taken hold of him. He opened his eyes, and there on the right side of the altar was a light, emanating outward from within the smoke, as would a flame, and yet its glow was purer and more white than that. It did not blind like the sun or burn like flame, and even through his tears, he could see it had taken the form of a man—or a woman; he could not tell—but he knew at once it was the presence of the Holy Place. It was the angel of the face, appearing now before him. And he might have turned away, not feeling worthy of its grace, but just the same as he could not summon his voice, he could not turn his eyes. The light would not be denied or refuted. It was the light that refuted all other light, and it was speaking to him, though again the sound did not seem to flow into the room so much

as rise from within him, with a radiance that was as pure and soothing as the glow, telling him not to be afraid, telling him what he knew
already but had refused to hear: that his brothers had not lied to him;
that what the hermit said was true. His prayer was heard, and he,
Zechariah, would know great joy and gladness now, and many would
rejoice over him at what was to come. The voice even pronounced the
name for him, the name he was to give his son, and it was the same
that the hermit Lilyukh had written.

Zechariah would have covered his ears—the words were much
too sweet, and hope had only ever punished him—but as before, the
angel's voice would not let him turn away. She said to him that for his
doubt, she would appoint the sign: that from this moment he would
be silent. He would not speak or utter a sound until the day her words
had come to pass.

The light then rose and hovered for another moment. Its radiance burst anew, inviting him to look and see the truth. Then just as
quickly it withdrew, was swallowed back into the little wicks within
the lamps and back inside Old Father's galloping heart.

Outside, the worshipers all were waiting with their offerings. The
Levites stood ready with their trumpets and cymbals. The guards, the
Nazarites, and all the priests were still bowed, but glancing up.

Should Old Father not have appeared by now?

Jaozar was concerned as well. He was back behind the golden door,
listening. He whispered through, but hearing no answer, he entered
in to find Old Father on the floor.

He went to him. He called to Gamla. Old Father was trembling
and white. They lifted him up. His legs were weak beneath him. They
walked him from the Holy Place back into the sanctuary.

Jaozar whispered in his ear, "Old Father, can you speak?" He
asked, as the Law required that Old Father offer a final prayer before
the worshipers, to conclude the evening service.

Old Father looked at him, his mouth agape, his tongue a helpless
bird in nest. He could not speak. He dared not speak, for fear that if

he did, then all that he had seen inside the Holy Place would become a dream, and all that he had heard would become a lie.

Nor did he speak that evening at the Sabbath meal. Nor again when he returned to his home in Ophel. But Elizabeth was there when he arrived. She was in her bed, having returned from Hebron, and the door to her room was open.

⚛9⚛

Ein Karim

A STORY WAS TOLD THROUGHOUT THE HILL TOWNS OF JUDAEA, of an older couple who came to live in Ein Karim, a little village just to the west of Jerusalem, balanced but barely on vineyards, terraces, and sloping orchards.

The couple brought little notice upon themselves. Their home was built of stone and looked out across a hushing grove of olive trees, and there was a narrow staircase leading down to where they ate and slept. They were humble and quiet in bearing. Some said the wife was a peasant, though others said no, she was of noble birth, and her husband was a priest. They knew this because other priests often visited him and brought him gifts from the Temple. They called him Abba Zabba, Old Father, and they treated him with great respect, although he could not serve now, as he was mute. He never said a word.

Still, the villagers brought him all the firstlings of their fruit, as they would any priest, and the firstlings of their livestock, which the old couple accepted only to share among their neighbors. Sometimes the villagers came to Old Father with their disputes as well, or questions about the Law. Old Father answered them by writing on a tablet.

In time the villagers noticed they were seeing less of the wife. They glimpsed her out in the groves when the heat of the day had passed, or sitting by the fountain of the vineyard, but otherwise very seldom. Some wondered if she was ill. They asked her young maidservant, Battai, and she said no, that she was well, exceedingly well, and with such a blush that some were now suggesting that the wife was with child. Given her years, this was hard to believe, but had the priests not brought her a lambskin this past visit?

Again they went to Battai and asked her, and this time she confirmed. There was no point in hiding. Her mistress had begun to show.

"How is it possible?" they said.

The maidservant did not know. She was as amazed as they, and yet she herself had felt the child, when her mistress's cousin Mary came to call. Mary was carrying as well. She was not showing, but the glow was in her cheek, and the moment she entered their door, the child in Elizabeth's womb had kicked in welcome. He danced within his mother, as she herself had said, as if he wanted to come and play already.

"He has great life," the servant said.

"He?" the neighbors remarked.

Battai nodded. There seemed to be no doubt

"Then she should rest." The neighbors clucked. "A woman like that."

"But she carries him lightly," said Battai. "Never did a mother carry more happily. Never did a child sit more lightly in his mother."

No midwife was there the day the child was born. Only the maidservant came and testified when it was done, that just as ably as the mother had carried the child, she had given birth and it was a boy.

Eight days later the customary feast was held. All the neighbors came, and several priests as well. They brought gifts of fruit and bread, and when they saw the child, they all were amazed, not just that this woman should have given birth but that she had given birth to this boy here.

How strong he was, how like his father and his mother both, there were no blemishes or imperfections on him, how unlike his father, he cried out with a great voice. The neighbors laughed when they heard.

"But tell us, Old Father, what name have you chosen for your son?"

"Will it be Jacob? So he may teach the Book?"

"Or Zatan the Pillar so that the people may swear by him and never lie?"

"No, no," said another. "Surely they will call him Zechariah, so that he may follow in his father's service and be ready with the Book to give our Lord."

They smiled and looked to him. "Tell us, Old Father, what will his name be?"

Elizabeth answered, saying, "Of all these names, we shall not give him one. His name is chosen, and it shall be Yohannan."

The neighbors were confused. "But is this name found in your family?"

The mother said no. "But Yohannan is the name the Lord has given him."

The neighbors turned again. "Is this true?" they asked Old Father.

He wrote the answer on his tablet: "His name is Yohannan."

The circumcision followed. Again, the child proved his voice, but when it was done and the time had come for the benediction, the guests all looked to the priests in attendance, thinking one of them would speak.

Instead Old Father stepped forward. He took his son into his arms. He set his hand upon the child's head and for the first time since his vision in the Holy Place, he opened his mouth and spoke aloud.

"Blessed is the Lord of Israel!" The first words rasped from his throat, but soon it cleared, and he proclaimed so all could hear.

"For He hath visited and redeemed His people. He hath raised the trumpet of salvation in the house of David. He has spoken through the prophets, that we shall be saved from our enemies and the hands of those who oppress us. He has shown great mercy."

Then he lifted John high above his head. "And you, Yohannan, you shall be called a prophet of the Most High, for you shall go before the

Lord to prepare his way, to tell the children of their salvation through his grace and tender mercy. You shall turn the hearts of children back unto their fathers, and the hearts of the fathers back unto their sons. A new day is come, and it shall light the way for those who live in darkness and in the shadow of death, and it shall lead them in the way of everlasting peace."

Amazed and afraid, all bowed their heads before Old Father. Most of the guests did not understand what he had said. They did not know where the words had come from, only that Old Father had been filled with an almighty spirit when he spoke them.

Even after they had gone back to their homes, they asked each other what was to become of this child, Yohannan. And their neighbors asked the same when they were told, as did the villagers all throughout the hill country. Who will this child be? they wondered, for those who had seen him and those who had heard Old Father speak all agreed the hand of the Lord was surely at play.

≡10≡

The Star

H EROD WAS NOW IN HIS SEVENTIETH YEAR; THE THIRTY-FOURTH of his reign as king of Israel, the second since the blister had appeared, which it did innocuously at first, as an ashy spot the size of a pinhead down on the underside of his scrotum.

He had not given it much thought at first, other than to note its itch, and that the direct application of a warm—or preferably very hot—sponge sent searing bolts of pain out to every extremity, including his navel.

He'd assumed it was this, his helplessness to resist the lure of such exquisite agony, that accounted for the fact that the thing was never really permitted to scab, but continued to fester and to grow to the point where only months removed from its first appearance, he had come to accept it as a basic condition of his existence—like the hump of a hunchback or a cripple's limp. He could not remember life without it, the aching needle down beneath his loins, nibbling away at him, the gentle sewing of mortal dread.

In less than a year's time the little speck had fulminated into more of a festering island, which, though it did not seem to be traveling inward—his testes were apparently unaffected—was expanding across the surface of his body at a faster and faster pace, devouring his flesh and leaving in its wake a pinkish-greenish pulp that, like the little spot that had given it birth, was irresistibly and addictively painful, especially when scratched.

Doctors of various schools had been brought in, but there was little they could do other than offer balms and palliatives that often as not set off more systemic disruptions: a chronic blocking of the bowels, soaring fevers, and withering intestinal cramps, such as those that found him down in his secret commode this evening, the one he'd had installed beside the baths last year; small, but well appointed, with marble seats, and a little canal of warm water running through, between a standing statue of Narcissus on one side of the room and, on the other, his beloved Echo.

Herod was seated, of course. In his hand was a scepter with a sponge fastened to the far end. He dabbed it absently in the canal, only wishing the water were hotter.

He groaned. It had been three days since he'd last passed anything. He thought he'd felt a movement awhile before, but no. Nothing, just the throbbing in his gut.

He leaned down and used the gilded end of his scepter to lift the hem of his robe. He was used to it by now, but the image that met his eye was still a horror. The rot extended halfway down his thighs, and up into his groin. He looked as if he'd sat down naked in a coal fire.

"Just tell me," he said. "I know you know. Is this what does me in?"

He didn't look up. He knew he was there. He could feel him, standing over by the threshold, tall and lean: Menahem, the Essene, the only one truly trusted anymore or allowed to come with him on his nightly rounds.

For the moment Menahem was not answering, though. He seemed to be either standing watch or sound asleep.

"If you would tell me," said Herod, "then I could end my suffering now. I've half a mind as is."

Menahem still gave no reply. He did not need to. They both knew that Herod could not take his life. Not today. The kingdom was in too much disarray. Ever since the business with his eldest, Antipater, and the revelation of all the lies he had been telling, the line of succession had been in flux. Herod had amended the will two times already, and he still wasn't sure he'd decided correctly.

He lifted the sponge and without thinking applied it directly to his wound. A wormy shiver instantly shot through him, down into the soles of his feet—exquisite and excruciating, the stems were all so deep inside. He moaned and shuddered and dug the sponge in harder, as if he could exhaust the pain this way, by enduring all of it at once.

In some ways it worked. The moment he removed the sponge was one of inexpressible relief and release; more than once the maneuver had caused him to evacuate, but apparently not this time. Only tears and sweat—

"Sire?"

And heaving breath.

"Sire?"

And stringy drool. He looked up, only just now hearing, the buzzing in his head was so loud. It was his steward, Pannaeus, standing there between the marble lovers.

"Are you all right, sire?"

"No." He slumped further. The muscles in his stomach were sore from clenching.

"I only came to let you know, Your Majesty, the room is ready."

"Which?"

"The Cedar."

"The Cedar? No. No, no, no. They'll be waiting there."

The steward looked at him, uncertain. Was His Majesty referring to Antipater's minions again, the ones his son had apparently paid to infiltrate the palace (this, according to Herod) and kill him?

"We've posted several guards," said Pannaeus. "We could post more."

No, sighed Herod. He did fear Antipater; that was true. At this point he put nothing past the boy. But it wasn't Antipater who had driven him from his bed chamber this evening, or from the Crow's Nest, or all the way down here.

He would not admit aloud who it was, or what. He only looked at Menahem, who knew very well, but who by that token understood: It did not matter if Herod was here, or in the Cedar Room, or hiding in the dungeon. They would find him eventually.

Herod took a deep breath. "Give me a moment." He used the sponge and scepter to push himself up. Pannaeus came to help him back out to the baths, where another guard, the largest they could find, was waiting. He hoisted Herod up like a child. He set his elbow beneath the crook of Herod's knees, while Herod wrapped his arms around his neck. It was the least painful way.

Together they ascended the back stairs, Pannaeus trailing. Herod spoke to him over the beefy hump of the guard's shoulder. "But are you saying you think there's cause for more," he asked. "Protection, I mean. From Antipater?"

"No, Your Majesty."

"He is still in custody?"

"Yes."

Herod was silent, thinking, as they ascended another flight. "And what of Archelaus?"

Archelaus was another son, and next in line after Antipater, at least according to form. He had arrived the day before, all the way from Rome, they said because he was concerned about his father's health. More likely he had caught wind that Herod was tinkering with the will.

"Asleep," said Pannaeus, "I would assume."

Herod assumed the same, regretfully. He still couldn't make up his mind about Archelaus. He always seemed so glib and entitled, which is why the latest version of the will assigned the crown to his younger brother, Antipas, even though that made no sense at all.

Herod sighed again, as they continued to ascend. The truth was, Herod *wished* Archelaus were up to something. If he could have believed that—that Archelaus was off somewhere bribing someone or plotting to do him in—he'd have considered it a point in the young man's favor.

The Cedar Room, so named for the seven sanded pillars that divided it, was halfway up the highest tower, with a balcony facing south. The sun was still a good hour from cresting, but just in case the king did manage to fall asleep, the curtains had been drawn.

The guard laid him down on the canopied bed, while Pannaeus tried to make him comfortable, propping pillows beneath his knees.

"Did you want to see Prospil?" Prospil was his current physician and a complete imbecile so far as Herod could tell.

"No," he moaned. "Just that." He pointed across at the tea.

There was a bowl already steeping.

Pannaeus poured. Herod drank and waved him away. "Go," he said. "And leave the lamps as they are."

He set his head back down. It was pounding now. He tried to put his mind on something other than the pain and the will, but as his head began to swim, he remembered the hyssop tea was as much to blame as anything. Not only did it leave him in a constant state of urgency, but it had been laced with several other much stronger relaxants and elixirs, which, when they did not succeed in smothering his mind entirely, had the opposite effect, of seeming to render his brain a kind of open wound, sensitive to movements he could not otherwise have seen and voices he would not have heard.

"They are here already, aren't they?"

He turned to Menahem, who had quietly taken a chair over by the curtain. He didn't answer, but there was no need. Herod could hear them, the brothers. They were standing down at the foot of the bed, snickering.

"Cur." That was the elder, Alexander.

"Swine." And that was Aristobulus, taking pleasure in his pain, his every throb and spasm eliciting another snigger or a snort.

"Good," sniffed Alexander. "And again. Yes, that's for all the pain you have inflicted."

Their mother was there as well. Herod could smell the rancid blend of her perfume and death.

"Goatherd."

How was he to sleep with this? It was impossible. He thrashed his way to an upright position, as if clearing a net of cobwebs above his head. "Will I never know a moment's peace?" he cried.

"No," she said flatly.

To the left, a vanity had been shoved up against the bedside. He caught sight of himself in the mirror and groaned. There was a time

he had enjoyed his reflection. Now it was only a reminder of how time
and this disease were ravaging him. Still, he took up the brush and the
jar of henna. He would be breakfasting with Archelaus in just a few
hours. He didn't want the boy getting his hopes too high. He dabbed
the brush into the sticky black and started sweeping it through his few
remaining wisps—briskly, and in clumps. The brothers snickered.

"Look at him. Who does he does he think he's fooling?"

"And don't forget the eyebrows."

"Oh, shut up!" Herod turned, prepared to fling the brush in their
direction, but just then he felt a burning lance down in his loins. He
was apparently peeing again. The urine was seeping into his rot. As he
doubled over, the boys both burst out laughing.

"And you had better get used to it," said their mother, also delight-
ing, "as there shall be nothing but misery and suffering for you—"

"My misery is the sound of your shrill voice, woman."

"Good to know," she said, and she began howling at him like a
banshee. They all did.

"Shut up!"

And sniping and barking.

"Shut up, I say!"

And hissing now.

"Can you not get *rid* of them?" Herod whirled on the Essene, who
was still sitting impassively by the curtain, apparently deaf to the din.

"No, he cannot," said the wife. "Of course he can't. This is destiny,
my dear. And he's the one who warned you, is he not?"

The boys fell silent too, for this was true. Menahem had warned
him, that first day down on Tyropaean Way, though this was the part
of the story that Herod never shared with the courtiers—the real reason that "strange Essene" had smacked him on the rear.

"Remember that sting," Menahem had said, standing over him on
the street, "and let it be a reminder that though you will be king, and
though history will remember you, you will just as surely forget yourself. And when your life is through, be assured your crimes will be
revealed. The Lord sees all, and He will punish you, but with a firmer
hand than mine, I promise."

That was exactly what Menahem had said. Herod never forgot the words, and he never forgot the sting. He certainly felt it now, only magnified and red and swollen and smeared with jagged glass.

"And this is only the beginning," said his wife.

"It's just too bad the people can't see," Alexander seconded. "How they would delight in this."

"They would be giddy," said his brother.

"They will be giddy."

"Oh, quiet, the both of you," said Herod, turning back to the mirror once again. "If you're so clever, why are you not still alive?"

"Why?" The specters both seemed to redden at this and loom in over his shoulder. "Because you *murdered* us," said Aristobulus. "Because you preferred the lies of that conniving bastard son of yours, rather than a true prince!"

"It's no wonder that they laugh at you in Rome," said Alexander. "You are a joke."

"They do not laugh at me," said Herod.

"They do," said Aristobulus. "Have you not heard? That it is safer to be Herod's pig [*huis*] than son [*hos*]?"

"It would funnier if it were not true," said Alexander. "But that is why the people *hate* you. That is why they cannot *wait* for you to die, because you have robbed them of their rightful kings."

Us they meant—themselves—and they *all* were there now. Herod could see them in the reflection: not just the boys but the others as well, hovering behind the dark pillars. Hyrcanus, with his mangled ear. And there was Jonathan, the golden child, sitting in the corner like a pale blue angel.

"Yes, just look at him," spat Mariamne. "That's what the people want. You know it's true because you want it too. You cannot help yourself, how you are drawn to what's pure and noble. You fuck it to try to disinfect your line, but all you end up doing is polluting it with your filth. Or killing it instead."

The boys agreed with nods.

"For make no mistake," the mother went on, "that is what you've done. And not just to the royal line but to the people and to the nation. You have murdered it. You have strangled it. You have drowned it in the tub, as everyone can plainly see now."

"That's right," said the boys, turning to Menahem. "Have you shown him yet? Does he know?"

"Shown me what?" said Herod. "What are they talking about?"

"Oh, you will see," said Mariamne. "But better you understand the meaning first, which your ghoulish friend there is apparently too scared to tell you. I will tell you gladly.

"Yes, you cur, you scab, you pox, this is the end. You are dying. You are rotting to death, as is everything you ever touched with your filthy hands: your forts, your ports, your precious Temple, now that you've finished dressing it up like a common whore. You might as well have built it out of dung." She scoffed. "Antipas. That urchin will not last a day. Or Archelaus, or Philip, or any of them."

"They're obsolete already," said Alexander.

"It's true," his brother chimed in, "as all the neighbors seem to have figured out."

"Which neighbors?" said Herod. "Who?"

"Oh, but they're here already. Were you not aware?" Alexander looked back at Menahem again. "Do you tell him nothing? Even now they're prowling the streets like dogs, sniffing at the carcass. They know. They can smell it."

"They can see it," said the brother.

"Who?" said Herod again, now turning to Menahem. "Who is he talking about?"

"Who is he *not* talking about?" said Mariamne. "The gentiles. The pagans. The Philistines. Every heathen tribe from Vienne to Pura has come to lay its claim—"

"—to place its bid."

"They are not blind."

"Not like you."

"Please, can we show him?" asked the boys. "Please, Mother?"

"Show me what?" Herod sputtered. He wheeled on Menahem. "I demand you tell me what they are talking about!"

The Essene still said nothing. He might have been asleep, but it didn't matter anyway, as now the old king saw. Just above Menahem's head, the curtains were slightly parted to reveal the purpling shades of another passing night. There was something there he hadn't seen before.

He stood. "What is that?"

He rounded the bed and peered out through the crack.

The balcony looked out upon the southern hills, in line with Herodium, the family shrine that he himself had built just east of Bethlehem. The morning light was creeping up, the merest hue of gold sitting on the black horizon, but there above it, up where the darkness still held sway, there was a strange light.

"When did this appear?"

It was in Zeus's eagle, Aquila, and standing out from all the stars surrounding: brighter, faster, and leaving a silvery plume behind it, like the whisk of a magnificent heavenly broom, burning through the sky.

"Why did you not tell me?" he asked, agape.

Then suddenly his entire frame was shot through by searing bolts of pain, originating in his crotch. Probably he had begun to leak again. He wasn't even sure, the pain was so excruciating, but he could not take his eye from the star. It only grew and shifted as he teared in anguish, making the impression all the more vivid: that this heavenly light above and this hellish fire below, the one devouring his flesh, were somehow one and the same, conspiring now to visit him with this agony and the certain knowledge of his end and the end of everything he'd given his life to create.

He called out once, wordlessly, and then collapsed, taking the curtain down as well. It fell overtop of him like a burial shroud, and the last he heard was the uproarious laughter of all the ghosts that he himself had made.

⨭ 11 ⨮

The Eagle

BUT EVEN THE SUGGESTION, THE WHIFF OF AN INFERENCE OF the tyrant's demise, was a spark on dry kindling.

The final gust of encouragement came several hours later. Archelaus had stepped out on the royal balcony to dispose of a melon rind, but the sight of him there, shielding his eyes from the sun, combined with numerous reports of the king's collapse at dawn—dozens throughout the palace claimed to have been awakened by the terrible wail—was more than enough to start the rumor on its way.

It sprang from the court in a dash and proceeded by shouts and whispers from corner to corner, window to window, bridge to bridge. It eddied in the muslin shadow of the stalls, giving way to tears here, jigs there, drawing strength from doors and alleys, but still heading in the general direction of the Temple.

By far the firmest shove came from the doors of the secret synagogue across from the old Hasmonaean palace. This was where the students of Judas and Matthias gathered every morning to hear the rabbis speak. The moment the news reached them, the plan was clear. They only needed a sufficient number, which, as soon as it arrived, spilled out in the street and joined the larger current headed for the mount.

Word was already circulating within, but mostly as a question:

Was it true? Had any official pronouncement been made? The Levites could only shake their heads. They turned to the merchants, who turned to the urchins, who likewise shrugged. They'd heard what they'd heard.

All took note when the students entered, so fiery and determined and still led by the two rabbis. They cut though the crowd like a swarm of bees, headed straight for the higher courts, and many onlookers followed, not quite knowing why, but just to see their purpose, for clearly there was a purpose.

The Levites were caught off guard. The students broke through the line at the priestly court. They pushed past the priests and commandeered the steps. The Levites went to call in the guard, and the ensuing row of scratching and shoving and random, triumphant cries provided just the needed diversion.

The six most agile of the students had already been chosen and equipped with ropes and hammers. They quickly reached the roof of the Temple and were lowering themselves back down toward the transom and the apparent object of their outrage, the golden eagle, a gift of the emperor and as such a gleaming emblem of Herod's rule and all that was wrong with Israel and the house that was supposed to protect it.

"Crush it!" cried the mob.

On touching down, the six immediately took up the axes and hammers from their belts and began pounding at the scowling eyes and half-spread wings of the statue. The crowd below went into a frenzy at the sight—not just the students, but the worshipers as well, most of whom also hated the eagle and were only just now hearing that Herod was dead. They pumped their fists and roared so loud they could not hear the more rhythmic stomp behind them, of one hundred heavy boots marching through the gate, a column of soldiers—Temple guards, Roman issue—with spears and plumed helmets.

The mob was oblivious, their eyes and ears upturned, watching with a rabid glee as the students up on the roof continued thrashing and hacking away. The statue bent and yielded, folding its wing beneath their hammers. Another two blows, and suddenly it tilted. The bolts cracked free, and with a horrible groan, the twisted bird toppled from its perch, turning over once as it plunged toward the shrieking crowd, which scattered just in time. The eagle struck the steps with a dull clang, then tumbled pitiably down to the foot of the marble stairs.

The mob pounced. They started kicking it and beating it with their hands and feet as if the thing had been preying on their children. They crowded around it for a chance to leave their dent, so drunk with fury most were still unaware of the soldiers pushing through to get at them.

Some fled when they saw. Some turned and made a stand, but the soldiers were armed. A mace descended, a skull caved in, and the protest ended that quickly. The eagle was reconfiscated. The students, taking signal from their venerable rabbis, let themselves be seized. To be arrested was a large part of the reason they'd come, after all.

⋛12⋚

The Magi

HEROD WAS INDISPOSED WHEN THE RIOTERS AND WITNESSES arrived at the palace. He had canceled all meetings for the day and finally managed to sleep for a few hours, but upon learning of the incident at the Temple, he roused himself.

The students, apprised that the king was alive, were separated, deposed, and then made to wait, first in the pens in the bowels of the palace, then again in the theater where Herod had taken to holding his official meetings.

His council was present as well, including the new High Priest, Eleazar, as the crime at question had taken place at his "house." All waited and watched as a large marble tub was wheeled in, up onto the stage, then hoisted onto a grate that had been set above a bed of coals. The coals were fired. The tub was filled.

Only when the water had begun to roil did Herod himself finally enter—to an audible gasp. The students could see: If this morning's report was premature, it was hardly unfounded. The king was bloated beyond recognition. His muzzle and neck were flushed and mottled. He required the help of two servants to walk. His breathing was strained. He could put no weight on one leg, requiring the help of the same two servants to sit again, upon a long divan where he could lie flat while three physicians treated the bath with carefully calibrated measures of salt and oil.

"And hot as you dare," he mumbled. "If the flesh burns free, so much the better."

His mind was apparently alert. He listened to the lawyer offer a capsule of what had taken place earlier.

"And where were the Temple guards?" he asked.

"Overwhelmed," the lawyer replied. "It would seem the rioters have been planning the act for some time."

"And what about the eagle?"

"It's being attended to even now, Your Majesty. It is with the smiths."

Herod sniffed, turning back to the bath. "Is that not ready yet? I am losing my mind."

It was. The servants came to assist him. They took his robe; they led him over. As he lifted his leg over the side of the tub, all in the room turned away—some too late. They gasped again: He was a green-black scab from thigh to belly, oozing pink.

But the bath was apparently a balm. As he lowered himself in by gingerly increments, he for the first time glanced over in the direction of the protesters.

"Are the rabbis here?"

The rabbis were indeed, but before they could make their way to the front of the group, one of the students, a broad-chested young redhead, spoke up.

"What was planned, we planned together. What was done we did together, and happily, for we serve that which serves the glory of God, which is the Law as spoken through Moses, and we know that this is a higher law than any that you or Caesar commands!"

Herod half admired the display. He bounced his tattered underside once, then twice, on the ruffling surface of the water, then settled in with a hiss. "Awfully brash," he said, "for one whose life hangs in the balance."

"If I am bold," the youth replied, "it is because I know that I, and all of us, should enjoy greater happiness in death. And we will gladly die, as we know in our hearts that we die not for crimes but for our faith."

"What is your name?"

"Eli ben Kozar."

"Well, Eli ben Kozar, since you are so brave, let me ask you one question: Why did you do this thing today? Why this day and not yesterday, I mean, or the day before?"

The young student was caught short.

"Let me see if I can help you then." The king shifted, for the moment distracted from his discomfort. "I believe the reason you did this today and not yesterday is that today you believed that I was dead. Is this not so? And that if you'd known I was alive, you would be back in the library, trimming rolls. And so I suppose my question is, why does someone who is clearly as brave and as virtuous as yourself have to wait for a man to die before you summon up the nerve to act against him?"

Again young Eli had no answer.

Nor did his teachers.

Herod waved them away like gnats. "To Jericho. All of them."

Even after the students had left the theater, however, and there was only his council remaining, the king seemed unusually stricken by the episode.

"I do not understand how such a thing is permitted to happen. Who were the guards on duty?"

Pannaeus replied that he would endeavor to find out.

"Do that. And I want them sent to Jericho as well. It is not right that I should have to suffer these insults after all that I have done. Tell me, when before has the nation known such wealth, such security and esteem? When before has it seen more magnificence? One hundred and twenty-five years the Hasmonaeans ruled! Not once did they lift a finger to restore the Temple or beautify it! Now it knows a greater glory than it has enjoyed since the reign of Solomon, adorned with gifts that *I* have made and *I* have paid for with *my* own money, so that it might stand as a monument of my good faith, that I be remembered as a good and generous ruler. But here, even as I live, even as I suffer, you let these men vandalize it in broad daylight! Then you let them stand in front of me here, insult me to my face, saying their purpose has been to affront me and my law. I tell you they affront Jehovah, and anyone who supports them affronts Jehovah as well—"

His eyes were flashing in all directions, but landing often enough on the High Priest Eleazar that he felt moved to speak.

"Sire, I can assure you, no one is more disturbed than I at what has taken place this morning, and I agree entirely. The actions of these men are a heresy, and an example needs to be made."

Yes, yes, all agreed.

"But for that very reason," the High Priest continued, "so that the example may serve, it follows that the penalty should be imposed upon those who are responsible. If the many are made to pay for the actions of the few, the lesson will be lost."

All agreed with this as well. "If we had known . . . If someone had come and told us, then surely . . ."

Herod was hardly persuaded. He appeared to be slightly nauseated, in fact. He looked down at the water surrounding him. A layer of scum had formed on the surface. He began to shudder slightly; it wasn't clear at first if he was acting voluntarily or not. His hands began a palsied shake. His arms and legs entered into spasms, flailing at the sides of the tub and swishing the water over the rim. Then came the coughing, uncontrollable and highly productive. His entire head turned purplish red as he now began hacking the phlegm from his chest.

Accordingly, Pannaeus stepped in and asked that the room be cleared.

By the time the king's spasms had subsided and his throat was clear and raw, the theater too was nearly empty. The councillors had excused themselves, or all but one, Menahem, as was not unusual. He often remained after the others had gone. His purpose this morning was no mystery. He was standing over by the eastern entrance, the one that opened to the courtyard.

"Are they here?" asked Herod.

The Essene had only to stand aside, and the men at question entered: three, and of evidently diverse stripes. One wore a turban in the Persian style. The others, he was not sure of. Was that the headdress of the Ethiopians? Their robes, though all embroidered, were also different—one green, one gold, one purple.

As they came nearer the stage, Herod could see their faces were likewise distinct: One was an African, with skin as black as coal and eyes that shone like diamonds; the next was from the north, with fair skin and a pointed beard the color of wheat; the third was of a distant Oriental mold, smooth, with feline eyes on high, flat cheeks.

The likeness was in their countenance and carriage. As they approached, looking all around them at the ceiling and moldings, the same faint smiles played about their lips: an eerie mix of innocence and knowingness; an open awe, untouched by envy. Herod himself was aware that a pleasing stillness seemed to have entered the room with them. The cypresses outside in the courtyard had gone still.

As one the three guests bowed, the fairest farthest forward. He spoke, but in a tongue that Herod had never heard.

Menahem obliged. "They are extending their thanks and gratitude," he said, "for granting them such welcome."

Herod could see they'd brought gifts: jeweled boxes, ollas and carafes for potions, it appeared. The Oriental offered the smallest first, an alabaster vial.

Herod gestured for Menahem to take it. "What brings you to our land?"

The three replied by pointing skyward. The star, they seemed to say, but so absent guile that Herod wondered if they were mocking him. He played along.

"So you are familiar with the prophecy as well?"

The question caused all three men to smile. Of course.

Herod said, "Tell me what you know?"

The darkest answered this time in an equally foreign tongue. Herod looked to Menahem.

"They say the new king has been planted from the heavens."

Herod glanced back down at the remaining gifts. These were not for him then. "Here in Jerusalem?" he asked.

All three shook their heads.

"They were thinking you would know," said Menahem.

Again, coming from anyone else, Herod might have taken offense at this, that they should come to him, into his very own court, for direction to the newborn king. In another mood, he might have asked for their heads, but it was as if these three had breathed a kind of salve into the air. He turned to Menahem.

"And do I?"

Menahem only had to look at him. Of course. The image of the star, burning through the sky above the southern hills, came to him once again. Herod remembered the prophet Micah, and said, "Of course. He was to come from Ephratah, which we now call Bethlehem."

Menahem confirmed with a nod.

"Yes, go and look," said Herod to his guests. "You have our blessing. I only ask, if you do find him, that you return and tell us where. We too would like to welcome him."

Of course. The three visitors bowed again, most grateful for his kindness and assistance. He had proved himself a gracious dying king.

That was all. Menahem now turned and led the three men from the room, their feet so silent beneath their robes they might have been floating just above the flagstone.

As they stepped out, the cypresses stirred again.

Herod called, "Pannaeus!" and the servants came to help him from the tub. He was tired now and would rest. The rash seemed better, though, becalmed.

"Send word to Jericho," he said, his throat clear, his voice serene. "All the students from this morning should be executed." He slid his arms back inside his robe. "The ones who watched, by rope; the ones who tore the eagle down, burn them in the public square. And the teachers too, Judas and Matthias."

Pannaeus bowed; he would convey.

"Oh, and also—" Herod pointed vaguely toward the courtyard. "Have those three men followed."

Pannaeus looked at him, a blank: Which men?

"The ones who were just here. The Magi," said the king. "Menahem will show you."

The loyal steward gave one more bow, now equally relieved and concerned:

Menahem had been dead for seven years.

≋13≋

Tab-Yumin

THE STAR WAS REAL. THEY SAW IT ALL THROUGHOUT JUDAEA. They saw it in Sheba too, and Persia, and Harran. Some took heed. Most took heart. Anywhere people lived in hardship, they also lived in expectation of a savior who would come and recognize their obedience and reward them for it, and punish their oppressors. They looked for signs that this savior had arrived, and the place they most often looked was the sky at night.

The Jews, as avid students of prophecy, bowed to no one in this respect. The Pharisees were well aware that a shining sword had long been prophesied to appear out of Jacob's line, to smite the corners of Moab and vanquish the children of destruction. Its corresponding star had been seen many times over the centuries, only to burn and fizzle out without event.

Now, about this light in Aquila many were wondering, Might it be the harbinger they were waiting for? Had it not appeared the year before in this same place? Some priests had taken note as well, though they tended to disdain all talk of saviors and resurrection. But even they, when they looked out and saw the silvery broom, could not help wondering: Had they not seen this very light in their mind's eye, bursting loose from all the rest and dropping down into the Temple?

Did the sky not crack soon after? Did the earth not heave and overturn the city?

In Ein Karim they saw the star, but they were not disturbed as yet.

"Look at him!" said Battai. "He sees it too." She showed the mother, Elizabeth. Even as he nursed, John's eyes were wide, and wide-set like hers, so that he could see the distance.

"He even points," the nursemaid said.

He did, outside the window where they sat. And Elizabeth did not doubt that he saw, or that he heard as well, for she remembered what the ibexes had told her that night out on the Bitter Sea, about how the pure of heart could hear the heavens pray. No heart could be more pure than his.

He gave *her* milk. He brought color to *her* cheek and music to her voice. As lightly as she had carried him in her womb, she carried him in her arms. She followed him about the smooth stones of their home. She carried him out into the olive grove, and there again Battai marveled at how his eyes danced about the dappled shade.

"The leaves too," said Battai. His expression was the same as when he saw the stars at night.

"Of course," his mother said. "All things pray."

He renewed her weary bones. She rose from her chair to follow him when he began to crawl, when he first stood, when he stomped his feet and clung to the wall, and when he began exploring—every corner, every rock and leaf. He tasted the world, and he named it in a great loud voice. The little home in Ein Karim resounded with the sound, day and night. He called Old Father Abbah-Abbah! He called Elizabeth Amam!

She gave thanks, each and every moment, for she had not forgotten her barren years and their time alone in Hebron and in Ophel. She had not forgotten how hard they had worked and the children they had cared for, including sweet Mary, whom they had loved with all their hearts. Only now their hearts seemed to have grown, and she gave thanks for all, for having led her here, as the love she felt for John had made a shadow and a cutout of any love that she had ever known before.

She knew the same was true of Zechariah; when she handed John to him, she could see it. And she felt the welling in her heart to see her husband finally holding his son and to see that his son should be John; John tugging at his father's beard, and Zechariah singing to him in his low, resounding voice. And she yearned for the day that he would take John to the Temple with him and present him to be blessed.

For she had not forgotten her vow either. She had no doubt that was why the star was there, to remind her of the promise that she had made, the same as her aunt Anne, and Hannah before her, that she would render him, her child, back unto the service of the Lord. So she took care to see that John was pure. She made sure the water he bathed in was taken from the purest well, that Battai's milk was pure, from myrtle leaves Elizabeth gave her, that no juice of the vine ever touched his lips, that no iron tool ever touched his hair, and that nothing dead ever came near him. He slept every night on lambskin. As she had done for Mary, so she did for John, and more, and all in preparation for the day that Zechariah would take him and present him at the Temple.

She had thought that he would take him in his first month, as soon as he was strong enough to make the journey to the Holy City, but the month passed and they did not go. Then again, when the turn of Abijah had come, she had thought that they all would go together and present him then, so that his brethren could look at John and see the one who was to follow Zechariah. Surely he would want for all his brethren to see.

But again, the eighth turn came and went, and Zechariah made no mention that either she or John should come with him.

Then came the Feast of the Tabernacles. What better time, she thought. She remembered Mary on that same day, when she was only three, and how she had danced before the lights. Elizabeth told Battai to prepare their things, for surely they would go, but when Zechariah saw their trunks set out, he told Battai to put them away. He told them they should stay. Only he went to the feast that year.

But when the feast was done, two other priests returned with him.

They wanted to see how John had grown and to offer their blessing. One was Ashabel, whom they had known since Zechariah first began to serve. The other was a younger priest whom Elizabeth did not know, Tab-Yumin.

The first day Old Father had gone to take his noontime rest. John was sleeping too. Elizabeth found Ashabel out on the terrace and asked him plainly, "Is it right that Old Father should be waiting so long to present John at the Temple?"

Ashabel said it was for Old Father to decide when he should present his son.

"I do not question my husband's prerogative," Elizabeth replied. "I only ask, is there some reason he would wait?"

Ashabel conceded she had cause to wonder and that she was not alone in doing so. "There are those among the course who have asked the same. But there are others who wonder why Old Father has himself returned, given his doubts."

She did not know what Ashabel was speaking of, so he sat her down and told her the story of the order of Malchijah.

During the first siege of the Temple, when the Romans took over the city in support of John Hyrcanus, the brethren of Malchijah were the ones responsible for seeing to it that the rites continue. Even as the Romans pounded the walls from the outside, the priests within negotiated for new lambs to be sneaked in and lifted over the walls in harnesses so that the people's offering would not be neglected.

More famously, when the northern wall finally buckled and fell, and the Romans and Syrians poured inside and began laying waste to everyone and everything, even then the priests were said to have continued with the rites. They went on pouring the wine, sacrificing the lambs, praying and lighting the incense, while all around them their brethren and their compatriots were being run through and hacked to death. Pompey's soldiers reported back that they had never in all their days seen such devotion to worship, or such indifference to life.

"And ever since that day," said Ashabel, "the order of Malchijah has been much revered among the priesthood as paragons of fearlessness and commitment to service."

"As one can understand," said Elizabeth.

"Yes," said Ashabel. "Only your husband confided to me once he never understood such praise. To him, it did not seem the priests had had much choice. He said to me, 'It is not for us to choose whether and how we serve. That way is chosen for us by our fathers and our teachers. It is our task to make it of worth.'"

Elizabeth still did not understand. "Why are you saying this to me?"

"So that you might understand why Old Father has continued serving at the Temple," said Ashabel, "and why he has not brought John with him."

Zechariah appeared in the door then, and the conversation ended.

Awhile later, the younger priest, Tab-Yumin, found Elizabeth at the well. He had already said good-bye to Old Father and to the child. Now as she was lowering down her skins to fill, he spoke to her in confidence.

"I hope you will hear me, good woman, and know I mean only good for you and for your son."

"Say what you mean," she replied.

"You must make ready to leave this place," said the priest, "to take the child and go. I have heard you speaking with Ashabel. I have heard the questions that you ask, and I am answering you: You must be ready."

"Tab-Yumin, you should not say such things. You should take care that I not repeat them to Old Father."

"Old Father knows what I am saying, and this is why he does not bring John to the Temple. The child's name is too well known—"

"Tab-Yumin, I am asking you to be silent now, or I will tell him. I will tell him you came to me this way and spoke threats about the child—"

"I do not threaten the child, good woman." The young priest knelt before her. "If he fulfills his father's word, then may I eat Yohannan's bread. May I drink from Yohannan's cup, but so that I may, you must make yourself ready. Go, and not any place where you are known. If you would go to Hebron, then to Hebron you should not go."

"Silence, Tab-Yumin!" She withdrew her hand. "Tell me why I should not cry out to my neighbors now, and to my neighbors' dogs, that you have said these things."

"You will not cry out to your neighbors or to your neighbors' dogs because you love Yohannan," said the priest, "and you have seen the star as well."

Just then they heard the child's cry back at the house. He had awakened.

Tab-Yumin stood. "And now I must go. Only beware, and be ready, good woman, for Yohannan's sake and the sake of all who would follow him."

With that, he took up his skin, lifted his hood, and continued on down to where the tree line met the road.

⋛14⋚

Jericho

HEROD'S BODY NOW BEGAN TO FAIL HIM IN EVERY IMAGINABLE and disgusting way. The putrefaction of his loins had exposed him to an infestation of mites and countless other parasites, some of which wormed their way up into his stomach and were stealing his food as fast as he could eat it. Day and night he gorged himself, without satisfaction. His bowels were not moving. His lower abdomen was distended. His rectum was nearing a state of complete prolapse. His feet were the size of two gourds. He was having trouble breathing, and his breath, such as it was, smelled like days-old milk. He was also beginning to suffer violent tremors in all his limbs, which only aggravated the rest of his conditions.

"For what he has done to the rabbis Judas and Matthias," whispered more than one diviner, after seeing him.

His physicians took him across the Jordan to a place called Callirrhoe in hopes the hot springs there might relieve his suffering, but he nearly choked on the vapors when they lowered him in. He was rushed back to Jericho, and it was there at the royal residence that all the poisons swarming inside him finally took hold of his mind completely. The ghosts of Mariamne and her sons tracked him down, more amused than ever at the idea that he could hide from them, their message the same as ever: that the kingdom he had given his life to building and defending would soon be rubble, would belong to the gentile masters, and that concerning his own demise, the people remained giddy with expectation.

"Not here in front of me, no." He'd sneer at the eunuchs who brought him heaping plates of lamb and dates. "Now you grovel. But I have seen you from my own bier, pretending to wipe the tear from your eye. You think I'm fooled? You think I've forgotten? I'll leave no account outstanding, I promise you that."

Though far from clear to the bowing eunuchs, this was reference to the three mysterious Magi who had come to worship the infant king, and whom Herod was now convinced had meant to kill him as well. He asked about them every day, whether they had gone to Bethlehem and what had they discovered.

Neither his steward, Pannaeus, nor anyone else in the court had a good answer, but Herod was adamant. He sent team after team to Bethlehem to see what they could find: Germans, Thracians, finally a small brigade of Gauls. "The Gauls will not fail me."

He also at this time began drawing up a mysterious list. No one was sure of the purpose, only that it included the names of all the most prominent Jews in the land—priests and Pharisees, lawyers, landowners, businessmen, and governors as well. Herod asked that they be brought to Jericho at once. Runners were dispatched to all the various regions and cities, from Hebron to Capernaum, from Caesarea to Philadelphia.

Back in Jerusalem, the High Priest Eleazar had taken note of this with some dismay. His own counselor, Elohim, had been asked to go, as well as several members of the Sanhedrin. Eleazar assumed that Herod must be making gifts of some kind, tokens not covered in the will, but then how could it be that he, the High Priest, had been overlooked?

It came as some relief, then, when his summons finally did arrive. No time was given for packing. The messenger said his presence was required at once, so Eleazar left a letter for his family, explaining his departure and promising to return with arms full.

On arriving in Jericho, he had assumed he would be taken either directly to the palace or to the High Priest's residence. He was a bit

surprised, then, when the carriage stopped in front of the hippodrome. He gathered there must be some entertainment in store—a
chariot race, perhaps, or a ceremony of some kind. It wasn't until the
handlers led him down into the cages below the arena that a proper
sense of dread descended. He saw Elohim penned in with all the rest,
like slaves, or athletes, or animals.

More and more of the family was gathering in Jericho. Archelaus's
brother Antipas came all the way from Rome; their half brother,
Philip, from Antioch. The wives were there, and cousins, nieces, and
nephews, all to make sure their interests would be served when the
day did come.

"Vultures," Herod spat, even at the wide-eyed grandchildren.
"Have a bite. I'm sure I'm poison."

Good news had arrived from Rome. Caesar had reviewed the case
against his son, Antipater, the one detailing all his half-hatched plots
against Herod, as well as the whole campaign of lies and subterfuge
that had led to the (admittedly wrongful) execution of Alexander and
Aristobulus. Caesar recognized the criminality of such behavior and
was prepared to sanction any punishment Herod saw fit to impose,
including death. Herod immediately had Antipater transferred from
his cell in Jerusalem to one there in Jericho. Everyone expected the
execution to follow shortly, but for some reason Herod delayed.

His sister, Salome, herself just arrived from Jamnia, went to him
out of concern. (Her husband, Alexis, went as well.)

"Why?" she asked. "You do know that even now he is trying to
bribe his way free."

Herod nodded. Nothing about Antipater surprised him anymore.

"Then I suggest you act," she said. "He can be persuasive, as you
know, and your hesitation is making others nervous."

"Nervous how?"

"They fear that you still harbor feelings for Antipater, even after
all his lies, that you still judge him to be the worthiest of your heirs."

"If this is their fear, then perhaps they should be afraid."

It was not exactly clear what he meant by this, but his expression let her know the subject was closed, so she broached another, nearly as troubling. "And what is all this at the hippodrome, if I may ask?"

"No, I am glad you did." He roused. He sat upright in his bed and patted it for her to sit beside him.

"It is no secret I shall be dying soon. No, it's true. This pain is not the sort that goes away, but the Lord has seen fit to grant me a glimpse of my own funeral, and so I know: The people will not mourn as they should mourn their king. They will be happy at my death—"

"Brother, you cannot believe such—"

"No, please, let me finish," he cut her off, but with an unnerving calm. "They will not mourn me as they should. I know this. And so I had thought, perhaps a sacrifice upon my death—a child from each family. Such things are not unheard of, after all. And if the people were made to pay this way, then they'd weep, would they not?"

Salome agreed they would.

"But then I thought no, perhaps the priest is correct. If an example is to be made, it should be made directly. It should be made of those responsible."

He drew her even nearer now, or near as she would come, repelled as she was by the rancid burst of every syllable upon his pendulous lips. "I am asking you to bring me peace on this matter, as there is no one else I trust. I want you to promise me. Promise me that you will remain here by my side. Be with me until the end, but then, upon my death—tell no one—but I want you to go to the hippodrome. Go to the guard, the Germans, and give them the order to round up all the men inside, and before my death has been made public, see that all these men are slaughtered."

Salome searched her brother's eyes for some fleck of irony.

"If possible," he said, "I would prefer they be shot with their own arrows. If not, so be it. But in any case, you see. You understand that if upon my death these 'great' men die as well . . . these so-called 'leaders of the people' . . . then my funeral will surely be remembered for the river of tears that flowed. They would not mock me then, would they?"

Salome shook her head no, they would not.

"You see it, sister." His features softened fondly. "You see that I am right. And if you would do this for me and promise me, it would relieve me half my suffering. Please, do not deprive me mourners at my funeral."

Salome could find no words. Her husband did. "But, Herod, what have these men done? Of what are they guilty?"

"Of hating me every step," Herod answered readily. "Of denying me what is mine. Of telling lies about me and my father. My sister knows. Did they not call him Philistine? Did they not accuse him of stealing from the palace, or escorting Pompey into the Temple and raping the Holy Place? They killed him, as they have tried to kill me, every day of my reign.

"Tell me, if they were not guilty, then why is my death a cause for celebration? How is it not the fault of these men, for having turned the people against me, and having mocked me, and lied to me? Or for sending spies and conjurers to kill me and then bring gifts of worship to my successor? Do you think I am not aware? Am I to let that go unanswered?"

"Brother, you are not well," said Salome. "You need to rest—"

"Don't!" he said, his volume suddenly rising. "Don't you be like the others. These men were here. They stood before me. They handed me the poison, and I can prove it. Pannaeus!"

"Brother, stop—"

"Pannaeus!"

Pannaeus, never far, entered. "Sire."

"Where is that vial? And have you spoken to the Gauls yet? About the spies, the Magi."

The steward's eye met Salome's for just an instant, but it was enough. "Yes, Your Majesty, I have."

"And?"

"And they could not find them either, I'm afraid."

Herod turned back to his sister with a dumbfounded expression. "Do you see? Do you see the level of treachery? It is inconceivable these men could not be found in Bethlehem. They'd be orchid among rush!"

Pannaeus agreed. "Which is why the Gauls came to the same conclusion as the Germans."

"Which is?"

"Either that the men at question left before the Germans got there—"

"—Or?"

"Or that they never went there in the first place."

It took a moment for the apparent fatuousness, the sheer vapidity of this deception, to settle in, but once it did, Herod began to writhe against his pillow, grimacing.

"Brother, calm yourself."

But he could not. He began to pump his arms and legs like an upset beetle. "Get him in here!" he growled.

"Who, Your Majesty?"

"Alaric!"

Alaric was captain of the Gauls. Salome and Alexis moved to excuse themselves, but Herod tried to keep them.

"No, I want you to see." His eyes were rolling in his head, even as he reached out to his sister. "I want you to see just how serious I am. They are not going to get away with this!" His great jowls were trembling like a pair of udders, his lips spewing white. "They think they can fool me? They think they can just come and steal what I have made? Oh, I will see them mourn! I will see them wail—" He burst out coughing. His head went beet red, and his conniptions were suddenly so violent he looked as if he were astride a wild horse trying to buck him.

Pannaeus summoned help, even as he sought to reassure Salome. These things looked worse than they were, but perhaps it would be best if they left.

News spread soon enough of the order that Herod was said to have delivered Alaric once the Gaul had been fetched and His Majesty had sufficiently recovered.

As with his plan to slaughter all the "leaders" in the hippodrome, Herod had stressed that he wanted the mission kept a secret; the outcome would make his point clearly enough. Still, word descended along the usual byways—not Pannaeus, soul of discretion—but down through the guards, the lower stewards, and the various echelons of family and court, who treated the rumor with varying degrees of credulity.

Some accepted it. This was vintage late-vintage Herod, they said. How could one deny he meant it? "Meant it, yes," said others, but that was no reason to take the order seriously. Since coming to Jericho, Herod had threatened to kill every living thing in the kingdom. Why should the firstborn sons of Bethlehem be an exception?

"It's just another spasm of his age," they said. "And his disease." They clucked their tongues: poor thing.

Of all the ditches and gutters into which the rumor eventually found its way, none drank more thirstily than those in the cages beneath the hippodrome. There, amid the growing stench and the dread, Herod's alleged order served only to confirm their worst fears.

"Oh, he'll see it's done," said Elohim. "I heard he even threatened the soldiers, saying if they failed him, he'd make sure they paid with their own sons."

Eleazar had thought this an unnecessary embellishment. He had no doubt the order was real. He had seen the king. He knew his state. He also knew the men he'd called upon, the Gauls, would hardly need coercion. They looked upon the Jews as animals. They'd think no more of slaughtering their young than they would a herd of swine, except to resent the fact they couldn't enjoy the flesh afterward.

And that the flesh at question belonged to the youngest firstborn sons made all too clear—to Eleazar, at least—what the king was up to: hunting for the Promised One, the one appointed by the star, the one who was supposed to come and fell the high and mighty. Herod was not above such superstition.

And Eleazar knew of such a one, did he not? He had heard the stories. He had seen the star, both in his dreams and in the sky.

He sat a half day with his dilemma. That was all he needed to take its measure: Sit the faceless child on one tray of the scale; then heap upon the other the lives and works of all the good men surrounding him. For it did seem possible, if Herod could be satisfied on this count and shown the loyalty of his subjects, he might abandon whatever plan he had in store for them. And after all, the augur had implied the child's purpose was to save.

So let him save.

"But what would be the proof?" asked the guard, a Syrian whom he and Elohim had taken into confidence.

"What do you mean, proof?"

"That this child you speak of is the one the king is looking for?"

"Just ask," Eleazar replied. "Ask the people in the village. The story is well known, and what concern is that of yours in any case? I should think your pot is sweet enough."

The guard merely turned and left the cage.

"But make sure the king understands," Eleazar called after him, pressing his face against the bars. "Make sure he knows where the word has come from, that it was his faithful servants in the hippo-drome . . . all of them!"

All of them. He made sure that final phrase was heard. It was the final phrase, after all, that made this a good deed.

⋛ 15 ⋚

The Veil

ABIJAH'S TURN HAD COME AGAIN, BUT ONCE AGAIN OLD FATHER had given no sign that either John or Elizabeth should make the journey with him. First he said good-bye to them out on the terrace; he kissed them both. Eizabeth carried John to the ledge, and together they waited for him to appear out in the orchard below.

The sunlight sifted through the quiet limbs and leaves to find him stepping out.

"Abbah!" John called.

Old Father glanced back once to wave good-bye again, then turned and continued on his way, the shadows dancing on his hood and shoulders.

"Abbah-Abbah!" John teetered in his mother's grasp, but Old Father had disappeared from view. "Abbah!" he cried again, so loud the neighbors could hear.

Strong boy, they smiled.

That evening, when Old Father failed to show at bedtime, John once again made his objection known. He stood in the washbasin, looking around at every sound, expecting it was Old Father, only to realize it wasn't.

But where is the white beard for me to pull? He frowned. Where are the wrinkles to trace?

"Old Father is gone to the Temple," his mother said. "You'll see him when he returns." As she poured the water over his head, he shivered and he stamped. "Why, just because he has a handsome son at home, does that mean he should forget his other duties? Someday you'll know the same."

John stamped again. He teethed at the cloth but accepted. He would do without the beard this evening.

The third night after Zechariah had left, Elizabeth sat beside John's crib, well after Battai had gone to sleep.

There was a full moon, hanging outside the little window like a silver plate, casting a crooked shaft of light along the floor. She watched it slide across the mat, row by row. The same as the two nights prior, she listened to the grove, praying that every snap and falling leaf was Old Father returning to tell them, "Come. Gather your things. Never mind what Tab-Yumin said." And he would take them to the city.

It was near midnight when the neighbors' dogs began to howl. Elizabeth thought they might have seen a fox at first, and yet the wailing was of a different, more bewildered kind. And now the neighbors themselves were stepping out onto their roof, the husband and wife, arm in arm, looking up at the sky. Elizabeth did not understand the reason why until she noticed that the patch of light on the floor was beginning to dim.

She went to the window, and when she saw directly, her breath caught in her throat. There was a great black shadow passing over the moon, like a giant veil drawn across its pure white face.

She could hear the neighbors' voices now; the husband's, low and meant to comfort. "Not the first time, no," he said, but he couldn't quite disguise his fear. "You'll see. She'll show again. As it comes, it goes."

The dogs were not consoled. They continued moaning as the shadow grew and the moon went dark before their eyes. Soon it was covered over completely. Only the nimbus could be seen, while all around, the pinprick light of a thousand stars and planets took on an extra glow.

As Elizabeth gazed up at them, she even thought she heard a hum, but not the song she had heard that midnight out upon the Bitter Sea. This was more of a buzzing, and it wasn't coming from the stars. It was coming from the distance, from the hillsides to the south, like locusts.

But could the others not hear? Battai was sleeping through, as was John, peaceful as a lamb. Outside, the husband was unaware. He stroked the shoulder of his wife and waited patiently for the veil to pass, but Elizabeth's ears were bursting with the sound now. These were not locusts. These were voices, shrieking, howling, faraway voices of mothers weeping. She turned away. She tried covering her ears, but it was no use. It was as if the gates of Sheol had opened beneath her, and the sound of the grief was more than she could bear. But just when she thought she might collapse, the wailing began to subside and drift, like a wind passing through.

And she could see the light on the floor again. Just a sliver at first, but the neighbor was correct. As surely as the veil had come, it continued passing over, and the brilliant moon began to wax again. Its light washed out the stars and muted all the awful shrieks and cries. They faded down and away, back into the distant valley until the night was bathed again in moonlight and silence.

"There," said the husband, none the wiser. "There now, see? It's passed. Now back inside. All's well."

The dogs agreed with snorts. They circled their beds and finally curled up again. The moon was round and full above the little sloping village, casting its silvery light across the hills, down on all the olive leaves and limbs and through the little window of John's room, slanting in across the floor to find Battai, still braying softly under cover; Elizabeth's chair, now toppled; the crib beside it, empty.

≋16≋

The Steps

EARLY ON THE MORNING OF THE SEVENTH DAY, THE SABBATH day, Zechariah was delivering fresh oil to the Temple. He did this every morning he could, going back to his youth, even though his stride was shorter and less even now, and his hands were not so steady. He had to stop several times to keep the vessel from wobbling on its base.

"Is that Old Father there?"

He did not recognize the voice, only that it bore a foreign taint.

"Don't be afraid," came another, much nearer now. "We come as friends."

Zechariah continued at his pace, his eye fixed on the mouth of the decanter.

"I say we come as friends, Old Father. Stop. That is, if you are he, father of John, whom the angel named."

Zechariah did well not to turn or even pause. He had been fearing this moment. He knew it well. "I am a servant of the Temple," he answered. "Now leave me be."

"You would not stop to save your son?" came the second voice, still feigning confederacy.

Old Father's feet replied that he would not, but having reached the steps of the priestly court, he was obliged to slow. There were just three stairs, but he could take them only one at a time, his right foot meeting his left before the left would climb to the next.

The two strangers took advantage, drawing even closer now. "Listen to us, Old Father. They are coming for him."

"They have spoken to your neighbors."

"They have spoken to the nursemaid. They have not found him yet, but they are still looking." The voice drew so near that Zechariah could feel its breath against his ear. "If you know where he is, only say, and we will see that he's safe."

"I am a servant of the Temple," was all Zechariah replied. "Away."

"Away?" The stranger's hand now took him by the wrist. "Did you not hear me, old man?"

"And did you not hear me?" Zechariah turned and for the first time looked both strangers in the eye, leaving him no doubt as to their true intention. "If you say my wife is not in her home, then I do not know where she is. If you say my son is not there, then neither do I know where he is. I know the lamps have fallen low, and so I will ascend these steps, and you are not to follow, or you will stand in violation of God's Law."

He released his hand and resumed his purpose, his right foot rising up to join his left atop the steps. Then he started across the sacred court, as slow and steady as a turtle, trusting the Law to keep him safe, and Elizabeth to do the same for John.

⋛17⋚

The Cave

ELIZABETH HAD TAKEN JOHN OUT INTO THE HILLS. SHE DID not use the roads or paths, and she told no one where she was going; she did not know herself. She took no money with her and no scrip. She took bread for John but otherwise entrusted herself to the wilderness, fearing more what men might do.

During the day she moved from shade to shade. She found a running stream and a ripe fig tree, but as soon as the sun fell low again, a chill set in, and a wind, and she began to fear.

She found herself at the foot of a great mountain, too high for her to climb, too broad for her to round, and she had not yet found a shelter for the night or anywhere she and John would be safe from animals or the robbers who were known to dwell in the caves there. Her arms felt slack and leaden, and the wind was lashing now and riffling her tunic, pinning it against her legs. John was crying. He was hungry again and frightened.

Still holding him in her arms, she knelt and prayed: "O mountain of God, receive a mother with child."

When she opened her eyes again, she was amazed, for there in the looming darkness of the mountain above her, she did see a light, growing clearer as night fell all around. There was a golden glow, hewing out from a hollow in the rock—and not so far above. More than ever it seemed to her that an angel was watching over them.

Bent against the wind, and with John's arms wrapped around her neck, she climbed. Her feet were cracked and bleeding by the time she came to the mouth of the cave, but the light was still shining from within.

She set John down. She took his hand in hers and entered. They followed around the turn into a larger space, but there was no fire burning, or any torch or lantern. Just a man and a woman, standing before them, waiting.

The woman she recognized. It was the Lilith, the one who'd called to her out by the locust tree and ministered to her at the Bitter Sea. Seeing her, Elizabeth knew that she had found the place she should.

The man she did not know, but as with the Lilith, the light seemed to be coming from within him.

He was looking down at John and smiling. And John was looking back at him, his little arms raised, his eyes wide open. Elizabeth thought of Mary again, when she was a girl, dancing before the maidens at the Temple, and her own eyes began to fill with tears, for she knew now why she had come.

The man spoke. Elizabeth was unfamiliar with the words, but she understood: "Be calm, good woman, and firm."

She felt weak. She knelt. She set her head on the ground so they would not see her tears.

The Lilith came to her and put her hand on her. "Do not fear," she said. "The Lord has heard your prayer, and your vow as well, which we have come here to fulfill."

Elizabeth could not speak. She knew that she was heard. And she knew that she would not break her word to the Lord, but was it for this, she asked, that her womb had been shut? Was it for this that her womb was opened? Was it for this she had been brought to the sea and given to drink from the living water and allowed to hear all the stars and planets sing? Had she been blessed to hold John and care for him, only so that she would have to let him go?

Again the Lilith told her not to fear. She said they would help her find her strength. Then Elizabeth fell into a deeper sleep than she had ever known.

The next she knew, the stone was cold against her skin, and it was morning. The light was the light of the sun outside, but the man was gone. The Lilith was gone, and so was John.

⧦18⧦

The Stain

ZECHARIAH DID NOT APPEAR AT THE SABBATH FEAST THAT NIGHT.
Tab-Yumin was aware, but he was not the only one. Others in
the order found their reasons. Perhaps he wasn't feeling well. Perhaps
he had been detained. "Perhaps the wind has swept him away." They
smiled, for it was true, a savage wind had descended on the city that
evening and was thrashing at the mount. Even in the banquet hall
they could hear it swirling through the courts, howling though tur-
rets and cloisters, and whistling from parapets. They had to raise their
voices to be heard, lending the meal an extra festive air, and false.

When the meal was done, the brethren conferred. No one had
seen Old Father that day. The last anyone had spoken to him was the
night before. Perhaps he had gone home to Ein Karim. None ventured the reason why. None had to. They too had heard the rumors
about Bethlehem.

It was not until the next morning that the brethren of the subse-
quent order, the course of Jeshua, entered the Holy Place to find the
stain on the floor. It was only the size of a hand, there on the marble
at the foot of the seven lamps. Not all agreed that it was blood. They
knelt and tried to scrape it with their nails, but it would not come off.
They brought brushes and saltwort ash and tried to scrub it, and in

the weeks that followed, many more came and did the same, but the stain wouldn't lift.

"And even if it did," said the Temple elders, "do we believe it would bring Old Father back?"

In time they gave up trying. The stain remained, and Old Father was never seen or heard of by anyone ever again.

⇒ 19 ⇐

The Will

HEROD SPENT HIS FINAL DAYS IN UNREMITTING AGONY, THE combined result of all the complications he had been suffering—the constipation, the sores, the gout—exacerbated by constant tremors, frequent coughing fits, and dry heaves. At one point he tried killing himself with a paring knife, but a cousin named Achiabus stopped him. Herod was only bloodied in the effort, but the incident once again prompted rumors that he had died. Among the misinformed was Antipater, still imprisoned in the city jail. He responded immediately by trying to bribe his way free, promising the guards horses and land as soon as he became king.

When this in turn was reported back to Herod, his wounds now dressed, he slumped. "Has any man ever been afflicted by such an ungrateful and treacherous brood?" he asked. Receiving no reply, he gave out a long and mournful sigh, raised himself up on one arm, and finally delivered the order that Antipater be executed.

Five days later Herod himself died in bed.

Before the news was made public, Salome and Alexis went to the hippodrome and freed all the prisoners, telling them to return to their homes and affairs, which the crown, as ever, judged to be of great value to the kingdom. No explanation was given for either their detention or release, but Eleazar took quiet credit for the latter and would include Old Father's son in his prayers for the rest of his days.

Otherwise all of Herod's final intentions were respected. The day of his funeral an extensive mourning party gathered at the palace in Jerusalem. This included the entire family, the army in regalia, the spearmen, the Thracian Company, the German guard, as well as more than five hundred house slaves and freedmen, bearing spices. Herod's body had been laid out on a golden bier. All took part in the procession, escorting it through the streets of the city and out into the countryside. For miles on end the people lined the road to see, all the way to the man-made hill just outside Bethlehem, Herodium, where the king was finally entombed.

No one present was openly giddy, but many were pleased. The final will had been read the day before in Jericho, and Herod had been generous. The emperor Augustus received most of Herod's finest clothes as well as ten million silver coins. Salome received three cities and half a million silver coins. Otherwise, gifts, districts, estates, and moneys all had been liberally and evenly distributed.

Of utmost interest, of course, had been the kingdom itself and who would rule, as this had been the subject of so much rumor and amendment over the course of previous year. In the end Herod had decided to divide the country into three parts: The lion's share, consisting of Judaea, Samaria, and Idumaea, was to go to Archelaus, who was also to assume the title king; under the lesser designation of tetrarch, Archelaus's half brother Philip (by Cleopatra of Jerusalem) was granted Trachonitis and the surrounding districts, leaving just the unjoined provinces of Peraea and Galilee, which, likewise attendant to the title tetrarch, had been assigned to Archelaus's younger brother, Antipas.

Part Two

YOUTH

≋20≋

Par'am

OUT ON THE FAR SIDE OF THE JORDAN, WELL BEYOND THE RIVER valley, tucked in the caves above a hidden wadi, there lived a small tribe of potters called the Subba, so humble and profitless in their trade that neither Israel nor Nabataea nor the Syrians, the Parthians, or even Rome made any claim upon them. They paid no tribute other than to the Lord, to whom they offered bread and gathered fruits and in whose name they prayed three times a day.

They placed no stock in the accomplishments of man, not in the monuments or the fortresses he could build, or the fabrics he could weave, or the perfumes he could manufacture. To them, such things were, like the jars they made, ultimately clay and dust. They possessed no life, and what the Subba worshiped above all was Life, which they found in the wilderness surrounding them, in their own children, and in the living water that flowed through their valley and in which they purified themselves three times a day.

The most learned and holy members of the tribe were called Nasurai. According to Kharsand, the eldest of John's disciples, Par'am had been one of these. He had learned the abaga. He could read the etchings in the magic bowls, and the scrolls that they contained. He had read the Book of Souls and knew the other priestly crafts by heart, all the prayers and incantations. When he and the other Nasurai came together and called the names of the dead, the dead heard them and answered. Par'am had studied the splay and interplay of all the heavenly arks, the stars and planets alike; he knew the secret souls that guided them. He could interpret dreams and recognize omens. If a raven cawed while flying past a given house, Par'am understood. When the fire hissed or snapped, when the door groaned a certain way or the clouds made shapes, Par'am recognized them and their meaning. When the moon took veil, or the dust cloud kicked up, either black or red or white, Par'am saw the sign.

But Par'am was not yet a Perfect. He had not achieved that state of holiness that abides among the dwellers of the Mshuni-Kushta, the blessed realm where spirit lives unfettered.

Par'am went to the chieftain of the village, Ahura, and told him he wished to be a Perfect.

Ahura neither encouraged nor discouraged him. He only cautioned that there could be no returning. Once the thing was done, it could not be undone. Par'am said he understood, and so the following day Ahura led him away to a cave out in the wilderness. He left him there seven nights, returning once a day with food, three loaves of bread and the flesh of a dove.

When the seven days had passed, Ahura went to him again and asked if he stood by his intention. Par'am said he did, so that night a feast was held in Ahura's home. All the other villagers came with their children. They had tea and myrtle, bread and lamb. They spoke their devotions together, and the Nasurai called out the names of all who had come before, all the forefathers leading back to Adam.

When the feast had ended, the Nasurai all took one last bit of food in hand and formed a circle around Par'am. He lay down with his hands on his chest, and together they said the prayer for the dead: that God be good to the good, that He bless those who praise His name, permit those who seek to find, those who listen to hear. They prayed all glory and honor to the fathers and forefathers, and mercy and forgiveness for all, but especially for Par'am, their brother who died today.

Then they ate the last handful of food to nourish Par'am's spirit on its journey, giving all thanks and praise to Life, which reigns eternal over all things and deeds.

Par'am did not leave the village after that. He went about his business as he had done before, building his boats by the river, washing his pots and leaving them out to dry in the sun. He continued performing his various devotions as well, his purifications and his prayers. But now, though he lived in the midst of his brothers and sisters and cousins, they took no notice of him. If he passed them on the riverbank, they did not meet his eye or avert their step. If he needed something, he had to get it for himself or do without. He could not speak, even to offer help to another. If he saw an elder stumble, he could not lend his arm. If he saw a child hungry, he could not offer food. If he saw fire headed toward the village or the river flooding its banks, he could not call and warn them. He could only stand and watch, a smile of fixed gaiety on his face.

In this way, like unfired clay left in the river, Par'am gradually dissolved. Like the tribe from which he came, he was not counted. His kin no longer recognized him, and he learned to go unseen, a living ghost among them.

One day Par'am was bathing in the middle of the river when a small band of men approached, soldiers and surveyors, all speaking Greek. Par'am did not understand them, but knew that they were census takers, discussing whether they should cross.

"Is there not a village beyond?" they were asking.

Par'am stood before them, smiling, but they evidently did not see him. They continued pointing past him and discussing, even as the current picked up and encircled him. They did not see him descending or his head slipping down beneath the surface.

Par'am sat upon the bottom of the river, his eyes wide open. Two silver fish, Nidbai and Shimai, swam up and greeted him. They said they had been sent to find him and that he should follow, so Par'am let the water lift him up. He did not need to move his arms or feet. He did not need the air to breathe. He closed his eyes and flowed with the current until it stopped again and all was peace around him. The fish swam off. He touched his feet against the shallow bottom and stood up straight, emerging up to his waist.

Surrounding him were trees in blossom and lambs on the hillside. He had never seen this place before, but he knew that he had found the Mshuni-Kushta, the land of Life itself.

And now he saw the Lilith was standing there: Zahara'il, the bride of Hibil-Ziwa, who first divided the heavens and the earth. She welcomed him and sang his praise for having found this place at last. She let him know that his seat was awaiting him. But first, she said, a mystery had been revealed in the house of Jacob.

Par'am did not understand, but even now a figure of light was descending from the sun like a shard. Par'am knew at once that it was the Uthra Anush, who never died but walked with God. He could feel the warmth of the Uthra's presence as he came near and hovered before him, and he could feel the light as well. He looked down at himself, standing there in the living water of the river and saw that he was clad in the same light, more brilliant and pure and white than any fuller could bleach.

"You see this radiance upon you," the Lilith said. "It is the spirit of the Uthra, which you have now been given to wear as you should need, just as your own flesh is now the Uthra's, to assume as he should need."

So did Par'am and Anush become each other's vesture, the body and the spirit, in order that the mystery might be revealed in all its fullness.

Par'am gave thanks for the great mercy he had been shown, then the Lilith took his hand and lifted him out of the water. Unbound, they crossed back over the river to the land of Canaan. As the daylight faded, they passed over the holy city, and the Lilith led him into the hill country beyond. As the winds began to stir, they descended upon a great black mountain and entered into a cave. They waited there inside, the only light in all the wilderness, while outside the windstorm howled.

The mother appeared not long after nightfall. She had the child with her, a boy, strong and bold. When she set him down, he looked directly at Par'am. He saw the body of Par'am and the light of Anush all at once, and he was not afraid.

The mother wept. To give her the strength she would need, the

Lilith went to her and let her glimpse the mystery. Then Par'am took the child's hand, and together with the Lilith, they departed.

By dawn the sky had calmed again. They took John to the white mountain of Parwan, which was bursting with yellow and purple wild-flower. They brought him to a stream, beside which lambs were suckling from the fruit of the Thadi tree. Par'am took the child into the water there and baptized him. He let the water wash over him. He spoke the word of life upon him and kissed him on the forehead, to seal him and protect him.

The Lilith blessed the child as well, and then she left them there. Only Par'am remained, both as guardian to John, and as earthly vesture—the Uthra Anush, who was to be the child's spirit-guide and light. For one more night John nursed from the fruit of the Thadi tree, then the following morning Par'am took him on his arm, and together they started east.

⋞21⋟

Archelaus

THE REIGN OF HEROD'S HEIRS MEANWHILE BEGAN INAUSPI-
ciously.

As soon as the king's death had been made public, custom provided
that seven days of mourning be observed throughout the land, followed by a feast to which all the subjects, presumably spent of their
grief, were invited to partake.

Chief responsibility for offering the feast fell to the eldest son of
the departed king, in this case Archelaus, the same whom Herod had
named to succeed him in his final will. The feast was to be Archelaus's introduction to the people, and it posed a special burden in this
instance, since Herod's death had come just before Passover. Jerusalem was already overflowing with pilgrims. Even a week before, they
were clogging the streets, spilling outside the walls and living in tents
in Bethpage and Bethany. All would want to be served.

Archelaus saw to it that that they were. He was very generous, in
fact—as far as food and drink were concerned—and the people were
for the most part appreciative. Judaea was in blossom. Stocks were
full. Herod was dead.

Still, in any gathering of such a size, there was bound to be trouble. Too many different interests had been assembled, with too many
rival agendas. There were the Sadducees, of course, the nation's upper

crust, who occupied all the highest offices in church and state. They were there, protecting theirs, taking far more than their share of all the incoming tithes and offerings, if only to make clear that their continued cooperation with the new regime was entirely dependent upon this, the steady flow of more favors and privilege.

Their political opposition, the Pharisees, were there as well, in greater number and passion. Comprised of businessmen, teachers, lawyers, and scribes, they were hardly a seditious bunch—they had too much to lose—but as self-appointed protectors of the Law, they were more than willing to stir the pot and inveigh against the corrupting influence of gentile rule and the compliance of the royals, the priests, and the high ministers.

Of greater concern were the more radical elements. The Zealots —or the *Sicarii*, as they were called, in reference to the daggers they carried into crowds—were rabid enemies of Rome and anyone who did business with the empire. For a generation already, they had been engaged in a low-grade guerrilla war against the powers that be, to assassinate, sow terror, and create chaos, all to the end of making the nation seem so ungovernable that all foreign interests would leave for good, and Israel could once again stand on its own, independent, armed, and pure.

That was the appeal, at any rate, which tapped the basic grievance shared by nearly all who'd come—be they fishermen, tradesmen, scribes, or shepherds—that the sacred homeland of the Jewish people, willed to them by God, had, under the departed king, become little more than a vassal state, a client kingdom beholden to the interests of a brutal, heathen empire.

Of all the agitators who had come, the most effective on this day turned out to be the students of the martyred rabbis Judas and Matthias. They were still in the throes of grief at the loss of their beloved teachers and comrades, and still furious at the manner in which they had been executed, burned alive in the public square at Jericho. As the festival approached and the streets began to swell with pilgrims, the students stationed themselves throughout the city, on the roads leading in and at all the Temple gates, so that anyone who entered was forced to hear them rail about how the High Priest was a criminal and about all the false tears that had been shed for Herod, while they had been denied their grief.

"Who denies your grief?" the pilgrims would ask, annoyed by the obstruction.

"Who denies me justice denies me grief!" the students fired back; then they'd ask for money in support of their cause.

Their presence was not felt acutely, however, until the opening ceremony of the festival itself. According to tradition, the first offering was to be made by the king. There was no king as yet, officially— Herod's will had yet to be ratified by Caesar—but Archelaus assumed the privilege, donning the sacred vestments and taking the place of honor at the heart of the royal procession that made its way through the streets and to the Temple Mount.

Again, the people were generally supportive and enthusiastic— that is, until the procession reached the Temple itself and the Court of Priests. Here the students were lying in wait, and Archelaus obliged them by turning and speaking to the crowd. He thanked them for the respect they'd shown during his father's funeral. He said that as soon as his crown was confirmed, he would remember their generosity and return it in kind, as he recognized his father's ways were not always as charitable as they might have been.

"Then ease the taxes," a voice called out.

"And lift the duties on wheat," came another.

Archelaus smiled. He said he would take their suggestions under advisement just as soon as Caesar confirmed him, but that today was a day of celebration.

"And what of Judas and Matthias?" one of the students shouted. "How are we to celebrate in our grief when the High Priest has blood on his hands?"

Archelaus pretended not to hear and proceeded quickly to the rite. He sacrificed the lamb, which did briefly quiet the crowd; then he descended into the private banquet hall in hopes that that would be the end of it.

It was not. In his absence, arguments erupted between the students and the worshipers, many of whom agreed with Archelaus that this was not the time or place. Even if he had wanted, they said, Archelaus could not depose the High Priest. He hadn't the authority yet.

"Wait until the crown is on his head," they said.

"But listen to yourself," the students answered. "Why should he need Caesar to crown him? If he must be crowned by Caesar, then he is not a Jewish king! He is an extortionist working for Rome, just like his father."

The point was well taken, in particular since all this was taking place beneath the glare of the golden eagle, newly restored for the occasion.

Down below in the private banquet hall, Archelaus was at first dismissive when told that the agitators were still agitating. He was surrounded by friends and family. The wine had begun to flow. Twice he sent legates up to repeat his answer, that he would he happy to consider any and all complaints at the appropriate time, but that in recognition of the day the protesters should now refrain and let the rites proceed.

When the second legate returned, telling him that the protesters were not merely disrespecting the rite but openly interfering with it, the would-be king's impatience began to show.

"Who are these people?" he snapped.

He was told, the students of Judas and Matthias.

"And do they not understand that what they are doing is illegal?"

"They say the rite is illegal," the legate replied, "just as what happened to their teachers was illegal."

"But how could it be illegal?" Archelaus sputtered. "It was ordered by Herod. Herod makes the law. Now tell them to desist at once, or they shall be subject to the same law!" And here, recognizing a certain familial resemblance in his tone, he could not resist. He screwed up his face and, in a sudden fit of comic palsy, shouted, "Now where is my fucking bath?"

Some laughed. Some made note.

No mirth, however misplaced, could change the fact that the situation up in the court was growing worse by the minute. Inspired by their own defiance, the students were now actually surrounding the priests and shouting at them. The worshipers, come to make their sacrifices, were piling up behind them and growing more and more angry, which only fed the students' sense of power. Other agitators could see the effect that they were having. The Zealots—always present, always armed—had joined in the protest as well, lending it far more menace. Now when the king's men appeared from below and issued their warnings, accusing the people of riot and sedition, the students beat their chests. "Yes, we are seditious!" they cried.

It was the Roman procurator of Syria, Sabinus, who finally recommended a more forceful response. Sabinus found Archelaus, mid-dance, and suggested sending in a regiment to clear the court. Archelaus agreed, but it was already too late. By the time a full complement of troops could be brought in, the crowd around the Temple was entirely out of control. When they saw the soldiers, they began pelting them with stones, while others descended on them, overwhelming them by their sheer number and driving them back. The Zealots actually took hold of the centurion and began beating him, kicking him and clubbing him. They let him go only for the pleasure of watching him scramble away, "like a limping dog," they called after him, howling in triumph. "Go and let your master see!"

And finally it was this, the sight of the officer staggering into the royal dining hall, bleeding, that sobered Archelaus enough to put aside his cup. He flew into a rage.

"How do we stop this? Now!"

Sabinus told him, calmly, it was only a matter of bringing in sufficient force. "Merely say the word."

"Word, yes," said Archelaus. "Do what must be done."

The full force of Jerusalem's standing army was summoned forthwith and given orders to treat what was taking place up in the Court of Priests as an open rebellion. They surrounded the mount. No more civilians were permitted to enter in. The way was cleared for a legion of footmen to enter by the steps, while a second legion, with cavalry, entered by the eastern gate.

Up among the students and protesters, the warning was brief. The cavalry fell upon the crowd without regard for guilt or innocence. The footmen likewise made no distinction. Those who were able fled to the safety of the street, where officers were already ordering the people to return to their homes. The feast had ended. Those still trapped inside were either arrested or killed, their bodies heaped in piles around the sacred Temple. According to the count of the priests, more than three thousand Jews were sacrificed before the riot was finally put down.

And only seven lambs.

≋22≋

Antipas

THE REST OF THE FAMILY HAD WATCHED ALL THIS UNFOLD WITH some dismay. They did not see the bloodshed or the dead bodies, but most had witnessed the scene out in the court when Archelaus addressed the crowd, and they had observed him down below in the banquet hall, losing control of the situation, chalice by chalice.

Most of them also convened at Caesarea in the days that followed. Their boats were there, waiting to take them to Rome, where their interests were more or less the same: Until Caesar approved the will, none of its gifts or appointments could be claimed.

Private dinners were served in various houses and halls—it was a large family—but the conversations all eventually reverted back to the same topic.

"Mark it, the people won't soon forget."

"No, this will not die in a day."

Archelaus had never been particularly popular within the family, for all the reasons now in evidence. He was petulant, haughty, and much too easily provoked. The generally accepted view was that Herod had only named him king as a way of getting back at Antipater, who'd always been very negative about Archelaus.

"But Antipater was not always wrong," said Varus. "He was often quite right."

In this case, certainly. Archelaus's conduct had been as typical as it was regrettable. All that giddiness at dinner, and the mockery.

"Disgusting," said Antipas. "What happened to those tears he was shedding all afternoon?"

His handling of the rioters? "Execrable," sniffed Achiabus. "He should have responded much more quickly."

"And with a firmer hand," said Varus, though all agreed the real mistake had been that pointless show of graciousness up in the court.

"He should never have engaged the people's questions."

"He should never have engaged them at all," said Salome, now the undisputed family eminence. "Let them see the robe, offer the sacrifice, and go."

Exactly.

Late on the second night, she asked to see her nephew Antipas in private.

Antipas was then seventeen years old. He had spent the better part of his youth in Rome, the younger tagalong to Archelaus and Philip (their half brother). He was, as such, among the least surprised by what had taken place, though in some ways the most offended, as had apparently shown.

"You loved your father," said Salome.

"I did," replied Antipas. They were standing out on a veranda, overlooking the beach and the boats. "I revered my father, and I grieve his death. I am thankful it took him from his misery, but I do not like to see his memory mocked this way or his legacy subjected to such abuse."

"Good," said Salome. "This is why I sent for you."

It was only at this moment that Antipas saw they were not alone. Ptolemy, his father's lawyer, was there as well, in the shadows.

His aunt began. "It is hardly news that there is little appetite within the family for living under Archelaus's rule. In light of what has just happened, I think it's safe to say there is very little appetite among the people either. Varus claims there is a delegation headed for Rome even now, prepared to challenge your brother's succession before Caesar.

They are proposing that the nation be united with Syria under the governance of a Roman regent.

"Well. Clearly, the family cannot be expected to accept such an arrangement. At the same time, we can hardly offer a full-throated defense of Archelaus. There is, however, an alternative."

Here Ptolemy stepped out, armed with scrolls.

"I expect you are aware," Salome continued, "Herod spent much of the last year revising his will. According to our friend Ptolemy, he drafted no fewer than five separate codicils in that time."

The lawyer so confirmed.

"What many may not know," said Salome, "is that Archelaus was named king only in the very last of these, which Herod wrote just days before he died. Prior to this—and I am speaking of the *third* codicil, drafted this past spring—he named you."

The lawyer presented Antipas with the document at question so that he could see for himself his own name conjoined to the word "basileôs."

There was a sudden mad rush of blood to his head. "What are you suggesting?"

"We are suggesting you let us go to Caesar now," said Salome, "and make the argument that Herod was clearly not well at the end of his life—clearly—but that when he was of sounder mind and body, he deemed you, not Archelaus, most worthy to be king."

Antipas was speechless.

"Obviously, it's a great deal to take in all at once," said his aunt. "I don't expect you to decide here and now. On the other hand, the sooner the decision is made, the better, just so that we can gather together all the necessary letters and testimony."

"Of course," said Antipas, but vaguely. He was stunned, not just at seeing the will but at the idea that his father had apparently thought of him this way, and that others in the family did too.

"You seem hesitant," said Salome

"No, it's only . . . the enormity. I am aware of what my father accomplished. I honor it, and I would want nothing more than to help it flourish, but"—his eye searched about the moonlit sand below—"it was my father's *destiny* to be king."

"Who told you that?"

"Why, but this is known," said Antipas. "Menahem told him when he was a boy—"

Salome smiled, not kindly. "And was it destiny that rode with Herod into the caves of Syria and killed the bandit Hezekiah? Was it destiny that hacked your grandfather's murderer to death on this very beach here? Was it destiny that chased the armies of Antigonus all through Palestine and then laid siege to the Temple until the men inside begged for mercy? Destiny belongs to those who seize it, young man. What I am offering you now is an opportunity."

Early the next morning Antipas recounted the meeting to his oldest and closest friend, Manean, who also happened to be the son of Menahem the Essene, Herod's most trusted (and storied) adviser.

Manean had not inherited his father's faith. Like Antipas he had been sent off to Rome to be educated, and was in all ways a more worldly, more moderate offering than his father had been: of average height and stature, bristle-headed, clean-shaven, and sensible in his thinking. He had shown no inkling in the direction of prophecy or divination. Still, his friendship with Antipas represented a kind of generational mapping from which both seemed to derive a certain tacit pleasure.

"So what do you think?" asked Antipas.

"About which aspect?"

"Any of it. What I should do."

Manean was surprised. His friend was still clearly in a state of shock. There was a pallor surrounding his blush and a subtle, involuntary shake of his head that suggested he had never truly considered the prospect before.

"I think you should be honored."

"I am. Obviously."

"But if you're asking me to venture what the future holds in store—"

"No, I don't want that, but . . . what is your *opinion*?"

Manean hesitated. In point of fact, he considered it a poor bet that

Caesar would ever overturn Herod's last will, but he did not say this. "My opinion is that this would be a very difficult proposal to refuse."

Antipas agreed. That same day, he sent word to Salome, consenting to her suggestion.

The trip to Rome took roughly three weeks, during the course of which Antipas grew more and more comfortable with his decision. Several other members of the family had come aboard, either in person or in the form of a letter, to offer their support. Irenaeus, an excellent orator, said that he would speak at the hearing, which was good news. By boat Salome also sent over the various testimonials that she had been able to collect against Archelaus.

In reviewing them all, Antipas came to regard the case as being fairly simple. The massacre had made his brother's rule impossible; the Jewish delegation would make that clear enough. If one accepted that, then Antipas was the only real alternative, inasmuch as his father had willed it.

"Not to recognize this would be an insult to Herod," he said.

"True," said Manean. "If one accepts the premise."

Of course the more convinced Antipas was of the legal merits of the case, the more certain he grew of its righteousness as well. By the second week of the voyage he firmly believed that he *deserved* to be king. "Both justice and the nation require it," he said. Whenever any doubt crept in, all he had to do was think of Archelaus dancing at the funeral banquet, laughing and mocking his father. That, or refer back to the final will.

"Because remember what he did give me," he would say, "even in his dementia: Galilee." Galilee had been his father's training ground, where he first served as governor back when he was only seventeen. "Clearly it is a sign. Salome is correct. This is a test, and I accept. As your father was to mine, so Salome is to me, my messenger."

The Jewish delegation had already been in Rome for several days when the family arrived. Caesar, recognizing the situation required a timely response, agreed to hear all three sides—the delegation's, the family's, and then Archelaus's, in that order, before the Senate.

The delegation represented itself very well, first laying out the case against Herod, detailing the history of his tyranny. They said the people had been looking to Archelaus for a new beginning, but that the incident at the Temple only served to show that their hopes had been misplaced. Archelaus was every bit as brutal as his father.

"Pity the remnants of the Jewish people," they said. "Do not throw us back to the beast."

The family's turn came next. Unfortunately, Salome's son Antipater (not the executed scoundrel) presented the case instead of Irenaeus. He opened by pointing out that Archelaus had already insulted Caesar's authority by assuming so many of the king's responsibilities, reassigning the top posts in the army, granting dignities, and so forth. He said Archelaus had treated Caesar as "lord of words, not things."

He then offered his own account of what had occurred at Passover, backed up by witnesses who all painted a clear picture of the carnage and how the blame lay entirely with Archelaus.

But this was part of the problem—at least in Antipas's view. The family's position was presented as having much more to do with Archelaus's *unsuitedness* to the throne than with Antipas's suitedness. Even in introducing the third codicil, the one naming Antipas as king, the point seemed to be that Herod's sounder mind had had the sense to pass over Archelaus, not that he had recognized the virtues of Antipas. Antipas himself had fallen into the same trap during his own testimony. He'd been very nervous and ended up spending far too much time describing Archelaus's behavior at the banquet—the false tears, the excessive drinking, the joking and dancing—rather than demonstrating his own merit. In retrospect, he conceded that had been a mistake, though he somewhat blamed the examiner.

Finally came Archelaus's turn to defend himself, which he did in the person of Ptolemy's brother, Nicolaus. A good lawyer, he took full advantage of going last, answering each of his predecessors' complaints, one by one: Methods notwithstanding, Herod's books sufficed to show how the nation had prospered under his rule and how Rome had prospered in turn. Regarding any liberties Archelaus might have taken—appointing officers, hearing petitions, and such—he had done only what was absolutely necessary in his father's absence. (A nation could not run itself, after all, as Caesar himself well knew.) As for the incident at the Temple, it had been a terrible thing, of course—a tragedy—but for all the reasons the family had already pointed out, Archelaus's hands had been tied. He was not yet king. He had been reluctant to assert a king's authority. Indeed, if he had erred one way or the other, it had been on the side of restraint, insofar as he had resisted the impulse of the rest of the family, who had been urging him toward violence from the very beginning of the evening.

Finally, as to the validity of the fifth codicil, the one naming Archelaus king, what more need be said than that Herod had chosen Caesar to ratify it? "How can we now question the judgment of one who openly and willingly yielded his authority to the 'Lord of the World'?"

It was at this point, and obviously on cue, that Archelaus himself approached the emperor, presented his father's ring and seal, and promptly fell down prostrate. From his seat beside Antipas, Manean could see that Caesar's eyes welled.

The verdict was announced two days later and came as no surprise. The final will would stand, with the one amendment that Archelaus would not be allowed to assume his full title yet. Where Herod had bestowed the name "king" and full sovereignty over all, Caesar for now granted Archelaus the more limited title "ethnarch," thus confining his authority to the districts named in the will. Caesar did not preclude the possibility of Archelaus's someday becoming king, but first he would have to prove himself and make amends.

Among the parties present, the general consensus was that Caesar had once again shown his wisdom. All sides were more or less satisfied. The public delegation had succeeded in exacting a certain measure of accountability for what had taken place at Passover. The family had managed to knock Archelaus down a peg, such that he enjoyed no real power over them. As for Archelaus, he could hardly complain after what had happened. He may not have been king, but he was still the preeminent ruler in the land, with the possibility of promotion.

Only Antipas had been left out in the cold, but the worst of it was not the ruling itself. He'd been prepared for Caesar's decision. What stung was that his claim had basically gone without mention. Caesar had said nothing. Not a single member of the family came to him to offer thanks, or consolation, or regret.

"It's as if the whole conversation with Salome never happened."

Manean wished that he could have disagreed. "I'm sure they're grateful," he said, but the silence that ensued was far more resonant and telling. His friend had tasted ambition. He had tasted humiliation. Only time would tell which taste would linger longer.

⇒23⇐

The Sacred Grove

IT FELL TO THE NURSEMAID, BATTAI, TO OFFER THE NEIGHBORS IN Ein Karim an explanation for what had happened to John. She told them what her mistress had told her: that the morning after the eclipse, Elizabeth had taken John out into the hills to collect hilazon. Somehow they had gotten lost, and then the storm had come. They had taken shelter in a cave and spent the night there. When she wakened, he was gone. She searched. All she'd found was his lambskin on the rock.

Some of the neighbors refused to believe. "Why would she go out alone so far? No woman is so careless."

"But she is old. And look at her. Look at her."

"I do look at her, and what I see I don't believe."

They did not believe because they knew about the soldiers too, the Syrians who'd come asking after John, saying they had been sent to take him back to the Temple.

All agreed that they'd been liars, those two; they'd been thieves, or worse, for by then the news had come of what had taken place at Bethlehem, how the hooded fiends had come in the middle of the night and slaughtered the children of the town. A dozen boys, none older than two. Who knew why? To feed the Romans. But the villagers of Ein Karim would never believe it was an animal that had taken John, or even an "angel," as the maidservant was also heard to claim.

"An angel with a spear," they said.

"But leave the woman be. What she tells herself she must."

They cast dust on their heads. They rent their clothes, for John and for Elizabeth. They wept for her, as this was only half the woman's suffering. For on returning from the hills without her son, she waited for Old Father. All the village waited. They dreaded his return even as they prayed for it, but only the Levites came, and then the other priests from his order, saying that they had hoped to find Old Father there. None knew where he had gone. And then came the news of Herod's passing, and the riot at the Temple, and the horrors in Bethlehem, where the mothers were now begging for Death to come and take them as well. They hurled themselves from hilltops. They drowned themselves in wells. They ate dust until they choked and died. The world was mad with suffering. The world was ruled by demons.

In Ein Karim no feast was held. The villagers kept vigil for Old Father and waited, and finally it was Elizabeth who entered the circle and told them to go home. She was reconciled: Her husband was not returning.

In the days and weeks that followed, there was talk of her moving back to Hebron. She still had family there.

"But even there how will she endure?" the neighbors asked. They questioned a God who would heap misfortune like this, and they looked at Elizabeth in wonder. Every morning she could be seen walking in the olive groves, and every evening, weaving out on her balcony. Yet they perceived no grief in her. The expression on her face was mild, and wan.

"She is beyond sorrow," they told themselves.

When they saw Battai descending to the well, they would go and ask her, "And how is your mistress today?"

Battai would tell them, "She abides."

And they would shake their heads; they did not see how. "Every day we are prepared to hear you say, 'She is gone,' to be with them, to be free of her grief. No one here would blame her. But every day you say that she abides, and we do not know how."

The nursemaid gave the only answer that she could. "By prayer," she said.

"Tell me that prayer."

"By faith," she said.

"Lend me that faith."

And there were those in the village whose wonder turned to disbelief and then into suspicion.

"Does it not trouble you," they asked, "that Old Father should have vanished as well? Or that a mother should stray so far for no good reason? She knew. She had been warned. She fled the demons. She met Old Father in the hills. The child is with his father."

Battai heard them, and she despised their saying such things, but in her heart she was confused as well. She too, when she looked at her mistress, did not perceive the grief she thought she should, for in herself the pain was more than she could bear; she could barely walk. She could not look where the crib had stood. She could not be in the same room as the lambskin; his scent was like a claw thrashing at her heart.

One evening Elizabeth found her. "What is it, Battai? Why do you weep?"

Battai tried hiding her tears, for shame at the presumption that her grief should spill out and whimper and wail, while her mistress carried herself with such calm and grace.

"But I can see your cheeks are damp, Battai. Dry them. Tell me."

Battai confessed. "I weep because I miss him. I look out at the terrace, I miss him. I miss him in the grove. I weep because the silence here is a wound that will not heal. I want to serve my mistress, but I cannot bear the silence."

Elizabeth took her aside. "But did you not hear me when I said he was with the angel now? I told you this because you were there, Battai. Out on the road to Hebron, where you saw the child and I saw the maiden. They were one and the same, and you must believe it was to that same maiden that I entrusted him and to the messenger beside, for he had heard my prayer as well."

Battai turned away. It was all she could do to keep silent when she heard her mistress speak this way.

"But do not think that I am cold. Do not think that I don't grieve his absence. His absence is a wound in me as well.

"But when I am given to doubt or to despair, when I lose faith or I forget, there is a dream that comes to me, of the mystery I was given to see that night inside the cave, and I will tell it to you, as you did love John, as you were there when the angel first appeared and then again when John awakened in me.

"We are in a grove, John and I, and it is morning. My cousin Mary is there with her son, Jesus. And we are watching the two of them and how they play. But you should see the look on John's face, and how tenderly he takes his cousin's hand. And Mary and I, our hearts are like springs. They are like rivers overflowing. We marvel at our deliverance and at how blessed we are, for we know we are mothers of long-promised sons."

Her mistress's words made no sense to Battai. "But where is your consolation if every time you must awake?"

"Because I know what I see is the truth, and Mary can see as well. It is not strange that we should be there, for all has been written, and there is nothing here the prophets have not seen, and none are more blessed than those who believe the Word shall be fulfilled. It shall be as Old Father said; he did not die in vain . . .

"But do not weep, Battai. Do not think me cold. Know that if I am not with him in that grove, if he is not with me, then I am in the cave again, and I am always in the cave. I burn inside with jealousy at those who hold him now and feed him, who hear him cry at night and sing him back to sleep. I would give my life for just one night to do the same.

"But the same as I burn inside, I know that he is out there. I see the moon. I know it shines upon him. I have seen him in its light, Battai. Oh, and he is beautiful. More than you remember. I only pray he hears me. I pray he knows there is not a moment passes I do not think of him and wait for him. For he shall return, Battai. We shall see him again, as all has happened for a purpose. I promise you, as they have promised me."

But Battai could not help herself. When she heard her mistress speak this way, she took no comfort, nor when she heard her mistress pray. She could not join her. She only thought, Listen to the old priest's widow. Listen to the mother without child. She hangs her hopes on desperate, foolish dreams.

24

The Subba

AFTER A JOURNEY OF A FORTNIGHT, PAR'AM BROUGHT JOHN through the wilderness to the far side of the Jordan, all the way to the hidden wadi and the little tribe of potters who lived among the caves there, the Subba.

The village was still asleep when they arrived, as was John. Par'am laid him down on the threshold of the cave of the chieftain, Ahura. With his finger he wrote John's name in the dirt. Then he sat and waited.

Ahura's wife, Taraneh, was first to awake. Thinking the light outside was dawn and not the mantle of the Uthra, she started out with all her pots and jars in arm to wash them at the stream, but then she saw the sky all dark, and she saw the child asleep.

She awakened her husband at once to show him. Like Taraneh, Ahura did not see Par'am. He did not see the light of the Uthra, but he could feel its warmth and knew, just as he had known when Par'am left the village, that he had returned and that he had brought the child to them.

His wife said, "We should look for his mother. Perhaps the child is lost and she is searching for him. She may be ill."

Ahura told her no. "The mother is not searching for him, nor is he lost." And he told her his name, which had been written in the dirt.

Yahya-Yuhana.

So the Subba took in John as a pride takes in a stray cub. He was cared for first by Ahura and Taraneh, both elders among the tribe, and by their sons and daughters, who had children of their own. And because the Subba took so little stock in earthly things and man-made things, because they took only what they needed and shared among them what they had, they gave little thought to sharing in the care of John as well.

They fed him and clothed him, bathed him and cared for him. And they loved him as they loved life, for in John the life was abundant. His eyes danced. His voice was full. A seed of celestial fruit, they called him, and they counted themselves blessed that the heavens had planted him among them.

They taught him how to tie his tunic around his loins and how he should bathe, wash his hands and arms before eating, and always from the "living" water, the water that moved and flowed. They fed him lamb's milk, and manna, carob beans, locusts, and honey. If he fell and bloodied his brow, they cleaned his wound. They kissed it and dressed it.

And their children played with him and squabbled with him. They called him brother. He was their brother. And so in time his memory of the life he had known in Ein Karim began to fade: the cool slate of the terrace and the shadows of the olive grove; the smell of Old Father's beard; the low sound of his prayer; the lilt of his mother's lullaby and how she stroked his temple with her finger; how Battai kissed his foot. All drew farther back in the recesses of his mind, until all that remained was his memory of the light, and the reason he remembered the light was that the light remained with him. It was the same as belonged to the Uthra, the same as issued from the mantle of Par'am, and Par'am did not leave John's side. He was with him day and night. He was with him when he fell asleep. He was there when he awoke, standing silently by in the presence of the others.

How Ahura and the others failed to see, John could not imagine. But they could not, even when Par'am would come and join them by the river.

"He is right here." John would splash. "Right here!"

Ahura would shake his head; he saw nothing.

John would take Ahura's hand and set it on Par'am's knee, but still the old chieftain would only shake his head and smile. And the others would shake their heads, agreeing. Nothing.

John would laugh. "Show them," he would say to Par'am. "Make the light. Show them the Uthra."

But Par'am would put his finger to his mouth. And Ahura would put his finger to his mouth as well, as the other children gathered around.

"Come!" he would cry out. "Sit! Listen!" This was the first lesson always. The rest all followed from this:

"The good man sits and is in search. The wise man is the one who lets himself be taught, who looks up full of hope, as Adam did, and asks, 'Who will tell me the truth? Who will set it forth for me and make it so I understand?' So did Adam give his ear and hearken, and he was first to ascend. And all who do the same, they shall ascend after Adam. Praise be to Adam and all who follow him!"

And the children would reply, "Praise be to Adam!"

"Praise be to the children who sit and listen to their fathers! Praise be to him who says 'Teach me! Tell me!'"

"Teach me!" the children would cry. "Tell me!"

"Tell you what?" Ahura would turn to one of them, the youngest. "Tell you what, Azha?"

"Tell about the kings," Azharan would say.

"Ah, the kings." Ahura's eyes danced among the shining faces. "But you have only to look up at the stars and see there are two realms, and always have been, ruled by rival kings. There is the king who wears the crown of darkness. He girts a sword around his waist. He unsheathes his sword in his right hand and slays his sons with it, and his sons slay one another. Behold!

"Then there is the king who wears the crown of light, a crown that shines in glory. He girts no sword around his waist. In his right hand he carries a book, and from this book he reads the Truth to his sons and to his daughters.

"And his sons and daughters, they have stood upon this very bank, and they have taught your fathers from this book. They said to them as I say to you:

"'Be not a liar! Be not a thief! Nor a cheat or a conjurer be!

"'Observe the heavens and take heed. Become not of the darkness a portion. From the evil unto the good separate thyself.

"'Honor thy father! Honor thy mother! For he who honors his mother and father has not his like in this world.

"'See that ye not pray to godlings and to idols! For those who cheat and thieve and lie, and those who pray unto other gods, they shall not ascend.

"'See that ye not practice magic or poison the soul with lies and deception. For those who deal in sorcery and deception, they shall be cast into dungeons and forgotten.

"'See that ye observe the boundary—be it of your neighbor's store, be it of the darkness and the light, be it of this world and of the one that waits. Do not think that you can go and then return. Do not think that you can move the stone aside.

"'But stay and sow, and gather up kind deeds and mercy. Load up your arms with acts of charity and goodness, and give from what you have. For he whose arms are empty, he shall ascend, while he whose arms are full with the riches of this world, they shall drag him down like an anchor to the bottom of the sea!

"'Woe to him who had it in his hand and did not give. Woe to him who heard the call but did not answer. Woe to him who hears the truth but does not pass it down, who lets himself be taught but does not teach. He is a glutton. As you would be taught, so must you teach. Help them who seek. Teach them who ask.'"

This, then, was the final lesson, always. The first: to sit, to ask and to be taught. The last: to love and to instruct.

"Love and instruct one another," Ahura said, "and your sin will be forgiven. Then you will ascend.

"Praise be to them who sit and listen to their fathers. Praise be to them who stand and teach their sons."

John was a good son. He sat and he listened and learned, and not only from Ahura. From Ahura's son Nasim he learned to fish, with the net and with his hand; from Seroush he learned to herd the goats, how to tap the stick, and how to find the stray; from Kharsand he learned how to calm the hive and drain the comb; he learned from Merdad to catch the locusts in the morning, when the wings were still heavy with dew; from Taraneh he learned the songs and dances; from Aram he learned the hills and where to set his foot; and of course he learned to make the pots and jars as well.

Still, for all he learned, he assumed that he would grow to be a holy man one day, a Nasurai like Par'am. John felt it in Ahura's embrace, and he felt it at their meals, where he was never given any meat to eat, or juice of the vine. They kept him pure. Why else but to be a priest?

When John turned seven, Par'am took him to the river and drew a circle in the sand.

O

He told John that this was the first and last, the symbol of perfection, and of light and life, and he said it made a sound. *Aaaah.*

And John repeated *aaaah.*

Then next to the **O**, Par'am wrote:

ﺝ

"The great father," he said. "And the sound it makes is *baaah.*"

Baaaah, repeated John.

Next was:

ﻉ

"*Ga,*" said Par'am, "the messenger Gabriel."

And so forth along the strand, Par'am wrote every letter until he came around to the **O** again.

So began John's lesson in the secrets of the abaga. He did not tell Ahura, but every day he went out to study with Par'am, and every night the river rose and erased his tablet.

As with his other lessons, John sat and listened, and he learned quickly. Soon enough, when he looked out upon the water, he could see the letters dancing in the reflection, like a bridge crossing from one side to the other. Par'am taught him how all the vowels were different phases of the sun, rising and setting. He taught him how they combined with the other letters, and the sounds they made together, and how these sounds made words, and how these words could open doors and yield the past, how they could unlock mysteries and reveal the heavens.

When John was ready, Par'am took him up into the cave where the sacred bowls were kept, high above the village, where they could protect all the people below. Par'am showed him how some of the bowls were inscribed with names and prayers and how if he closed his eyes and put them to their ear, he would see the angels, whom they called Melkhi. Par'am showed him how the other bowls contained papyrus scrolls. He let John open them and read from them all the spells and legends they contained.

One morning Ahura found him there. He told him, "Yahya, you should not have entered in this place. This space is sacred. These bowls hold mysteries inside them that should not be tampered with."

But John showed him the inscriptions were no mystery to him. He read the spells aloud, and all the prayers and the names of all the fathers, from Zihrun to Ram, to Simat, to Anhar, and Noah. He showed him he had seen the Melkhi, Nirigh, Bel, and Liwet.

"And tell me what they look like," said Ahura. "How does Sin appear?" (Sin was the spirit of the moon.)

"He has seven heads," said John, "branching out like a tree."

Afterwards Ahura went to the other Nasurai and asked if any of them had been teaching John. They said no. They would not have taught the spells or the letters to one so young. They were concerned, but Ahura told them they should not be.

"This child is blessed," he said.

One night when John was eight, Par'am came to him and awakened him and took him up onto the plateau just above the caves. He pointed to a bright star out in front of them.

"Merikh is the morning star," he said. He pointed to another. "Thuraya gives rain."

So began John's lessons in the secrets of the heavens. Par'am showed him which of the lights were the stars, and which were planets, how they were aligned in constellations and how their paths were fixed. He told him they were like arks, that each possessed a guiding spirit, and that these were Uthras, too, just like Anush. He showed him how they turned and intersected with the planets and what this meant for all things below.

"And do they see?" asked John.

Par'am told him yes.

"And do they sing?"

"They do," said Par'am, "but you must be still and silent to hear," and he showed him how to do this as well.

Later Taraneh's sister, Dariyah, found John sitting with the other children and pointing to the sky.

"The northern stars pray twelve butha," he was saying, "and the rest pray the seven buwath." Then she heard him reciting in the language of the stars.

She went to Ahura and told him what she had heard. Ahura did not dispute her. Again he asked the other Nasurai if any of them had been teaching John these things. Again they shook their heads. They would not have taught the heavens' secrets to a child so young.

"But surely he is blessed," they all agreed.

John knew that he was blessed, not just because of what Par'am was teaching him but because of what the Uthra let him see.

One time John's uncle Nasim, a young father in the tribe, was bitten by a snake. As he lay dying, and all the priests were gathered around him, dressing him and praying, the Uthra waved John around. He opened his arm and shone the pure light of his cloak on Nasim. John saw the angel of death, Azrael, sitting on his uncle's chest and peering in his mouth.

"The soul is not like the blood," the Uthra said, "which runs warm until it stops and goes cold. The soul is not like the dew, which vanishes beneath the sun. It is not like the wind, which yields to the mountainside."

Then John saw Azrael draw the spirit of Nasim into the flames of his trident. He saw him steal away and leave the body there, a husk, while the widow and the mother wept.

Another time Taraneh's daughter, Pareesa, was round with child but ill. Again the Uthra came to John and shone his light where the daughter lay. John could see there was another Uthra there, sitting beside Pareesa, pouring silver smoke into her mouth.

"What did she look like?" asked his brother Azha, when John told him of it later.

"She was tall and slender, like a mantis," said John.

"Did she speak to you?"

"Yes," said John. "She said, 'Behold. The soul is rendered well before it enters the body. If it is kept pure, then it will ascend.'"

Azha did not doubt him. He said, "Will you pray for me, Yahya, when you are a Nasurai? Will you remember me and say my name?"

"Of course," said John. "But you will not be far."

"Say my name, Yahya! Say my name and they will hear."

"Azharan!" John cried out. "Azharan!" And Azharan danced in circles, laughing.

One day Kharsand, who was a young Nasurai, took John aside. He said, "I hear you speak to the others. I hear the others speak. But you understand that you will never be the chieftain or a priest."

And Kharsand showed him why: how beneath his loincloth, John had been circumcised, while his brothers and cousins had not.

John knew this, as he had always known that he was not the same. Soon after Pareesa's child was born and baptized, John was there when all his cousins gathered around.

"Look," they said. "Already she has Pareesa's eyes. Already she has her father's chin."

John saw too, the eyes were like his aunt Pareesa's. Her chin was like his uncle's, and yet when he looked around, he found no likeness to himself among them. And when he bathed with them, his difference was there as well, which the other children could see.

"Who carried you, Yahya?" they would ask.

His cousin Kerbah pointed to his mother down the bank. "She carried me."

"And she me," said Dariyah.

"Who carried you, Yahya?" They smiled and waited. They meant no harm.

But he did not know. And so even after he had learned all the hidden wisdom, all the prayers and the secrets of the heavenly arks, and how to read dreams, and what it meant when a raven cawed while flying past a certain house, or when the fire hissed or snapped a certain way, when the door groaned, or the clouds made shapes or the dust kicked up, even after all of this, the one question still lingered.

He went to Par'am one evening and asked him, "Who was my mother who carried me?"

Par'am brought John down to the river. He walked him to a spot along the banks, set apart among the reeds, and left him there.

John sat until the night had fallen and the moon rose up, and while he waited, he prayed. He gave thanks to the Heavenly Father for all the blessings that had been shown him—for the wisdom of Ahura, and for the care of Taraneh, for the guidance of Par'am and the treasures of the Uthra's light. He gave thanks for all his brothers and his cousins, for their laughter and their embrace.

The heavens heard. While he prayed, the river swelled up its banks. The water reached out to the moon, and all around, the stars called down to him: The one who had carried him was still beside him. Not for a moment had he left her heart, or her prayer, which she was praying even then; their light so testified.

But John could not see them through his tears. He could not hear them for his weeping.

≋25≋

Herodias

FAR AWAY, BACK ACROSS THE JORDAN AGAIN, BEYOND JERICHO AND Jerusalem, out along the coast of the Great Sea, a reasonably pretty young girl could be found traipsing the halls of the palace at Ascalon, sighing on the balconies of Jamnia and Ashdod, playing hide-and-seek and keep-away among the palm trees of the family groves up in Phasaelis.

"Give it! It's *mine*."

"Don't worry, you'll have it back. I just want to—ow!"

She'd grabbed her brother's wrist and was digging in her nails.

"Ow! Here, then. Take it." He flung the vial.

She caught it before it fell and, in the same gesture, tilted the little porphyry mouth against her wrist. And there, in that single acrobatic, its viciousness and elegance combined—the essence of Herodias.

There was, and always had been, this battle inside her, between the ermine and the fox. More than any child in the clan, Herodias seemed to be the product of its rival sides, the Herodean and the Hasmonaean, perhaps because those sides reduced so cleanly—in her mind, at least—to the persons of her two grandmothers.

There was, on the one hand, Salome, the last surviving member of Herod's generation, his sister and by all accounts his only equal, Salome, whose eye missed nothing, whose sidelong glance meant all, who stood as living proof of what succeeded in the war between cunning and entitlement. (And by whose graces, it should be noted, young Herodias lived the life she did; she did not take that for granted.)

Yet there was her father's mother as well, Mariamne. Herodias had never met her. She'd died long before Herodias was born, but still her legend loomed: the great and beautiful Mariamne, whose veins had run with the bluest and most valiant blood in all Jewry, whose purity was preserved in the honey of a tragic death. Herod had apparently loved her so madly that he killed her out of jealousy at the thought that she would ever be with another.

As proud and grateful as Herodias was to be the granddaughter of Salome, she prized every drop of Mariamne's blood as well. She often bragged that when she had a daughter, she would name her Mariamne, in tribute to the line. In her room she kept a ruby-encrusted box filled with the coins of the Hasmonaean dynasty, left her by her father. She treated them as jewelry. She painted her eyes to look like Mariamne's because she had been told once that they resembled hers. And when she learned that Mariamne's favorite scent was susinum, she demanded a bottle of her own. When she was told she wasn't old enough, she arranged to receive it anyway, by back channels, and then proceeded to wear it, as now, whenever her grandmother was not near.

"Where did you get it from?" her brother asked.

"Egypt." She lifted her wrist. "Hermina brought it."

"You don't think you're a bit young?"

"I am not young. I am a woman, as everyone seems to know."

Agrippa smiled. He too had heard. "To be impregnable is one thing. To be worth the trouble, quite another."

Such eyes he had. It wasn't fair. Like Jonathan's, her mother said.

"In any case, I'd suggest you be more sparing."

She doused some more, to spite him. "Grandmother hates it. She says it's vulgar."

"It *is* vulgar."

"You should talk. At least I'm not the one who's been ogling the harlots in Baalbek."

"But this is my point. They are not harlots. They are worshipers, offering themselves."

She scoffed. "At their Temple."

"Outside their Temple, yes."

"How? How are they offering themselves?"

"With their eyes," he said, batting his his own again, though with his long lashes it was more a taunt than a demonstration.

She sniffed. "So they catch your eye and then what?"

"And then it's settled."

"*What* is settled?"

"Well, I think it's Philip's place to tell you that."

"Because you don't know."

"Because it's Philip's place. But you see, if that is how you are going to act, you make my point. You are too young. Different people see things differently." He smiled. "The goddess in the window, the one in Cyprus."

"Aphrodite."

"Yes, but in Susa they don't call her Aphrodite, they call her Kilili sa abati. They pray to her as well, but they don't think she's peeking out the window."

"No, what do they believe, O wise and knowing brother?"

"They believe she is *revealing* herself at the window."

"Stop it!"

"They do. She is. You can see for yourself at the shrines. She is plainly letting herself be seen."

"How? What is she revealing?"

"I don't have what Aphrodite has to show. But the point isn't *what* she's showing. It's that she *is* showing and that she is doing so in secret. It's the same thing that these women do at the Temple. When they look at you, they look at you openly, but *in secret*."

"Oh, riddles. Show me."

"I'm not going to *show* you."

"Yes. If it doesn't matter what they show, then show me. Prove it."

He pondered, and the fact that he pondered at all let her know he would. "Very well." He sighed, another pretense. "But you have to look at me. In the eye. If you look away, that proves it: You are not ready."

"Fine."

He took her behind a pillar. "Are you ready?"

"Yes."

"All right. This is how they look at you."

And he looked at her. Their eyes locked, and she wasn't sure at first if he was actually doing it or making fun, and she would have looked away—the game was silly—but she didn't and he didn't, and it was in that moment, that stubborn instant of not wanting to be the one to relent, that something did happen. A warm wave rushed through her. He *was* looking at her in secret, and she was letting him, and they both knew what the secret was. The secret was that there was a flame inside her. There was a candle inside her.

And it was melting.

"Hmm." His lids relaxed. He looked away.

"What?"

"Lucky Philip."

Lucky Philip. Philip had once been luckier than that. Grandson of the former High Priest Simon, this Philip (not the tetrarch) had been Herodias's intended from the time she was three and he, twelve. The marriage had seemed like a very good idea at the time, particularly for Herodias, as Philip had in fact been in line for the throne.

However, this was during that period of flux immediately following the execution of the two brothers (the younger one, Aristobulus, being Herodias's father). The line of succession was under constant revision, and when it was learned that Philip's mother was among those who'd known about all the lies Antipater had been telling (the ones that led to the execution of the brothers), Herod took revenge by promptly blotting her son Philip's name from the will. He was to receive nothing, and just like that, a marriage that had held out quite some promise for little Herodias held out none at all.

Herodias knew all this, of course. This had been explained to her many times when she was growing up, but she had never been too bitter. The rest of the family had been generous to her and to her mother afterward—Salome's kindness was a kind of compensation—and she was hardly the only member of the clan who could moan about what might have been. They all had their stories. She bore her loss like a handsome scar, sustained before she'd been old enough to feel the pain.

Also, as intendeds go, Philip was not so bad. He was good-looking, and he had manners. Whenever he saw her at the festivals, he gave her gifts—pomegranates and honey jars—which was especially thoughtful when one considered he really didn't have much money. Best of all, he was of the priestly line, which made her think of Mariamne and how this would have pleased her.

It wasn't until the days immediately preceding the wedding that the bloom fell off the rose. Herodias was sixteen. The hope had been that the wedding might take place in Rome or Jerusalem, but Salome's health had been failing, so it was decided the feast should be moved to the villa in Ashdod.

As a matter of custom Herodias liked to bring flowers to her grandmother every day. This morning she was doing just this, and was on the point of announcing herself, when she overheard her mother and her grandmother talking.

With the wedding day approaching, Herodias's mother had been doing a worse and worse job hiding her disappointment, not just at the venue (which was in fact spectacular) but at this last reminder of what they had lost and how different a celebration this would have been had it marked the nuptials of her daughter and a king.

"I cannot help it," she was saying, near tears. "If only his mother had gone to Herod and begged his forgiveness, surely he would have—"

"Oh, silence," said Salome, but with such a sibilant hiss, it stopped Herodias in her tracks. "Let me explain something to you so that I never have to hear this ridiculous whining again: If Philip's name had remained in that will, he would surely *not* be king today. He would be dead. Do you understand? The only question is who'd have been the one to kill him."

Herodias stepped back from the threshold, stunned not only by the frank admission of the family's habit—she had never heard it put so bluntly—but by the instant apprehension that what her grandmother had said was almost surely true. And though in part her reaction was one of relief—that the life of her soon-to-be husband had in fact been spared by fate—she would in the years to come look back upon this moment as having been the one when, assuming she ever had been in love with him in the first place, she decidedly fell out.

The wedding went ahead in any case. Her grandmother's illness lingered for two more years before she died. It was another two years after that that Herodias gave Philip his first child, a daughter, whose name he let her choose. She did not trouble long, but she did not name her Mariamne after all.

She named her Salome.

⋚26⋚

"Herod"

ACCORDING TO LEGEND, THERE WAS A SPARTAN WARRIOR NAMED
Xianos, famous for the ability to deliver a blow to his opponent's
chest that, though it left no lasting mark on the flesh, apparently did
so much damage to the underlying tissue that the deeper bruise never
healed but rather spread, slowly eating its way through meat and bone
until it reached the victim's vital organs and eventually killed him.

In the case of Antipas, Caesar's decision to honor Herod's will and
install Archelaus as ethnarch of Judaea could hardly have been called a
deathblow, but to those who knew him—and none knew him better than
his old friend Manean—it was clearly an injury that took some time to
develop fully. Whether it ever healed entirely was open to question.

To be sure, he from that point forward always bore a certain resent-
ment toward the other members of the family, the ones who'd put him
up to challenging the will in the first place. They'd clearly gotten
what they wanted, while he'd been the one to put his name on the line
and suffer the consequences.

Manean did his best to lend perspective. "I think everyone agrees
they'd have done the same as you."

"But the point is they did not," Antipas shot back. "I did, and tell
me, what chance is there that I should ever be restored in Caesar's
eyes?"

132

It was this, then, that bothered him most: that he would always be thought of as some sort of jealous usurper, and disloyal, when in fact there was no one more devoted to the family or to his father's legacy. Antipas tried to prove this in how he governed his two provinces. He delivered all tributes in full and on time, always. No banditry was tolerated, or extortion, or even the whisper of sedition. And like his father, Antipas built whenever and wherever possible: Caesarea (by the Jordan), the two Julias, and then of course Tiberias, which was to be the new capital of Galilee and his showpiece.

All this, while down in Jerusalem, Archelaus was using his power to settle old scores and pay off cronies. The people loathed him, but they did not fear him, and so the whiff of anarchy and insurrection was always in the air. It pained Antipas having to watch, to see what was becoming of his father's kingdom, what was becoming of his father's name—literally. The tetrarch Philip had recently taken to calling himself Herod, apparently adopting his mother's nickname for him as his new title.

"Can you imagine?" said Antipas. "If Philip is Herod, my toe clippings are Zeus."

In light of all this, it should hardly have been surprising that Antipas eventually set his sights on other game.

In addition to Galilee, the other territory that had been willed him by his father was Peraea, an oblong stretch of jagged, mostly uninhabitable wilderness that sat between the Bitter Sea on one side and the vast Arabian Peninsula on the other. Peraea was essentially a buffer zone, there to put a safe distance between Judaea and the neighboring land of Nabataea, which was itself a rather uninviting expanse of rock and dune, of no inherent appeal other than that it furnished the straightest path between the spice traders of the Orient and the wealthy markets of the empire.

Ruled for as long as anyone could remember by the formidable line of Aretas, Nabataea's relations with the Jews had been a mixed bag of natural enmity and strategic alliance. The Hasmonaeans had once had designs on Nabataea—as had Rome. But the Nabataeans had also proven useful in lending support during Israel's various internecine struggles. In particular since the Herods had come to power, the two kingdoms had enjoyed a generally peaceful coexistence (Herod's mother had been Nabataean royalty, remember), the only point of controversy being the region east of Gadara, the exact border of which was the subject of chronic dispute.

It was in fact this minor matter that Antipas used as a pretext, in his twenty-sixth year, to embark upon a diplomatic mission, traveling for the first time to the hidden jewel of Aretas's kingdom, the legendary city of Petra.

He came back a changed man.

"I have never seen anything like it! I tell you it is like entering another world."

Antipas was not the first to have been so moved. Hidden in the valley of the wadi Musa, the same through which Moses had led his people, the city was well known to have been a marvel, having actually been carved into the fissures and clefts of russet sandstone.

"It is ingenious. I don't see how the place could ever be taken. The entrance—it's true what they say: The corridor they've chosen can't be any wider than two arm's lengths. We had to leave several of the litters outside. But once one enters in! The columns and colonnades and porticoes, all with the whorls and waves of the living rock still showing. It's as if the whole thing had emerged on its own. And in the twilight, I cannot express to you the red, it beams. It is the color of a rose, and everywhere the air is heavy with the scent of frankincense, galbanum, and myrrh."

It did not escape Manean, as he listened, that his friend spoke of the city as if it were not merely a woman, but a woman's nethers.

"Sounds extraordinary."

"It is. And they have everything. There is an amphitheater, a market, and a public fountain. You must come with me next time."

Manean said he would, though he understood that Antipas's enthusiasm was born of more than architectural appreciation. There was also the fact that he had been received so warmly. The main square had been packed apparently. "In my own home I have never been treated with such respect."

"And what of Aretas?" asked Manean.

"Oh, very impressive. Small. Quite small, in fact, but only in stature. A man of an ageless wisdom and power. He greeted me as an equal. As a brother, I tell you! He himself took me to the royal tombs to leave a gift. And these are holy places. One can feel it. And the temple! It's built entirely from massive blocks of yellow sandstone—who knows how they got them in? And just across the way is a second temple, the temple of the bride, with the most extraordinary winged lions out front."

Here again Manean suspected that the reason the temples had made such an impression had less to do with the craftsmanship than with the fact that it was here—in front of the second temple, of Atagartis—that Antipas was introduced to Princess Phasaelis, Aretas's as yet unmarried daughter. No words had passed. All he had seen were her eyes above the veil, but what with all the frankincense and the peculiar light and enchantment of the place, Antipas was smitten. He admitted as much and said he understood right away—from the cast of those two dark eyes—that this had been the real purpose of the visit: She was being offered to him.

"I suppose I was a fool not to have understood in advance, and this is why the crowds had been so warm, of course. Which is fine. If the people should want our lands to be joined . . ."

Manean was surprised at the ease with which his friend was discussing the prospect. Antipas said he'd been tempted to propose that first evening. "And if you'd seen this city, my friend, you would credit me my restraint."

But he had demurred, managing to leave the question open by extending an invitation to Aretas, and to his daughter, that they should come see Sepphoris when the renovation of the palace was complete.

Manean approved. Such matters should not be entered into on account of mere passion or the intoxication of the moment. Still, he was surprised to learn what the true nub of Antipas's hesitation had been.

Apparently King Aretas had taken note of Herod's polygamy. In principle, he could hardly have complained—Aretas himself boasted a stable of no fewer than thirty brides—but for his daughter, he had let it be known that if and when she married, she should be the only wife of her husband.

"Which would be one thing if Phasaelis were in the family," Antipas later confided, "but as a foreigner . . ."

Manean was confused. "But isn't that the point, to see the two kingdoms united?"

Antipas granted. "But one wouldn't mind seeing the crown and the Temple united as well."

It took a moment for Manean to read his old friend's meaning. He meant that since Phasaelis was not a Jew, no child of theirs could serve as High Priest. That was Law, and indisputable, and it was equally indisputable that the people yearned for their king to be High Priest again. What Manean had not been aware of until just then was that Antipas apparently still entertained notions of reuniting the two thrones himself.

At the very least he seemed willing to give the idea one last chance.

As usual, the feast of Passover had given the family an excuse to convene and review the state of the nation, which was not good. The latest scandal concerned Archelaus's decision to divert the waters outside Jericho from the farmers' fields to his own palace; this, coming on the heels of his marriage to Glaphyra, the former wife of Archelaus's late brother Alexander, and as such legally off-limits. The Pharisees were beside themselves; the family was disgusted; Archelaus, entirely unrepentant. He and Glaphyra were a pair of lovebirds.

"Apparently she knows tricks," said Achiabus.

The family had also learned that now another public delegation—of Jewish, Syrian, and Samaritan constituents—was preparing to go to Rome and ask that Archelaus be removed from office in favor of a Roman procurator, not on account of the marriage or the water but the more general complaint that he was a crooked tyrant.

Antipas went to his brother Philip—"Herod" Philip—to discuss the matter. They agreed that Archelaus was hopeless and that Judaea was a mess. The best thing now, said Antipas, was for the family to separate itself from Archelaus. "If we don't go stand with the people, we are liable to be dragged down with him."

Philip agreed, and so they went to Rome together in support of the delegation.

Manean joined them for the trip over, mostly to boost morale but also because he was curious: Was there any part of Antipas still clinging to the hope that if Archelaus was deposed, that he, Antipas, might be given the throne? Manean tried subtly to ply his friend's intentions, but Antipas was uncharacteristically tight-lipped. Even after they arrived, he gave no signal of any ulterior motive.

The hearing went forward. The Jewish delegation, comprised of many of the same lawyers who'd spoken nine years prior, delivered much the same argument as before: that the people should be spared any further punishment by the Herods.

For his part, Antipas was far more restrained in his testimony this time around. He resisted attacking his brother personally but credibly confirmed that Archelaus had been overtaxing and skimming, imprisoning his political enemies, and that the region as a whole was at constant risk of falling into lawlessness.

He did one more unexpected thing as well; Manean had had no clue. Once the hearing of the delegation was concluded, Antipas went to Caesar and formally petitioned that his title be revised. He did not ask for more land or more power, only that from this point forward he be referred to not as the Tetrarch Antipas, but as Herod Antipas.

Caesar did not offer a ruling right away—either to the delegation or to Antipas—but he did ask that Archelaus be summoned at once from Jerusalem, which most took to be not a good sign for the sitting ethnarch. As to whether this boded well or ill for Antipas, no one could be sure, and he himself gave no sign of any hopes he might be harboring. He waited patiently for the six weeks it took Archelaus to arrive, and that same day Caesar announced his ruling before all interested parties:

Archelaus was indeed to be stripped of all authority and sent to Gaul.

While the much-relieved leaders of the Jewish delegation broke out into spontaneous whistles and shouts of thanks to almighty Caesar, Manean stole a glance at his old friend, just to see if any glimmer of either excitement or dread could be detected in his eye.

He found none, and just as well. The further ruling was that both Philip and Antipas would retain jurisdiction over their territories, but that a Roman procurator, Coponius, was to be put in charge of Judaea and Jerusalem.

Antipas had survived. No more or less.

As for the other request, the one regarding title, this too Caesar granted. From that day forward, Rome formally recognized that the former tetrarch Antipas should be referred to by the moniker Herod.

Antipas gave thanks with a bow and a gift of Peraean salts, then returned directly to Galilee, but only briefly. He had already sent a messenger to Petra to let Aretas know that he was on his way and would be asking for his daughter's hand in marriage.

≡27≡

Qumram

NOW THAT JOHN WAS NO LONGER A CHILD BUT A YOUTH, NOW that he had learned all the secret wisdom of the Nasurai, he went to the chieftain, Ahura, and told him that he would be leaving the village, journeying out on his own, as was not unusual for boys set to become men.

Ahura did not try to dissuade him. He gave his blessing. "But continue to give ear and listen," he said. He did not doubt John would.

A feast was held in celebration. Afterward, after all the villagers had prayed for John and bidden him farewell, Ahura went further and sent out two prayers alone: first to Par'am and to the Uthra, that they should let no harm come to the boy; then he gave thanks to Hibil-Ziwa for having humbled him with this gift, of planting for him a son out of the heavens, and letting him be father and teacher to one as blessed as Yahya-Yuhana.

Par'am stayed with John but let him find his own way. They went out into the desert. John stayed clear of most villages and cities, but his path eventually led him to the Jordan and across. He journeyed down into the wilderness beside the Bitter Sea for a time, but finally his wanderings found him on a strand along the western shore and to the north.

Down by the water, two men were gathering stones. Nearer by, a collection of clean white blocks had been set out in rows. Par'am told John it was a cemetery but that he should not fear. They sat beside it and looked out upon the two men at the water's edge, and as the sun descended, the Uthra revealed himself to teach John one more lesson:

He said that long ago, back beyond the Jordan, beyond the desert there and the river Parath, the worship of the One and Only God began. There they called the One God Brahm, and so long as they remembered his name and included it in their thoughts and deeds, their laws remained just; they lived in peace; they walked in wisdom's ways, a pure and devout people.

But as is the way of all things—that the pure should have to fend off corruption—so it was beyond Parath that the holy men entrusted to preserve the people's worship forgot themselves and forgot Brahm. They succumbed to falsehood and to the appetites of the world and the flesh. They twisted the Law to suit their selfish ends. They bound burdens on the poor. They spurned the truth and in time became blind to it. They made idols out of birds and beasts and creeping things, while the unseen God of all was forgotten by them and by those who followed them.

But even in the face of such corruption, he said that there had always been enlightened men who stood as beacons before the world, who came to preserve and to renew the faith. Beyond Parath, the greatest of these was called Zoroaster. Zoroaster beheld the Truth on high, and when he looked back down and saw what the holy men had done, he raised his voice. He spoke so others could hear, and those who listened to him were redeemed.

In time some of their children and their children's children did stray and tainted their worship with smoke and lies, but just as surely there came enlightened men to testify, to draw aside the pure of heart so that they might teach and beget and, in this way, see that the worship of the One God survived. And of all the flocks that remained devout, the Uthra said none was more pure than the Subba who had raised and cared for John. He told John that he was blessed to have been their son.

But he also said that Zoroaster and his line were not the only ones who stood firm. In Ur of the Chaldees there had lived a pious man named Terah. Terah so loved Brahm he named his own son A-brahm. While Zoroaster and his followers preserved their faith east of Parath, Terah took his wife and his son and all his kindred and their flocks and herds and traveled west into Harran. There Terah died, but his son Abrahm took his father's flocks and herds and with his kindred journeyed down into the lands of Canaan. Droughts and famine forced them farther down into the plain of Zoan for a time, and they learned many secrets there, but Abrahm's sons returned to Canaan with their flocks, to pitch their tents in the plain of Mamre, to live and die there and to remain.

And the Uthra told John that it was to this same flock that he had been born; that his blood was the blood of Terah and of Abrahm.

And he said that just as had happened beyond Parath, the children of Abrahm were beset by many trials—not only droughts and famine but unholy priests and wayward shepherds who led the flocks astray, into storms and pestilence and to the charnel house. Some fell asleep while the wolves and lions closed in. But as with their brothers of the east, there had always been good shepherds too, who raised their voices and drew aside the purest of the flocks, to graze and sow in peace so that the worship would endure.

And the Uthra told John that of all the flocks of Abrahm that had survived down to this day, the purest still remaining were to be found here in this place.

The two men from the shore were now headed back in, approaching a long, smooth wall built entirely out of mortar, all but for a single door made of cedarwood, behind which it appeared a small village had been fashioned from the low hillside.

In fact there were several more men emerging from the surrounding slopes, all wearing the same white tunics, all headed for the same door. They only had to knock and the gate would open.

John went and knocked twice. A moment later two men answered. Neither took notice of Par'am, but seeing John, they opened the door farther. They gazed upon him as if a pure white shell had been left there for them, and finding no fault in him, they took him in.

Par'am did not follow.

There was a kind of village inside, with various different court-yards and low buildings, more finished than the settlement of the Subba, but the spaces were still simple and clean. Dark wood beams provided the only contrast in an otherwise bone-white landscape of clean lines and turns.

There were more men as well, of varying ages, but all wearing the same coarse tunics and well-worn sandals. They seemed to be coming in from their labors for the day, greeting one another with nods but few words.

Most were funneling into a cool, dark building. John followed. Inside there were baths, dug out and filled with caught water. The men were cleansing themselves, and John could see it was as Par'am had said: They all were circumcised as he had been.

John bathed himself. When he was done, they offered him a tunic to wear, this one of a much finer, whiter cloth, the same as all the others were now putting on. Then in groups of two and three they crossed another court to a larger hall, a dining hall, lined end to end with long wooden tables. No privileged place was apparent.

When all had come, they spoke a prayer together. John did not know the words but understood it was a prayer of thanks. They ate quietly and quickly: no bread, no meat, but raw sprouts, gourd, and honey. When their bowls were empty, an elder rapped the table, and all stood. As one they funneled out into an enclosed courtyard to pray again, kneeling and setting their heads on the ground.

When this prayer was done, the same two men who'd let John in came to him again and asked if he wished to stay the night. They showed him where the novices slept in another low building. The spaces inside were more divided, but no room had more than a dozen beds in it, and again no privilege was in evidence.

John looked around. Evening was upon them. The bone white of the walls had given way to blue. He had not seen Par'am since entering. He did not see him now. He nodded he would stay.

They asked his name. He told them, "Yahya-Yuhana," so they called him Yohannan, which is the Hebrew for John.

This is how John first came to live among the Essenes at Qumram.

These were the same Essenes as had counted Manean's father, Menahem, a member, though Menahem had studied at another settlement called Sakara, near Alexandria. In fact there were dozens of different Essene communes scattered throughout the Holy Land, among which minor differences existed: Sakara was not celibate, Qumram was, which is why there were no women there, or children.

Generally, though, all Essenes subscribed to the same basic code. They all were faithful to the Book. They believed in the prophets. They lived in expectation of a savior—or two, in fact, who would come in tandem, to recognize all those who honored the covenant, and lead them up into the higher realm.

In this prospect, the Essenes considered themselves alone among the Jews, the rest of whom they judged to be living outside God and the Law. Ever since the beginning of the Hasmonaean dynasty, the Essenes had rejected the authority of the Temple in Jerusalem, its calendar, and its priesthood. They opposed blood sacrifice, and they ate no meat, including fish and birds. They drank no wine. They renounced all worldly claims and things and were required to give up all their possessions upon joining the sect, which they did voluntarily. Legacy and blood bonds were immaterial to them. They believed true faith and understanding could be achieved only by example and through practice, by adherence to the True Law, and by absolute loyalty to the sect. Once one became a member of the Essenes, he could not leave, nor could he pass on their secret wisdom to any outsider. He was committed to his brothers and to a life of utter simplicity and devotion, the sole aspiration of which was to become one with God, through constancy, labor, prayer, and purification.

In many ways the Essenes were not unlike the holy men whom John had grown up with, the Nasurai, and so because of this, because he trusted the Uthra when he said that these men was the purest surviving flock of Abraham, and because he judged he could find no better teachers than they, John remained with them as a novice.

Their days were very structured and all the same, except the Sabbath, which they observed with an extreme devotion (some members going so far as to bury themselves up their necks to ensure their passivity). After the morning prayer, they all put on the coarse tunics and set out to their given chores and labors, which rotated among them according to a fixed schedule. All served as potters and carpenters, tanners, cooks, fullers, bakers, scribes, farmers, and herdsmen. No matter the station to which they had been assigned, all the members worked five hours in the morning, as either masters or apprentices. Then came the noontime meal, before which everyone would bathe and put on his whiter linen. The initiates ate separately from the novices; then all would resume their day, donning the coarse tunics again and returning to their various stations to work another five hours, either in the fields or in the workshops. The second half of the day proceeded much as the first, with the one difference that everyone, initiates and novices alike, ate together at the evening meal.

There was one other station at the settlement where all members were required to spend at least some portion of their day: the library. Of all the rooms and prayerful spaces at Qumram, none was more sacred than this. The library was their treasury; the books were their treasures. The books contained the Word, and the Word, not blood, was what the Essenes passed down. So they copied their books, and copied them again, and they did not keep them out on the hills above the settlement. They kept them there at the center, so that all could go read. And all did, every day, aloud, so that the words would be imprinted in their minds.

With the help of an older initiate named Perida, John taught himself to read Hebrew, and soon he was able to sit among the other novices and read with them. They had many books there, but the first that was opened to him was the Law of Moses, which they called Torah, which set out the rules by which they lived. John soon mastered all the five parts of Torah, and others remarked when they heard him reading, how the words seemed to flow from his lips and rise. Others fell silent when he read.

One day John went to Perida and asked that he be allowed to read the books that followed, for there were many still awaiting him—the psalter, and Joshua, and all the prophets—but Perida refused him.

John asked why.

Perida said, "For the same reason I would not throw an infant in the deep end of the river."

"Then let me show I am no infant."

Perida tested him, and John proved there was not a word of Torah he did not know by heart.

"Now let me see what follows," he said, but again Perida refused him.

"I cannot let you see beyond Torah, Yohannan, for the reason you well know."

John did. No one was allowed to see the later books until he had sworn allegiance to the sect, as John had yet to do.

"But if the words of the prophets are true," he said, "then tell me why they should be guarded. Why should we not go share the truth with others?"

"Because they would not hear," said Perida. "Because the ground must first be ready before the seed will take."

"Then we should go make it ready."

He waited, as if this argument might gain him entrance to the other books, but Perida replied, "First tell me why you would not surrender yourself and come to us."

John did not answer him there but took the question outside the wall of the settlement. Often, after evening prayer, he walked north to where the river fed the sea. The shoreline there became a thicket of driftwood, so encrusted with salt it looked like a giant nest blanketed with frost.

There he sat, a lonesome bird beneath the low-slung moon, the waters swelling up the banks and the driftwood. His mind turned to the village of the potters, to his brothers and sisters, and how he missed them, how he missed the high vault of Ahura's voice when he taught his lessons by the water's edge and the dance of his long hands; how he missed Taraneh's songs and the sound of the younger children laughing, Azha's laughter, most of all. He had been happy there, east of the Jordan. He had known his purpose there, and when he ceased to know, when he began to doubt, he had left.

Within his heart, he called out to his protector and his guide, Par'am. "Then come and tell me. Help me. Make it so I know. Is this where I should be?"

He called out to the Uthra as well: "You who have shown me all the hidden things, show me now. Make me see. Is this my place, and if it is not, then where else should I be?"

He closed his eyes and listened. He opened his eyes and sought, but the heavens above were as silent as the sea beside him. All he could hear were the crickets calling out to one another, from rock to rock.

Now, many of the elders at the settlement were aware of John. They knew he had come from the east, that he had spent his youth among the Subba, and they knew that he brought special knowledge with him. The astronomers among them had taken note of his learning. He said many things they recognized and many they did not. Likewise, the apothecary had remarked John's way with healing stones and with the hives, how he removed the combs by hand, not wanting the smoke to taint the honey. John was often sought as an interpreter of dreams, and of course all remarked on the authority with which he read.

One day a brother just returned from Jerusalem observed John during his purification, how he washed his hands and arms and how the water seemed to cling to him and gleam. He asked who this one was, and when the others told him, he reminded them of the story of the old priest and his wife, how beneath a star of prophecy a child was born to them in the hill towns, a son who then vanished into the wilderness. He said there were many who believed that the child had survived.

"And do they say his name?" the others asked.

"Yohannan."

The others pondered. "But even if he were he," they asked, "would we treat him differently?"

They all agreed that they would not.

"If it is written," they said, "then let it be writ."

One day John was working in the scriptorum, the hall adjacent to the library. Here the scribes sat all day and copied books so that they could be trimmed and rolled and set aside for safekeeping.

John was there, building new shelves, as the rest were already crowded and full. As usual, the voices of the brethren could be heard through the wall, reading aloud from their scrolls. John had not meant to listen—these were the very books he had been forbidden to read—but he could not help it. Amid the confusion of murmured prayers and songs, laws and tales and histories, there was one voice standing out, not because it was any louder than the rest but because John recognized it.

As he stood there, Perida went to him. "We have spoken of this, Yohannan. You should not intrude, even with your ear." And he ushered him from the door back to the table. John did not protest, but that evening, after all the rest had gone to sleep, he rose from his bed and returned to the library. He knew where the key was hidden. He took it, and he used it, and he went inside when no one else was there.

All the books were kept in clay jars. The jars were set in rows, in racks along the wall. There were hundreds of them, all arranged in order, from the oldest to the most recent, but John knew the one that he had heard, as there was one jar glowing among all the rest. Its clay was red and gleaming, as if a candle had been set inside. He could see the glimmering from beneath the lid.

He took it down, and when he opened it, the light burst out, just as it had from the Uthra's vesture. It flooded the room.

John rejoiced within. "But have you been here all along, hiding while I called to you out by the river? Have you been here waiting while I gathered stones and tilled the rows? Have you been here while I was sleeping over there?"

He unrolled the scroll along the bench. He could feel the warmth of its light against his skin, and as he gazed down at the words, for the first time since he had come to Qumram, he heard the Uthra's voice again.

And do not pretend you do not know, or that you do not see,
how every deed is every day recorded in the mind of the
Almighty.

He continued reading. Much of what the Uthra said John recognized from when they would sit together by the river or on the high plateau. The book spoke of visions John himself had seen within the sacred cave. But there were other visions too. That first night the Uthra told him of his journey through the seven heavens and in Gehenna. He described the throne of God and the fire of the luminaries.

John was overjoyed. He put away the book at dawn, but he returned the following evening when all the rest had gone to sleep. This time the Uthra spoke to him of all the eras and of the seventh era they were entering even now. He introduced John to the host of angels and archangels, the watchers and holy ones: Raguel and Uriel and Gabriel. They appeared before him, and he was not afraid, and in the nights to come, he met Raphael as well, and Michael, and Saraqael. One by one they opened all the rest of the books to him. The Uthra let him hear the psalms and prayers, the stories of the patriarchs, of Abraham and Isaac, of Jacob and Joseph. John was told of all the shepherds, the good and the bad, and of the flocks that were devoured and of the flocks that survived; of Solomon and the Ark, and the Temple, and the captivity.

John no longer questioned that he should be at Qumram now. He spent his days out in the gardens and the fields, gathering stones and pulling the combs, but then at night he would return. He sat at his teacher's feet, and jar by jar, scroll by scroll, the Uthra, whom those at Qumram called Enoch, opened the mouths of all the prophets to him: Isaiah and Daniel, Elijah, Malachi, and Micah. Each revealed his wisdom. Just as Par'am had taught John all the secret knowledge of the Nasurai who lived east of the Jordan, so the Uthra now taught him the secrets of the holy men who lived to the west.

The other brothers were aware. Perida had followed John one night. He sat outside the door, and he was amazed by what he heard inside, the sound of the voices conversing within. And he was not the only one. Others came as well, to hear, and none who heard was moved to interfere. By the silent consent of the scribes, John came to know all the prophets and the fathers. He sat before them. He listened and he asked and he took their answers to heart. As he knew the Law, he came to know the songs and psalms, the prayers and prophecies.

Yet even after all this, after all the fathers had come and made themselves known, and revealed their wisdom, John was not filled. He still had one more question left, as the Uthra could see.

"Ask," he said one night.

"But who then was *my* father," said John, "the one who planted me?"

The Uthra did not answer him directly. He had John put back all the books, set them in the jars and seal them, and set the jars back on the shelves. But the following morning, as John went out to gather stones with the apothecary, there was Par'am waiting for him just outside the gate.

"Let us go to Ur-Shalem," he said.

⟩28⟨

The Holy City

I T WAS LATE IN THE DAY WHEN JOHN AND PAR'AM ENTERED THE shade of Bethany, at the eastern foot of Olivet. They had left Qumram in the morning and reached the road from Jericho midway. From there it was a six-mile walk, the length of which Par'am used to let John know what he would need to know and that he should not be going with false hope.

John was thirsty now. They found a public well at the center of the village and so paused beneath the shush of lazy palm fronds. Perida had given John a purse of coins before he left. John used the first to purchase a cluster of dates from a peddler who was blind. The peddler could not see the offerings John brought: a branch from the first blossoming fig tree, three jars of honey, and a parcel of grain. Still he knew.

"You are going to the Temple?"

"I am," said John. "For the first time."

"Then it is a great day," said the peddler, smiling. "A magnificent house, so I am told."

"My father built it," said John.

"Did he? He is a priest?"

"He was," said John. "He served his whole life there."

The peddler bowed in deference.

John saw his basket was empty. He handed him another coin for his kindness, but the peddler gave it back.

"Be on your way," he said. "The evening service will be upon us soon."

Just then three trumpets sounded in the distance.

Over the top of the hill, there was a dip in the road, so John's first glimpse of the Holy City was only that, a glimpse. He saw Mount Zion and the roof of the royal palace before the hill intruded again. Three dwarf palms sprouted up from the roadside, offering red and yellow fruit in clusters. John did not see. He hurried to the second rise and stopped.

All Jerusalem spanned before him, painted in two colors by the descending sun: the one, a warm and brilliant gold, slathered across the western face of every cobbled building, every wall and tower, every bridge; the other, a cool blue, washing the valleys and wandering streets, twisting around wells and squares, dipping, rising, and finally bowing down again before the brilliant crowning glory of the city, a man-made mountain of gleaming marble, all steps and massive walls ascending to the western peak, where even now the sunlight could be seen glinting off its golden front, and a trail of smoke whispering into the sky.

John felt something swell inside him. He could not imagine that man could make something so wondrous.

"How?"

"Time," answered Par'am. "And devotion."

John's gaze fell next upon the eastern wall, the one directly facing them, a vivid blue rectangle, so large and flat it tricked the eye, became the window on another sky, which from its sheer intensity flung another darker blue across the roll of Olivet, a blanket tossed across four sleeping brothers, patched with flower beds and vineyards, orchards and fields, groves of myrtle, pine, and stately cypress.

The fringe fell upon two little men in black robes and talliths, just now descending from the shoulder of the second sleeping brother.

"Pharisees," said Par'am.

Above them a spray of catacombs pocked the hillside. Both men turned and offered one last supplication, lest anyone misunderstood: They were parting with expensive gifts. They kissed the ground.

"To whom?" asked John

"The prophets," Par'am answered.

He led John down to the foot of the hill, where just inside the city's eastern gate, they came upon a market. John had attended the bazaars in Jabbok, but he had never seen so many tents and stalls all together, each one overflowing with its keep—of fruit or robes or silks. The swirl of colors dizzied him, the embroidery and the sheen, and all the scents, the frankincense and cinnamon perfuming the air, and the men as well. Their hair and skin were anointed with oil. The aisles were clogged with buyers and peddlers and beggars and children. Their fingers were like leaves and branches, snatching at him. One, a stammerer, his mouth open, his tongue stiff and trembling, grabbed hold of his garment. John pushed the remainder of his fruit at him, which brought a swarm of children and beggars down upon him. He tried to show them he had nothing more. The coins he had to keep. The gifts were for the Temple. The people still cursed him, for having given once.

There was a fountain. He went and sat on the edge. Across the way a group of children were gathered around an injured bird. One was beating it with a stick. Beyond, a woman wearing an open robe stood in a window, talking to two soldiers below.

John turned away to dip his hand, but Par'am stopped him. A bloated rat was floating in the water. He took John by the elbow. He pulled him through a second gate to the steps of the Temple Mount. But how many stairs did they climb? How many pure white slabs passed beneath their feet, polished by how many heels? And how many men must it have taken to bring each one here and shave it and set it? If his father was one, he was one of thousands, or tens of thousands.

John had hoped to find more calm inside, but the public court was another open market, roiling with pilgrims, preachers, merchants, lambs, goats, and doves. The smell was the smell of livestock and manure, mixed in with the syrupy sweet of incense, also there for purchase. The sound was not of prayer but of haggling and argument. The men attacked each other with jabbing fingers. They spit as they spoke, but John could not hear the words; they jumbled together like rubble.

He came to a long table, set before a pen of lambs and cages. The man there motioned for the gifts he'd brought—the jars, the branch, the bundle of wheat.

"What offering?"

John told him, "*Olah*."

The man held out his hand for more. His nails were black underneath. He snatched John's purse and dumped the change. There was enough, but barely. He slid three temple coins to him and waved him farther down the table to where a soft-whiskered boy was already lifting a lamb from the pen, a small and trembling thing, with brittle legs and a blood blotch in the eye. Seeing that John saw, the boy returned a coin to him and pointed him on, signaling to one of the Levites standing by the great brass gate.

Par'am led him through the crowd, past two men fighting over a cage of pigeons, and another beside them in a great black robe, embroidered all around with images of fauna. On his fingers were so many rings it was a wonder he could close his fist.

The Levite stopped them at the second gate to check the lamb. He saw the blotch. He waited.

"The coin," Par'am advised.

John gave it over. The Levite waved him through, but here Par'am let go of John. There was a stone tablet on the wall beside the gate. LET NO GENTILE PASS, it said.

The people behind them were pushing now. *Go. Go, or get out of the way.* The lamb was trembling in John's arms and bleating.

"I will wait," said Par'am, and John felt himself swept up and in.

This higher court was smaller than the first, and the pilgrims were herding in one direction, straight ahead, but all around, it felt as if the ornaments and images were grasping at him, snatching at him like the hands outside: all the carvings on the walls and porticoes; the flash of the coins below, whole heaps of them, glittering, tarnishing mounds, choking silver trumpets; mothers with children in their arms, others with doves; widows, with their hands out like beggars.

Outside, on Olivet, John had felt such pride and awe. Here, within, all that wonder had turned to fear: fear that the stones might fall; fear of the crush of the people; and fear of something else he did not yet know. The crowd kept pulling him forward, but the nearer he came, the stronger he could feel it, a kind of revulsion, or stronger, a repulsion, as if something foul were already pushing him back and away, but he could not stop, for now as he moved past the kneeling suppliants, the Temple itself appeared through the gate ahead, rising up before him, its marble front pink in the evening light; its pillars and roof trimmed with glimmering gold. And an eagle there, looking as if it had been dipped in the same pot as all the moldings.

As he passed through the final gate, he felt a push from behind but held his ground. He had come to the steps of the highest court, the Court of Priests. Here before him was the very altar where his father had served, the very laver where he had washed his hands and feet, and here were the priests as well—his father's cousins and his brothers—all in their white linen, moving from station to station with their heads bowed beneath their miters. Dozens of them. More. A hundred? It was difficult to tell, they looked so much alike, ascending and descending the Temple steps. Some stood around lambs, offering bowls of water, examining the coats and hooves. Others passed by, bearing away plates of coal or ashes.

Behind, the lank, lissome body of a just-offered lamb was being taken off into a chamber in the corner, to be stripped and drained. John could see the flash of cleavers through the oriel, rising and falling.

It was all as he had been told, and if he closed his eyes, he knew this was the place he had sought. The scents of woodsmoke, lamb, lamb's blood, and frankincense all burrowed deep inside him, in search of his remotest memories, yet there was something more.

He opened his eyes, and there was a priest standing directly in front of him, reaching down to take his offering. His beard came near, and John was flooded again. Again the scents all wove and slithered deep inside him, like snakes twisting into knots. He released the lamb. He tried to find the old man's eyes, but they were cold and blank. The priest handed the offering over to two younger brethren, who set to work with a butcher's speed, binding the front legs first, then the back. They ran a pole through the fetters and hoisted it up onto their shoulders. The lamb swung down, upside down, its woolly crown grazing the floor as they made way for the ramp of the great stone altar, which stood like a dark behemoth in the middle of the terrace, a Goliath's tomb.

There were more priests up there, tending to the fire, setting the meat just so, their faces lit from beneath by the smoldering coals, intermittently obscured by billows of smoke. John watched it rise up into the darkening blue. But was that the scent that pierced him? Or something coming from behind, from within an antechamber?

The lamb had reached the rack now. Quickly they hung it in place. Its mouth opened helplessly. John saw its pink tongue and white-rimmed eyes; terrified and innocent, unaware that this was the very purpose for which it had been born. The priest took hold of its throat with one hand, a silver lance in the other. A moment later the blood spewed up in pulses. John turned away, and his eyes for the first time fell directly on the Temple. He looked through the pillars and into the shadow of the sanctuary, and that is when it came to him, in a sudden noxious rush, what else it was that he was smelling. Death. The same stench he'd smelled on Nasim's breath, but multiplied and magnified a thousandfold. It was flooding out from the heart of the Holy Place, as if the space inside were clogged with rotting corpses. And now it was all he could smell.

His knees turned to rope, and the pilgrims behind him were pushing around. He felt himself being swallowed back into the crowd. He did not resist. He let himself be pulled away. He did not pray. He did not supplicate himself as the Law prescribed. He let the others shove their way through while he retreated, his ears buzzing now. Another Levite was directing him. Out, out, the way he came.

Par'am was still standing just outside the great brass gate, silent and unseen amid the throng. He took John's hand and led him back out through the public court and down the marble steps. Together they passed through the city gate and the market in the valley. John followed his light. The rest all dimmed.

Evening was falling fast. The sky was a simmering blue behind the black leaves of the olive trees and the spires of the cypresses that crowned the hill. Par'am led him up through a small vineyard until they stopped beneath an olive tree, beside a stone.

Par'am sat with him. He laid his hand on John's head. John laid his head in Par'am's lap. He closed his eyes, but the images still whirled, the sounds still rang in his ears, and the fetid stink of death still lingered.

His stomach turned. He yielded up the dates he'd eaten in Bethany, his pride. They fell in clumps on the sticks and dry leaves.

When his stomach was empty and his eyes were dry, he said to Par'am, "Why did you not tell me?"

"What should I have told you?"

"That they have turned their backs. They are lost."

Par'am did not deny. "Why do the messengers come from age to age," he said, "but to pour fresh water into the well—"

"But only to those who will drink," said John. "They are nothing but maggots and vultures inside. Did you think I would not smell it? Sooner could that peddler see, sooner could he set his eyes upon the palace, than that this house shall rise again."

His voice could be heard down in the valley below.

"From my childhood I have asked, Why should I be kept from them, the ones who planted me and carried me? Is this the answer, that if I knew the wickedness from which I'd sprung, then I would see it in me? I would find a poison well in me and drink from it?

"Then look at me. I am ill. It would be better I had tasted this bile, then it would not sicken me like this, but I am sick because you have raised me in a lie, because you took me, and hid me, and kept the truth from me. What choice had I? It was you who took me out into the desert to live with your kind, you who brought me to the cemetery, only then to bring me here and show me my people's corpse, that I might watch the scavengers pick at it. I say the whore will have back her virgin skin before these people see the truth. And yes, this stone would sooner turn to marble.

"Now get away from me! And the Uthra too, who raised me in the same lie! I am going, and you will not follow. If you follow, I will not see you."

With that he turned his back and left Jerusalem, the tears still hot in his eyes, and Par'am let him go.

⊰29⊱

Villa dei Pini

HERODIAS HAD NOT BEEN AWARE THAT ANY VISITORS WERE due. It wasn't until that very morning she was told, in fact. Not that she minded the surprise. She welcomed any disruption to the torpid rhythm here.

It had been less than a year since they had left Palestine—she and Philip and Salome, who was nine. They had been living along the coast, splitting their time between Azotus and Jamnia. There was no real reason they'd had to go, except that Philip preferred it here. He was a favorite among the royal family, and he seemed to function much better in Italy than in his homeland.

The villa was proof. It could hardly have been more ideally located, right between Ostia and Rome. A hundred hectares if you counted the wood. The emperor's villa was just the other side. One could hear the Tiber, smell the pines. The land was gorgeous, the vineyards legendary. They were living better here than they ever had in the territories. And yet for whatever reason—the isolation or the fact that Philip seemed so content, dawdling among the vines—the whole situation was driving her mad.

"When did you say my uncle will be here?"

"He's already here," the steward explained.

"What?"

"He's been here for an hour already, touring the grounds."

"Does my husband know? Is he with Salome?"

The steward shrugged. Most likely. Riding.

"Well, someone should go tell them, don't you think? Tell him his brother Antipas is here."

The courtiers at hand, Livia and Priopy, let it be known that they, at least, were not so pleased by this unexpected intrusion. While the servant dressed their mistress's hair, they vented their derision.

"But he can't be serious," said Livia.

"Oh, deadly," said Priopy, her sister and identical twin. "He seems to me to be quite humorless when it comes to such things."

At issue was her uncle's habit (which apparently he had just put on public display again) of actually sitting in the sukkah during the Feast of the Tabernacles. All good Jews were expected to go build a bamboo hut somewhere near the temple, to honor the nomadic existence their ancestors had endured in the desert. The royal family played its part. Their sukkahs were usually made of imported cedar and were generally used for entertaining. Only Antipas actually made his out of bamboo (or his spearmen did) right on the palace terrace for everyone to see. And only Antipas actually *slept* in his.

"It's all to be like his father," said Priopy.

"Herod didn't sleep in the sukkah," said Livia.

"No, but you know what I mean. He liked to make a show of his piety."

"True."

"And that's all Antipas is doing."

"*Herod* Antipas."

"Excuse me, yes. *Herod* Antipas."

Herodias notably held her tongue. In the past she might have joined right in, for there was something about her uncle that seemed to lend itself to ridicule. A certain neediness, a desperation. Yet of late she'd found herself rethinking him. Not long before they'd left the territories, she'd had to go up to Galilee. She decided she wanted to see Tiberias, which was supposed to be Antipas's great showpiece, and it was a lovely city—very new, very cosmopolitan. But what most caught her attention was the story about the graves, which she hadn't heard until then.

Apparently there had been an old cemetery where her uncle had wanted to put the main residential district, to have the best possible view of the water. He ordered that all the graves and sepulchers be secretly dug up and moved, but of course the Pharisees found out, and of course they were beside themselves. They said the whole space was contaminated now, that no good Jew could possibly live in such a city. They threatened to boycott the place entirely. So what did Antipas do? According to Faisool, the eunuch, he actually paid the people to come live there. He made it worth their while.

The consensus among the family seemed to be that this was another example of her uncle's ham-fistedness, but Herodias couldn't help feeling the episode had a certain charm about it too. At the very least, it seemed to make the point: Any man who would build his capital on Jewish graves and then pay people to live there couldn't be all that serious about sitting in a sukkah. If he was, he was deranged, and that seemed to be the question.

"Do we know why he's here?" she asked.

The twins both shrugged. "To get away from Phasaelis."

"She is not with him?"

"Is she ever?"

Their titters were cut short by Salome bursting through the curtain, smelling faintly of the stables and telling them that Philip would meet them all at the wine press in an hour.

"An hour?"

"He says he has to bathe."

"He's not the only one."

After an hour, then, and another half hour of searching, Herodias and her courtiers finally found him out at the vineyard. Right away she was reminded what an odd bird he was physically, knock-kneed, and he had that unfortunate way of holding his hands, as if he were waiting for them to dry. And yet as the courtiers lined up to greet him, she watched him make his way from one to the next and realized she felt somewhat the same about his looks as she did his ambitions. She'd always found him rather repulsive—by comparison to Philip, say, who verged on being beautiful, but whose beauty, like all beauty, had begun to fade. Antipas's ugliness, on the other hand, seemed to be aging rather well. Those features, which sat so ill on his more youthful face—so petulant when plump—now, without elastic, seemed to have assumed a more fit expression of earned disdain.

"My niece." He bowed and motioned to his aide to present her with a token. Perfume. "From Alexandria."

"How kind."

The tilt of his head seemed to express apology, as if the gift lacked imagination.

Just then Salome whirled to her mother's side. She hadn't been aware that presents were in order.

"Ah, yes," said Antipas. "Did we not have something for the girl?" He reached into his scrip himself and began rummaging around. Salome was bouncing on her toes.

At last, he produced it. "Here."

A porcelain ethrog.

Salome stopped bouncing.

World's pithiest and most hideous fruit.

"Tsk-tsk." He chided her disappointment. "You don't think it's remarkable? I do. Look how they got the ripples just right." He held it up to the light, and the resemblance was unmistakable—of the fruit to him, that is—but was he aware? Herodias couldn't tell. She even wondered, Was he drunk?

"Oh, but wait, there was something else." Again he motioned to the second, who this time removed an onyx box.

Salome didn't linger over the packaging. Inside was a small bracelet made of hammered silver.

"Also from Egypt?" asked Herodias.

He shook his head. "Petra."

Her feelings divided. "It's lovely."

It was. A snake swallowing its own tail. Salome wasn't quite sure what to make of it.

"Why don't you go show your father?" said Herodias. "And tell him to hurry. This is unconscionable."

Salome skipped away without a word of thanks.

"The girl is a jewel," said Antipas.

Herodias detected a plaintive note. "Is Phasaelis not with you?"

"No."

No plaintive note there. The twins were right. That woman was always ill and indisposed, complaining of woman's problems, never justifying them.

They decided not to wait for Philip. She and her retinue escorted their guest (and his) down to the wine cellar. She had the steward open them a cask, and they made small talk. He asked about Philip's mother, who had recently taken a turn for the worse. Herodias was impressed he was even aware.

"So remind me again," she said. "What brings you?"

"The vineyards," he replied. "I've been thinking of starting some of my own."

"You didn't come all the way to Italy to see my husband's vineyards."

He seemed a bit put off by her prying and might not have responded at all except that the answer brought him such obvious pleasure.

"Also money," he said. "Literally, I mean. I think it's time the districts had their own coin."

"Galilee?"

"And Peraea. The people deserve a currency of their own."

"No question." She could not hold her smile. How of a piece with everything he seemed to do.

Just then a thought occurred to her—or two, in quick succession, the first popping into her brain so utterly out of the blue she had to believe it was true—answer to an old and long-suspended question: Who'd have been the one to kill Philip if his name had somehow remained in the will as Herod's heir?

Was it Antipas?

"What?" he asked.

She shook her head. "Just that that sounds like fun. A new coin."

He didn't disagree. He scanned the space again. They'd come

upon a shelf of empty casks. "Do you know what these are made of? Is it oak?"

"I wouldn't know. I'm sure Philip could send you some."

She was looking him in the eye, and that is when the second thought occurred—as an experiment almost—to play her brother's game and see how long she could hold her uncle's gaze.

So standing there among the casks while their various courtiers traded gossip just up the steps, Herodias continued looking at Antipas, and Antipas continued looking at her. He would not look away, and the refusal on both their parts to be the one to surrender—the very force required to stave that impulse—was like a magnet between them. They both could feel it, so powerfully it was as if the others were suddenly receding, or were standing up on dry land, while the two of them were floating in a calm black pool where no one else could see below the surface.

"Brother!" came Philip's voice from the door, all good cheer.

With that, Herodias let her uncle go, but that night upon her bed someone left a rose.

⋟30⋞

Redress

MANEAN HAD NOT BEEN PART OF THE RETINUE THAT ACCOMPAnied Antipas to the Pines. He met up with his old friend in Rome, but right away he could see Antipas was in a fog, smiling and grunt-humming at nothing in particular. Manean did not learn the cause, however, until very late that night, when over a fourth helping of honey wine, Antipas confessed: He was completely obsessed.

Manean had to ask three times with whom. He knew Herodias more by reputation than acquaintance. High-chinned, barbed. Her features had always struck him as being rather large and mannish. She would never have occurred to him as a candidate for such starry-eyed pining.

"But it happened in a moment." Antipas snapped his fingers. "It was like a thunderbolt, but there was no mistaking its intention. Or the refusal to retreat. It was . . ." He struggled for the word and happily settled on "obscene!"

Manean could see his friend was excited, but his own enthusiasm was tempered by common sense. Whatever had occurred, whatever that moment had betokened, he did not see that anything could be done about it. The woman was his brother's wife.

No doubt that was part of the appeal, but the other part he attributed to the accrual of disappointment that had come from so many years with Phasaelis. Indeed, if any man had earned a moment of caprice—even an "obscene" one—it was Antipas. He had remained quite true to his Nabataean princess over the years, despite the fact that theirs seemed to have been one of those marriages that peaked on its wedding day.

A glorious day, granted—in Petra. Manean had gone and finally seen for himself the hidden splendor of the place, and it *was* like a different world. Enormous tents had been set in the central square, but they could hardly contain the crowds. Not so much of the family had come, but Rome had sent an embassy, and that's what counted. The ceremony took place before the great Temple of Dushara. A band of maidens performed ritual dances for the bride, then the entire party crossed to another temple just up the rise, the one with the winged lions out front. There, beneath blazing torches, with the walls of the city cooling to a brilliant crimson and the ribbon of sky above turning an electric blue, the couple invoked the blessing of Dushara's bride, Atagartis, goddess of fertility.

Would that the newlyweds could have remained in that eerie, beautiful space. Together they returned to Palestine, making nest first in Sepphoris, then in Tiberias. Neither found its purpose. Phasaelis wilted, visibly and before her husband's eyes. Like a flower uprooted from her native soil, what beauty she possessed fled suddenly. Her expression soured. Her skin lost all luster, and Antipas, though many things, was no gardener. He treated her like a kind of ornament, a broken toy, which she clearly resented. She openly detested Jerusalem, and one could hardly blame her. They only ever went during the festivals, and the rest of the family made no secret of their revulsion. A "lizard-eating cave dweller" they called her, often within earshot.

All such antagonism might have been overlooked if an heir had followed, some offspring who could plant one foot in Petra and another in Tiberias. Unfortunately, Atagartis had been unmoved by the nuptials. The pregnancies were few and fruitless. Physicians were brought in, and soothsayers and magi from Nabataea, to burn their incense, take her blood, prepare their potions. To no avail. "Dry as a dune" was Antipas's phrase, but a dune to which he was now exclusively bound. There was talk of divorce, of course, annulment, but Antipas would not have it. He had given his word before God, the one true God, and several pagan gods as well, to say nothing of his father-in-law, the king, whom he may have feared most of all.

Hence the grain of salt with which Manean now listened to his old friend speaking of his niece.

"You don't believe me, do you?"

Manean knew better than to answer, and he did believe. He believed a coal had been stoked, and he was glad to see it—he'd assumed his friend had died in that department—but he also believed that Antipas's excitement would fade as the days and miles expanded between him and his obsession.

The rest of the trip seemed to be going very well, in fact. In Rome, the emperor received Antipas quite warmly. He invited him to sit in on a Senate hearing. He dined with him, conferred with him on purely local matters. Antipas was pleased. There seemed little doubt he would get his coin.

The same day that he was formally to submit his petition, an unsigned gift arrived. Manean was there when the messenger appeared—with a flat acacia box.

The note read, "Fortis." *Good luck.* That was all.

Antipas was stumped at first, but his face went red the moment he opened it and saw seven polished coins.

He held them up to the lamplight. "Hasmonaean," he said, squinting at the year, "from the reign of Alexander."

Manean was confused. "But who are they from?"

Antipas looked at him, chuckling. "Who do you think?"

Antipas had toyed with the idea of returning to the Pines immediately. Herodias's gift had driven him mad with passion. Through envoys, however, he learned that she was already on her way to Ashdod. Her mother-in-law's illness was apparently worse than imagined.

Antipas's course was therefore set. Once again Manean was made to watch while his friend used the three-week journey across the Great Sea to let his imagination run, and it ran farther than Manean would have thought advisable. Antipas was not talking about a mere affair. He was talking about a realignment.

"It is the right thing," he said repeatedly. "This—this marriage, it was not right. Ever. Have I not honored my vow? Clearly the Lord has spoken, and the woman is miserable," he said, referring to Phasaelis. "This is redress," and he would point to the gift, the coins of Alexander, last Jewish king to unify the crown and Temple.

"What about Aretas?" asked Manean.

Antipas allowed that Aretas was the rub. "I will make him understand. The gods have not looked kindly. To continue with this for the sake of our avowals becomes an act of pride. I wish her well. I wish him well. But at a certain point one must yield."

Manean nodded, but as he looked at his friend, braced against the wind, he couldn't help wondering if Herodias had even the faintest idea of what she had done.

Philip, needless to say, was most surprised by his half brother's appearance in Ashdod. And touched.

Herodias was encouraged. She had not been driven to quite the same state of distraction as Antipas, but she was no less determined. When she learned her uncle had arrived, with gifts and words of support, she knew very well why he was there, and it was not her inclination to be coy. She regarded only one point as being nonnegotiable.

They stole their first moment alone in the nave of the Temple of Dagon. This was where most of the Jewish visitors to the city were taken, to see for themselves where, according to legend, the Ark had briefly been hidden after the Philistines had stolen it from Jerusalem.

Herodias and Antipas trailed behind the others. "I haven't had the chance to thank you in person," said Antipas. "For the coins. They have given me lots of good ideas."

"I'm sure they have." She met his eye again. His heart leaped.

"Is this the spot?"

She nodded, pointing to the marble stone between them. The story went that when the Philistines first set down the Ark, the statue of the temple god fell from its pedestal and broke in two.

"I will not be a mistress," she said.

"I would never ask you to be."

As determined as they were, neither Antipas nor Herodias had any illusions about the risks of such an undertaking. Archelaus had already blazed this trail somewhat, marrying Glaphyra, his brother Alexander's former wife. That hadn't gone over very well, and in that case, Glaphyra had been a widow, somewhat mitigating the offense.

For her part, Herodias didn't appear to be too concerned. If they ruffled any feathers, so be it, she said. "Let the hens be warned." Antipas was more cautious and set about about lining up support among the priests and the Sanhedrin—quietly, of course—to see if the marriage to Phasaelis could be annulled. He made it clear he would be willing to pay.

Most striking of all, to Manean at least, though he wasn't sure if it testified more to the romance or to the calculation behind the whole affair, was Antipas's admission that even upon leaving Ashdod, now fully committed to a plan that would likely brand them both as pariahs, he and Herodias apparently had yet to touch.

When Antipas finally did get back to Galilee, Phasaelis was in a foul temper as usual. The day he arrived, she asked permission to leave, to go to Machaerus, his southernmost palace down along the coast of the Bitter Sea. She'd been known to retreat there from time to time, her servants said because the high balconies offered a view of her homeland.

Herod was only too happy to see her go. Her absence gave him time to devise a strategy and a settlement. He sent for Chuza, his chief financial minister, to discuss what sort of package they could afford. Aretas had conceded the region east of Gadara at the time of the wedding. Perhaps they could give that back. Perhaps Machaerus, if Phasaelis really liked it so much.

They were in the midst of these very deliberations when word arrived from Ashdod: Philip's mother had died. This was good news. She had been old and miserable, but also this gave Antipas an excuse to see Herodias again. He was just preparing to leave, in fact, when another breathless messenger arrived, this time from Peraea.

Phasaelis had disappeared.

"What?" Antipas was confused, but Manean wondered if he didn't detect a hint of relief in his expression. Had tragedy happily intervened? Did he picture her body crumpled at the foot of the cliffs?

"What do you mean, disappeared?"

The envoy reported that the queen had retired at the usual hour the night before last. The following morning she was gone. No one had seen her since.

"What are you saying? She was kidnapped?"

No, said the envoy. There had been no sign of struggle. But her trunks were gone, as were all her personal servants.

Antipas still did not understand but seemed oddly detached from the implications. Herodias was waiting. He asked Manean to go find out what he could and send word back as soon as possible.

It was a three-day journey from Tiberias to Machaerus, which was every bit as dreary as Manean remembered. The idea that someone would actually *want* to come to such a place should have been clue enough that the woman had been up to something, but in fact the mystery had been solved by the time he arrived. The local governor, Naaman, said they had received a message from Petra the day before.

Phasaelis was safe and sound. She was with her father and would not be returning. Apparently she'd found out about Antipas's intention with Herodias. That was was the reason she had asked permission to go south. She'd arranged for one of her father's generals to meet her at Machaerus and help her escape from the palace; then a string of Nabataean officers had escorted her from checkpoint to checkpoint all the way to Petra.

This was all most unfortunate, thought Manean. "So I take it Aretas is upset."

Naaman nodded.

"How upset?"

"He has vowed revenge."

"What kind of revenge?" asked Manean.

". . . eternal."

⧽31⧼

The Wilderness

IN JUDAEA AND THE REGIONS SURROUNDING, THE WILDERNESS WAS never far. It might be made of sand, or rock, or mortar. It might be made of granite or porphyry. It might be flat or rolling or jagged or smooth, as high as a mountaintop or lower than the sea. Only the land must be barren, not arable, and therefore absent man.

Now John, following his first pilgrimage to Jerusalem, chose the wilderness. He could, if he had wanted, have returned to Qumram and joined the brethren in their white tunics. He could have made his way back beyond the Jordan to the Subban potters, to be among his cousins and brothers and sisters, but it was not his purpose to return. He had been a child among the Subba, a youth among the Essenes. He would become a man out in the wilderness, as far from the poisoned wells of Jerusalem as he could get. Like the stench of carrion or a low din rattling inside his head, the hollow worship he had witnessed at the Temple of his father drove him away. It filled him with a fury he could not extinguish and a sorrow that only the farthest distance seemed capable of soothing.

He wanted to forget what he had seen, not just at the Temple but everything that had come before. He wanted to burn the page that had been written in his name: of the tribe that had taken him in but whose holy men would never let him pray with them; of the quiet sect that had hoarded secrets; and of the mother who had given him away and the father who had served his life in a charnel house.

He wanted none of this. He wanted to go back before the lies and set his sight on the one true thing he knew, which was the light. In this alone he continued to believe, as it was the first thing he had ever known. It was the one thing that had remained constant, but he wanted to see it directly again and only so that it might enter him and fill him and purify what was poison in him.

Of his former worship, he brought with him the rudiments: his prayer. He prayed three times a day. He drank no ferment ever, nor ate meat. He honored the Sabbath by fasting, and where he came upon the living water, he purified himself as he had been taught.

To all the rest he died. To the Word. To the Law. To savor and to scent. To comfort and contentment. In the pastures he earned wages. On roadsides he collected alms, but he entered no house twice, nor sat upon a chair, nor slept beneath a roof. He let his ceilings be the dome of stars or sandstone; his floors were flinty hammada. He lived upon God's mercy in the waste howling wilderness, a child without father, a fruit without tender. He fed upon the increase of the field; he sucked honey from the rock and oil from the flint. He still sat and listened, but it was the unfettered wind that taught him now, and the asp, the pill bug, and the scorpion. He became a stranger to the world. No one pronounced his passing. None came and prayed for him, but veil by veil he passed from sight. In the places where he was, he went unseen. In places where he was not, he was remembered and remarked.

In the mountains of Harran a man appeared to a small brotherhood of holy men called the Darawish. They did not know where he had come from, and yet he knew their prayers. He prayed with them. He tilled with them and harvested with them. (They had no wives or books.) He sat with them in their holy house, and they had never seen so many visions as when he was with them.

But he did not stay, despite their pleading. "Are we not avowed as brothers to remain as one, never to leave each another, to pray, to live and die together? Do not go." But he took heed of the living water, which stays pure by flowing. And they did not see him again.

Out on Mount Carmel, a master appeared, whose voice was

delightful and fair, who never spoke falsely or in presumption, whose body and soul were incorrupt. They said he was invulnerable, that he could not be made to bleed or burn or drown. Many students and seekers went to learn from him, but when they came to the place where he had been, he was gone already.

A pupil appeared at the temple in Zoan. He learned their secrets, just as Joseph did, and he shared his own with the masters there. According to his disciples, it was there the heavens tested him.

One night while he was praying, they cast down a wreath of roses before him, and as seven ravens they surrounded him.

"Yahya," they cawed, "you are a scorched mountain. You bring forth no fruit."

They circled him, with their black eyes and shiny wings.

"You are like the dry creek bed," they said, "whose banks yield up no reeds."

"You are an untilled land."

"An abandoned house—"

"Who shall remember your name, Yahya? Who will follow after thee when Yahya is in the ground?"

"Take a wife," the ravens said, "and found yourself a family. Fill your quiver. Do not let the world end."

John gazed upon the wreath before him. He drew its fragrance near. How pleasing it would be, he thought, to take a wife and raise a child, and he would gladly have done so, but he was wary of the desire it would wake in him, and of how he might neglect his prayer.

"But then divide your time," the ravens said. "On the first and second night, devote yourself unto your wife and to your marriage bed. On the third and fourth, devote thyself to prayer. On the fifth night and the sixth, trade off again. And on the seventh, rest. Only see that you are not cut off."

John was tempted, but finally he set the wreath aside. He would not be distracted from his prayer even for a day.

He left Zoan. He went and walked among the bitter lakes and the papyrus. He found the twelve springs of Elim and the seventy palms. He went to where the quail fell down. He did not gather them. He found the tree that Moses did, in Marah, but he did not cast its branches in the water to drink. At En Gedi, he found the wood where David had strengthened his hand, but he did not sleep inside his cave. In winter he wandered to the gorge at Cherith. There the ravens discovered him again and brought him carrion and bread to eat. But John refused them. In the springtime he climbed down into the great ravines of Gilead, but he found no balm. He traveled into the wilderness of Shur, and found his way back through the Negev. He hardened his heels upon the limestone bed in the valley of Ramon. He cooled them in the wilderness of Ziph. He ascended the ruins of Shiloh. He wandered in the Sea of Reeds and farther on through Jeshimon.

Finally he went to seek his end in Arabah. He tempted death, as life had tempted him. He journeyed out to the most barren place of all, beyond the manna and the morning dew. He went out alone into the desert, where there was no river and no well; beyond the camels, and the camel spiders, where not even the vultures dared gather around the carcasses. With nothing but a staff of linden in his hand, he went to where the only living thing was the sand, where the wind thrashed and sun pounded down, and together they devoured, they sucked and dried to the bone.

This is where he stopped, with empty arms and nothing in his stomach. The sun beat down on him, wave upon wave, and he surrendered himself. He said, 'Take root,' but he did not burn. His flesh did not yield; he drank the heat. And held it inside him, and he felt it catch. He felt the page within him burning and the smoke drift up and leave his mouth, a pure breath. A prayer was freed from his lips like incense:

"My life be thine," he said. His words rose up and up. They touched the ceiling of the sky and cooled it. The colors all exploded. The stars peered down. They pierced the veil, poured through their light and sang to him.

"But tell us, Yahya. Answer us. Enlighten us."

One after another, the planets called down. First, Shamish: "Tell us, Yahya, can a stammerer then become a teacher and profess?"

"He can," John said, though he did not intend the words. It was his voice, but the words were spoken through him, coming from the burning light within him, which did not hesitate. "As a child is born a babbler from his mother's womb, but grows and blooms before her."

Sera asked, "And can the blind man become the scribe?"

"He can," said John, still listening as he spoke, "if the villain can find virtue, if he abandon his lies and thievery and seek his faith in Almighty life."

Then Nirigh, Bel, and Enwo called down from their heights, in turn:

"But can the widow become a virgin?"

"Can the foul water be made fresh?"

"Can a stone soften unto oil?"

John answered them: "The widow can become a virgin if only she be pure before her children.

"The fetid water can be made fresh again, and sweet, if the wanton girl would cover herself.

"And the stone will surely soften unto oil, if the sorcerer descends the mountain; if he abandon his magic and become father to the orphan, if he fills the widow's pockets and surrenders to Almighty Life."

"Then tell us this, Yahya," called Liwet and Kiwan, speaking now as one. "Do you say the fallen house can rise?"

"The fallen house can rise," said John, now more clear and certain than ever, "if it abandon the hill, if it pull up its stakes and build itself anew beside the sea; if it open its doors to the stranger; if it lay out the table of its bounty for all who are hungry, and beds for the weary, and never seek to keep them, but teach its children the way of Truth."

Hearing this, the heavens were filled with joy. They answered all as one, the stars and planets alike, "Well for thee, Yahya! The heavens decree you are a prisoner no more. You are free. Thou hast won thy release and left the world an empty cell. Now plant thy staff."

John heard them clearly. He planted his staff in the sand, and where the tip had stabbed, there first appeared a tear. It came seeping up and made a small puddle, and that puddle began to spill in one direction, first a trickle, then a stream, and as the earth turned beneath him, the stream gave rise to banks on either side, and the banks grew brush, the brush gave way to willows and rolling green hills. And while he stood knee deep in the running water, the mountain rose up beneath him, with forests and meadows to feed the wakening sheep, and there were lilies and wildflowers to cover the fields and quench the bees. And the sky was scattered with clouds to spell the sun, and in the sky were both the sun and moon at once, but the moon was meek in the blue and descending, and the sun was rising, and everything was singing, every blade of grass. All Life was looking down at him and up at him, and back at him, rejoicing. He knew that he had found the place of Truth. He knew he was in the presence of Almighty Life, and he knew this was the light that he had seen from the first. The same that had appeared before him, but in all its glory, the light that he had always known.

And while he stood beneath it, basking, a beam descended from its heart in the form of a man, a perfect and radiant man, whom he recognized as Hibil-Ziwa, who first divided the heavens and the earth. In his hand, he held a cloak of pure light, and John recognized this as well. It was the same as the Uthra wore. It was the same he gave his son Methusalah; the same Noah gave to Chus, and that he passed on to Zoroaster; the same worn by Ram and Shurbai, and Shum bar Nu before him. It was the same as Adam wore, only it was being given to him now.

So he understood his journey was only half finished. Having sat and listened, the time had come for him to stand and teach; as the heavens had lent him ear and let him see the Truth, now he was to go and bear witness to the same: that what had been corrupted could be made pure, what had fallen could rise, what had died could know life again.

So John took the mantle from the messenger. He draped it over his own shoulder, and when he turned, he saw there was a boat waiting for him, carved of mashkil wood, and that sitting in the boat was his guardian, Par'am, ready to take him on one last journey.

⋛32⋚

The Kiss

IN HER WINTER YEARS ELIZABETH OFFERED HERSELF AS A SISTER and an aunt, as a teacher and a seamstress for the Temple, a friend and grandmother to the children of Battai, all of whom scampered across the stone floors of her home. They sat on her knee. They heard her quiet song and grew into young men and women before her dimming eyes.

But she never relented with her prayer to her born son, John. Every night that the moon appeared, she prayed. When it rested, she was silent. She let the heavens ponder and weigh, but when the moon appeared again, then she resumed.

Battai remained true to her mistress, even with her doubts. She had followed her from Ein Karim when she grew too old to be alone. They moved to Hebron. With a full heart Battai watched Elizabeth with her own three children, singing to them, teaching them, walking with them in the vineyard. With broken heart she watched her pack John's lambskin on every pilgrimage, and then unpack it first thing. With a bleeding heart, she watched her mistress kneel at night, her lips moving silently.

———

Just before the wedding of Battai's eldest daughter, Battai and Elizabeth went to the markets in Jericho. Battai had made a trip down to the river to see the mongers there.

As usual, they were bickering with the customers and the fishermen alike, accusing them and threatening them. But above the normal give-and-take, she heard another voice, of an old man calling out.

"What woman had a son who then was stolen?"

He was old and haggard. He looked like a beggar, but there was a young man beside him, a hermit stepping from the boat, and already he had attracted notice for his appearance. His hair was long and tangled; his beard likewise. For a garment, he wore nothing but camel skin, bound at the waist by a leather strap. But his body was straight and upright. His shoulders were broad, not thick. His neck was long and sinuous, as were his arms and legs. He stood tall, looking out above the heads of those surrounding him. His eyes scanned the crowd, but they did not descend, and there was a faint smile on his face.

The old man continued calling out, "What woman has made for him a vow and been careless about it?" And he pointed back to the young hermit as if he were a prize calf. "What woman had a son who was stolen? Let her come and see after him now."

Battai looked at the young man again. His skin was of a deep olive tone but without blemish. His brow was dark, his eyes deep-set, but when he turned them down on her, she went still.

She knew these eyes. So wide and wide apart—the better to see the farthest distance. These were the eyes of her mistress.

She knew the mouth as well. The lips were full, well framed. His mouth was the mouth of Old Father.

She dropped her basket there and ran to where Elizabeth was sitting with her young. She fell down at her feet.

"Forgive me, my mistress. Forgive me that I have ever doubted."

"Be calm, Battai, what is it?"

"Forgive me, my mistress, but by the river, by the market, he has returned. On my life, a guardian angel stands by him."

"Calm yourself, Battai, and breathe."

"But his eyes—his eyes are yours. His mouth, Old Father's. His hands—"

She looked up. Elizabeth was already gone without her veil.

The young hermit was still standing beside the beggarman, and a crowd had gathered around, on account of his appearance and the harping of his companion. Elizabeth could see only his head and broad shoulders, but she fell down before him. The crowd parted, and when the young hermit saw her, he awoke from his daze.

He took her hand, and there among the marketers, the mongers, and the fishermen, he set a kiss upon her lips.

They all were taken aback. Even the beggar. "Is it right that you should kiss this stranger?"

John smiled. "Is it not right that a son should honor his mother?" he said. "Nay, hail and hail again to the man who honors his father and mother. The man who honors his father and mother has not his like in the world."

When Par'am heard this, he knew that John had remembered all his lessons, and so he left them there, the son and his mother, just as he had found them so many years ago.

None saw the old man go. He returned to the wilderness, to the hill country east of the Jordan, and there he offered up a prayer, first to the sun and then again to the moon and all the stars that night, that they look down and take care of him whom the Almighty had sent. "Keep him safe," Par'am said, "until we ask for him again."

Then he entered inside the cave and laid down the mantle of the Uthra. The Uthra laid down the mantle of the man, and each ascended to his place and to the seats awaiting them.

John stayed with his mother that first night, and with Battai and her children. They had supper together. The old mother's heart was full. She saw how his fingers held the bread. She saw how he washed his hands and arms. She saw how he glanced about at their lamps and floorstones, a stranger to her world. She heard the songs he sang the children, melodies she did not know. And if he glanced to her, and if that glance reminded her of Old Father, and how his head would turn, she did not say.

She heard him pray before he lay down, and how the words were strange, but the voice familiar. He had his father's voice. He had his father's mouth and hands. They were the same as held him once. They were the same as had prayed for him.

After all the rest had gone to to bed, she went and sat with him.

"Have you no questions?" she asked.

He did, many. "But which would you have me ask?"

"About your father," she said.

A shadow fell across his eyes. "My father was a priest at the Temple."

"He was," she said.

"Which he also helped build."

"He did," she said again, "and which he would just as soon have razed."

The shadow lifted from her son's eyes.

"You he loved," she said. "For you he gave his life, at a dearer price than I have given mine."

John heard, and stood, and kissed her again. Then he went and spoke a final prayer outside.

After he had gone to bed, Elizabeth remained awake. In all the years her eyes had been dry, not wanting to affront the Lord with her doubt, but now with the sound of John asleep inside her home, she wept as she had not wept in all the years of her vigil, so much so that she removed herself in order not to wake the children.

Battai found her outside.

"My mistress," she said, "why do you weep? Tell me it's for joy. Surely it is cause for celebration that John has returned to the land of his father. Tell me, who did not fear that he was dead? Who did not fear your prayers were in vain? And yet we see he has returned, and look at him. Has a more perfect man yet been created? Tell me thy sacrifice has ended."

Elizabeth took the nursemaid's hand.

"I know not why I weep," she said. "I weep because my heart is full, and I am full because I know the Lord has always looked upon me. And I am too small for all that he has given me.

"I weep because I see a scar upon his brow. And I do not know how it came to be. But I know that he has not returned to be my son. And I shall no more be his mother now than I was before. And I know he has placed that kiss on me to protect me and to gird me, for he has returned for a greater purpose than I can know.

"I know the road behind him has been filled with sorrow and with loneliness. And I know the road ahead will be the same, and worse. I fear what lies ahead for him.

"And so I pray that he not suffer, but I am too weak to follow now. I want only to be with my husband."

Elizabeth did not follow John. When he left again, she stayed in her chair. She continued to sit with her family and with Battai's children, and she continued to pray for him until the day of her own passing, which came not long after. Battai was there to witness how peacefully she departed, and how hopefully, that she might see Old Father again and watch over John from the heights.

Later, when John was told by one of his followers that she had passed, he knelt. He said, "Let us give thanks and praise to Elizabeth, and to the Almighty Father that I was born to one of such faith and such forbearance."

Ever after he would speak her name in all his prayers, giving thanks to "Elizabeth, who carried me lightly, in whom I first beheld the light of my creator, and who then bore me twice—unto the world and unto Him, the Heavenly Father."

Part Three

THE MISSION

⇛33⇚

Agrippa

UP IN GALILEE, THE HONEYMOON DID NOT LAST FOR LONG. For all the passion and impulsiveness that stoked it, the union of Antipas and Herodias had been entered into with certain expectations also: bluntly, that Herodias might provide an heir, and that Antipas might provide that heir a worthy kingdom—more worthy, that is, than the mere tetrarchy willed to him.

Two years removed from their vows, it didn't look as if either expectation was likely to be met.

On the queen's side, the explanation seemed clear enough: She was past her years. None dared murmur such a thing, and the queen herself threatened to disprove the theory any number of times with nameless guards. But the reason was there, and blameless.

As for Antipas, his failure to expand the domain was attributed— by him at least—to the fact that the marriage had turned out to have been far more controversial than he had anticipated. The family had sided squarely with Philip; Antipas had had no idea how popular his brother was. The Pharisees were outraged on principle. They did not care what the High Priest said (the High Priest having, for the price of one hundred talents, given his blessing to Antipas and Herodias). The Sadducees and the Romans were merely confused. The politics made no sense, which—in the absence of an heir—was true.

Worst of all, the unfortunate manner in which the whole affair had been revealed—that is, before Antipas had time to explain himself or offer compensation—had overnight turned the nation on his eastern flank into an avowed enemy that needed fending. Antipas felt this keenly. He was spooked by Aretas and lived in constant fear of attack. Far from being in position to expand his footprint, Antipas felt more surrounded than ever, and more isolated, and he held the marriage to blame.

In their mutual frustration, he and Herodias compensated each other's grief with toleration. Herodias put up with her husband's various Jewish pieties and superstitions. She turned a blind eye to his drinking, to his preference for spooning with eunuchs at night (another aping of his father), and of course to his shameless doting on Salome.

Indeed, he seemed to have taken a strange sort of solace in his new stepdaughter, all the more as time passed and it became clear that she would likely be his only heir. It struck Manean that Antipas was in many ways prouder of Salome, and more delighted by her, than he would have been had she been his own spawn, precisely because she was *not* of him. He took open pleasure in the endowments she possessed that he did not.

He would watch her skip along a narrow ledge of the wall, as she was wont to do. "Look how she moves," he'd say. "The high chin is an air. What marks her pedigree is *that*," and he'd point at the feet, the legs, and how nimble they were, and the eerie stillness she could maintain in her torso, while below she traipsed so freely. The feet again: "One can picture them—can't one?—hiding in the passes of Ebal, lying in wait, then pouncing like tigers on the armies of Antiochus." He was referring to the Maccabees, of course, the fathers of her line.

He lavished gifts upon her. If she so much as glanced at something— a necklace, an Egyptian kitten—it was hers. Not that her mother held out much hope anyway, but she complained the girl would never learn that way, never be "clever," if everything was simply handed to her for the asking.

"And what's the good of being clever?" Antipas would reply.

For his part, he put up with his wife's many airs (perfumes included), her tastes in design, which ran to the grotesque, and the abusiveness of her courtiers to staff. The bulk of his patience, however, was expended on the person of her older brother, Agrippa.

Antipas had never liked him. He did not consider Agrippa a good man or a man of his word. Raised in Roman privilege, the same as he, Agrippa seemed to have taken precisely the wrong lesson from his youth—that is, to take no responsibility. The years he should have devoted to building something from his advantages, he had instead wasted, being far too generous with other people's money, gambling and giving it away. He'd spent ten years touring the empire, escaping debt and incurring more. Finally, Herodias had come on his behalf to ask if Antipas would take him in. Again, as part of the new bargain, Antipas said yes, but it still galled him, having to sit and watch how she treated him. The two were like lovers, batting eyelashes, cooing, and laughing much too hard. But the worst was how she talked about Agrippa when he wasn't there. She spoke of him as if he were the standard against which all other men should be measured, which was absurd. The man was a wastrel.

The third year of the marriage a banquet was held in Sepphoris, the wooden city, to celebrate the restoration of the palace there.

The day was near enough to the wedding anniversary that special attention was given. Herodias hired the well-known Roman caterer Temiculus to organize the whole event, and he did not disappoint. The palace was resplendent with lilies and lanterns like the ones they used at the Temple. There could well have been a thousand people in attendance, but the menu had been ample and excellent. The entertainment likewise, with dancers and musicians roaming the courtyards. Salome had even come out with two of her maidens to perform one of her dances, more of a romp, really, but Antipas still repaid her with a coral necklace all the way from the Himalayas. He gave Herodias a fountain.

It was proving to be a very pleasant evening, all things considered —that is, until the wee hours, when well into his cups, Antipas happened to overhear Agrippa complaining about the wine, saying that Temiculus might want to "rethink whoever sold him this."

Antipas informed him that the wine at question had come from his own vineyards at Ascalon. "If it's not to your liking, perhaps you could go run them yourself."

Agrippa made some joke: that with wine, he could certainly claim some expertise. The people laughed. Antipas went off to stew in the corner with Manean: "He comes here, lives for free, drinks my wine, then has the impertinence to complain."

He finally worked himself into such a lather that he went back to Agrippa and started berating him in front of the other guests, telling him he was a disgrace and a family joke. He called him a mooch and a welcher and a bad influence on Salome.

"If it weren't for the family coming to your rescue time and again, you'd be derelict."

To his credit, Agrippa did not seem to take offense but kept deflecting the insults, conceding they were "probably true," "probably so," "well said," "note taken," but with such an ease and a charm that it only provoked Antipas all the more.

"But this exactly your problem," he said, "thinking you can simply charm your way out of any situation. You rely on the indulgence of others, all because you're pretty to look at, but the truth is you're useless, just like your sister."

Again, Agrippa had been remarkably patient up until then, but this last bit stopped him.

"Say again?"

"You heard me," said Antipas, seeing he'd aimed the arrow well this time. "I said you're as useless as your sister."

This Agrippa parried. "Oh, as if my sister is the useless one. My sister has proven her worth in Salome, as I'm quite sure you've noticed. But tell me, what have you to show for ten years with that she-goat?" He smiled, turning to the others. "No, methinks the problem is with the seed, not the soil . . ."

Agrippa was removed from the grounds that very night and forbidden ever to set foot in Antipas's territory again.

≋34≋

The Market

ACCORDING TO HIS DISCIPLES, JOHN WAS THIRTY YEARS OF AGE when he finally returned to Jerusalem. He first appeared near the spice markets in the valley of the cheesemakers the eighth day before Passover, just as the streets of the city were beginning to teem with early arrivals.

He was already there when the merchants began setting up their tables and scales. As he had chosen a place in the shade of an overpass, they took little note at first. They could see he wore no veil, and that his hair was a long dark drape. The merchants nearest by assumed he was another Nazarite who'd lost his way, as happens.

The first to pay him any mind were the children. They came racing through as usual but stopped when they saw him—how still he was and how strange in appearance. He wore a pelt of camel skin. Only one shoulder was covered. His arms were bare. His eyes were open, but they did not follow. The children waved. He did not blink. He sat as still as a dial, knees splayed, his legs crossed at the ankle, his arms crossed in his lap at the wrist.

The guards asked if they should move him.

"Leave him be." The merchants all agreed. "He isn't begging."

He did not beg. He did not budge. The children drew closer, making faces, gnashing at the fruit in their hands. They tossed bread-crumbs at him to see the pigeons climb up onto his knees.

As the day drew on, customers began taking note as well.

"How long?"

"Since we arrived this morning," said the merchants. "He was here when we came."

They peered.

"Is he breathing?"

They watched his ribs.

"He is, but slowly."

"And look how pale he is."

"He isn't pale. He beams."

So it seemed in the waning light. To some at least.

". . . he's pale."

They left him blankets for the night, and bread and water.

The following day the blanket was there where they had left it. The bread was gone.

"See? He eats."

"Or the dogs do."

The bowl of water appeared to have been untouched.

Again, the guards asked if they should move him. "If you think he's slowing business."

"Slowing business?" The merchants gestured around. The market was abuzz, in part because the feast was drawing near, but also because so many customers were lingering to see if they could catch the hermit moving or blinking.

Some were even saying that they recognized him now.

"It's John," they said. "The Baptizer."

"This one? No. John rejects the city."

They stood before him, speaking aloud as if he could not hear or see.

"But look at his garment," they said. "My cousin heard him speak in Damascus and said he is possessed by demons."

"Is he a Syrian?"

"No," said one. "He comes from farther north."

"North? No. East. His followers are out at Bethabara, beyond the Jordan—"

Others merely shook their heads. They had not heard of him, or of the garment, or of the word—"Baptizer"—not used that way at least.

The following day, the customers were coming with slightly better information. None could confirm that this was he, but as for John, he came from the east. He was a Nazorean, they said. His followers had been seen out to the west as well. They had a cave there where they purified themselves and others who came, but they'd recently moved again to Bethabara, out beyond the Jordan.

"But what does he preach?"

They shook their heads. They were not followers, though some did venture. "Repentance. He preaches purity for the sake of salvation."

They peered again at him.

"He cleanses them."

"Who?"

"Whoever comes."

They left him more than blankets now, and bread. They left him flowers and bowls of locust.

"That is what he eats. They say."

They left him carob and nuts.

But still the hermit did not move. The crowd around him grew some more and continued trading stories, but eventually, just as his stillness had first drawn their attention, it lost it. By the fifth and sixth days they had come to accept his presence there as if he were a statue, and now the festival was upon them. They went about their business, buying and selling, gossiping, complaining. The guards looked away. The children ran on by.

Then on the eighth morning, the first day of the feast, he was gone.

≍ 35 ≍

The Temple

THE STREETS WERE PACKED AND CHURNING NOW. THE TEMPLE was a hive. Rumor of the Baptizer's appearance in the city had made its rounds but was subsumed by the sudden tide of pilgrims, most of whom had yet to hear of him or of the rite he offered.

"Right there," said the spice merchants, pointing to the now empty spot beneath the overpass. "Not a murmur. Not a budge."

Some customers refused to be impressed. "Seven days. I've seen seven days. The masters down in Alexandria will sit for seven days as habit."

The merchants shrugged. Maybe so. They tried to put him out of mind, but later, when the children's voices called down from overhead, they knew instantly the reason why.

"Come!" The boy was jumping at the guardrail of the bridge. "He is inside!"

"And he is speaking!" said his brother.

The spice merchants dropped their sacks. They left their scales and went to see. They barely tied the canopies.

As it was now midday, with the sacrifices already well under way, the public court was swarming with pilgrims and traders and more than the usual share of proselytes, there to take advantage of the crowd, competing with the barter and the beggars, blocking their way to say their piece. But even in the bustle and din of all the bodies, the spice merchants could hear one voice cutting through the rest:

Where is Adam? . . .

"That one?"

. . . Where is the mother, Eve?

"I heard that voice last night. Was it not in my dream?"
A nearby stranger shook his head no. "I looked out my window. It
was like a cricket in a crack."

Where are Seth and Râm and Rûd?
Where are Shurbai and Shar-hab-ẓl?

"But it was more a chattering than this. A jabbering."
Yes. They listened again. This morning the words could not have
been more clear.

Where are all the bygone ages—
of the sword and the fire and the flood?
Where are all the fathers and forefathers who stood
guard for you, protecting you?

The voice called out, firm and loud. It neither rose nor plunged.
Its pitch stayed even, but with a hoarseness that at its greatest exertion
gave him the sound of seven men:

They have all abandoned you! They have turned
their backs on you, as you have turned your back on them!

It was coming from the entrance to the Court of Israel. He had set
himself where all the pilgrims would be forced to pass. He had been
there since the gates had opened, the people said, calling out to those
who would hear, and different ears were struck by different phrases.
The Zealots heard him say the nation of Israel was a "home-born
slave." A scribe claimed he had spoken of the judgment day and how
it would leave the wicked neither root nor branch. A shepherd said he
had dismissed the sacrificial lamb as carrion.

When the spice merchants finally pushed their way through to see him, they still weren't certain it was he, the man from the market. The pelt was the same, and the beard, but the hermit in the market had been so still and serene, so barely there. This one seemed to be exploding with life. He stood with his feet apart, one before the other, and his right arm thrust forward like the prow of a ship. His eyes were beaming out like lanterns.

> *The heavens look down, aghast, appalled by the desolation! They see by the coming light: Your fields have gone to waste. Your rivers have dried up! Your cities are in ruin! They are not fooled. Your noble houses are but sties of rubble and dung, pens for filthy swine! Your royal palaces are brothels, rife with whores and adulterers and the diseases they carry. And here your sacred Temple is, in heaven's eyes, a tomb— more fouled than the bat caves of Mount Carmel! Your incense is a whore's perfume, sent up to disguise the stench of death!*

A train of noblemen approached. The Temple guards and Levites parted the crowd before them, so they could be seen in all their fineries—Sadducees and Pharisees alike, and members of the royal court—all come together to show their unity on this holy day. Herod Philip was there, with his wife, Livia, as well as Gamaliel, the rabbi, and Caius, brother of the High Priest.

They heard the voice as well. It was a ranting to their ears, but they did not look, even as he pointed at them directly.

> *Awake, ye nobles! Awake, ye gentlewomen, who will not lift your heads. Awake from your slumber!*

They pretended they did not hear. Livia smiled. How could she awake when she had never been asleep?

"*Awake and heed unto Jehova!*" the voice cried out.

"Return unto me," he has said.
"And I shall return unto you."

But how could he return, thought Caius, if he had never left?

"And yet ye rob from me!" the voice replied, as if it had heard his thoughts aloud.

What holy man would wear such robes? Or
dress his temple up in gold, while widows and
their children crawl out in the gutter? What
shepherd feeds on his own flock?

Here they turned. They had not come to be insulted or accused. *"You have forsaken the living spring!"* he called.

You have hewn out cisterns instead,
which crack and break.

But the man was a lunatic; could the people not see? Standing there in his pelt, with nothing on his feet. His hair looked like a lion's.

But when the true light shows itself, be warned:
You who rule by the yoke, by lash, and by letter,
you shall burn by heaven's light. You shall be
rendered stubble
and all thy riches, ash!

The royals told the guards, "Remove him," and the guards did start in his direction, reaching for their clubs, but the hermit stayed them with an unearthly howl. *"What is that bludgeon?"* he cried.

A sparrow's wing! What is the arm that carries it?
A reed! Cut out my tongue! It will grow back
and back and back again!

The soldiers pretended to be amused, but the crowd could see that they were uneasy, even as their masters urged them on.

"Go shut him up," they said.

But now the people were stepping in, and some of the rabbis and younger scribes as well, who had been taking pleasure at this, the sight of a hermit cowing the leaders of the Temple. As savage as his appearance may have been, they agreed with much of what he was saying. Who could deny that the priests had overseen the denigration of the people's house, that they ignored the Law and the prophets and stole from God? Who could deny that the royal house was rife with incest and depravity? They themselves had been saying these things for years, just never so bluntly and never so directly as this wild man.

They stepped up to his defense, and yet no sooner had they cleared their throats than the hermit turned on them as well.

> *And you, do not console yourselves! You*
> *doctors, you lawyers and teachers, you are*
> *slumberers as well, cumberers of the ground, and*
> *tumors of the body of the people.*
> *You neither till nor spin. You worship God with*
> *lip; your hearts are hidden miles away,*
> *set on gold and station.*

And now the scribes and rabbis, the very same who had been so pleased a moment before, reconsidered. Who was this man to speak to them this way?

> *You gnash your teeth at Caesar,*
> *then go twist God's Law into a labyrinth.*
> *You rend your clothes when they set a crown upon*
> *a harlot's head, while you yourselves have made a*
> *kept woman out of Torah. She is your mistress.*
> *She knows your tricks and you know hers, and*
> *these you keep.*

The spice merchants smiled. They and the Zealots nodded as they watched the Pharisees turn red. Again, the wild man only spoke the truth: The priests were thieves; the Romans, thugs; the royals, a disgrace—who could deny it? And who could deny the sanctimony of the Pharisees?

"But there is a time and place," the scribes were grumbling. "No man of God would seize upon this day—"

"But this is just the day that he should seize," said the Zealots. "You should listen to this one."

"*But those who follow me,*" he was saying now:

> *those who follow the way of the pure,*
> *they shall be uplifted.*
> *They shall feel the breath of life*
> *And behold the realm of everlasting light,*
> *As it has called to them*
> *and to all their brothers and their sisters!*

The rabbis and the priests had heard enough. The man had gone from insult to blasphemy. They made way for the guards, but now the Zealots stepped in.

"Stand clear," the priests commanded.

The Zealots replied with spit. Much lunging and shoving and hair pulling followed, which gave the guards their entrance. Names were cursed, garments torn, and several teeth dislodged. The scuffle didn't last for long, but when the parties were separated, the hermit was nowhere to be seen.

"Did they take him?" asked the spice merchants.

No. Not that anyone had seen.

They looked for him the remainder of the day—they and many others—all throughout the Temple and back at the marketplace, but they could find no trace of him.

Back in the hills, they guessed. The hermit had returned to the caves from whence he'd come. Many said good riddance. "Let him bray at the moon." But there were others who were already whispering to one another, "The prophets are not dead."

⋛ 36 ⋚

Bethany

JOHN HIMSELF WAS NOT HEARD FROM AGAIN UNTIL THE FOLLOW-
ing evening. Word had come that he was in Bethany, on the far side
of Olivet. This is where Andrew first saw him.

Andrew was a young fisherman from Galilee. He had come down
to Jerusalem two days before with his brother, Simon, and Simon's
family to make their offering, just as they had done every year since
Andrew could remember.

But he had felt himself at a distance this time, and stretching back
awhile. The journey down had taken five days, which was longer than
usual. Their mother had not been feeling well, and they had had to
stay the night at Sychar to find her some balm. Three full baskets of
fish had spoiled on the way, all meant for the house of Caius, whose
brother was High Priest. Simon had put the blame on Andrew, saying the fish had not been well enough salted. As punishment, he had
Andrew make the delivery, which was quickly rejected. The servants
hurled the baskets into the gutter, and Andrew had spent the remainder of the day at the open markets, trying to sell the rest, but by then it
was no use. The fish stank. He returned to the family empty-handed,
which meant they had that much less to bring to the Temple, which
meant their offering that year would be meager.

Again Andrew was held responsible, but it wasn't even this that weighed upon him, or his brother's harsh words. It was how little they affected him, or any of it: his mother's pallor in her bed; the sound of the waves lapping against the boat; the blank black stare of the fish in the gutter. All seemed strange to him and unaffecting. Not since he was a boy had the questions come to him so acutely: Why this way? Why this garment? Why these people all around him? Why should Simon be his brother?

Even in the wearying turmoil of the Temple Mount, the same queer sense persisted, as if he were observing it all through a muslin gauze. A flock of heron thrummed overhead, and it was not so much that Andrew wished that he were one of them, as that he might as well have been, looking down at the little priests and Levites, all so intent, so busy with their anthill tasks, burning birds and bowing, scurrying from gate to gate with oil and bundles of wood; the women waiting in the Women's Court, infants wailing in their arms; the sinners bending down to supplicate and peck, while all surrounding them the other daily rites were observed in equal faith: the moneychangers at the tables changing money; the pilgrims purchasing their doves; the sheep, confused, shuffling in their places, taking comfort in the nearness of the flock, while lazy oxen chewed their cud. Andrew watched their lazy eyes and felt the same.

And he felt the same when the family gathered in the evening to eat their paltry feast of bread and olives. A neighboring tent had offered their lamb, but Simon refused, too proud, and more interested in casting blame on Andrew. Andrew didn't care. He left his family there, not out of shame, but to try to shed the veil that seemed to be surrounding him. He made his way up and over Olivet to Bethany, in search of strangers like himself. That was when he came upon the small crowd gathered in the road, all squinting in at a well-appointed house. It appeared a banquet was taking place inside.

Just to see what was so interesting, and to confirm that it would not interest him, Andrew peered over their shoulders and into the home. Lamps were lit inside and out. He assumed there must be some high official, a judge or maybe a rabboni, in attendance.

"Who?"

"John," replied the man beside him. "The Baptizer."

Andrew shook his head. He did not know the name.

"The one who cursed the priests in the Temple."

Andrew looked back in over the low stone wall. It appeared to be the home of a Pharisee. Most of the guests were Pharisees, still at this hour wearing the taliths and the little scrolls on their foreheads.

But now as he looked again, he saw the one. A Nazarite, or so it appeared. His hair was long and thick, his beard, the same, and while all those around him were dressed in their finest robes, this one stood in their midst in a simple pelt, like a man who'd wandered in off the street or from a cave, the sort of man whom servants turn away, and yet the learned men within were all gazing at him, nervous and awed.

"This one?" he asked.

The men surrounding him nodded. "And there's word they are looking for him, the Temple guard."

That hardly seemed likely. "Why?"

"For telling the truth," a man behind him said. "He called priests thieves."

"He called the palace a harlot's den."

Andrew looked in again. This man here?

A woman of the house was handing him a cup, a rounded Roman cup that had no base; he could not set it down. It balanced in his palm, drained of all enticement. When she turned away, he stepped out on the terrace, where all the vessels and wine craters stood.

The gathering in the street let out something between a murmur and a cheer of welcome.

"Praise be to John," they said.

"And when will you return to the river?" another asked.

He did not answer them at first, other than to pour the wine back into the crater. He did not seem to hear them until another called out, "And have no fear, John. We're standing watch."

At this he did look out. With the torchlight behind him catching the stray locks of his hair, his silhouette was rung in gold.

"From whom are you protecting me?" he asked. His low voice cut clear through the murmur of the guests behind him.

"From the Temple guard," the men in the street answered.

"And the palace guard."

"Your words have disturbed them, John."

"Your words disturb them because they are true."

John did not move. "Do they not disturb you?"

The gathering was silent.

John continued. "I did not come to awaken just the high and mighty. The fishmonger sleeps if he sneaks his elbow on the scale. The farmer sleeps if he plunders his neighbor's field. Both the soldier and the publican, if they skim and extort, are asleep. As is the harlot.

"And the husband is no better than the king if he covets his brother's wife, if he washes himself before entering his door to hide her smell, and only then so he may return to his sister's bed. And his wife is no better than he if she complains, if she works the Sabbath, thinking, What does it gain me to rest? What does it gain me to give?"

The men all stood silent. Finally it was Andrew who spoke, though the voice might have belonged to someone else, it came so freely, so unexpectedly from his throat. "What should we do?"

John looked back at him directly, his eyes black; the whites a simmering blue. "The Lord God Jehovah hath said, 'Bring ye the whole of thy tithe into the granary, that there may be food in my house. Show me now with all ye have to give, and I shall open you the windows of heaven and pour you out a blessing greater than this world can hold.'"

Andrew had not heard these words before. He did not know where they had come from, but he knew that he was obliged to heed them now for simply having heard.

The following day Simon started the family back to Bethsaida, but Andrew went with them only as far as Jericho. He did not tell his brother why he was staying.

"Tell Mother I'll follow," he said.

"Should I tell her you are chasing shadows?" asked Simon.

Andrew was not offended by Simon's words. He let them pass. It was now just two days until John had said he would be at Gilgal.

⇥37⇤

Gilgal

GILGAL WAS THE OLDEST TOWN IN THE REGION. IT MARKED THE ancient oaks of Moreh, where Abraham set the first altar. It was here that the Israelites, on their return to Canaan, took twelve stones from the bed of the Jordan—one for each tribe—and set them down as witness to their arrival. It was here that Elijah had parted with his pupil Elisha.

But Gilgal's day had long since passed. Now it sat low in the Jordan Valley, baking dry and empty, most of the people having moved elsewhere, to the greener pastures of Jericho, Bethel, and Galilee.

Andrew understood therefore that the several dozen pilgrims now waiting on the outskirts had most likely come for the same reason as he. Almost all were common folk. A small troop of Essenes was there as well, but otherwise they were farmers and peddlers and fishermen like him. Some had clearly made the journey from Jerusalem. They had brought their offerings with them. Andrew only wondered, had these others any better sense of what they were doing here?

There was one he knew from Bethsaida, another fisherman named Nathaniel. He was sitting with a family that had traveled all the way from Damascus, two brothers and a sister, who was with child. They shared their bread with him, and fruit. They said they had heard John speak awhile before, that he had been throughout the region preaching, and so they had come here to be "reborn."

This was the first time Andrew heard the word, but when they asked him why he had come, he said the same.

John appeared midday, coming from the east. Even as his image flickered and wavered in the rising heat, all could see it was he, from the length of hair, the beard, the pelt.

Two others, dressed in simple linen tunics, were following him. The pilgrims gathered around the stones to wait and bowed their heads as John came near. He regarded none in particular but took his place before them, standing on the largest of the rocks. The two disciples sat one on either side.

His countenance was not as grave as it had been in Bethany. He cast his gaze above them, on the sky and the horizon. Likewise, his voice when he spoke was like a sail or the sheath of an enormous tent, flung far and high above their heads, so that it would fall upon them all.

"*A radiant boat descends upon the waters,*" he said.

> *The other fishermen do not see. They do not see the sail of gleaming white or the beams, which shine like gold. They do not see the lamp on its prow or the fisherman standing beside it, in a golden crown of glory.*
>
> *They do not hear as the boat touches down. It does not make a sound or stir the waves, and they are too busy cursing one another—their house, their customers.*
>
> *Not until the radiant fisherman takes up his trumpet are they aware. The sound of it blasts across the water. It riffles the waves, warning all the fish to stay away, stay clear of this reef and the tangled nets these fishermen set.*
>
> *The fishermen are terrified at the sound. They scramble back, but now they see the ship that has descended in their midst. They see the pure white sail, the golden beams, the glowing lamp upon its prow. They see the crown upon the fisherman's head.*
>
> *"Welcome!" they say. They put aside their differences for now. "Sit. Drink from our cup. Eat from our bowl. Let us work together. Let us*

tie our boats to yours," they say. "Let us show you where to drop your nets and how to bait them best, with withered dates and olives. We can help you. Between us and all that we have learned, and you and your fine nets, we will catch all the fish, the good and the bad, and we will let you have the lion's share. We will give you three parts to our one."

The golden fisherman sets down their cup. He gives them back their bowl.

"You will not tie your boats to mine," he says. "You will not foul my nets with withered, rotten bait. Take your boats, and set them on the distant shore.

"The fish I seek, will not be caught up in your nets. They will not sink down in the mud. They will never be tempted by your withered bait, for they are the pure. The fish I seek I do not gut, or eat, or trade. The fish I seek will follow my lamp, and they will follow me, and the heavens will clothe them in glory."

Now John stepped down from the rock where he had been standing and started back in the direction he had come from, east toward the Jordan.

Those who had come to hear him were not sure what they should do. John had offered no direction, but when his two disciples stood, then so did the rest, Andrew among them.

They followed the disciples, who followed John all the way across the plain to the banks of the Jordan, which was shrouded in that part by willows leaning down to drink.

John had crossed already, but the disciples showed them the river here was shallow, at no point deeper than their chests, and there was a rope as well, stretching from bank to bank with two small boats beneath. Some of the women and the older men climbed in, and some put their fruits and bread inside. Most forded the river on foot, as the disciples had shown them.

This was how Andrew crossed. He felt as if his heart were lifted in his chest, was floating on the surface of the cold and bracing water. He looked at the faces of those beside him, the sister from Damascus and her brothers. He thought of all the gray faces back at the Temple, how twisted and veiled they had been. Here every countenance was open and uplifted. Here all was hope, even the current tugging at them lightly, the ruffle of the surface, the breeze in his ears, the titter of the swallows looking on from their branches, watching them all return again, to begin again.

An older man, one of the peddlers from the roadside, refused the boat. Halfway across, the water rose above his chin. He swam. He paddled like a dog. The river carried him down, but gently. He did not panic. Another younger man caught him and carried him until his feet could touch again.

There was a smaller stream on the far side, feeding the river from the east. The pilgrims followed the disciples alongside it, past supplicant rows of more hunchbacked willows. Then, after a mile or so, the banks opened out to reveal a small valley, shaded here and there by locust trees and willow and acanthus flower, carved and watered by the same little stream as it rounded a stubborn hill, riven with caves.

There were men here already, more disciples, standing in the water washing jars. A small looping canal had been dug as well, to circumvent a hut that had been built from the displaced mud. Smoke drifted from a hole in the top. The air smelled faintly of flat bread.

One of the disciples was standing on a rock inside the stream, looking back over them, straining to watch the descent of the sun as it fell between the two slopes that formed the little valley.

Perhaps a dozen more were sitting up on the hill, all dressed simply but not the same. Some wore linen; some, a coarser fabric. Some were in turbans; some, veils. Some covered their faces. High up, one more sat in the mouth of the utmost cave: a woman.

None spoke. The flow of the water was all that could be heard, and the gentle stir of the willow braids, and locust leaves, and prayer.

This was the settlement at Bethabara.

⤜38⤛

Bethabara

NOW SEVERAL OF THE DISCIPLES WERE CROSSING THE STREAM
from their side—the side of the hill and the caves—over to the
more gradual strand where the pilgrims were gathered. They entered
their midst and sat with them.

The one who came to Andrew was among the oldest. His beard
was long but not so full, and he wore a turbin that, like his tunic, was
a clean white. He was slender and dark in complexion. His eyes were
black and fierce, and there was a mark upon his forehead like the
shadow of a fig.

Despite his years, he crouched down before Andrew and spoke to
him firmly and eloquently, but in an accent that Andrew recognized
as coming from the east.

"You wish to be baptized by John's hand?"

Andrew answered, "Yes."

"And you know the price of his baptism?"

Andrew hesitated.

"Of what do you repent?" the disciple asked.

Again Andrew wasn't sure he understood the word.

"To what do you confess?"

Andrew looked around him. The other disciples were speaking
to other pilgrims, to the siblings from Syria, and to the old peddler

and to Nathaniel. Their words came fast. The disciples all listened intently. Andrew thought to contrive some sin of his own, to say that he wished his brother ill or to burn the family boats, but his tongue was tied.

The elder disciple revised the question. "Why do you wish to be baptized?"

The answer came naturally. "So that I might be awakened."

"You repent of your sleep then."

Andrew nodded yes.

Beside them now the young Syrian woman was weeping, saying she did not know the father of the child she carried.

When the shadow of the tallest sycamore finally reached the rock in the middle of the stream, the disciple there gave signal up to the woman, who was still sitting before the highest of the caves. The others then stood and started leading the pilgrims down the bank, now as the waters began to sparkle in the low angle of the sun.

A moment later John emerged from the same high cave.

The valley fell still and quiet as he descended, using the stones for steps. The disciples did not bow, but their heads were low as he came near.

He entered the water directly and did not stop until he was waist deep in the middle. There he dipped his hand, and cast a spray of light around him. His lips were moving. Then he faced them all and the sun as well, as it beamed between slopes behind them, bathing him in gold and amber. He raised his right hand and called a name:

"Man-DAH-dei!"

And though his voice was hoarse, Andrew once again remarked its resonance and music.

> *"O Heavenly Father,*
> *O house of life incarnate,*
> *O great radiance and light*
> *that is mightier than all the worlds,*
> *O first and founding realm of all,*

before whom none existed,
who art Thyself the light that shines from thee,
hear our prayer that we, thy servants,
might abide with Thee.
Have mercy on us.

The disciples all bowed their heads, but Andrew kept his eye on John. He had heard the rabbis pray at Bethsaida. He had heard the preachers on the steps at Jerusalem, but by comparison to this their prayers had seemed to rise and drift, like dust cast in the wind. John's words were all like arrows in their purpose, or birds bound for their nest.

Poor are we who are apart from Thee.
Have mercy on us.
Forgive us, whose eyes look ever to Thee,
whose minds turn ever to Thee.

Look not upon our faults and our missteps.
Look not upon the thoughts and offenses that weigh us down
But upon those acts that lift us up.
Look upon our charity and on our struggle.
Look upon the purity we seek and vow to keep this day.
Give us strength who praise Thy name,
that we be constant in our prayers.
Do not turn from us who seek and serve Thee,
but have mercy on us.

Clothe us in Thy glory,
Bathe us in Thy eternal light.
Keep us free from fear and dread
and from the terror of those who would oppress us.
Deliver us from all evil and temptation,
And free us from the hunger of our mortal flesh,
as Thou art Life in life,
the living water in our cup,
and the bounty on our table;
as Thou abides within, and reigns over all.
Amen.

The first to be baptized that day was the mother with child. John gave his blessing to the child. He asked the mother's name, which was Syrah. He spoke her name aloud in asking that there be forgiveness for her, then lowered her down. The round of her belly dipped beneath the surface then rose up like an egg. He called out again before lowering her a second time, and then a third, setting his thumb on her forehead and kissing here there, to seal her.

When she emerged the final time, she stood up straight before them all, and the sunlight danced upon her. And she seemed to be glowing before them as her brothers came to help her up the banks.

Three more were baptized before Andrew: the brothers, and the old peddler. Then came Andrew's turn. He was thrilled and he was frightened. The sun was hot upon his back and shoulders. His heart was thundering in his chest, and the blood was pounding in his ears as John held out his hand to him, but the moment he took it he calmed, and eased, and slowed, for in John's touch and in John's eye he found affirmation all at once of everything that he'd been feeling during the weeks and the months leading up: that all this was shadows, and false. Yet whereas before, Andrew had felt abandoned by this, stranded and alone, here in John's eye he felt embraced. He felt this same truth as cause for celebration, not despair, for if there was shadow, then there was light, and he could see that light reflected in John's eye, and he could see that it was near.

John asked his name, and Andrew told him.

John then asked the same question as the older disciple had, but this time the answer seemed simple, as if he'd been offered a drink after a night in the desert.

"I repent of my sleep," Andrew said. "I repent of my slumber."

John stunned the water with his open palm. "Let there be forgiveness and awakening for Andrew." Then with the same hand he leaned Andrew back against his arm and lowered him beneath the surface.

Andrew's ears filled. He could hear the pebbles and the sand tumbling on the bottom of the river, and yet he did not feel he was in a river—or only a river—but something much deeper and wider than that, and more bracing. It was as if he had been thrust into a current of light, but that his eyes and ears and all his flesh were so encrusted he could not feel it fully yet. He felt like a mud-caked jar that had been buried for ages but that had been found and dug up and plunged into the water. Even now the filth which had been encasing him was beginning to dissolve and drift away, but before the light could reach his skin, he was lifted up again out into the sky.

He heard John's voice. "Let there be purity for Andrew!" he called, but all Andrew wanted was to return into that place, into that beam of light. He wanted more, and so John leaned him back down into the water again. It swept over him and swallowed him, and this time he was aware not only of the energy and of the life coursing through the water but of the place where it was coming from, like another realm surrounding this one, as John had said, like another kingdom standing at the gates, teeming to come in, peering at them through the cracks. Just as the world above—the stream and the willows and the hill—was surrounding the dark of Syrah's womb and the child inside, so there was another world surrounding this one here, and Andrew was its unborn child, but with each caress of the water, and each layer of mud that it was drawing away, and death and dead skin, he felt that he was being released into it, the world from which he had come.

But now John was lifting him up again into the open air.

"Let there be sealing unto Andrew!" John's voice called out. Andrew felt his thumb upon his forehead, swiping down and then across, and then more firmly than before he thrust Andrew back down into the water, and deeper as well, and now that all the mud and crust were gone and he was nothing but the jar, Andrew felt that he and the water, the light, the coursing beam of life, were one. And he knew that he was not alone, that he had never been alone, as the light within him was the same as shone within everyone and everything, only he had been covering his own eyes.

And now John was pulling him back up, back out into the air and the sun, and the water was like a brilliant blazing cloak of light upon him. He felt it bouncing off his chest, and he gasped and shouted aloud. He burst out laughing, and seeing him laugh, so did some on the shore. They cried out for him as he stood naked before them, covered in this shining light.

John spoke into his ear: "May your thoughts be of the Lord, Andrew. May your deeds be the fruit that you would bring Him."

Then he let him go. Andrew climbed back onto the shore. The disciple who had spoken to him before met him there and helped him up onto the strand with all the rest of the pilgrims. Nathaniel was there, raising his hand to him and smiling, but for now Andrew sat alone.

He still felt raw, but he could feel the sun's warmth healing him. He closed his eyes again to see if he could hear the pebbles or the current from below. Not quite. He heard the surface of the water and the birds, the trees, and the other pilgrims as they descended, and the Baptist calling out their names, one by one introducing them to the light and to the life that shone within it.

When he opened his eyes again, the sun was nearing the bottom of the valley slopes. Andrew watched the remaining pilgrims take John's hand and enter the water: a widow, a farmer, a merchant from the city. He watched them each emerge like fawns, laughing, weeping, gingerly climbing up onto the strand again. He called out his praise to them, and he could feel the joy of the others surrounding him, sitting up and down the bank like washed jars set out beneath the sun.

⇥39⇤

The Disciples

MOST OF THOSE WHO HAD BEEN BAPTIZED BY JOHN LEFT Bethabara soon after. They were welcome to stay, to sit and pray with him and his disciples, to hear more of his lessons, and many did, but usually by the second or third day they would begin making their way back, whichever way they had come. They would return to their homes avowed to live lives more pure, more devoted to the Lord, and bound to share what they had learned with their neighbors and their kin, many of whom would come down to the Jordan as well, to see the prophet and determine for themselves whether the things they'd heard were really true.

Andrew expected he would do the same. He yearned to tell his brother and his mother and the other fishermen what he had seen and felt. He wanted them to see and feel it too, to make them understand that nothing should come between them and the light that he had seen, but he feared they would not listen to him.

The third day after their baptism he and Nathaniel, the other fisherman from Galilee, started back together. More pilgrims had begun to appear, presumably in hopes of being baptized the coming Sabbath. Andrew did not want to burden the settlement, so he and Nathaniel had walked along the bank of the smaller stream, but even there Andrew felt as if a rope had been tied to his waist and was pulling him back.

When they reached the ford of the greater Jordan, they stopped. The water passed, smooth and silent, right to left. Beyond, and over the top of the drinking willows, he could see the distant hills of Judaea; to the north, the gradual rise to the softer, greener slopes of Galilee and the Beautiful Sea, where at this hour his brother would be returning with his boats.

Andrew could not bring himself to cross. He feared that if he returned, then so would old thoughts and old ways. The veil would descend again. All the emptiness and the loneliness would close back in.

He sat and waited for his fears to pass. Nathaniel waited with him. They watched the water flow by, as if its gentle current might carry his doubts away into the sea and choke them. All day and then into night they waited, but when the dawn arrived again, Andrew felt the same.

Out to the west a small band of new pilgrims appeared, led by more disciples. Andrew watched them cross the river, the same as he had just a few days before, not knowing why, only that they felt drawn. He and Nathaniel helped them ashore, two elderly brothers, one with a palsied arm and leg. Andrew pointed the way to them. They started off, arm in arm.

Andrew turned and told Nathaniel he should go. "Tell my family they are in my thoughts," he said, "but that my place is here now."

Then he went and joined the brothers headed back to Bethabara.

He sought no one out at first. He sat on the near bank and watched. He watched the black mouth of the cave where John prayed, the one the woman guarded. He watched the pilgrims as they came. John baptized only on the seventh day, so the pilgrims grew in number day to day. They appeared along the banks of the smaller stream, but they came from the north as well, and the east, and the south. Andrew watched them confess. He watched them weep. He saw how they looked at John and how they listened to his prayers and to his lessons. He watched them be reborn in the water, how some emerged dazed and dreamy. Some embraced. Some cried out. Some danced.

Most of all he watched the disciples. He studied how they went about their days, how and when they rose for their morning prayer. He prayed when they prayed. He ate when they ate, and as they ate: no meat, no wine. Only bread, and locust leaves, carob, and manna, which they gathered from the tamarisk leaves. He fasted when they fasted. He listened closely to their prayers, and his voice joined in, though he often did not understand the words. Three times a day he bathed, just as they did.

He did not impose himself, but he did speak to them, and in time he learned their stories of how they had come to follow John.

There were nearly thirty of them—that is, who dwelt in the caves on the other side of the water and who joined with John in the evening prayer. Most knew him from the desert, from Harran and Mount Carmel, and Zoan. Most had been holy men before finding John, though not all. Samuel was a shepherd. Kanufar, the Nabataean, had been a warrior in Aretas's army, then by his own admission a thief along the trade routes. That was how he first came by his horses.

Several had been Essenes. Perida, with his long, gaunt face and sleepy eyes, was the eldest of these. He said he had known John from his youth and that he had taught John to read Hebrew. Others called themselves Mazbutians; some Darawish (Shurbel and Nidba); three were priests from the Temple in Jerusalem (Benyamin, Ismael, and Neri, "the swift"). The woman was Annhar, a maiden from the temple down in Zoan.

There were a number of Nazoreans, some of whom came from the very same tribe that had raised John, the Subba. The eldest of these, eldest of all the disciples and the one who had first heard Andrew's confession, was Kharsand. But there was also Azharan, well named after an ancient fire temple, as he was clearly fiercest in his loyalty to John (or Yahya, as the Subba called him). Azharan said he and Yahya were brothers from their childhood, though he did not look like John. He was lower to the ground, broader in stance and more bowed. His face was set in a constant grimace, but he spoke often of how he had loved John and followed him, as even then the children of the village had known that John was blessed. He said John had had not one but *two* guardian spirits growing up, Par'am the Perfect and the Uthra Anush, neither of whom could be seen by anyone but Yahya.

They all had their tales to tell about him. The Darawish told of the visions that came to them when John was living with them in Harran, how all the Uthra had appeared through the windows of their clay prayer room, and all because John was not frightened in their presence.

Kanufar, the Nabataean, said that he had first come upon John at one of his wells in the desert. He said he had been prepared to make an example of John, as one could easily picture. Kanufar was by far the most physically imposing of the disciples, bronze skinned and standing a head taller than the rest, with a crimson turban that he also wrapped around his neck. He said that he had raised his sword and was ready to bring it down upon the lowly hermit, but that John blunted his blade with a single word.

Annhar had first encountered John down in Zoan, where she was a temple maiden and therefore pure like him. She left the temple after him and wandered the wilderness for one year until seven ravens found her and told her of the man at Cherith who had refused their offerings. They led her to Mount Parwan, where she found him again, sitting among the lambs.

The disciples from Jerusalem told of John's birth, how he was born beneath a star of prophecy to an elderly couple from the Temple and how Herod's men had hunted for him in the wilderness before he was taken in by the Subba.

The Subba also believed that John was born beneath the star. "A seed of celestial fruit" they called him; none spoke of him more movingly. Kharsand would crouch upon the plateau above his cave and point at the sky. "A blessed one is Yahya, whom eternal Life has given ear and granted him its treasures to see. As life has lent him ear, so shall he lend his ear to us. As life has let him see the truth, so shall he let us see."

Andrew believed this. He believed the priests and the Subba and all of the disciples, for though each of their stories began very differently, they all ended the same. All found their way to Bethabara, where there was no dispute. Here they recognized the heights which John had attained. When they looked upon him, they knew the Truth was near at hand, and they understood their place was with him, to serve him and follow him and serve all those who came to him.

Early one morning after Andrew had been there a month, Neri, the former priest, came out to him and asked if he wished to join them in their evening prayer.

Andrew did not hesitate. He followed Neri back across the stepping-stones and up onto the small plateau where they all were sitting. John was there. Andrew entered the circle. John welcomed him by name. His eyes were bright and playful.

"A poor man is Andrew."

"A poor man am I," Andrew replied.

> *Be thou free, poor man.*
> *Do not lament that you stand alone.*
> *For thy sake was this firmament spread out.*
> *For thy sake have the stars been hung.*
> *For thy sake have the clouds been brought to gather and rain.*
> *For thy sake are the seas filled.*

> *Look upon thy right hand, and behold the glory of God;*
> *Look upon thy left, and behold His countless lamps.*
> *For thy sake do they shine, poor man.*
> *For thy sake is the dawn come.*

As Andrew listened, he perceived that John's words were being heard above. As ever, he perceived that he and all of them were being watched, that the stars above were pinholes in a great black veil, behind which an entire realm of light was yearning. And Andrew knew from that moment when John spoke his name among the rest of the disciples, his former life had ended.

⹀40⹀

The Pharisees

THOUGH JOHN HAD BEEN PREACHING FOR SOME TIME THROUGH-
out the region, it was his appearance at the Temple at Passover
that first stirred the imagination of the Jews and their leaders. Out in
the markets, in their homes, and in their hearts many were now asking, Who was John? Was he just another madman-preacher come in
from the hills? Was he a sorcerer? A prophet? Might he even be the
One, the anointed one of whom the prophets and the teachers spoke,
who would come and lead the children of Abraham to their salvation?
John himself had proclaimed the day was here at hand, only in ways
that they had never heard.

"He says that it shall be like a feast day, a banquet for which the
worlds and the aeons are waiting."

"He says the children of this world are like fatted rams standing
in the markets for sale, but that the sins of those who follow him will
be forgiven."

Even among the Pharisees, there were some now asking themselves
these same questions, for though John had publicly castigated them,
they too lived in expectation of a Chosen One, and many believed the
time was ripe. They had gleaned it from the stars; they had read it in
their books. Enoch had said the angel Azazel would be bound beneath

the rock for seventy generations before the day of judgment. And that
had been seventy generations ago, by certain counts.

So they met in their homes and synagogues to collect their thoughts
about the Baptizer. They traded many of the same stories as were told
in the markets, saying he was a nazir, or no, a Nazorean, that he had
studied down in Egypt or taught on Mount Carmel. Some contended
that he was plainly mad, a rabid dog, they said, while others murmured no. They had heard from those who had gone to Bethabara,
and they said John was the One.

"But has he not denied this himself?" asked Joshua ben Sekar, who
had been a student of Matthias.

His own students conceded he had.

"Then you are not listening," said the rabbi. "Put away your books,
and look at what is before you. How does he appear? Where does he
set himself? Did he not denounce the marriage of the king?"

He did. Plainly.

"Then ask yourself who else did the same. Who never died but
went to that very place where John has gone and ascended into the
heavens to walk with God?"

They did not need their books for that. Elijah had; Elijah, whose
return had been foretold by Malachi, as harbinger of the great and
terrible day.

So they went to Bethabara, Joshua ben Sekar and his most faithful
students. They made the journey from Jerusalem, not to challenge
John or lay traps, but in hope. They crossed the river where the other
pilgrims did. They took the boats, so as not to soak their robes or talliths, but they followed the rest alongside the banks of the wadi to the
gentle slope where the crowds were gathered.

John was speaking to the throng about the very day they feared
and hoped for. The pilgrims had been asking him when exactly it
would come.

"But why do you ask this question other than to tarry?" John
replied.

When Azrael came for the keeper of the inn, he did not offer warning.
The angel entered in his door, though it was locked. He crouched upon the

innkeeper's chest, though he was asleep. He called down to his soul, "Come
out. Do not make me wait. The hour is at hand."

The innkeeper awoke, trembling when he saw. "But I am not
ready," he said. "I did not know. Give me two days, that I might settle
my accounts."

Azrael laughed. "What child has returned into his mother's womb
that the angel of death should grant you two more days? Why do the
widows and their children weep if the gravestones of their fathers can
be so easily set aside? I will not grant you two more days, or two more
moments to settle your accounts when you had your life to do so." And
he drank the innkeeper's soul from him and spit it out upon the blazing
coals of Gehenna.

Hearing him speak, seeing his appearance and his hold upon the
people, Joshua ben Sekar and his students had no doubt this was Elijah, and they made themselves known. The other pilgrims cleared the
way as they came forward, for as yet no one so learned had come to
Bethabara, and the people wanted to see how their leaders and teachers would treat John.

The Pharisees humbled themselves before him. They knelt and
bowed their heads, and many of the pilgrims could not help smiling at
the sight of such fine robes dragging the mud, while John in his pelt
stood tall before them.

The Pharisees even laid gifts of oil and balm down at his bare
feet.

When John saw this, his brow darkened. "What are these?"

"Offerings," said the rabbi. "Emblems of our welcome and
respect."

John grew more disturbed. His nostrils flared as if a rotting,
half-devoured carcass had been laid before him.

Then his voice rang out. "Brood of vipers!" but with such a sudden
force, the students flinched. He glared at them. "Who warned you to
flee the wrath to come?"

The rabbi was stunned. "But, Rabboni, we have come in hope, to
celebrate our baptism by your hand."

"And by what account should you be baptized?"

"As we are faithful sons of Abraham," said the rabbi, "children of the covenant."

"And so the heavens hold a place for you?" John looked down at them, one to the next. "Do not console yourself, saying, 'We have Abraham as our Father.' Do you not think the Lord can raise up children of Abraham from these very stones? Only they must bring gifts befitting of repentance."

He turned to the others now. "And you who ask, 'When?' and 'What shall we do?' I say take heed that even as you stand and listen, the ax blade hovers at the foot of the tree. And the wielder shall judge the yield, not the root. For the tree whose fruits are withered, or whose limbs are found to be bare, that tree will be hewn. It will be chopped into kindling and thrown into the unquenchable fire. But the tree whose limbs are full, whose fruit is ripe and pure, that tree shall be saved. That tree shall know life everlasting and behold the glory of the Lord."

John said no more that day, but he did not accept the gifts the Pharisees had brought, nor did he baptize them.

⋛41⋚

The Flock

THIS INCIDENT ALSO WAS WIDELY SPOKEN OF: HOW THE BAPTIST had turned away the Pharisees. John and many of the disciples left the camp at Bethabara not long after, to travel through the region so others could hear his voice. They went to many of the same places John had gone before—to Damascus and Sebaste, Philadelphia and Pella. They went to farms and villages as well, but now the people knew better who John was. They knew not only of his crude pelt and his call to repent but also that he was the one who had sent the Pharisees away. The most pious of the Jews John had refused, even after they had come to him and supplicated themselves.

He had said it did not matter the gifts one made at the Temple or to the prophets. John required no offerings, no firstlings or coins. He had said it did not matter one's command of the Law, or the house to which one belonged, or even the tribe. John said all that mattered was the purity of one's heart, which could be attained by repentance alone, borne out by deeds of kindness, righteousness, and charity.

"See that your arms are empty from all that you have given," he said. "For he whose arms are empty from all he has given shall ascend, while he whose arms are full with the riches of this world shall be dragged down."

The noble and the wealthy did not hear him then. But to those who had little, those without voice or purse, John offered hope. He asked nothing that they could not give, and in return he promised them a kingdom where the high and mighty would be laid low and where the neediest and most humble would be uplifted and exalted. And he said that this kingdom was here at hand. He said the earth was pregnant with heaven, and they believed him. They had only to look at him to feel how close. They could see it reflected in his eyes. They heard it in his voice when he spoke. He made them understand.

When they asked him how they should prepare themselves, John's answers were simple. Let the sinner name his sin and then abandon it. Let the proud abandon pride. Let the thief abandon thievery. When the publicans asked what they should do, he said, "Take no more than has been assigned you." When the soldiers asked what they should do, he told them, "Be content with your wage. Do not accuse. Do not threaten or extort." He did not condemn them. "Treat others as you would be treated," he said. "If you have two coats and your neighbor has none, give him one. So be it with the bounty of your table."

The people understood this. What the sacred books had kept shuttered away behind letters and laws, John opened. What the Temple kept hidden behind walls and veils, John revealed. "Come to the river," he said, and others said the same on his behalf. They stood before the synagogues and called, "Away!"

> *Away from the Temple!*
> *The Temple is a tomb.*
> *Away from the palace.*
> *The palace is a brothel.*
> *Look not to the rabbi or the priest.*
> *The priest is a thief,*
> *The rabbi, a babbler.*
> *And Herod is a slave, the servant of his loins.*
>
> *But go out to desert and you will find him.*
> *Go to where the fish all swim to greet him.*
> *Go to where the sheep flock down to hear his voice!*

From their pastures they have come.
Go to where the birds fly down at the sound of his call!

And so they did, from all around the region. The scribe and the fisherman alike set down their books and their nets. They came with open hearts to hear John speak, and to pray with him, not just at Bethabara but up at Aenon too, near Salim, and farther north at Yarmuk by the Beautiful Sea. The merchants left their tables full. New brides threw away their jewels, just as the wanton came and cast aside their shame, to confess their sins, to surrender themselves and be cleansed and released from their miseries.

And they came not only from Judaea, but from Samaria as well and from Syria and Assyria. Gentiles came from from Gadara; pagans came all the way from Idumaea; Philistines from Phoenicia. They came from Nabataea, some not understanding a word John spoke, but just to hear his voice, to see his countenance in prayer and the light in the eyes of those he baptized.

And when they returned to their homes, they praised him as well.

⋚42⋚

The Voice

OW HOW ALL THIS UNFOLDED, AND HOW JOHN'S FOLLOWING grew as quickly as it did, was as much a mystery to the disciples as to the flocks and droves now going to see him.

The younger disciples, and those who came from Judaea, were thrilled. The more pilgrims Andrew saw coming through the willows, or over the eastern ridge, the more convinced he was that the hand of the Lord must be at play, in carrying John's word on the winds, in stirring the hearts of so many different people from so many different walks. When he heard them confess, how eagerly they surrendered themselves, he felt more than ever that he was right to have stayed.

Among the older disciples, however, or those who had known John the longest, there was more misgiving. They were not as surprised that the people came. No one else was speaking with John's voice. But having known him since his days out in the desert, having heard him pray when there was no one else to hear, they were troubled that a man should go from a life of such solitude and devotion to this, surrounded by so many people he did not know, clamoring to see him and hear him, all coming to him with their own reasons and stories and expectations.

These disciples—the former Subba, the Nazoreans, and the Darawish—did not go as often into the cities with the others. They saw how John's anger seemed to flare the farther he was from the river and how those passions calmed again when he returned, so they preferred to stay at Bethabara, or at Aenon when he was there, and let those who chose to come and see come and see. And this was not because they lacked faith in John or the truths he spoke, but because they lacked faith in those who were listening, as was only common sense.

"The more people hear," said Kharsand, "the more people misunderstand."

"What do they misunderstand?" asked Perida, the former Essene. "Tell us."

Shurbel, an elder among the Darawish, answered, "When we first came to Yahya, it was to be his pupil. It was because we recognized the heights he had attained, and we had hoped that he would lead us to those heights by teaching us."

"And now?"

"And now he does not teach the people. There are too many. He can only warn them and cleanse them."

"And is it wrong, you think, that he should be so confined?"

"I do not know," said Shurbel. "I wait to know."

Nidba, Shurbel's brother, said, "When we first came to follow Yahya and he spoke of the kingdom that was here at hand, we understood that this kingdom was surrounding us but that we could not see it. This is why we followed him and prayed with him, so that our eyes might be opened."

"And now?"

"And now we find the kingdom is not waiting to be revealed but is waiting to reveal itself, like the dawn, and that this was why Yahya has come, to proclaim the new day and prepare the people."

"And do you think that this is wrong?" asked Perida. "Do you think we have misunderstood?"

"I do not know," said Nidba. "I wait to know. But we should not be surprised when people hear what they expect to hear."

The disciples looked to John for guidance, and he showed no doubt or hesitation. He continued to speak in a voice that was loud and clear. He drew strength from those who came to hear him and from their joy as they emerged anew from the water. He continued to go about his own worship the same as he had always done. He prayed at dawn; he prayed at midday; he prayed again at night. He purified three times a day. He fasted on the Sabbath.

He asked the same of all the disciples, that they should continue their prayer and their purification and that they should also see to the needs of those who had come from far away: to hear them, to see that they were fed and sheltered. But he was never troubled that there might be too many.

"If we cannot baptize them all this day, we shall baptize them the next."

Or he would say, "So long as the river continues, so should we."

Also, he withdrew from time to time, taking several of the disciples out into the desert so they could pray together. No one ever questioned this. All understood that whatever powers or enlightenment John possessed, he came by through prayer.

And so they, the ones he chose, would go pray with him and stay with him as far as they were able, but then John would always go an extra length. He would ascend to heights where they could not follow, where only the purest of hearts could go. He saw aeons and archons that only the purest of souls could see. The disciples went with him as tethers and as bonds, for however far John traveled in spirit, he always returned to them, and together they would return to Bethabara, where they always found more pilgrims waiting than there had been before.

Neri observed, "It is as if by removing himself, he only increases the people's hunger for him."

"So it is well he goes," replied Kanufar, the Nabataean, "to gather strength."

"But he does not go to gather strength," said Azharan. "He goes to find stillness." He said John had been taught this stillness by his guardian, Par'am, whose stillness was such that the Uthra was able to enter him and reveal himself to John when he was still a boy.

"It is this stillness that lets Yahya stand before the people and tell them what they should hear," said Azharan, "and bless them as they should be blessed. Tell them, Kharsand, is this not so?"

The eldest disciple answered simply, "We should not inquire into Yahya's innermost prayer."

All the disciples agreed, however, that among the increasing numbers now gathering on the far bank, more and more were coming with a tainted purpose. The Zealots had made an appearance, in hopes of drafting new members. Kanufar had had to drive them away on horseback. Oglers were coming as well, to see if John was as wild and rabid as they had heard. And the worshipers were just as much a distraction, wanting to see a prophet in person, maybe even the One, the Chosen One, as many still believed John was.

"Moths" Azharan called them. "They feed upon the garment, but when the closet door opens, off they'll fly to nearest lamp." He shooed them away with fallen branches. He had no compunction. "Better the flock be pure than large," he said. "Noah had a single boat."

The Sadducees had also turned their ear, though predictably, they had been last to do so. Given all the privileges this life afforded them—as foremost governors in the land, and judges and priests— the Sadducees did not hearken unto prophets or to prophecy, or look to other realms for restitution. John—or the "Dipper," as they had taken to calling him—they at first dismissed as being just one more in an endless line of rabble-rousers and fearmongers. Early on, when they were told that he had left the settlement at Bethabara, most assumed that they had heard the last of him and that his followers would scatter like dust, as had happened countless times before.

However, they did hear of it when he returned, and they were aware that his influence seemed to be growing, and changing. Before, it had merely been the commoners invoking his name: hermits, Essenes, and peddlers with their empty baskets. Now John's followers included

some of the more prominent agitators as well. The Zealots, led by
Galgula, were standing on their usual corners, admonishing the people as they always did, warning them about the unwashable taint of
empire and how the nation was rotting from its head like a fish; calling
the priests thieves, the royals whores and Jezebels, only now the rants
all ended: "So saith the prophet. So says John the Baptist!"

The priests and their counselors conferred, debating whether it
was fair to hold against a man the words that others put in his mouth.
Some said no, how can a man account for what others will do or say?
Others disagreed, asking what better way was there to judge a leader
than by what he let be said on his behalf. And what he let be done.
"And if he avows their actions, good, let this be known. And if he dis-
avows, then likewise good, let him say so."

And so they sent their envoys, Levites all, down to Bethabara to
examine him, and their questions were not so different from those of
the scribes and Pharisees who had come before, only their purpose
was clearly to entrap.

They asked him directly, "Are you the Messiah?"

John said no.

They asked him, "Are you Elijah?"

John said no again.

They asked if he was the prophet foretold by Moses.

John said, "I am not."

"Then tell us who you are," they begged. "So we may go and tell
those who sent us."

John said, "Tell them I am the voice in the wilderness."

But even here John's answer divided his disciples. The Subba and
the Darawish were gratified at first that John had given the men from
Jerusalem so little. "He has sent them back empty-handed," said
Nidba.

But the Judaeans said no. Both Ismael and Perida observed that
John was still speaking in the language of their prophets. They said
Isaiah had spoken of this same "voice" as harbinger of the day the
savior would come.

"John has served warning," Perida said. "And that is what the
priests will hear."

Not long after this, several of the disciples began to talk of heading north again or maybe east. Bethabara could no longer accommodate the numbers coming, or the temper. If John left, more people could hear him; he would not be so easily preyed upon by doubters and entrappers. Also, the settlement at Bethabara could itself be cleansed, in absence of the crowds.

Kharsand agreed with much of this, but waited. "If we should go, he will tell us."

Annhar also expressed wariness. The "last" disciple—or the "twenty-ninth," as she was sometimes called—she rarely spoke or was spoken to. There were many disciples who did not know the sound of her voice, but as she was the one who sat outside John's cave when he retired at night and again when he emerged in the morning, she was believed by many to be the disciple in whom John confided his innermost thoughts. This is why the former priests Ismael and Neri had sought her out.

"But he is already weary," she said.

"And that is why we would go," Ismael explained. "To revive him. We have been at Bethabara awhile now, longer than we were before."

"And if the journey tires him," said Neri, "then he can go into the wilderness and pray and take solace in the presence of the aeons and the archons that he alone can see."

"And do you believe he still takes solace in such things?" Annhar asked.

They did, and the following day, when John said the time had come to leave again, they were reassured.

Most of the disciples went with John this time, including Annhar. He led them north, a three-day journey back to Aenon, which John favored because the water there was abundant. It gushed and pooled amid all the rocks, and there were springs as well, just to the south.

But they had been there only a matter of days when John asked the Darawish to come with him farther into the wilderness. Together he, Shurbel, Benyamin, and Yaquif walked another three days and nights, all the way to Mount Carmel. There, above the Valley of

Kishon, they sat beside a spring together, beneath an overhang of limestone, and prayed.

As always, the disciples remained with John as far as they were able, in expectation that he would go farther, to heights where they could not follow.

This time, however, just as they were finding their own place, they heard a voice. Benyamin turned his ear. He did not even recognize that it was John at first. It did not sound like him. The voice was gathering neither strength nor stillness. It was beseeching.

> *Teach me, O Heavenly Father,*
> *thou who is first and last*
> *and from whom nothing is hidden,*
> *tell me. Stand I alone?*

"Is this Yahya?" Benyamin asked.

Yaquif affirmed.

"Then we should not intrude."

"Unless he has brought us for this purpose," said Yaquif, "so that we might attest to what he hears."

John himself had fallen silent now, as if to listen for his answer. The disciples did the same, but they heard nothing, until John's voice rang out again, this time calling out to his first teachers.

> *You who taught me, you who raised me up,*
> *you who walked with me and showed me what is hidden,*
> *tell me now, Was I mistaken? Is there no one who will follow*
> *me, who will speak the truths which I have spoken, and take my*
> *voice from me?*

Again, Benyamin and Yaquif listened as their master waited for an answer, but the hills and heavens remained silent. The disciples' hearts were filled with sorrow to hear John's anguish, to think they could have been so deaf to his utmost prayer.

"We should go to him," said Yaquif.

But then the prayer resumed. They heard his voice again, even more yearning than before, though this time they were not sure to whom he was speaking.

> *You, in whom life's treasures were first shown to me,*
> *show me now.*
> *Is this a dream I have been keeping?*
> *Tell me now: Have I no kin?*

> *You, who once did ransom me from the heights,*
> *ransom me again. Bring thy jewels,*
> *bring thy pearls and coins, and ransom me again,*
> *that the others might look on him and forget me.*

Now they knew, it was to his mother he was praying—to Elizabeth, who had carried him. But hearing how he called to her, the two disciples could not bear that he should suffer so or that they should hear his suffering without his knowing. They could not bear that his question should hang in the air without answer.

But then it begun to rain, and the rain roused them from the heights, as they could smell it in the air and hear it on the rock. They opened their eyes to the spring and to the valley, and they saw John was still beside them, sitting beneath the overhang, and Shurbel was there as well, never having left.

Yaquif looked to John, to see if he had yet descended. He wanted to confess what he and Benyamin had heard, and to tell him they would pray with him.

"Rabboni . . ."

John did not answer at first.

"Then leave him," said Benyamin. "So he can listen."

But then Shurbel, the third disciple, spoke. "Yahya is here," he said.

And so he was. He eyes were open, and he was looking down at the water before them. But even in the half-light and the rain they could see there was no sorrow in him. His face was alight. In his eye there was no cloud.

They wondered, Had they misheard? Had they been deceived?

They turned, as the rain was coming harder now, gathering on the stone above them and spilling down more heavily into the spring, so that it was as if a drawer of jewels and pearls and coins were being emptied into the water.

And as they looked at the surface dancing before them, all sparks and shards, they were amazed, for they could see now how the light was making shapes, and the shapes were making words, as clear as if a scribe had written them there.

"Do not weep," the water said. All three Darawish agreed.

> *Do not weep,*
> *or let your splendor fade.*
> *For you, I have sent my image into the world.*
> *For you, I am come.*

≡43≡

The "One"

Azharan was among those who had not gone north to Aenon. He remained at Bethabara to cleanse the space and see to the pilgrims who came there.

Still, he could sense the difference when the others returned. He could see that John himself had been revived. He happily met Azharan's eye. The grace and the lift had returned to his arms and hands. His voice during the prayer that first night was clear and strong, and the others said he had used it mightily at Aenon. They said the pilgrims had come from all over to hear, though they had told no one he was there.

"He was aglow," they said. "And the people were drawn to him."

The following day Azharan went out early with Neri and Andrew to the tamarisk trees to gather manna. He asked if something more had happened while they were away.

Their answer did not surprise him.

"He spoke of Him again," said Neri. He did not need to say whom. More and more the younger disciples and the ones who came from Judaea were looking for signs of the one they now believed was coming after John.

"What did Yahya say?" asked Azha.

Neri told the story. He said some students had come from Bethel, and they had been trying to provoke John. "They were saying, 'If you are not the prophet, if you are not the Messiah, then by what authority do you baptize others?'"

"And how did Yahya answer?"

"He said they should not be so concerned with him or with his baptism, as it was only a cleansing by water, but that there was One coming after him who would baptize them in fire."

Azha said, "But he has said this before, as he was taught: All was wrought from water and fire."

"Yes, but never in this way," said Neri. "He said, 'He stands among you'—"

"And so he does," said Azharan. "The Heavenly Father stands among them as he stands within them, but they do not see."

"No, but John meant that he was here, out there," said Andrew, pointing west.

At this Azharan bristled. "Yahya *meant*? And tell me how a fisherman has come to be so certain what a rabboni means?"

"As he has said it clearly," answered Andrew. "He said that he is out there now, one greater than he. He said that he was not worthy to carry this one's sandals."

Azharan scoffed.

"You were not there, Azha," said Neri. "Those were his words."

Azharan looked at them both. He could sense the stubbornness of their belief and their yearning, and he could feel the fire flaring inside him. "Very well, then you should go look for him. If there is one greater, then go. Find him. Leave us here with less the burden."

He turned and made his way back alone, but not long after, he found Kharsand again.

"They are intent," he said.

Kharsand acknowledged as much. "Remember, he is to us our brother and our teacher. He is to them their prophet."

Later Andrew sought out Azharan at the fuller's stone, as it disturbed him to see a fellow disciple so upset, and Azharan was not one to hide his feelings.

"Azha, why are you angry?" he asked. "Why do you not rejoice at the things John says? None of us thinks we know better. We follow John because we believe he speaks the truth. But if you doubt the things he says, then how is he your teacher?"

"I do not doubt the things he says," said Azharan. "I doubt the things you hear and how they become twisted in your ears."

"But they are not only my ears," said Andrew. "Others have heard the same. Perida has said that John has spoken to him plainly of the One who came before him—"

"—and who will come after," said Azaharan, "who is first and last, who is the Heavenly Father. But of course Perida does not hear this. Perida believes that Yahya is speaking of another because Perida has long believed that there would come two Messiahs. It says so in his books, and he believes Yahya is the first. He has said this.

"But this is what I fear: that you go to him and you hear what you will. The farmer comes and hears him speak of a thresher and a winnower. Samuel hears him speak of a great shepherd. You hear him speak of the fisherman, and you believe this fisherman is out there. You believe that he wears sandals and that he will save you and redeem you. But Yahya did not say this, and I will tell you why I know this.

"Because there is *no redeemer*!" Azharan was shouting now, so that his voice could be heard throughout the valley. "There is no redeemer! There are fathers and there are sons. There are enlightened men, and we can follow them. We can separate ourselves and see the truth survive, or we can flounder in the darkness. But there is no one out there who will come and see to your salvation. And whoever waits for such a one, whoever looks to the horizon so that he might be saved, he will *never* be saved!"

John had heard. Awhile later he found Kharsand and sat with him.
    "The others are disturbed."
    Kharsand answered, "They are disturbed if you are disturbed."
    John said, "I am not."

"Then is it true?" asked the oldest of his disciples. "Are we now waiting for another?"

John answered, "I cannot attest the truth of what I say. I have said it. I only know that when I say it, it is what my soul wills."

Hearing this, Kharsand knelt before him. "And we will follow you, Yahya. Only do not cause us to stumble. Do not lead us astray."

≡44≡

A Fly

THERE WAS NO WAY OF KNOWING EXACTLY WHEN ANTIPAS FIRST heard John's name. The Jordan was the lifeline that connected his two provinces, Galilee and Peraea. It was entirely possible he'd been told in passing about another cult leader who was using the river to purify himself and others, but Antipas could hardly be expected to keep straight who was who, whether John was the one who wore only grass or camel skin, ate locusts or locust leaves.

He had more pressing concerns. Archelaus's reign in Judaea, though happily a thing of the past, had left the whole region a tinderbox. There were still many scores that had yet to be settled, and the presence of new Roman overlords did little to brighten the people's mood. Antipas was constantly looking over his shoulder for fear that he was about to be ousted, either from below or from above. Ever since the incident at Sepphoris, when he had expelled Agrippa from his territories for having publicly impugned his "seed," Antipas feared he had fallen out of favor in Rome, where Agrippa was very popular (though recent reports were indicating otherwise, that the emperor Tiberias had apparently just *jailed* Agrippa for relishing the prospect of his death too openly). Also, Antipas's brother, Herod Philip, was making him nervous, building up his army for reasons no one quite understood.

But his greatest fear by far remained King Aretas, whose vow to avenge his daughter's reputation still loomed. Antipas simply couldn't figure out: Had Aretas taken his revenge already, in cursing Herodias's womb, or was there was more to come? An ambush? A military strike? He kept a constant eye on the border. He brought in an endless stream of seers and diviners to try to determine what the future held, but they all disagreed, which only made him more nervous.

"My father had your father," he liked to lament. "I, alas, have you."

Manean did not take offense. It was true he was not his father. But absent any gift for divination, Manean did what he could by more pedestrian means to set his friend's mind at ease, assigning agents and spies to go find out what they could about his various concerns. Manean would then digest these reports and pass them on in private conference.

It was on one such occasion that the subject of John was first broached between them, though not, as it turned out, by Manean. They had met in the royal box of the hippodrome, where Antipas had recently taken to spending his mornings. Some months before, at Sepphoris, Antipas had bought Salome a stableful of Arabian horses. There weren't many open spaces in Tiberias, however, so the hippodrome was set aside for an hour each day for the princess to ride and her stepfather to watch.

"And they're just going to keep him there, in jail?" Antipas was speaking of Agrippa and his curious incarceration back in Rome.

"Only for a time," said Manean. "Word is, he's drafting an apology."

Antipas cocked his head, not sure quite what to make of this. "And what about Gadara?"

Manean allowed the Nabataean troops were apparently still close by. They'd been gathered along the border for several months now. "But I don't think there's cause for concern. It's all a posture."

Salome rode past at that moment, as if to say, "Now, *this* is posture," with her hair flowing behind her while she stood tall in her stirrups, but so perfectly still a chalice would not have fallen from her head, or lost a drop.

Antipas watched her round the track. His eye did not stray. "And what do you know about this man, the Dipper?"

"The Dipper?"

"The man at the Jordan. John."

"The Baptizer, you mean?" Manean was vaguely aware there was a Nazarite attracting crowds along the banks of the Jordan. "What of him?"

"You tell me. There was something in Tyro's last letter I didn't understand." Tyro was one of Antipas's men in Jerusalem, a member of Pilate's council, who periodically sent back detailed accounts of their meetings.

"He said that the Dipper, the Baptizer—whatever you call him— that his name came up at the council, and how much sway he had among the people now, but that Pilate had said there was nothing he could do since the man was not in his jurisdiction."

Manean waited. "And?"

"And he is in *my* jurisdiction, is he not?"

Manean thought. He supposed he was.

"So I just don't understand," said Antipas. "Are they asking me to swat their flies for them?"

"Did Pilate send you a letter?"

"No. Just Tyro."

"Then I don't think you've much to worry about. It sounds to me as if Pilate is doing what Pilate does."

Stay out, he meant. Pilate was the latest of the Roman procurators sent to oversee Judaea. Just after taking his post, he had tried hanging banners of Caesar throughout the Holy City, in clear violation of the Jewish law against graven images. A contingent of protesters had marched straight to Caesarea and camped out in Pilate's courtyard. When he threatened to have them all beheaded, they exposed their necks. "Take us then," they said. The banners were removed the following day, and Pilate made a mental note not to come between the Jews and their faith again.

"But even so," said Antipas, "why would it come up? Isn't he supposed to be an ascetic?"

He was referring to John again. Manean nodded; this was his

impression as well. In fact on a recent trip to Philadelphia, he had seen some of John's followers washing themselves in the river, wearing white. He agreed with Antipas. To him they'd seemed more glazed than angry.

Just then a shadow descended.

"So is it true?"

Herodias was standing behind them, having come to pick up Salome. "Is my brother actually in prison?"

Manean stood, squinting, and was reminded in that glance that the queen had taken to painting her face rather thickly of late. "So far as we know," he said. "It sounds like an overreaction."

"It's ridiculous," she sniffed.

Antipas pointedly did not second the sentiment or rise, noting which the queen started down the steps to her daughter, who also had seen her and was slowing her horse to a trot.

Antipas asked after her, "Have you heard of John the Baptist?"

He had made it sound like an afterthought, but the queen stopped and turned. "You mean the one who all the birdies and the fish like to sing to."

"Yes. What do you know about him?"

"Why, he's the one who calls you the goat and me the Jezebel, is he not?"

Antipas offered no reaction, so she let this be her exit and continued down the steps.

Antipas turned his eye. "Is that true?"

Manean shrugged. The insult frankly struck him as being far too popular to lay at the feet of any one man. "I can look into it."

Antipas slumped, finding one last glimmer of consolation in Salome's dismount down below. Manean watched as well, how absently, yet gracefully her hand remained on the horse's lathered neck. It occurred to him that the days of these rides should probably be numbered. She was hardly a girl anymore.

"Lovely," he said.

Antipas sighed in agreement, looking at the two of them now, the queen and her daughter. "But see how it is happening moment to moment. Everything that's leaving Herodias is entering Salome."

Manean went to Simon-Matthew, an Essene living in Tiberias, and also a former priest. Simon-Matthew confirmed Manean's impression: John was a hermit recently emerged from his cave, an itinerant preacher whose message had found an audience.

"What does he preach?"

"*Teshuvah*," said Simon-Matthew. Repentance.

"How?"

"Turn from sin, obey the law, live more righteously toward one another."

"And what is the meaning of the baptism?"

"A sign," he said. "A ritual token of the cleansing that has presumably taken place within." Simon-Matthew made it all sound very simple, but he did not diminish the movement.

"He has great sway. I would not make an enemy of him, but I do not take him to be an agitator."

This all accorded with Manean's understanding, and he was intending to deliver Antipas the very same message the next morning at the hippodrome.

He was apparently too late.

"They say he is a prophet!" Antipas offered up, proudly almost. Salome had yet to make her appearance, but he was already quite excited.

"To whom have you been speaking?"

"To Faisool," he said, the eunuch. "He says they say the Word of God is upon him."

Manean shrugged. "They said Simon was Messiah."

"Some say that John is Messiah. They say he is invulnerable: that if you pierce his flesh, it doesn't bleed; that flame won't touch him. If you try to drown him—"

"I understand."

"And they say he heals. Did you not hear all this?"

"I have heard he is a man of great wisdom."

"They say he sees the future too!"

With that, in particular, and seeing the round of his old friend's eyes, Manean understood he would soon be traveling to Bethabara.

Part Four

THE MESSIAH

≋45≋

The Nazarene

NOTHER CAME TO BETHABARA, NOT TO ENTRAP, NOT TO OGLE or to bow down, or even to confess, but, as he himself said, to learn.

Andrew had not even been aware of his presence until he heard some of the other disciples speak of him. The Nazarene they called him, and at first Andrew had thought they meant another Nazorean had come, but when he looked to the far shore, he could find no one was wearing the tunic typical of the sect.

Only later did he realize the disciples had been referring to the young rabboni from Nazareth, and only when they pointed at him. He sat a good length from the riverbank, so that he was behind most of the other pilgrims. He was of a middling stature, more fair than John, a man of reverend countenance, to be sure, but one who brought little attention on himself. His tunic was simple, of earthen tone. He bowed his head when John came out to pray and teach, and he observed quietly as the disciples crossed the wadi and heard the pilgrims' confessions, though he himself had offered none. Neri said he had spoken to him, to ask if he wished to confess.

"And did he?" asked Perida.

No, Neri shook his head.

"Did he come alone?"

"He came with his mother and his brother," said Neri, "but they are gone."

"And where does he stay?"

Neri pointed to the northern ridge, and the others nodded. There were known to be more caves there.

The sixth day it rained through the night. The morning of the Sabbath the clouds were still slung low and heavy, but as the sun ascended, pockets of blue were punching through. The air was redolent of the scent of willow and the acanthus, and for a time a rainbow appeared, extending over the valley like a bridge. It drew the disciples out from their caves, those who weren't already down among the pilgrims.

John stepped out as well to meet the colors and fragrance of the day and the play of beams and light shafts shifting through the clouds. Across the way the Nazarene was sitting in his usual place. John gave welcome to all. He descended to the water and led them in his morning prayer, the same as he spoke every Sabbath morning.

When he was finished, all the new pilgrims stood and started down toward the water to be baptized, the Nazarene among them.

Several of the disciples, including Andrew, took note, as they had been making sure that those who'd been waiting longest came first. The Nazarene had been there awhile, it was true, but as yet he had offered no confession to any of the disciples or expressed any repentance, the only given price of John's baptism.

John knew this as well, and yet he did not move to stop him. In fact, even as the other disciples looked to John to see if they should intercede, he was opening his hand to the Nazarene and asking others to make way. He took him first.

Andrew looked at the Nazarene more closely now. Again, there was nothing remarkable in his outward appearance. His hair was parted in the middle, the hue of an unripe hazelnut. It fell straight down to his ears, then flowed to his shoulders. His brow was smooth. His face showed no blemish or furrow, and there was blush in his cheek, half hidden by a beard the same color as his hair and slightly forked just beneath the chin.

But then, as he passed, Andrew met his eyes, which were a light gray, glancing and clear, and which, with the sunlight glinting up from the water, seemed almost to be lit from within. More, they conveyed to the young disciple an expression the like of which he had never seen before, borne from a place beyond all joy and sorrow.

The Nazarene stepped into the water now, reaching out his hand to John and speaking to him as kin. *D'ahde*, he said, which means "cousin."

They exchanged words; Andrew could not hear them. Then John baptized the Nazarene as he had so many others before, only with a difference. He raised his hand and he spoke the name of Life upon him, and he called out his blessing, but this time in the tongue that he reserved for his most private prayer, the one that only the Subba and the Darawish could understand. Yet never had the power of John's words been so clear, for as his voice rang out, the distant clouds did seem to part in answer and to let the sun peer through and see.

As John lowered the Nazarene down into the water, the reflected colors seemed to shatter, to multiply and to deepen. Andrew was aware of how the fragrances of the valley, all the locust and acanthus flower, seemed to release themselves anew.

John lowered him once, and then again. He pressed his thumb against the Nazarene's head and kissed him there. Then a third time he lowered him down. The waters gathered around him and swirled, luminescent, and when the Nazarene arose the final time, the sun, still peering through its keyhole, seemed to hold him in its grasp. He stood before them all like a beam of pure light, but none along the shore moved to shield their eyes. Some exclaimed. Even the birds let out with song, and Andrew saw one, a dove, fly over with its wings outspread, curling above John and Jesus like a messenger from heaven.

Azharan saw this as well. He saw how the light clung to the Nazarene. He smelled the flower and saw how the colors of the water seemed to fragment all around him. But when the dove flew past, he also saw the shadow that it cast, and how it cut between the two men like a dagger.

John baptized all the others who had come that day, and there were many, but even as he purified and blessed each one, some of the disciples were already speaking of what had taken place before. They asked among one another what words had passed between John and the Nazarene.

Yaquif had been the nearest. He claimed John had deferred. "He said, 'You have come here, yet should you not baptize me?'"

"And what did the Nazarene say?" asked the others.

"He said, 'Let this be for now.' He said, 'Baptize me in the name you speak, and all will be put right.'"

When the hour had passed and the rite had ended, the Nazarene crossed over to the eastern side of the wadi. John welcomed him by his name. He called him Yeshu Messiah, and he took him up into his cave, where they were alone.

Andrew was standing with Kharsand. He remarked what John had said.

"Does this mean that he is the One?"

Kharsand shook his head. "It means the Nazarene has attained the highest understanding of the mind."

Andrew was not ashamed. He asked him what this was.

Kharsand said, "That all is One, and he is One withal, and all is light and life incarnate."

Andrew thought: Then John had seen as he had seen. "And what of the words John spoke before he baptized him? Did you understand him?"

Kharsand nodded, he had.

"What did he say?"

John had said many things. Kharsand chose the last: "'Receive thy son.'"

Higher up the hillside, John sat with Jesus alone. No one else entered past Annhar, who kept her place at the entrance.

John asked him why he had come to Bethabara.

The Nazarene replied, "To prove myself a student of Yahya." He said, "If I prove myself a student of Yahya-Yuhana, his name will forever be written in my book; if I do not prove myself, then my name will be blotted from his."

John replied, "But what has a Messiah to learn from me?"

The Nazarene replied, "I have learned much from you already. From Yahya have I learned how the blind man can become the scribe; from Yahya have I learned how the stutterer can become a preacher; from Yahya-Yuhana have I learned how the widow can have back her innocence, and how the foul water can be made pure. From Yahya have I learned an abandoned house can rise again."

Hearing this, John bowed down before him. "Blessed art thou, Yeshu Messiah. Blessed are those who follow thee. Blessed are the pure at heart, that they might receive thee."

When the Nazarene left, John took Annhar within, and together they prayed.

The following morning when the settlement awoke, the Nazarene was not there. The disciples searched, but unable to find him, they asked where he had gone.

John told them, "He is in the wilderness."

⋛46⋚

The Embassy from Tiberias

MANEAN WOULD HAVE MUCH PREFERRED TO GO TO BETH-abara alone and more discreetly. Given the nature of the tetrarch's interest, he felt he could have been of more use to him that way, observing.

It was for that reason he had presented the idea as an afterthought. He let the frontier at Gadara be the ostensible cause of the mission. He had said he wanted to go down to check on the troop positions along the border there, but that on the way he would be happy to go see John. Antipas agreed. Manean left the second week of Heshvan.

Manean had intended to bring Simon-Matthew with him, the Essene with whom he had first spoken about John. Simon-Matthew had volunteered, and Manean was grateful for the company.

He was very disappointed, however, when the day of his departure he learned they were to be joined by another emissary, a young Herodian named Jacob ben Dama. Manean knew him by face (of course) and by reputation. Jacob ben Dama was one of the more ambitious young Sadducees in Jerusalem. He was a procurator for the Temple, a shameless aspirant to the Sanhedrin, and would likely have been a priest as well—he was a son of the house of Ithamar—if not for a disfigurement he had suffered from birth, a cleft palate that not only twisted and encaved the middle of his face but undermined what was an otherwise eloquent and discerning mind.

What Manean found most disturbing about him, however—at least in this instance—was that he did not know why, or at whose suggestion, he had been added to the embassy.

It was a three-day journey, the better part of which he, Jacob, and Simon-Matthew spent together in the shade of the royal litter, the largest carriage of which required six slaves to carry and another seven guards as escort—hardly the quiet presence that Manean had been hoping for.

They spoke of John. Simon-Matthew, who had been a priest before becoming an Essene, told them the story of Old Father and his wife—of the visions and the star, of Old Father's prophecy, of the massacre, and the mother's flight.

"Pah," said Jacob, whose disfigurement rendered a certain sameness to all his facial expressions, a kind of bemused disgust such that it sometimes made his true feelings difficult to read. Not in this instance.

For his part, Manean had no reason to doubt John's parentage—as he said to Simon-Matthew, John would hardly be the first son to throw stones at his father's house—but he was dubious about the final part, having to do Herod's terror and the massacre of the infant sons.

"Why would I not have heard of such a thing?"

Simon-Matthew shrugged. "Herod's final days are rife with tales of horror. Some are true. Some are no doubt false. The latter taints the former, and all becomes legend."

"Well," said Manean, "I would only ask you to refrain from sharing such legends with His Majesty, as they are liable to prey upon his nervous imagination."

"And who is to say he shouldn't be nervous?" Jacob put in. "It hardly matters whether the stories are true or not. What matters is how they prey, as you say. Ask me if John is a prophet, I will say I do not know. I will say I do not care. But I care that he wears the prophet's robes. I care he plants himself where prophets do and riles the people with prophet talk."

"He has denied he is Elijah," said Simon-Matthew.

"Which only goes to show his cunning. They speak of him as if he were harmless, as if he were a sleeping dog. I put it to you: If a man came forward and said to the plowman, 'You need not till; we can live on sand,' would the plowman not take heed—especially if all his neighbors then started eating sand? Of course he would.

"Then tell me where is the difference here. If a man should rise to prominence saying the sacrifice of lambs is no longer required—'we need only dunk our heads'—what should the herdsman and the merchant do? This man says the same. He calls the people to the river, and they go to him to receive the atonement they would otherwise receive at the Temple."

Simon-Matthew smiled. "I am not aware the Temple is being abandoned."

"So said the pharaoh of his granary. The man's aim is clear, whatever his answers may be."

The conversation fell off there, but once again Manean was made to wonder at whose behest exactly their guest had come.

They stopped in Jericho, but only briefly. They had made good time, and there was a chance they might reach the settlement before the day was out. The way from there was well beaten by now. Stones pointed the way, as well as peddler stands and tents. More than one, on seeing young Jacob's face, offered up prayers of support, that he might be healed by the Baptizer's hand.

Manean thought it best to leave the litter in Gilgal and walk. The heat of the day had passed, and he was still hoping their presence could remain inconspicuous. Three guards came with them. They crossed by boat and followed the trail a half mile from there before coming upon the smaller encampments of pilgrims, sitting in circles and gathered around fires.

Even without the slaves or litter, however, someone must have sighted them, because when they finally came out into the clear again and to the bank where the greater numbers were gathered, two of the followers were already coming out to meet them. The first was a very tall and imposing figure. Manean wondered for a moment if it might be John, except that he did not wear the famous camel skin. He wore a dark crimson headdress that wrapped around his neck. His skin was a deep bronze, and his accent placed him as a Nabataean.

The other was a Jew, a former Essene to judge by his tunic, by the greeting he gave Simon-Matthew, and also by a characteristic evenness to all his movement. Manean's father had possessed it as well, a deliberate poise that in his brighter moods, Manean had always taken to be the natural result of the uncluttered life; in his darker moods, a grating affectation.

This one, Perida, recognized Manean as the ranking member of the embassy. "And what is your business?" he asked, knowing they had not come to be baptized.

"We wish to speak to John."

Jacob ben Dama seconded more forcefully. "We have come from Tiberias."

The Arab told them to stay, then crossed to the small hillock on the far side of the stream.

While they waited, another pair of followers came with water, to wash the hands and feet of each member of the embassy. It seemed less an offering than a demand, and here again Manean regretted not having come alone. He would never have sought an audience with John—at least not until after he had observed awhile. But here he sat, having his feet washed by the man's followers, and he took the point. He was a contaminant—he and Jacob and Simon-Matthew alike— and as he looked around, he didn't disagree. The pilgrims were strewn about the bank in various groupings, some still looking over at them, some eating quietly. There was a mother nursing underneath a small tent and farther down, a young man drawing something in the sand with his finger.

They appeared to have come from all over. He recognized headdresses from Syria, Idumaea, even a few more from Nabataea, goatherds down the way, and yet he could feel the sameness of their purpose. When Simon-Matthew had used the word "repent," Manean had thought of people renouncing their misdeeds, disburdening themselves of their deepest, darkest sins, and there was that, to be sure, but sitting here among the pilgrims, Manean was struck far more by a sense of surrender, of yieldedness, that these people were seeking to be purged not merely of their misdeeds but of the world from which they'd come, so that they might give themselves over to this: the clear and limpid water; the silence of the desert, which was not silence at all. The current played an undulating chord beneath the hush of the trees, the murmur of the pilgrims, and the occasional call of a swallow. And the air possessed the same hypnotic quality, in the way it seemed to sift the light and to hold it. There was to everything about this place a sense of suspension or readiness, only Manean couldn't quite tell: Was this the stillness of repose, or of the tiger poised to strike?

Now all were turning. John had appeared. He was coming across the water now, and here again Manean found himself strangely unsurprised; confirmed in every expectation, and yet entirely unprepared for its effect upon him.

He had been told about the garb, of course, and he had seen many men like this before—hermits—but he was struck by just how strange this one seemed, truly as if he had emerged from the wilderness, like Eve from Adam's rib. And he could feel himself succumbing to this quality of otherworldiness and the authority it conferred. As John came near, Manean felt more as if he were about to meet a military leader than a holy man.

When he finally reached their party, Manean was even surprised at his size, how of-scale it was, as if he had expected more. John was nonetheless taller than most, though not nearly as tall as the Nabataean. His camel skin could not have been more crude, a pelt, curled at certain edges, fraying at others, fastened by a leather strap, but here again, even beneath the most primitive of garments, there stood a clearly noble posture. It was not difficult at all to imagine this man was the son of a priest, just one who had set his temple here.

Simon-Matthew saw the same. His eyes were welling as he looked up at John. The young Herodian, Jacob, was likewise moved, though to an opposite extreme. The fixed expression of disdain was flushed by anger, which made sense inasmuch as this man before them, this blemishless specimen, had so brazenly repudiated the very privilege that fate, with one cruel twist at the mouth, had forever deprived young Jacob. He clearly despised this man.

Aware of the attention they had drawn, John led the party over to a more enclosed space, bounded on one side by a great boulder and the shade of a locust tree. Still, some followers did gather around to hear. John did not stop them.

It fell to Manean to speak, though all this now seemed superfluous. Already he had seen what he had come to see. He knew what he would tell Antipas.

"Are you John," he said, absurdly, "the one they call the Baptizer?"

John nodded. "I am."

With that, Manean was at a loss, searching for words; Jacob ben Dama stepped in, ready. "You are the same, then, who preaches the destruction of the Temple."

"I do not preach the destruction of the Temple," said John, keeping his eye on Manean's, so that he would not mistake the violence of his reproach. "I bear witness to it."

Jacob ben Dama pressed. "And do you then bear witness to the corruption of the royal house?"

"Which corruption?" asked John.

The answer drew smiles, but as Jacob had said they were from Tiberias, everyone knew which corruption he was speaking of.

"If Herod has taken his brother's wife," said John, "then the law bears witness."

"The law has borne witness," Jacob parried, "and it has given its blessing."

All turned back to John, who waited only a moment before answering.

"Then let the fruit bear witness," he said. Again he met Manean's eye, to let him know that he should feel free to take this answer back.

Manean's reaction was mixed. It pleased him, oddly, to find a posture of such defiance here at the heart of the enclave, to see a man who did not yield but who, offered the chance to rescind his insult, had chosen to double it.

But Manean was troubled too, as there appeared to be a look of smug satisfaction on Jacob ben Dama's face, at having elicited just exactly the response he had been sent to provoke. He could return with this and more than satisfy the one who'd sent him; only now did it occurred to Manean who that was. He chided himself for not having seen it sooner: Herodias. She had said go. *Go ask him. Challenge him. See if he blinks.*

The Baptizer had made it clear he would not, so Manean moved to step in. He wasn't sure what he would have said, but another of the disciples appeared from behind to interject.

"The prayer." He pointed to the light. The evening rite was apparently at hand.

John agreed. He turned, and for a third time looked Manean directly in the eye, but all the violence had vanished from his countenance. "If you wish to stay, you are welcome," he said. He was being neither cordial nor ironic. He had sensed the yearning in him.

Manean demurred. Out of decency he and the others withdrew. All six made way in a line back along the little stream. They did not speak again until they had crossed back over the Jordan, but Manean had little doubt that each had come and been confirmed in his particular expectation: in his own case, that Antipas should definitely leave this man be; in Jacob ben Dama's, that he should be made an example of; and finally in the case of Simon-Matthew, that John was surely the son of Old Father, the one born beneath the star of Jacob.

⋛47⋚

The "Lamb"

FROM THE MOMENT YESHU MESSIAH HAD LEFT BETHABARA, THE
disciples were looking to John to see if he would speak of him.
No one like the Messiah had come before. No baptism had been like
his. Yet John offered no word or sign that anything had changed.

Once again the former priest Ismael went to Annhar. He found
her in the little mud hut down beside the baptismal stream. That was
where the fire was kept, and the buried dove, and it was there the disciples made the pihtha, which was their bread.

Annhar was kneeling before a clay table, and she was in her veil as
usual, which was of a dark earthen tone and which framed her hair,
which was also long and dark. Before her were the bowls—of flour
and salt, of quince, and walnuts, and pomegranate.

Ismael brought water from the stream.

"Has Yohannan spoken to you of the Messiah?"

At first she did not look up from her kneading. "You should speak
to him yourself."

"I have," said Ismael. "We have, but he will say to you what he will
not say to me, as he will say to me what he will not say to Perida, or to
Kharsand. Because he will say to each of us what we will hear."

"Then you should listen," she replied, now taking up the bowl of

255

salt. Her hands, the only flesh that she exposed aside from the face, were long and slender and of two complexions.

"And so we are," said Ismael, "and we are trying to understand. Because he has said to Neri that he would know him, the one who was to follow."

"Then Neri is not listening," she said, "as Yahya-Yuhana was told that he would *not* know him, but that he would recognize him."

"And did he?"

Finally the woman set aside the bowl and met Ismael's eye, arresting him with the color of her own, which was a light topaz, set against the deep olive of her skin. "There can be no doubt that in Yeshu Messiah, Yuhana has seen the light of the Heavenly Father, the same as appeared to him from the first within the womb of his mother, Elizabeth."

Ismael filled with hope at hearing this, so she quickly cautioned him. "But he also knows that he has seen this light before and many times—"

"Where?"

"But you should ask, 'Where not?'" Annhar said. "He has seen him in the mantle of his Uthra; he has seen him in Merikh, the morning star; he has seen him in the lily of the valley as well and in the stones of Shiloh. He has seen him in your own Temple."

Ismael, who had served in Jerusalem for many years, was surprised by this. "How?" he asked. "Where?"

"You have said already he speaks to each of us what we will hear. So listen, and maybe he will say, and maybe you will understand why he does not leap to proclaim everything that he has seen."

With that, she took up the bowl again.

Later, when Ismael conveyed this to the others, they were still confused. If he had recognized the light in Yeshu Messiah, then why would he not proclaim it? The embassy from Tiberias had come not so long before, and he had said nothing.

"Perhaps he is waiting to see if the Messiah returns," said Yaquif. "He cannot point at one who is not there."

This was true, so a number of the disciples, including Andrew, did look to the wilderness. They listened for word, and word came, but

from too many corners: rumors that the Messiah had been seen in
Jabbok; rumors he had been seen in Jerusalem at the Temple; rumors
he had never left the caves where he was staying. Again Andrew was
among those who went to look for him, but they could not find him.

Then one day, late in the day, John was sitting with several of
the disciples high upon the knoll above the caves. Ismael was there,
and Azharan, and Andrew as well, when John looked down and said,
"Behold the lamb."

There below, standing at the water's edge was Yeshu Messiah. He
did not look up. John did not rise to go to him, but Andrew was certain now. Looking at his master's face as he looked down at the Nazarene, Andrew understood: To follow John was to seek the light that
hung before his eyes. To be near him was to want to see this light as
well. But the Nazarene was the light. Down below, he had entered
the water now and was cupping it to his face, and Andrew felt his own
expression transform as he looked at him, to become like that of John,
and having become like John, he knew that he could leave him.

Even as the others stood around, he went to John and asked
directly, "Would you have me follow him?"

John said, "Yes."

Azharan, who also had heard, went to him. "And I?" he asked.

Again John said yes.

⇥48⇤

A Bee

MANEAN UNDERSTOOD THAT ANTIPAS WOULD WANT TO SEE him the moment he returned from his trip south. However, it took him a full week to get back to Tiberias, which was yet another reason he regretted not having gone to Bethabara alone. Having met with John and fulfilled the actual purpose of the mission, he had been obliged to go honor the putative one, checking on troop movement along the border at Gadara. This had given Jacob ben Dama a three-day head start on him, to return to Galilee and repeat to Antipas what John had said, plant his seeds, and provide the queen whatever fodder she was looking for.

For the more Manean thought about it—and the journey down to Gadara had given him ample time—the more convinced he was that she had been the one to send Jacob ben Dama, and that she likely resented John far more than she let on, for reasons not difficult to imagine. The woman made no secret of the pride she felt at her Jewish purity. John, whom she likely considered beneath human, had not merely called her a whore but had called her Jezebel; that was the word she'd used. And Jezebel had not merely been a harlot, remember, but a heathen too. From his cave beyond the river, standing alone in his mangy pelt, John had struck out at the thing the queen most prized about herself, and

258

certainly nothing that Jacob ben Dama was going to report to her now was likely to assuage her anger. He had motives of his own.

Manean's fear was that by the time he got back to Tiberias, Antipas's opinion of John—as being a dangerous, avowed, and openly seditious enemy of the crown—would be basically set.

And so it seemed. The same day Manean returned, they met privately in the arboretum of the palace. There was a pleasant breeze, hushing the gentle gurgle of the fountain, but Antipas looked unusually grave. He was not a man who bore well under the weight of deliberation. He barely welcomed Manean and dispensed with pretext; no mention was made of the troops.

"So what was your impression?"

"Of John?" Manean affected as casual a manner as he was able. "I don't think he's anything you should concern yourself with."

"You don't?"

"No."

Antipas pondered, but dubiously, with whistling nostrils. "Let me ask you then. Who was there? Who was listening to him?"

"Among the followers, you mean?"

"Yes, were they all Jews?"

Manean hesitated. He hadn't expected this.

"I'm not sure. Not all."

"Who else?"

"We didn't take a census, but I suppose there were some others, yes."

"Were there any Nabataeans?"

Manean paused. So this had been the young man's tack. "Yes, I think so. Why?"

"Well, do you think that's appropriate?" Antipas asked. "Do you think it is permissible, I mean, that a man, claiming to speak for God, should be openly insulting me in my own territory and before my sworn enemies? I don't see that I can let that stand."

Manean paused. He knew that he was arguing against unseen adversaries and therefore stood little chance. "Well, that's one way of looking at it, I suppose."

"What's another way?"

"Another way is the same as I've been saying, the same as I said before. Given the nature of his mission, and that all this is taking place out in the middle of nowhere, I'm just not sure what the purpose is of opposing him. If you challenge him, you exalt him, and you vindicate the anger of those who follow him."

"Then you admit they are angry?"

"Some," said Manean. "But there are always people looking for an excuse to throw a stone."

Antipas stood to think. He paced, in fact, down and back. "You see, but I don't think this *is* the same as you said before. Before, you didn't think it worth the bother. Now you are saying you don't think he is worth the risk."

Manean did not answer. Antipas was not completely wrong.

"Would you say he is a holy man?"

"I'm not sure what you mean."

"Or mad? Which?"

"He is not mad," said Manean. "He is a man standing at a river, exhorting those who come to lead more righteous lives."

"You were impressed with him then?"

"If I was impressed with him, then it was with the simplicity of his purpose."

"Is he a prophet?"

Again, Manean was caught short by the bluntness of the question, and his answer was at least a beat too slow in coming. "I am not my father. I would not presume to speak with any authority on such matters. I only say his aim is not you. Or that his aim is only you if you set yourself in front of him."

"What does that mean?"

"It means he is a bee. Leave him be."

But he could see, no figure of speech could make up for that moment of hesitation, and clearly it was that—the hesitation and not some trumped-up fear of the Nabataeans laughing at his or at his wife's expense—that seemed to matter most. If Manean could not stand up and deny the man was a prophet, then the decision was made.

≩49≨

Parwan

SOON AFTER JESUS LEFT FOR GALILEE, JOHN WITHDREW INTO THE wilderness. He went out alone this time to the place where only he had ever gone, the mountain of white stones and the meadows covered with purple and yellow flowers. He sat beside a river there, beneath the Thadi tree, where the lambs came to nurse from the low-hanging blossoms.

He had guarded his joy up to then, but here he knelt and gave thanks. In Yeshu Messiah, his word was fulfilled. In Yeshu Messiah, his relief had come. His burden had been lifted. The one who had appeared before him in the desert had now taken on the vesture of the world, and so John gave thanks to Hibil-Ziwa, and he gave thanks to his mother, Elizabeth, "that the light which, even from thy womb, you first granted me to see has shown itself again."

When he opened his eyes, the seven ravens were surrounding him. He knew why they had come.

"Should I no longer be a scorched mountain then? Should I no longer be a vineyard without grape or a dry creek bed?"

"Do not let the world end, Yahya," the ravens said. "See that you are not cut off."

"Then show me," John replied.

They led him down to the water's edge, and he saw there was a woman there, made from the clay of the bank, and when he came around in front of her, he was not surprised to find it was Annhar.

The ravens raised their wings. The evening drew its curtain, and there beneath the stars and planets, John lay with her. He rained upon her, and she was fecund.

And in the morning she bore him a son there on the riverside, a boy named Haran, and a daughter, Sarah.

John said to Annhar as she sat nursing, "Teach her. Teach Sarah so she will know life and not death, and I shall teach our son the same."

"I will teach as I am able," Annhar said. "But I have only borne their flesh, not their heart. If they listen and let themselves be taught, so they will ascend. If not, they will perish."

Sarah and Haran grew before their father, and they did listen, and they learned well. They drank the milk of the Thadi tree. They swam in the waters of the everlasting Jordan. And as the ravens had once counseled, John divided his time, attending to them and to Annhar on the first night and the second, devoting the third and fourth to prayer, then trading off again the fifth and sixth, and always keeping the Sabbath holy.

In this way he raised them. He bathed them in the river. He carried them on his shoulders. He knew the proud love of the father for the son. He knew the fierce love of the father for the daughter. He taught them as he had been taught, of how the earth was wrought. He taught them of the two kings, the one who held the sword, the one who held the book. He read to them from the book, and he introduced them to the prophets and the fathers. He taught them how they should emulate the Uthra in the heavens and separate themselves from the darkness: never to cheat and never to lie; to practice no magic; to worship no idols; and always to heed the boundary. To be simple and be pure. They ate fish and manna, honey, locust, carob, and pithha. They worked hard at their labors. They rested on the Sabbath. They treated others as they would be treated. They forgave and made amends. They did not keep. What they were given, they returned. They emptied their arms, and their hearts were full.

And they were not alone. The ravens let John see what else might be. Both Haran and Sarah grew, and they had children of their own.

From their generation, Birham was born, and R'himath-Haiye, and they also grew up in that valley by the Thadi tree, and they grew strong in body and spirit, and they were taught just like Haran and Sarah, how to be simple, how to be pure, how to pray and to be silent, and to be still, to receive the light like jars upon the bank. And from their generation came Sam, and the radiant Anhar-Ziwa, and another Sarah.

At the end of the day John sat above the rest, weary and content. The sound of the children's laughter drifted up from below, and he took heart that the simple way had been revealed to him.

But as the darkness continued to fall, the stars came out, and he could see the ravens perched upon the boughs across the water. He waited until all was silent and the children were sound asleep; then he stood and gathered them each—from Sarah to Sarah and their mother as well. He returned them all to the clay of the bank. Then he descended the mountain again.

⌇50⌇

Aenon

NOT LONG AFTER JOHN HAD LEFT BETHABARA, SOLDIERS CAME— soldiers who had been baptized there—to inform the disciples of rumors they had heard. They said that Herod had apparently ordered John's arrest.

The disciples split up at once to look for him. Some went east of the river, some west, to the mountains and caves where he was known to sleep and to pray. In case he returned, some remained at Bethabara, while the rest traveled north to Aenon to set up camp there. They agreed, if anyone should find John, he should take him to Aenon, as Aenon was in the province of Decapolis and therefore beyond the legal reach of Herod Antipas.

It was Neri who found him, at the foot of Mount Parwan, which was not far from Aenon, only seven miles to the south, in Judaea.

John asked who was there, and Neri told him.

"And where is Annhar?" asked John.

Neri told him she was still back at Bethabara, as were most of the Subba. "But we should go to Aenon first," he said, "and let the others see you there."

Azharan had been up north in Galilee during much of this time, following Jesus, but he had left in hopes of returning and telling John the things he had seen.

He did not hear of the soldiers' warning until he reached Bethabara.

"And where is John now?" he asked.

No one knew. Kharsand said John had not been seen since his last sojourn, but he did not seem concerned as yet. "If they had arrested him, they would say."

Azharan agreed. That would be the point, to let the people know.

"So tell us about Yeshu Messiah."

Azharan did so. He told them he had been with Jesus since the time he had left. He and Andrew had followed him up to Galilee, to the villages along the coast of the sea, and briefly into Judaea as well. He said there was no questioning the heights the man had attained or his powers. He healed. He spoke with great authority, and the people, many of whom had been baptized by John, gathered around him.

"Then what is your misgiving?" asked Kharsand, as he could tell all this was prelude.

Azharan admitted, "I would not follow him. His example is lacking."

"Say how."

"He is impure. He is impious. He violates the Sabbath. He neglects his prayer. He eats from an unwashed hand. He drinks, and he does more than that. If I say to you he drinks, this is the smallest portion of his offense. He makes others drunk. I saw with my own eyes the people come and fill their cups.

"You may shake your heads and smile. I know you think, 'Azha, he sees the world in starker colors,' but I tell you, if Yahya had seen what I have seen, he would be disturbed as well."

"What else?" asked Kharsand.

"I will tell you what else. This 'Messiah,' he would cut men off from their seed and women from their womb. He says, 'Follow me and sow no more. Forsake your sons and daughters. Forsake your fathers and your mother.' Now tell me when did Yayha say this?"

The others were silent.

"And yet when others question him, 'Why should we listen to you? By what authority do you stand before us?' he will say, 'John. John has recognized me.' He speaks as if they are in league."

Kharsand asked, "Is Andrew still with him?"

"Yes, Andrew is with him. He is his disciple. The Messiah healed his mother."

Kharsand weighed the things he had heard, and then agreed that Azharan should go at once to Aenon, in case John was there. Kanufar volunteered to take him on horseback, to speed the way.

They stopped only once, at Gerezim, because Azharan and John had gone there in the past. They did not find him, and here for the first time Azharan began to fear that John might have been arrested. He cursed himself for having left him, and he vowed if he did see John again, he would never leave his side.

But he was soon uplifted. From Gerezim they rode together to its twin, Mount Ebel. They were not far from Aenon now. They followed the stream there down into the great valley, the wadi Far'ah. As they descended, they caught sight of pilgrims in the distance, making their way on the far side. Behind them was another string of pilgrims, and they were also headed in the direction of the river where John had often gone to baptize.

"Like seabirds," said Kanufar.

From there they galloped.

At the springs just to the south of the river they came upon the first disciples, Benyamin and Neri, who took them back to the grotto where John was taking his rest.

When Azharan saw him, he fell down and kissed his brother's feet, and all the fears he had been keeping fled. They did not speak of the Messiah. John asked after the disciples at Bethabara. Again he asked about Annhar, and they spoke of Herod's men as well. Kanufar told the others that no more soldiers had appeared at Bethabara. They asked Azharan if he had heard anything, either up in Galilee or in Judaea. He said that he had not, but that if the rumors were true, he did not doubt their reason.

"Herod fears Yahya."

All agreed. That night Azharan and Kanufar both slept at the entrance of John's cave.

The following day was the sixth day. Some of the disciples had begun to wonder at the fact that there were so few pilgrims anywhere near.

"It is better they stay away," said Neri. "Until the threat has passed."

Still, it did not make sense. The last time John had gone to Aenon, the people had come in droves and without bidding.

That morning Azharan and Samuel went to the nearby village of Salim to ask for flour for their bread. They were speaking of this as well and of how both Azharan and Kanufar had seen caravans coming through the valley, yet they had not shown themselves.

Two lawyers from Sebaste overheard the two disciples, and recognized they were followers of John. "But are you not aware?" they said. "Come let us show you."

They led them back to the river, but farther to the east, two bends from where John and the disciples had made their camp.

Even before the water came to view, Azharan could hear the throng, and when he and Samuel crested the rise, they saw the banks below were thick with pilgrims and worshipers. They were standing in the river as well.

"Make it a lesson," the lawyers chided. "A fisherman must keep watch of who's upstream."

Azharan was confused. He started down to get a closer view, but then he stopped. There among the bathers he saw Andrew's brother, Simon, then Andrew as well and several more of Jesus' disciples. And now he wondered at his own eyes, for it appeared that Andrew was lifting one of the pilgrims out of the water, an elderly man with his arms outstretched and his mouth agape.

"The price of success," said the lawyer, taking pleasure at Azharan's dismay. "If it's any consolation, it seems most of the people believe that he *is* John." He pointed. Yeshu Messiah was up on the bank but surrounded by another circle of pilgrims.

Azharan felt the fires in him flare. He could hardly bear to watch, but he could not tear his eyes away or close his ears to the sound of the pilgrims emerging from the water and the fishermen's voices declaring how they were sealed now and blessing them. He wanted to descend, to enter into their midst and stop them.

"This is profanity!" he cried.

"Leave them be for now," said Samuel. "We should return and let the others know."

John and the rest of his disciples were still back at the grotto, but they could see Azha's state as he and Samuel appeared.

John asked, "What has stoked thy fires, brother?"

Azharan pointed back toward the bend. "Did you know that he is up the river now, the Nazarene, and the people are going to him to be baptized?"

They did not know, but John did not seem troubled.

"Today," said Azharan, "which is not the Sabbath. And it is not even to him they go, but to his disciples, to Andrew. He is standing in the river now, pretending to purify and to bless."

The others were admittedly confused by this. They looked to John, but he still would not be provoked. "The better to accommodate their number."

"Yes, but they are fishermen! In whose name do they presume to purify these people?"

"Be calm," said John. "You sound like the Pharisee." He turned and sought to calm the others as well. "Nothing comes but comes from heaven. Who opens his ears will hear. Who opens his eyes will see."

But Azharan would not be consoled, so finally John asked the others to leave. When they were alone, Azharan told him what he had seen in Galilee and in Jerusalem. He said all the same things he had said to Kharsand down in Bethabara, of how Jesus did not wash and did not fast, how he drank, and how he tricked the others into drinking.

"And I have no doubt you asked him about this."

"I did."

"And how did he reply?"

"In circles," said Azharan. "That we should not use old wineskins for new wine. And why lament when the groom has arrived?"

"But have I not said these same things?" answered John. "The feast is at hand. A wedding shall take place between heaven and earth. And if the groom is come, then let us rejoice at the sound of his voice. . . . Do not look at me heartbroken, Azha. If one must recede for another to grow, so be it. Thus is our joy fulfilled."

"But, Yahya"—Azaharan clung to him—"would you not at least come and see? See for yourself what they are doing."

But John would not. He withdrew his hand. "Azha, you are my brother. No one's fears mean more to me or cause me more to fear. But for me, you must try harder to see. You say that Andrew is still with him. Then go and look with Andrew. See what Andrew sees."

The words were not easy for Azharan to hear. They pierced his heart, yet because he loved his brother, he did as John asked. That same hour he returned to where Jesus and his disciples were, despite the vow he had made the day before at Gerezim that he would never leave John's side again.

⋛51⋚

The Spearmen

THE NEXT MORNING JOHN TOLD THE REST OF THE DISCIPLES THAT he was returning to Bethabara. For his sake, some stayed behind, to scatter the pursuit of those who might still be looking for him. Kanufar went with John.

They were seen together outside Jericho. One of the publicans, who also owned a palm grove there, said his slave had given them a bunch of dates for their journey home. The tetrarch's spearmen had a runner there as well, who, hearing this, made the dash for Machaerus, where the spearmen had stationed themselves.

John and the disciples arrived back at Bethabara in the middle of the night. The disciples went to their usual dwellings. John climbed up to the cave where Annhar was sleeping.

She awakened at his entrance.

"Am I not dreaming?" she asked.

He told her no. He sat with her and shared with her what the planets had shown him. He told her of the way that lay open, and she confessed to him that this had been her prayer as well, and that it was in this hope that she had remained.

Later, as they were out upon the plateau, and the night sky was still high and ripe above them, John said, "But if you were to awake one day and I was gone, what would you do?"

Annhar did not understand at first. "I would do as I have done," she said. "I would look for you. If I could not find you, I would wait for you to return."

"But if I had been taken where I could not return, what would you do then?"

"Why do you ask me such questions when you know how they injure me? If I awoke and you were gone where you could not return, the world would be a prison to me. I would not eat. I would not sleep until I found you again. Only tell me where and when I should go—"

"But I say to you there will be no returning," said John. "What else makes this day blessed, Annhar, but that having passed, it cannot come back? If we could always go and then return, there would be no widows in Jerusalem. There would be no orphans. I ask again, by the bed in which we lie, by the light of the coming day, if I should be taken from this world before you, what will you do?"

"And I say again, this world would end for me," replied Annhar. "I would not eat or sleep, or wash or comb, until the day that I was with you again, Yuhana."

"But this is not true," said John. "Some days might pass that you would not eat, but in time your hunger would return, and you would eat and you would drink. And it may be that you would wear your mourning dress awhile, but by and by your grief would lift. You would put aside your mourning veil, and you would wash, and you would comb, and your mind would turn to the needs of the day. And so it should."

In the distance now, it was as John had said. The light of dawn was just appearing, shell pink behind the black outline of the locust trees. Neither of them saw.

"I will never forget thee from my mind, Annhar. If I forget thee, may the Lord forget me. But if I should leave this world before you, promise me you'll build no coffin. Bury me in the ground. Make no pageant or procession, but give bread for me, say the prayer for the dead, and see that Life is always praised and honored."

Annhar said she would, and they were silent again.

At dawn, the others came out to greet the day, and John led them in the morning prayer. When they were done, Kharsand followed John down to the water. He brought him bread and honey.

"Only tell me: Why are we here now?"

John said, "For the same reason as we have always been. To see the truth survive. To teach and to sow and to see our life renewed."

The spearmen descended moments later—not from the west, as would have been expected, but from the east, over the hillock. A full thirty men had been sent, far more than were necessary. They subdued Kanufar with their number, and seized John swiftly. They bound his hands; they took him by the hair and dragged him off, while the rest of the disciples looked on helplessly. They only asked on what account he was being taken. The spearmen did not say. The disciples asked where. The spearmen told them, to Machaerus.

Part Five

PRISON

≋52≋

Machaerus

THOLMAI, COMMANDER OF THE BATTALION THAT FINALLY
arrested John, was surprised by the ease of the incident. After
all he had been told about John and his sway, he had expected more
than that—a few clenched fists and a straggling band of ascetics in
rent garments.

He had determined already that they should bring John back to
Machaerus. There had been talk of taking him north to Tiberias—
Herod Antipas was there—but word of the arrest was bound to spread
quickly. Tholmai feared if they tried moving John up through Judaea,
they'd meet hostile crowds along the way, and demonstrators.

Machaerus was closer, just five miles down the coast, and far more
secluded, guarded by the Bitter Sea on one side and the equally barren hills of western Arabia on the other. Except for the lonely band of
disciples trailing after them, they encountered no one on the road.

The local governor at Machaerus was a former publican named
Naaman, a Jew who more or less ruled in proxy. Antipas came twice a
year, if that, and only for administrative reasons. So it was into Naaman's custody that Tholmai now delivered the prisoner.

Given the isolation of the place, Naaman had not been particularly aware of John and his followers. He understood that the charge
against him was sedition, but he had also been given to understand

the personal nature of the arrest—that is, that it had been ordered by Herod himself—and so refrained from hearing the case. Until Herod could come down and render sentence, Naaman turned the prisoner directly over to the head warden of all the jails at Machaerus, a Samaritan named Jacim.

Jacim had been at Machaerus longer than any of his superiors, twenty years, a fact belied by his appearance, which still hearkened to his days as a foot soldier in the renegade brigade of the Samaritan rebel Kuhath. His face was lean and long. His hair, too, was long and all gray, but piled up plumelike on top of his head. He wore a narrow pointed beard, also gray, but his figure remained a chiseled marvel. As sleeves tended to confine his shoulders, he rarely wore a shirt or tunic, making do with a pair of billowing purple pants wrapped at the waist by a sash of black and gold.

He knew even less of John than either Naaman or Tholmai did, only that he was leader of a cult and that he was a Jew. He was aware there were members of the palace guard who had gone to hear him speak up by the Jordan, and they testified to his wisdom, but Jacim himself was unmoved, being a Samaritan and one who therefore regarded all Jews as marauding heretics.

He accorded John no special treatment. The day he arrived the jailers stripped him of his camel skin and burned it for fear of mange and mites. For much the same reason, they cut his hair and his beard, despite the objection of two guards.

"But he is a Nazarite," they said, "like Samson."

Jacim paid no heed. He found another who was willing.

"But what exactly did he do?" the barber asked, taking up a fistful of the prisoner's mane.

Jacim shrugged. This was not his business.

Another replied. "He called Herod's wife a whore."

"Oh." The shears chomped down and a thick black lock fell to the floor like rope. "And the whores want an apology?"

It wasn't until they actually put John in his cell that the jailers came to understand whom they had in custody. They brought him to the cages down beneath the armory, where they kept most of the prisoners—robbers, swindlers, and the like.

When the other inmates learned that John was among them, they grew agitated. They called out to him through the bars, seeking his blessing. Some claimed to have been baptized by him, and they warned the guards of the wrath they would suffer for keeping this man, who was a prophet. They said he would never yield to them, as he was invulnerable.

Some of the jailers took this as a challenge. They dunked him, as they had heard he was a dunker. They held him under the water; he went limp beneath their hands. They tested his flesh as well, to see if it burned like other men's. It did, but he did not wail. They sliced his arms and sides, just to show the other prisoners the blood on their blades.

The inmates were suitably provoked. They went wild, vowing the Lord's vengeance upon their keepers. They lunged and clutched so that their arms and hands had to be smashed and mangled against the bars.

And yet to the jailers' ears, the riot was not nearly as disturbing as the silence at night. When evening fell, the cages all went quiet, the same as every night. The difference was that all the prisoners were listening, keeping as still as they could in order to hear the murmur coming from the Baptist's cell. He was praying.

The jailers heard as well. They could not understand a word, but they nonetheless summoned Jacim, who agreed it would be best to move the new one. They took him to the northern hall, which had long since been abandoned. There was a row of empty cisterns there that they sometimes used for the most hardened and dangerous of criminals. None was occupied at present. They led John down into the first and closed the lid.

⫷53⫸

The Following

BEYOND THE WALLS OF MACHAERUS, NEWS OF JOHN'S ARREST spread quickly. Among the larger following, there was the predictable mix of responses—anger and fear, resignation and confusion. Many were stunned that such a thing could happen. They did not understand why the crown would choose to act against a man whose purpose was so distant from theirs. Others were surprised it had taken the authorities so long.

They prayed for his release, but deep down they feared his fate was sealed. Some were saying he was dead already, while others claimed that he had escaped, that even now he was still in Judaea. They had heard him preaching in Capernaum.

The Zealots, not surprisingly, were the most exercised. Even those who had never heard John speak were still outraged, reserving no small part of their anger for the disciples. Why had they not taken better care to protect him? Why had they not hidden him? Or put up more of a fight?

Many of these same agitators were now determined to avenge him. They plotted various responses and demonstrations. A whole contingent from Jerusalem made the journey down into Peraea. They gathered outside the fortress to protest. They pitched camp at the foot of the ramparts, chanting John's name. They scrawled the word "whore" on the stones, but their resolve, for all of its stridence, proved short-lived.

The second night after they arrived, Naaman dispatched a cavalry brigade. They descended on the tents with clubs and torches. Six protesters were killed. The rest scattered like kindling. Their flames died out in isolation.

The disciples were more resolute, though the natural schisms that existed between them were further tested. Those who had remained up north were upset with the others, the ones who had accompanied John to Bethabara. Like the Zealots, they asked how John could have been taken so easily. The disciples who had been there had no answer other than to say that John himself had neither resisted nor shown any fear, and that they should trust in him now as they had trusted him before.

"And is this what she is doing?" Samuel replied, pointing up at the black mouth of Annhar's cave. She had not emerged since the morning of the arrest.

Intermittently, pilgrims were still appearing through the trees, coming to be baptized, wanting to be purified in the waters there, not just for themselves but in protest of the arrest. The disciples would not presume to administer the rite. They taught the pilgrims to pray and to purify themselves but set their focus south on Machaerus. They traveled down in rotation to sit outside the walls, not in the manner of the Zealots. They did not chant. They did not deface the walls, or instigate, or rally. They sought only to be as near as they could to John, and to pray. Led by Kharsand and Perida, they prayed outside as they knew he would be praying within. They prayed for God's mercy—for John and for those who had taken him.

Also, every morning two disciples went to the gate to bring him water from the Jordan, which they carried there in skins. They asked again if they could be allowed to see him. They asked if either the governor or Herod had yet determined what they would do with John, and when they were told no, and no, and no again, they handed the skins over to the guards and asked if they would deliver the water to John.

Some of the guards, moved by the disciples' display, saw the skins all the way to the northern hall. Some fouled the water and passed it along. Some drank it. Some tossed it in the nearest gutter.

⋛54⋚

Audience

Back up in Tiberias, Antipas was well aware of the expectation that John's arrest had created: that he, Herod, would finally come face-to-face with the man who had been insulting him so publicly; that John the prophet would have to answer for himself; that Herod Antipas would then deliver sentence and show the people the cost of such slander and defiance.

The problem was, Antipas had yet to determine what that cost would be, and every time Manean asked, Antipas answered—with reason—that he should probably wait until he saw the Baptist and let him account for himself, then decide.

The problem there, however, was that the trip kept being put off. "The prophet shall have to wait," he was fond of saying, even bouncing slightly when he did so.

Again, his excuses were adequate. A great jubilee had been planned to celebrate his upcoming birthday. Antipas had wanted all the most influential players in the region to come, to make a show of solidarity that might give pause to any potential enemies in the area, by which of course he meant Aretas. The city would have to put on its best face for the occasion. The streets would need sweeping; the temples, spiffing. A new aqueduct was being put in, and a pier. Even now new plumbing was being installed at the palace. All of which needed his attention and oversight.

Also, and to be fair, the patience Antipas was showing—regarding John, that is—seemed to be having the desired effect of calming the waters. There had been that one incident early on with the Zealots, then nothing. The Baptist's flock had drifted back into the hills, just as that cloven-mouthed Herodian had said they would.

"Perhaps I should never go," Antipas liked to joke.

Manean agreed. "But for the matter of the sentence."

Finally, it was Chuza, Antipas's minister of finance, who prevailed upon him to make the journey south, and only then for administrative reasons. There were quarterly tax reports that needed a proper audit, as well as all the various petitions that were piling up. These things needed attention too.

Manean seconded. It was one thing to let the man cool, "but if you are seen to be neglecting duty, it might appear that you are hiding."

"Yes, yes," said Antipas, as if Manean were a nagging mother.

So a full seven weeks after John had been arrested, Antipas finally deigned to make the trip to Machareus. Notably, he asked Manean *not* to come, to stay behind and see after the various reconstructions and face-lifts. Manean didn't object. He had no desire to go see the Baptist in a cell, but he did think it odd that his old friend should choose to do without his company on this occasion, when normally this was the sort of thing for which Antipas openly confessed the need of support. Manean could only hope the show of independence was a good sign.

As a rule Antipas liked to arrive at his destinations in the morning; the night was no way to meet a place, and better for travel in any case. So for much of the final stretch, he had slept. He was sleeping when they crossed the Jordan and passed over the smaller stream that led back to Bethabara.

He did not awaken until they were already on the King's Road, that pitiless strip of baking asphalt that snaked its way between the blanched hills of Arabia on the left, and that lifeless sulfurous lake of brine on the right, the Bitter Sea. He only had to take a deep breath to remember how much he loathed this place.

Up ahead the fortress was just now coming into view, perched high atop its bone-dry mountain, a crude crown chiseled into the last ridge of hills before the landscape plunged down into the trough. At one time it had played host to forty thousand soldiers, and that was its real purpose, of course. Machaerus was a lookout, a southern outpost, there to stand as warning against the interests lurking on the far side of the hills. His father had done his best to dress it up. As if to brandish the advantage of his mixed blood, he tried turning the place into a kind of citadel, a nest in which to entertain, enjoy the breeze and the nearby baths. He'd even managed to tuck a palace snug inside, with gardens, fountains, and arboretums, swimming pools, and spires. It didn't matter. All that hidden splendor only served to render all too glaring her affliction: The palace stood within the fortress walls like a bride inside a coffin.

The final climb up the mountainside was long and steep and mildly nauseating. Antipas drew the curtain until they came upon the village surrounding the fortress. His father had built most of that as well, but thanks to the embargo that Aretas had put in place ever since the divorce, it was now a ghost town. The markets were gone. It looked as if most of the people had left as well. As Antipas's litter ascended to the ramparts, the zigzagging lane that led directly to the palace, he was so aghast by the sheer emptiness of the streets he did not see the encampment of disciples just outside the walls. They offered little to the eye. They were praying.

Protocol dictated the next several hours. Naaman came and greeted him. They ate. Antipas then rested before his first council meeting, which was held in the Hall of the Wilderness, so named on account of the view it gave, looking out over the sea and beyond, to the eastern desert of Judaea. Chuza was there, and Naaman, and most of the rest of Naaman's council, as well as several landowners from the area.

He sat through various reports regarding taxation and the local crops. Harvests had been meager. It had rained once all season apparently. (Antipas couldn't help wondering if Aretas and his magi's spells might have had something to do with that.) He heard a number of petitions, then, and lawsuits, proposals for construction and recon-struction. Naaman had given his recommendation in each instance. Antipas signed off.

The criminal matters came last, late in the afternoon. Only three required his attention: The first concerned a notorious local brigand, applying for clemency (Antipas denied); the second, a horse thief whose sentence merely required his seal; then finally John.

He did not realize it was John, however. On seeing him, he assumed it was another petty thief. Even when they read the charge against him, sedition, he commented, "He sounds a bit like the Bap-tizer, doesn't he?"

Naaman had to tell him it *was* the Baptizer.

The guards confirmed. They turned him to the light; the sun was low now. They gave a tug at the back of the prisoner's head to let Antipas see.

"Did we cut his hair?"

"We did," said Naaman.

"And what about the pelt?"

The counsel shrugged; they were not sure. "I assume it's been dis-carded," said Naaman.

Antipas did not hide his displeasure. "And has he offered any defense?"

"No," said the lawyers. "He says nothing at all."

"But he understands why he is being held?"

They assumed.

Antipas peered at the prisoner, still not quite believing this was the one.

"Do you deny the charge?"

The prisoner said nothing.

"Do you deny that you foment sedition and excite the people against the crown? Make him look at me, please."

Again the guards tugged back his head. Their eyes did meet this time, and Antipas could see: This was the one they had been speak-ing of, only different than he had expected. He had expected to meet a fiery leader of men, a snarling, growling beast. He had expected to meet with condemnation, with disgust and fury. What he found was something much closer to indifference, much more like the glint one might find in the eye of a predator stalking prey—that is, no glint. No relish or expectation. Only purpose, and as with any predator, it made no difference the mangled flesh he left behind or the blood that smeared his paws and muzzle, he himself remained blameless. Pure.

"Take him away then. When he is ready to answer for himself, we will listen."

Antipas had trouble getting to sleep that night. His bedroom, high up in the southeastern tower, was the same one that he and Phasaelis had shared. She had liked it because its balcony looked south toward her homeland. He continued to use it only because it had also been the preferred room of his father.

Yet for himself he could have done without the view. One could not see Petra, of course, but he knew it was out there, a hidden coal, seething in the distant landscape. Even after all that had happened, just the thought of its rose-hued walls still stirred something in him. When the wind picked up, he imagined he could hear it whistling through her hidden rivulets.

Worse, when there was no wind at all, the silence was oppressive, pounding upward from the silent Bitter Sea. His imagination filled the void. Were those drums in the distance? But of shepherds or soldiers? Or was it the Baptizer? Was that his heart thumping away in his deep dark cell?

The following day Antipas attended a wedding of a ranking publican and the daughter of a local priest. Antipas was guest of honor. The feast lasted well into the night. He drank too much. He knew he would not sleep. Not long before dawn, he appeared at the apartment of the Samaritan Jacim.

"Take me to him."

He had never been in the northern hall. Entering it at this hour provided very little sense of what it must have been like in its day. There were seven guards assigned to the space, one at each of three entrances and four more who looked after the cell itself. Two kept watch during the day, and two at night.

The cisterns were all on the northern end. Antipas might not even have seen them but for the guards, and the fact that the lid of the first in the row had been wedged open, presumably to let in air

There was an alcove not far away. Jacim lit the wall torch and brought a chair. Just one.

Antipas sat and waited. He was still woozy. He might have fallen asleep right there but for the sudden groan of the bronze hinge as the jailers cranked open the lid.

Moments later the Samaritan introduced the prisoner into the alcove light. He knelt him directly before the king. His hands were bound. Dutifully the Samaritan excused himself, but only as far as the shadow. He wanted to be sure the prisoner felt his presence.

Antipas did not. In fact the shadow surrounding them was so vast and black he assumed they were alone now, floating and unseen, though nothing could have been further from the truth. In addition to Jacim, the seven guards were still there, and privy to the same affect. In an otherwise draped and darkened hall, the only light at all was the golden orb now surrounding Herod and the Baptist; the only sound was of Herod Antipas's voice, soft and then loud and soft again, clearing itself as he spoke.

"So tell me, I just want to be sure. You are the Baptizer. I know you are, but are you the one they say? Are you the old priest's son, the one whose tongue was loosed . . ." He lost the thought, then found it farther on. "But how would you know? That *is* what they say, though, that you were born beneath a star. Is that so? Can you see what's to come?"

The prisoner said nothing.

"Like father, like son, eh? If you do not answer me, what can I do? I cannot do anything."

He waited. The prisoner still offered no reply.

"On the other hand, if you speak to me, I will be kind. My father was kind. To seers, I mean. See for me, and I promise you . . . I am a loyal man. A man of my word. You can ask."

He waited another moment, and suddenly the sight of the

prisoner—kneeling there, shorn and silent—filled him with disgust. His patience turned foul. "Well, then, you'll have time to think about it, won't you?"

He stood, wobbled, and caught himself against the wall. Jacim stepped in to help him and summoned the other guards with a snap.

"Tell me." Antipas leaned heavily on the Samaritan's arm, his feet dragging behind them. "Is he eating?"

Jacim nodded. "We bring food," he said; even after twenty years, he did not speak their language comfortably. "Sometimes he eats."

"Make sure he does." The king nodded lazily. "It's important that he eats."

Jacim agreed.

The other guards pulled John away now. Antipas watched him disappear into the shadow. "Find out what he likes," he said. He teetered beneath one final thought, then fell back onto Jacim's shoulder, whispering much too loudly into his ear. "And do not cut his hair again."

⋛ 55 ⋚

Nain

AZHARAN WAS STILL WITH JESUS WHEN HE LEARNED OF JOHN'S arrest. They all were back at Aenon, having sojourned briefly into Samaria. He came upon several of the Messiah's disciples in the morning, preparing to take their leave again. He asked why.

"But have you not heard?" they said.

Azharan was staggered but not surprised. He asked the disciples where they all were going, and they told him, back to Galilee. It would be safer there, they said.

Azharan knew this was a mistake. If John had been arrested, it was by Herod Antipas. Returning to Galilee, Jesus and his followers would be retreating directly into the spider's web. Azharan did not say this, however, in part because he was angered too. If Jesus had been arrested, was there any question that John would have spoken out? He would not have skulked away into safer territory. He would have raised his voice.

Azharan yearned to go and do the same, to leave Jesus behind and go back down to Machaerus. If John was there, then Kharsand would be too, and Perida, and the Darawish, and he wanted to be with them now.

He struggled over what he should do, but finally he remained up north, out of loyalty to John. John had asked him to follow the Messiah and see what Andrew saw, and Azharan still had not. He still had doubts. So he followed Jesus back up into Galilee, to Chorazin and Bethsaida, and up into Capernaum. For John's sake, he opened his heart to the Messiah, and to his own dismay, it did begin to thaw.

He saw how the people came out to him. He saw they were the same as had come to John, the poor and the needy. He saw how the Messiah affected them, how he uplifted them and healed them—some wondrously. He cast out their demons. He cured withered hands and palsied limbs. He performed many signs beyond anything that John had done.

But it was not the signs that caused Azharan to reconsider. It was the Messiah's words. John and Jesus spoke differently, to be sure. Jesus never raised his voice to the level of John. He did not speak with quite the thunder. Where John's voice would go hoarse from the force inspiring it, Jesus' was always clear and never strained. Where John's eye hovered out above the heads of those who came to hear him and burned, Jesus looked at them directly, and his eyes seemed to cool whatever they touched. They gave shade.

But even with their differences, still Azharan began to hear John in much of what Jesus said and in the way he said it. Jesus did not ever talk down to the people the way the Pharisees did, or harangue them like the Zealots. He spoke in ways that they would hear and understand. Of the coming kingdom, he said it was like a grain of mustard seed, or leaven. He compared it to a treasure hidden in a field. John had not said this, but things like this. John had compared the kingdom to a net cast into the sea. Jesus did the same.

In Capernaum, some of his followers asked him to teach them how to pray. They said, "Teach us as John taught his disciples." Without hesitation the Messiah offered them a prayer to speak, and it was very like the prayers that John had spoken at Bethabara: a prayer for the coming of the kingdom, for mercy and forgiveness, for protection from all temptations of the world.

Yet whereas before, Azharan would have bristled at the likeness and regarded it as further proof of the Nazarene's thieving, now, knowing where John was, confined in Herod's prison, he began to hear his brother speaking through the Messiah.

And Azharan was not alone in this. Others were saying the same, how Herod had tried to silence John, but he had failed, as John was still speaking to the people, only he was using the tongue of the Nazarene. The more Azharan listened, the truer it seemed: in the consolations the Messiah offered the poor and in his castigation of the nobles. Like Yahya, Yeshu Messiah reserved his harshest words for them, and the scribes and Pharisees, all those who clung to their wealth and their station. Yeshu Messiah said they had received their consolation already, just as Yahya had said before. He cursed their hypocrisy, blaming them for cutting other men off from the truth. Yahya had said the same.

So Azharan had begun to reconcile himself. He saw how the truth must reveal itself in stages, how the lessons of tomorrow are built upon the lessons of today, which are built upon the lessons of yesterday, and so it was no wonder that teacher should give way to teacher.

Andrew helped him see this. "See how readily the people hear Jesus. This is John's doing. I know because I have felt the same, Azha, that John made me ready. The same as a jar, if it is to keep its water pure, must itself be pure or it will taint what enters in, so it was John who made me pure by my confession, who made me new, so that I could receive the truth of Yeshu Messiah."

Azharan heard him. Indeed many things that had seemed a mystery to him before, or a lie, now began to clarify in his mind and in his heart as he began to see the light in the Messiah when he spoke, and that it was the light that spoke, and not the man, as the Messiah himself had clearly said.

In Jerusalem a group of Pharisees had challenged him, saying it was not legitimate for a man to testify to his own self. Jesus answered them, but this time he did not cite John as his witness. He said, "If your law requires two witnesses, then there is myself and my Father who sent me. And if you knew me, then you would know my Father, but you do not."

Clearly the Pharisees did not. They sputtered and spat, but what struck Azharan most was his own reaction to the encounter: Seeing the Pharisees' contempt, he felt contempt for them, thinking to himself that they were blind.

But then did this mean that he too had seen the Father in the Nazarene? Did this mean he saw what Andrew saw? Just the question staggered him, and divided him, for he knew in recognizing the Messiah's light, he was fulfilling his brother's wish, but at the same time he felt he was betraying John, forgetting and forsaking him. Again, he did not know if he should go back and tell the others—Kharsand and Shurbel and Perida—or whether he should stay and see what followed. He did not know what John himself would want.

But then they came to the town of Nain, on the slope of Moreh, and what Azha witnessed there caused him to depart at once and return as fast as he was able to Peraea, to find the others and warn them.

⧼56⧽

The Venue

U P IN TIBERIAS A SEWAGE PIPE HAD BURST, ONE OF THE MAIN
arteries of the system just installed at the palace in preparation
for the jubilee. The Pharisees predictably blamed it on the apostasy
of the city's placement, that it was the belated revolt of all the corpses
that had been moved to make room for the streets and bazaars. The
more ostensible culprit was Chuza, who had chosen to purchase Syrian parts and labor rather than spend the extra money on Roman
expertise. Either way, the smell had invaded an entire wing of the
palace. The place was unlivable. Herodias let this be her excuse.

In fact, she had wanted to go down to Machaerus *with* Antipas, as
she still did not trust him when it came to the Baptizer. She'd thought
it curious how long he'd taken to arrest John in the first place, and all
the dithering ever since she found completely mystifying.

"He is an insult to his name," she said to the eunuch Faisool. "Do
you think his father would have hesitated two seconds before snap-
ping that filthy man's head off? He'd have shown the people who's
invulnerable."

She'd sent the eunuch down to be her eyes and ears, but his reports
still made no sense to her.

"But what on earth is he waiting for?" she fumed.

Now, with the brown froth fouling the shoreline just outside her bed chamber, she decided she would go down and see for herself. She took Salome with her. Just three weeks after Antipas, they traced his very steps, the Jordan their companion to the left, guiding them down into the scorching valley. They crossed over to the eastern side of the river just north of Bethabara. They both were awake and did glance briefly to the east. Two men had come out to watch them pass.

They were dressed in white tunics. One was standing on a rock, the other gathering water. In her gut, Herodias knew they were connected to John somehow; the veiled righteousness of such men, the willful, deliberate misery of their condition filled her with revulsion.

Salome must have sensed something similar. A short while later, as they were nearing the fortress, she asked, "So who is John exactly?" The expression on her face made clear that she knew at least he was a distasteful thing, but Herodias was surprised she was even aware.

"A rabid dog," she said.

"No, but really. I heard them say he was magic."

Herodias scoffed. "I say again, he's a rung above the animal whose skin he wears. But don't worry. I'm sure they've hidden him safely away."

Not far enough. The moment they arrived at the palace, she could feel there was something different about the place. The truth was, she had never liked Machaerus either. She always felt like an outsider there, as if she were violating a nest every time she went, but there was a strange new solemnity in the air. The guards, the trees, even the fountains all seemed to be in mourning.

Antipas was not there to greet them. One of his stewards explained, His Majesty had been having great difficulty sleeping of late, but he had just managed to nap and was looking forward to seeing them both at dinner.

Just as well. They proceeded to their given rooms. As promised, Salome's was the cupola in the southwest tower, without question the most spectacular in the palace, at least in terms of the view. The balcony wrapped half way around and looked out upon the sea and the southern hills. Flowers had been left: lilies, camphire, onycha, and roses.

As soon as Salome was settled in, Herodias and her retinue made their way across the high courtyard to the northeast tower, where her room awaited. No flowers, needless to say. But Faisool was there.

"What has happened to this place?" she asked. "It's like a crypt."

"It's the embargo. They don't even have those olives anymore, the ones with the cinnamon."

"And we are still awaiting a sentence, I assume."

"As I wrote." Faisool set aside his lemon water with a scowl. Sulfur. "Herod will not render any verdict until the prisoner answers the charge."

"That's ridiculous. Has he even seen him?"

"Seen him?" Faisool's chin retreated to his Adam's apple. "If you cared in the least, I'd say you should be jealous."

"What are you talking about?"

"Apparently he goes and sees him late at night. That is, if the guards are to be believed, and I can't imagine why they'd lie—"

"Wait. You mean to tell me the king goes to him, the prisoner?"

Faisool nodded. "But don't worry. I think he brings that mad Samaritan as chaperone."

That evening at dinner she waited until there were just the two of them. (Salome hadn't come at all; she wasn't feeling well.) But even at their greeting, Herodias could sense his gravity, the same faux solemnity that overtook him whenever he came near the Temple. It frankly reminded her of those two miserable wretches they'd passed on the way here.

"So I understand our friend the Baptizer is a stubborn one."

Antipas offered a nod.

"But you have heard him."

Again he nodded, though he had become quite preoccupied with his squab all of a sudden.

"And?" said Herodias.

He nibbled at the bone and mumbled something inaudible.

"Say again?"

"I said, 'They threw away his coat.'" He spat some gristle. "And they cut his hair." He returned his attention to the bird, but so intently now that his eyes began to cross.

Herodias weighed the goblet in her hand and imagined the dent it might leave in his skull if she hurled it across the platter at him.

"How disappointing that must have been."

She did not vent her feelings until several hours later, up in the cupola. She had the servants bring Salome a plate.

" 'They cut his hair.' Can you imagine?" She was stalking.

Salome was taking no evident interest, either in the food or what her mother was saying. She was lying on her bed, on her stomach, beading and unbeading her necklace.

"He is petrified of him, you understand. That is why he does nothing now, because he is scared. That's why he goes to him, because nothing could be more thrilling to his frantic little mind."

She looked over at her daughter, dawdling, scissoring her ankles. What was the point? she thought. Salome was frustratingly her fathers' daughter, both of them: lovely, as Philip had made her; artless, as Antipas had. Herodias had come to think of her as an almost entirely physical being, there for the satisfaction of appetites, her own and others'. Still, someone had to try to make her see.

"These men are mongrels wearing crowns, and they know it. 'I understand the street.' The gutter is what he understands because he *is* the gutter. He swallows every ounce of crap that winds up there, and the same was true, I hate to say, of his father, but—Listen to me! Put that down. Do not string beads while I am telling you the one thing you need to remember.

"My grandmother. Your great-grandmother Mariamne. Herod worshiped her because he knew she was too good for him. She was pure, like you, and that is what the people crave, not these groveling, sniveling curs, these slaves, who would rather kiss the feet of the beast they've locked up in the—"

"Then let's go!" the girl burst out finally, utterly surprising Herodias. "If you hate him so much and hate this place, why are we here? I can't stand it. Why can't I go to Rome?"

Her father was in Rome.

"I told you," said Herodias, more quietly. "It's too far. You would never be back in time."

"Then Sepphoris or Ascalon. I hate it here. It smells. It smells worse than Tiberias."

Herodias paused, pleased. It was good to see some life in her at any rate.

"It's just the sea," she said, suddenly calm. "The wind will shift." As if to show, she stepped out on the balcony and took a deep breath. She actually did not mind the sulfur. Her physician had told her it was cleansing. She looked south. She saw nothing, heard nothing but the wind ruffling in her ears.

Still that was when the idea struck her.

She brought it up the very next day, after a morning trip out to the baths.

Antipas thought she was joking at first.

"I'm quite serious. Tiberias will never be ready in time, so where else? Sepphoris has been done. Sebaste, you'd be a guest."

Antipas sighed. He knew it was true about Tiberias, but the thought depressed him. He had so been looking forward to showing it off.

"Here, look around you. It is spectacular."

She had chosen a good moment to make her pitch. They were out on one of the seaside catwalks. The sky was strewn with fluffy white clouds, low and sliding endlessly west.

"But it's a bit out of the way, no?"

"All the more reason," she said, "to find out who your friends are. But they'll come. The baths, and the breeze. We'll bring down Temiculus, see what he thinks."

"He's not the one I'm worried about."

He was worried about Lucius Vitellius, soon to be proconsul of Syria. Clasping hands with Lucius Vitellius in public, that was the whole reason he had wanted the jubilee in the first place.

"We'll make sure," she said. "They'll all come, everyone who should, and that will say everything that needs to be said."

He looked out across the sea. Perhaps she had a point.

"But what about Salome?" he asked.

"What about her?"

"She seemed a bit gloomy this morning."

"Oh, that's just the journey. She's always that way the first day, but she likes it here."

"She does?"

"Of course. Why wouldn't she?"

It was settled then.

⋛57⋚

The Proffer

MANEAN WAS OPPOSED TO THE IDEA FROM THE MOMENT HE first heard it. He was still up in Tiberias, overseeing the reconstruction of the aqueduct and now the palace sewage pipes as well. There was no question that the site of the jubilee should be changed; whole rooms of the palace would have to be pulverized. But Machaerus? He knew very well who was behind that idea, celebrating so close to Nabataea, and with John underfoot. He had already begun drafting a letter of dissent when a second messenger arrived from Peraea, requesting that he come down at once, as escort to a rather extensive list of items that would be needed in preparation, including Salome's horses and the entire palace kitchen staff.

He left the following day, heading a caravan more than a hundred strong, though the numbers continued to grow along the way, taking on spice merchants, shepherds, and droves of laden donkeys, all headed down to Machaerus for the same simple reason that *everything* would have to come from the north—and at special cost, no doubt—on account of Aretas's embargo.

He also saw some of John's followers, not at the wadi, but down along the King's Road, bearing water, and then again outside the walls.

There were a dozen or so, sitting vigil. Among them the one he had spoken to at Bethabara, the older Essene.

As the caravan passed by, the two of them looked directly at each other. Manean detected no malice in his eye. Still, he was first to look away.

Antipas was taking lunch in the private courtyard when Manean finally found him. Naaman was there, as were several of the eunuchs. They were choosing among gifts to send along with their invitations. A dozen or so cakes of hardened sulfur were arrayed on the steps before them.

"Which do you think?" asked Antipas. He wasn't looking well—flushed and jittery, overly excited. "For Vitellius, I mean."

Manean did not pretend to be interested. "Can I ask about John?"

Antipas kept surveying the cakes. "What about him?"

"Well, is the assumption that he will still be here at the time of the jubilee?"

"That's entirely up to him," said Antipas, now taking up the two largest chunks to compare the shape and weight. "If he is content to say nothing, I am content to do nothing."

"But have you decided what you're going to do about his followers?"

"His followers?" He didn't seem to be aware.

"The encampment down at the foot of the ramparts," said Manean. "I understand they've been there for several months now. I'm assuming we don't still want them there when the guests start arriving."

Meeting blank stares, Manean turned to the eunuchs for help. They agreed: One wouldn't want that.

Antipas said, "Well, I'm sure we'll have them cleared away. But better to wait, don't you think? Why, what are you suggesting?"

What Manean was suggesting was that they strike a deal. He recommended the terms right there. Antipas did not object, other than to ask how they could be sure these men would keep their word.

Manean did not dignify this with an answer.

The following morning, he descended the ramparts in the escort of Tholmai and three spearmen.

As before, there appeared to be a dozen or so followers there, perhaps a few more than the day before. All stood up when they saw the delegation coming. Manean could sense the dread in which they now were living. Clearly they expected to be told the worst. He raised his hand to set them at ease, and the leader, or the one he took to be their leader, the Essene, stepped out.

Manean spoke to him directly. "I assume you would still like to see John."

"Where is he?"

As the others now gathered around, Manean addressed them all. "Provided you clear away from here and return to Bethabara, Herod is prepared to let three of you in to see him."

"When?" asked the Essene.

"As soon as you like, but then you must go."

"For how long?" asked another.

"You must stay away from here and keep the road clear until after the jubilee."

The followers pondered this. Finally the Essene replied, "And after the jubilee, we can see him again, a second time."

This seemed reasonable to Manean, or a reasonable way of assuring Antipas that they could be trusted, so with somewhat less reflection than he would later deem wise, he agreed.

⋚58⋚

The Visitation

IT WAS UNDERSTOOD THAT PERIDA AND KHARSAND SHOULD BE two of the three disciples to go and see John. Between them, they agreed the third should be Azharan, who ever since returning from Galilee had been insisting on seeing John, but who had moved back up to Bethabara, such was his agitation. The others could not pray with him at Machaerus.

They sent Neri back that night to summon him and to bring water.

The following morning at dawn the chosen three—the former Essene and the two Subba—were met at the palace gate by an escort of five spearmen. The three were blindfolded and led in, across a courtyard, then down a series of narrow stairwells into a catacomb of low-vaulted chambers carved deep into the foundation of the fortress. The arsenal. They did not see the quivers or the greaves, the forks and lances, the grappling irons, the serpent-crested helmets, the poison jars, the axes, the javelins, the breastplates, the pincers, whips, or scimitars.

They came to a room that had been cleared of all. Their blindfolds were removed, and they were made to wait among the empty racks. They did not speak. The next sound was of boots approaching. John was barefoot. He also was blindfolded. The guards forced him down before them.

His hair, though it had grown in, was shorter than any of them had seen since his youth. In his sackcloth, he looked more slender, and was. His ribs were clear beneath almost translucent skin; the clean line of scars showed upon his shoulders.

The hands had lost some flesh as well, but the disciples recognized the length, the contour of the knuckles and how they hovered from his upturned wrist.

All three fell down before him. They removed his blind and bathed him with the water they had brought: his hands, his arms, and then his feet. Then they prayed. Kharsand led, and it was this, the sound of the familiar words, that seemed to rouse John down from his distant place and bring him to them.

"How are the others?" he asked. As with his flesh, the voice had waned in strength, and Azharan could not help crying out.

John asked again. "How?"

They were slow to answer. In the several months since he had been taken, their number had dwindled. Some had left the settlement—to seek, to preach, to wander. Their reasons were unique.

Kharsand said, "They are worried. At Bethabara they pray for your return. They pray here at the gate."

Who? he wanted to know. So Kharsand told him. He named them.

"And Annhar?" asked John.

The question fell to Azharan, as he was last to have seen her. "She does not eat since you have left, Rabboni. She does not wash or comb. She will not until you return. When will you return?"

John looked at him, but he was still a distance away. "You have come from Yeshu Messiah?"

"I have." Azharan bowed before him. "Only know that I have tried, Yahya. I have followed. I have listened. I have watched and I have prayed that I might see what you have seen, and what Andrew sees, and I do see. But he is false."

Azharan did not shy from his brother's eye, but he had trouble finding it.

"Hear me, brother, and know that I will not lie. May the Lord forget me, may the guardians all turn their backs if there is anything untrue in what I say to you, but I was there. I was with them, and I saw."

The other two disciples had lowered their eyes, so as not to distract their master from his brother's account.

"It was at Nain. We were entering the city, the Messiah and his disciples and many of his followers as well. There was a mourning party making its way out, headed to the cemetery, and on the bier there was the body of a young man who had passed. He was dead, Yahya, and his mother was beside him, weeping, but when Yeshu Messiah saw, he went to her and to the men who were carrying the bier, and he stopped them. There in front of all the people he laid his hand on the corpse and he said, 'Arise.' And before my eyes this man did sit up. The body took life again and spoke."

John had listened without moving. Now he turned to the others.

"We were not there," said Kharsand, "but Azha's eyes are clear enough, and others have spoken of this."

"They proclaim it," said Azharan. "They boast of it, as you would hear if you would only leave this place. They were taking him to his grave!" Once again he laid his head upon his brother's knee. "Be gone from here! Say the words they ask. They do not want you here. You are better in the desert. You are better by the river where they can hear your voice and not the voice of one who would cut men off— from their seed, from their mate—and one who would violate the tomb. We have been told of this one, Yahya, and those who follow him. They drink his wine today. They will be drinking his blood before he is through."

Here Kharsand set his hand on Azharan's shoulder to silence him. "Rabboni, tell us what we should do."

John was silent awhile. From his youth he had been taught the same as Azha and as Kharsand, that the boundary between the living and the dead was never to be violated, that it sanctified the realms on either side, and that whoever trampled it was therefore a corrupter and a deceiver.

Finally he stood. He held out the blind to the jailers, for them to take him back.

"Tell Annhar I think of her," he said, "and that I hear her. See that she is fed. See that she is bathed and clothed."

Kharsand said they would, and all the three took heart that John would tender hope to her.

Then John looked at Azharan directly. "You, go back. Find Yeshu Messiah and ask him for me: Is he the One, or should we wait for another?"

Azharan took heart at this as well. He kissed John's hand and thanked him, knowing his brother would not have sent him back with this question unless he had believed him, unless he had begun to doubt the Nazarene and whether his own work was done.

⇒59⇐

Good News

WITH JUST WEEKS TO GO BEFORE THE JUBILEE, TWO BITS OF good news arrived in quick succession. Or three, depending upon who was listening.

First came word all the way from Susa that though Artabanus (king of Parthia) would be unable to attend the festivity himself, he would be sending a representative in the person of Theortes, the satrap of Media. No small thing.

The very next day, a messenger arrived from Damascus saying that the proconsul, Lucius Vitellius, was also making arrangements to attend. In other words, it looked as if Antipas would be getting just exactly the birthday gift he had been hoping for, a show of regional unity to stick in the eye of Aretas.

Of somewhat keener interest to Herodias, Vitellius's attendance tendered the possibility that he might bring his son, Aulus, who would have been around fifteen, by her calculation, and as yet unspoken for. The family was very well connected, needless to say. The tree was teeming with questors and consuls, including Lucius himself. The highway leading from the Janiculum to the sea bore their name, and there were divine roots as well, the line deriving its name from Vitellia, goddess of victory.

Herodias had only to retrieve the vial from her cabinet of aromat-
ics and then made straight for Salome's cupola.

She passed Chuza in the courtyard.

"Did you hear?"

"About Theortes, yes."

"And Vitellius. See? They come. Is he awake?"

Chuza shook his head, not yet.

It was noon, but that was nothing new. Her husband's late-night
trips to the northern hall had apparently been getting later, but she
was determined not to think about that. The idea of him groveling
at that man's feet and striking deals with his followers stoked too
much rage in her. It was pathetic, but all the more reason to attend to
Salome, her only hope.

The lamp was on up in the cupola, but that didn't necessarily mean
her daughter was in. She kept it lit all day and night—for fear of John,
she said, "the beast." Apparently, she'd taken her mother's description
literally. Herodias saw no need to correct the impression.

Halfway up the spiral stairs she passed Salome's nursemaid, Cardea.
Beneath her arm was the third bit of good news. She was carrying
Salome's bedclothes.

"Is she up then?"

Cardea nodded but lifted the hem to let her see: a coin-size crimson stain.

"Hmm." Herodias took approving note. "And not a moment too
soon."

She entered to find the cupola a mess. It looked as if Salome had
been playing, vamping. Her traveling hamper was open, and the con-
tents seemed to have been flung about: girdles, veils, and headdresses.
Along the commode were all her bracelets and armlets. The girl herself was lying on the bed, a fresh linen pulled up between her legs.

Herodias had to admit she was somewhat surprised. Of course it
explained her daughter's mood of late, and sluggishness. Her own
menses had started early too, about this age. But she and Salome were
not the same. Herodias had developed much more quickly and more
fully. Salome was still a reed.

Herodias sat beside her. A bowl of lemon water was waiting on the bedside table. She doused a cloth and put it to her daughter's forehead. She stroked her brow, a kind and gentle mother. "You'll learn ways. Is Cardea bringing agnus?"

Salome nodded, groggy. "But why do we have to stay here? Can't we go?" She slumped back down.

"Don't take it out on the place. Have you seen what Temiculus is doing? With the pools?"

No, she had not.

"It won't be much longer. You'll see." She stroked her temple gently, soothingly, hypnotically.

"Here."

She removed the vial from her little silken purse and opened it. It took a moment from the fragrance to drift.

Salome stirred. "What is it?"

"Susinum. I had your uncle send it all the way from Alexandria."

Salome sat up to see. She wiped her eyes.

"He had them make one especially for you."

Salome lifted it to her nose and smiled.

"Is he coming?" she asked.

"No." Herodias frowned. Agrippa had been released the month before, for good conduct, but all agreed he should probably lie low for a while. "No fun, I know, but I promise you, as soon as the feast has passed, we'll go, you and I. Somewhere far. We'll go to the coast." She opened her arm, and Salome nestled in, still a girl, despite the apparent bidding of Ishtar.

≋60≋

Gladly

JACIM HAD GROWN ACCUSTOMED TO THE INTERRUPTION. IT tended to come some time around midnight. He would hear the telltale shuffle of the eunuch's slippers padding along the marble outside his door. More often than not he was up before the knock.

The king would be waiting in the hall—slumped, from drinking— but still intent. The eunuch would leave off and Jacim would take him from there, telling the guards one by one to stand down as they made their way, portico by corridor by cloister, up to the northern hall. Even the two that stood by the cistern were dismissed.

Late as the hour may have been, it still sometimes happened that the prisoner would be praying when they came. Jacim would set the king's chair there beside the lid so that he could simply sit and listen.

He'd close his eyes and a smile would cross his face, as if he were hearing birdsong, or watching a spider build a web inside his mind. The language was unfamiliar. Often the king asked if Jacim had ever heard such a thing; it had such a strange, almost chattering rhythm to it.

Jacim would shake his head.

"Some of the names," the king would whisper, "but otherwise . . ." Again he would tilt his ear. "There are those who say they can hear the stars pray, calling out to one another. And that this is the language they use."

Jacim would nod, if necessary, or stay until he heard the king snore, at which point he would have the eunuch summoned to come and take him away to bed.

More often the cistern would be silent when they arrived. The prisoner would be asleep. When this was the case, Jacim and the two guards would descend with torches, awaken him, bind his hands, and lead him back up.

The king would have taken his place in the alcove. Jacim would introduce the prisoner into the space, kneel him down, and then withdraw, again not far—close enough to act if anything should occur, far enough so as not to intrude. He preferred not to hear the words, though often this was impossible—

"I am a contemplative man, you know."

—the voice was always the king's, and he was voluble—

"I agree with you. I believe in a day of reckoning."

—too loud and too soft, rushing and halting, yet always determined, like a drunk making a run for the gutter.

"Of course I do. You say the day is at hand. I feel the same. There has never been a doubt in my mind. There is an eye. Of course there is, an eye that sees all.

"Why else did I go to the priests, do you think, and seek their blessing? Because I understood there is the eye, and it looked ill upon that marriage. . . . So I went to the priests. Should I have gone to the wilderness? Do you know I didn't? In my heart I lived there, prophet. And so I know, there is much that needs repair, and much that requires mercy and forgiveness. Of course I know.

"Why else do I give? I do give, you know. At the Temple every day, an offering is made in my name, though I gather that holds no sway with you. You think the place is a den of thieves, and there again I hear you. The priests should not be profiting as they do. It is unseemly, but I have spoken to the Pharisees as well. There is one who says our sins are like a dash out into the fens. You have heard this? That if one seeks to be forgiven, he must retrace his steps. Is this what you say? If a man repent of his greed, then he must give up his jewels. If he repent of his gluttony, he must give up his bowl.

"But then tell me, tell me because I believe you are a prophet. If I steal ten ducets, must I give them back to the man I stole them from? But then what if I stole them from a publican, and gave them back to a widow? What if I gave her a hundred? Have I not done better? I do not mean to challenge you, prophet, but to make you see these things are not so simple. And I think of them.

"What good am I, after all, if I give up all I have? Then I deprive myself of the means to do good, whether I want to or not. Do you understand?

"Tell me, does it even matter what a man wants if he doesn't act? Or if a well-intended act results in something ill? Such things happen every day. What does the all-seeing eye say of that?

"Have you answers?

"Does it matter what a man desires or only what he takes?

"Very well, then tell me, Who is more pure, the man who was tempted but resists or the one who was never tempted at all? And what of the one who was tempted but stood firm, must he be cleansed? Has he proved himself corrupt or pure? Do you see? I am not challenging you. I am asking. . . .

"Tell me of your baptism—because you know they disagree when they speak of you. 'Does John's baptism come from heaven or from earth?' From earth, says Simon-Matthew, and he is wise, but I have spoken to the soldiers too, and they say you are a healer. They say that when you speak, the heavens listen. Show me then.

"Baptize me. If I let you baptize me, will you then prophecy? Will you speak then? If I say yes? Take me. Where would you take me? To the pools out in the courtyard now? But no, then you will say the water must be 'living.' So then what if I took you back to the river? Would you? Or would you keep this infernal silence? Is my soul worth less to you?

"Baptize me. If you baptize me, I will let you go. Do you not hear? I am a man of my word. I will take you up. I will set you free, prophet. I will loose you back into the wilderness.

"But you would not let me. You would not take me. So it is *your* choice, because *you* say no, because you are proud. You think it gives you power to withhold from me. But you are mistaken, because I will leave here, prophet. I will tell them, 'Take him back to his little pit. He is dead to me,' and I will not return. I promise you that. I will tell the Samaritan, 'Leave him! Forget him. I am done with him. He had his chance, but he turned up his nose, and so let that be his tomb. He chose it. I am done with him.'"

With that, or something like it, the king would rise and go. He would refuse assistance. He would demand to be alone.

But every time the path back to his room would lead him past her tower, the southwest tower, where high atop, from just beneath the cupola, the lamplight beckoned—always—a flickering temptation, coming from the one who did not refuse him.

≋61≋

The Page

FINDING THE MESSIAH AGAIN PROVED MORE DIFFICULT THAN Azharan had expected. He traveled north with Neri this time, and all throughout the region they met with stories of more healings and baptisms and exorcisms, but they were too many, it seemed, and too scattered, so many that Azharan finally came to realize that the Messiah must have divided his disciples, endowed them with his powers and sent them off in ones and twos. He had cast his net, and its reach was felt. In the streets and fields, people were speaking of how the blind had had their sight restored to them, how the lame were walking straight, the lepers had been cleansed. And they were speaking of the one the healers all proclaimed, the one who raised the dead. Not just in Nain, they said, but in Sychar he had done the same, and in Nazareth as well.

Both Neri and Azha understood that this was Yeshu Messiah. Neri was not offended. He said that this had all been foretold by the prophet Isaiah.

"That the Messiah would come and violate the tomb?" said Azha. "If your prophet says this, then his book is not ours."

It was in Dalmanutha that they finally caught up with him. The Messiah was in the public square, speaking to a crowd outside the synagogue. His aspect had changed. His voice was louder and more forceful than before, and he was more aggressive in his stance. His gestures were larger, but when he saw Azharan and Neri, he calmed and welcomed them. He knew why they had come.

"Tell me of my kin?"

Azharan was blunt. He did not let himself be cowed or taken in. He spoke aloud so that the others could hear. "I have come from him just now, from Yahya-Yuhana. He has sent me here to ask you to your face: Are you the one the people have been waiting for, or should they look for another?"

The people all fell silent, hearing this.

Jesus took no umbrage, though he understood the moment as well, how it gave pause to his own followers to hear the closest of John's disciples questioning him in public. He spoke loudly in reply. "And you may go and tell John all the things that you have witnessed. Tell him those in need are hearing the word of the Lord, and blessed is he who is not offended by me."

The Messiah held Azha with his eye an extra moment, so that he would know this last statement had been meant for him. Then he turned back to the crowd and continued speaking in an even louder voice, though again Azharan had no doubt the words were intended for his ears.

"Why did you go to the wilderness?" he cried. "Why? To see a reed bending in the wind? No. To see a king, bedecked in robes and fine silks? No, you went to see a prophet. Nay, more than a prophet, for John is he of whom it is written, 'Behold, I will send my messenger before thy face, who shall prepare thy way before thee.'"

Azharan was looking at the people and at Neri. He could see the wonder in their eyes and how the words were searing into their minds, even as the Messiah spoke.

"No man born of woman has risen higher than John the Baptist," he said, "but I say to you, even the heights that he has attained are the depths of the realm that waits.

"Before John, the kingdom was locked away and guarded by prophets and by law. But John has come, and he has seized the gates, and all men clamber to get inside! So let those who will receive the truth hear it now: that he is Elijah who was to come.

"As for the rest of you, you are like children bickering in the markets. If we pipe, you do not join and dance. If we mourn, you do not hear and weep. For John came, refusing food and drink, and you said, 'He is mad! He hath the devil!' Now comes the Son of Man, who eats and drinks, and what do you say? 'Behold a glutton and a drunkard!' But the truth will be revealed in time, as Wisdom is proved by her children—"

Looking around, Azharan feared exactly this, the spawn of this man's words, and he grieved for his brother, that he could not be there to answer them. More, he dreaded that he should have to return and tell Yahya what he had seen. He did not know that he had the strength.

⋟62⋞

The Serpent

NOW THAT ANTIPAS WAS NO LONGER PAYING JOHN HIS LATE-
night visits, there was even less to divide the time down inside
the cistern. Just the feedings, which happened once a day, at midday.

John would normally be deep in prayer until the moment just
before, when out of nowhere the air surrounding him would seem to
shift or draw its breath, the subtle lift required to take a thing down
from its hook. The terrible groan would follow, of the hinges moaning in protest while the guards hoisted the lid above. The sliver of
light at the top of the shaft would expand into a sickle, then a crescent,
then a half-moon peering down.

The sound of the boots came next: two pairs usually, tramping
down the nineteen steps and stopping at the foot to leave the day's
serving, the bread and the water. Sometimes the men offered a word
or two. Sometimes not. If they were kind, they took up the previous
day's bowl, which doubled as John's washbasin and his chamber pot;
then up they'd go, another nineteen scuffs. The bronze rasp would
sound. The light withdrew like a puddle up a straw. The moon would
wane, and with one last creaky flutter—of the pigeons resettling their
wings—John was flung back into the darkness again, and the silence.

But these were not what preyed on him. Darkness and silence he
did not mind. Darkness and silence refined the mind, as did hunger,

as did thirst. According to the guards, John ate one-third of the bread they brought him. He drank one-ninth of the water. He put his flesh to sleep. According to his disciples, his heart beat seven times an hour when he prayed. His lungs drew seven breaths, and this was where he set his mind again: on breath, and life.

And so this is how the doubts would find him. Even after the echoes had died away, and the last of the crimson blots had vanished from his lids, the air inside the cistern was still alive and stirring with the scents of sulfur, and bread, of the must and the mold that was growing in the corner and spreading across the lime and ash; the slick along the floor where the mortar had cracked. All around him he could smell the infestation of the space, and after so many weeks of being trapped inside, he could feel how it had taken root within him like a fungus, like a serpent wrapped around his heart.

He felt it lift its head—like him, roused by all the scents. He felt it unravel from the little perch inside his ribs, glide up his throat, over his tongue and out between his lips. He saw it slither across the floor and over to the bowl, to curl around inside it, to make a throne of it, and face him, smiling.

"*Woe* . . ." it said.

Woe unto the prophet who speaks words that I have not.

John bowed his head, for he knew the Lord had said the same to Moses, as warning to the prophets who presumed to speak in His name, for they would be found out. If their words did not follow, if their prophecies should fail to come to pass, then they would be revealed and they would perish.

John knew this. Only he did not know what was to become of his own words now, or of those who had listened to them, for he was haunted by his brother Azha's voice as well, and the things he had said of the Messiah.

John feared that he had been weak. He feared he had been weary, too tempted by relief. He had given over all his gifts and all the newborn children of the kingdom to the first man who would take them, the first to prove himself enlightened, but who, as Azha said, might well be a deceiver and a corrupter, a scavenger or a wolf. John did not know.

He knew only what was here before him, and all surrounding him: that everything pure would eventually spoil. Everything chaste will rot. All fruit withered. All bread grew mold. And all the paths cracked; they filled up with rubble, with branches and weeds, all while the kingdom roiled behind the veil.

He prayed for mercy and forgiveness. He prayed his life was not as it now seemed: a waste, and worse, a lie. There in the shadow of the cistern, everything that had gone before now seemed a queer and distant thing, a disjointed stream of misbegotten vows, vanity and illusion, but finally the truth had found him, here and in this place: The moon to which he'd prayed each night had been revealed, a sliver of light peering in around the lid of a prison cell; the planets were seven gambling jailers; his guardians, a pair of sickly pigeons in a pipe; the Jordan, a crack in the mortar, seeping mold; and all the sons and daughters of Abraham were nothing but one wholly unrepentant man, begging to be saved just for the asking—as Azha said, just for saying he "believed."

John prayed to all the fathers and forefathers for mercy and forgiveness if he had ever spoken falsely; he prayed for mercy from his teachers and his guides if he had forgotten or mistaken the lessons they had taught. He prayed for those who followed him, and those whom he had baptized, if he had misled them or abandoned them. He prayed to his disciples for forgiveness if he had caused them to stumble; to Azha if he had not heard him; and to Annhar if he had squandered her.

He prayed to his mother, Elizabeth, begging her forgiveness if he had forsaken the vow she made for him, if he had let himself be deceived and then deceived in turn. He prayed to her in hope that if all of this had been a lie, all these visions and memories and voices, then let it be that they were nothing but a dream and that he was still within her now.

"Carry me, and I will sit within thee lightly. Let this be the shelter of thy womb, and let it be that I see one thing only, which is the light I saw within thee from the first. If you would grant me this, Elizabeth, then I will set my gaze on it and keep it there before me, and I will dance before it and hold it fast until it has filled me and consumed me and I am nothing left."

This was his final prayer. This was his breath, and the hope on which he set his mind, to fend himself from the serpent's tongue, and the shadows crowding in around him, and the unrelenting rot.

Part Six

THE BANQUET

≋63≋

Morning

AS WITH ALL GRAND FEASTS SPONSORED BY THE ROYAL FAMILY, Herod's jubilee was to have two faces—one public, one private.

The public celebration had begun the day before. The palace gates were opened in the morning. Herod Antipas appeared out on the balcony to welcome all men of goodwill to come in and receive his gratitude for their kindness and support. Selected halls and courts were set up with fruit and bread and (diluted) wine. Entertainment was provided as well: musicians, dancers, and various other theatrical amusements.

An impressive number showed. The whole surrounding village, as well as most of the people in the region, had put a great deal of work into the feast, providing meat, fruit, and service. Now they flooded in, cramming up the public courts and gorging themselves, congratulating themselves.

As for the more private festivities, final preparations were now in earnest. All throughout the interior rooms, the telltale clamor could be heard—of slamming doors, shuddering portieres, the screech and bark of massive mahogany tables moved here, divans there; the hiss of scrubbed marble; the rattle of stacked silver; the crack and splatter of toppled urns; the blast of the conch, sounding down from the highest towers, directing the various servants to go help at the eastern gate, or the north, wherever they were needed most.

Crucial supplies were still arriving. Heaping baskets of grapes sent all the way from Eschol, sesame from Carmel, antelopes in harnesses, and storks in cages, all were being hoisted up on various pulleys and winches and shoulders. Nightingales and dormice fattened on chestnuts and acorns; baskets of bluefish; melons and pomegranates from Sorek, and whole banks of snow were finding their way from nearby mountaintops down through trapdoors or up into kitchens where more than a thousand calves and lambs had already been slaughtered and flayed, their various parts pickled and sautéed, while down below, giant vats of wine—grape wine, palm wine, wines of tamarisk from Safed and Byblos—all were being transferred to the appropriate amphorae.

The menu was to be broad-minded, and broadly conceived, suited to leave no guest unsatisfied, no matter the taboos he brought with him. The Pharisees would not eat the swine, so for them, the lamb. The people from Sichem declined to eat turtles, out of deference to the dove Azima. So perhaps a ragout of wild ass. For the Essenes, gourds in honey.

Alongside the last-minute supplies, the more esteemed guests were still arriving. Most of Herod's court had been there weeks already; most of the entertainment, days. (The various dancers and musicians had been given lodgings in the village.) The Phoenicians, the Greeks, and the Thracians had also been there a while, having come the farthest. As usual, the nearest neighbors were cutting it closest—they and the most anxiously awaited guests. All morning the best eyes in the palace had been squinting down at the King's Road, trying to determine the color of the distant flags, and whose standard was that? Was that the purple of the Libans? Or down below, whose slaves were those, down there heaving their burdens from the carriages, their beds and sundries, and all the other necessities of lengthy highborn travel? Whose harems? Whose concubines, waiting to be told where they should go? Runners dashed, cutting through the common throngs to make sure the proper courtiers were ready to receive the proper guests.

"Who?"

"Some sailors from Eziongeber."

"Eziongeber? Go tell him. Now. Make sure he knows."

Lists and contingency lists had been prepared, but as much as one planned, such things invariably had to be decided at the last minute.

"Go, go, go!"

At the heart of all this—or serving as its brain at least—was Temiculus of Antioch, the same who had arranged the celebration at Sebaste two years before, as well as the welcome feast of the last Olympiad, as well as the coronation of Tiberias; Temiculus, whose ear could distinguish every conch blast and shriek and who, despite complaints about his increasingly too small feet, reveled in a nearly preternatural ability to keep straight, to coordinate, to attend to the large and small at once. Securing the services of Temiculus had been both a necessity and a coup. It was Herodias's first birthday gift to her husband.

Temiculus would probably not have taken the job, however, had it not been for the queen's brother, Agrippa, an old friend who had been expressly *not* invited, but who, for his sister's sake, had asked him to come and do his best. Temiculus's experiences in the territories were always a disappointment. The Jews were not particularly gifted revelers. They held their liquor poorly, and they were so chaste. Not the royals, but the rest. He would just as soon have done without them, and certainly without the awful setting.

"Again," he said, waving to a band of musicians. "And don't be bashful."

The musicians played again, another sampling of the dance that would accompany the presentation of Theortes's gift. Temiculus had wanted to check the acoustic of the space.

"Still a bit loud, no?" That was his second-in-command, Pithon.

"Not once all the bodies get in. Perhaps another drape over there, though. Something in the red family. Not brown."

They were putting the finishing touches on what Temiculus had come to call the inner sanctum, the most private of spaces to which the royals and court would ultimately retreat once their public duties had been served. The larger banquet hall was much too drab and obvious. He had determined this the moment he arrived, but his inspiration had come when he stumbled on all the old pools (literally—he'd nearly broken his neck). There was a whole maze of them running through the back half of the second level, all of various depths and sizes and shapes. Thanks to chronic cracks, they'd all been drained and covered long ago; one simply couldn't keep the salt away apparently, even at this height. But as soon as he saw all that Babylonian tile, he knew he couldn't let it go to waste. He had the idea of transforming the entire maze, through liberal use of pillow, veil, and torchlight, into a kind of multilevel labyrinth of debauchery and scandal.

It was to be hoped, at any rate.

"What?"

Another assistant, Flebus, had found him. "A number of things. First, Chuza wanted to check on the cost of the melons. Is it really seventy drachmas per?"

"That is correct."

"He doesn't seem to think that's possible."

"Tell him this is the price he pays for holding banquets in Peraea. If he has a problem with that, he can take it up with Herod."

"Or Herod's wife," Pithon side-mouthed.

Flebus smiled. "And still no sign of Agrippa?"

"No," said Pithon, "but the embassy from Philadelphia apparently just arrived."

"And some sailors from Eziongeber," added Flebus.

Temiculus waved the musicians to continue. "I thought the Philadelphians said they weren't coming."

"They did. Who knows?" Pithon consulted his list. "We could move the Thracians."

"No. We've moved them once already."

"Then what about Vitellius?"

"Absolutely not."

"But they're not even here."

"No. Vitellius goes west of the terrace; Theortes, north, catty-corner. The Philadelphians can go in the southern court."

Flebus tsked. "But isn't that where Agrippa was supposed to go?"

"For the last time, he isn't coming. I'm telling you, he loathes the place."

"Of course he does, but still . . ."

Flebus's insistence was function (in part) of a standing wager the three of them had: For any feast or banquet they were asked to serve, the question was what would be the incident, the outrage that people talked about afterward? And who would be the cause? Flebus was convinced that Agrippa, the uninvited, was going to make a last-minute appearance, on account of the row that erupted the last time these parties had met at Sebaste.

"He *has* to come."

"You're thinking with your prick," said Temiculus.

Flebus granted the point. "But then who? We haven't heard your pick yet, have we?"

Temiculus sighed. "If I tell you mine, Pithon here will just repeat it and spoil the odds."

"Fine, then let's commit," said Flebus. "I say Agrippa. You?" He turned to Pithon.

Pithon thought. "I say . . . Aulus."

"Aulus?"

Vitellius's son, and not that bad a choice, given the rumors. He was said to be a little sex freak and daft, having been broken in by none other than the emperor himself.

Pithon confirmed: Yes, Aulus.

"And what about you?" The two assistants looked to their leader expectantly.

". . . you're both idiots."

≋64≋

The Sixth Hour (Noon)

WITH THE DAY AT HAND, MANEAN KNEW ENOUGH TO BE AT HIS friend's side. Antipas had been having trouble sleeping—as usual. He was complaining of dreams, awful dreams and premonitions, the significance of which seemed clear enough to his waking mind.

"Pure madness, the provocation." He was referring to the decision to hold the jubilee here at all, so close to Aretas and his restless armies. The nearer to the event they came, the more reckless it all seemed.

Manean did his best to reassure him. Even if Aretas knew of the celebration—which, granted, he probably did—he would also know who was likely to be there. Staging an attack now would be tantamount to declaring war not only on the Jews but upon Parthia, Syria, and Rome as well.

"Yes, but Vitellius isn't here yet, is he?"

No, conceded Manean. But he would be. And they would know the moment he arrived.

"Talk to me about something else. Who else is here?"

"As of this morning, Herod Philip—"

"What about the Parthians?"

"They are all settled in—"

"No, but does anyone know yet about Theortes?"

The question was whether the Theortes who had arrived this morning was actually the satrap himself or the satrap's father, Theortes the Elder. According to witnesses, the man who'd emerged from the litter looked to have been at least eighty.

"No one knows yet. He's still napping."

"Did we make sure about the hunt?"

"Yes, tomorrow. Another contingent of soldiers from your father's guard arrived as well."

"That's good of them."

"Yes. On the whole, I'd think you should be quite pleased."

Antipas sighed. It was true, and yet . . . He sighed again. "Sometimes I think it is my lot in life, having to choose whether to be content with what's at hand—'pleased,' as you say—or dreadfully disappointed."

"You don't think that's the lot of every man?"

"Well, yes, but me especially, don't you think?" The whole idea seemed to make him suddenly very tired. "I think I am going to nap."

"Never a bad idea."

Just then, however, Naaman entered.

Antipas sat up. "Is it Lucius Vitellius? Is he here?"

No. Naaman had only to look at Manean, who took his cue. "I'll go," he said. "If there is anything of concern, I'll return. Otherwise, sleep." He directed the nearest steward to send up one of the eunuchs, then followed Naaman down.

In the mere fact of Naaman's summons, Manean knew it must have something to do with their other guest, the Baptist. In the last few weeks Antipas seemed curiously to have lost interest in the subject. "Dead to me," was his phrase, and it seemed to be true.

Still, Manean had taken measures. He wasn't concerned about the disciples. They would stay clear—if only so they could see him afterward, as had been the agreement—but he knew others were out there just waiting for an excuse to come rally. He ordered that sentries be posted all along the King's Road, and he put the palace guard on alert as well, even assigning several dozen to wear plain clothes and circulate.

He had done one more thing too, a strange thing, for him. Several horses had had to be sent north a few days before, so as not to steal the thunder of the sultan of Palmyra's expected gift. Manean had specifically instructed that the horses be carted off at night, however, and in an enclosed crate, the thought being that this extra measure of secrecy might further stoke the rumors, already circulating, that the Baptist was to be reassigned before the festivities began. Somewhere far away.

The maneuver had succeeded—tactically at least. The question of the Baptist's whereabouts was a live one, but apparently of no concern to this morning's protesters. Naaman's deputy led Manean down to where they were being held, in the soldiers' hall above the arsenal.

There were only two dozen, if that, and all bound, but they roused at his entrance.

"You'll burn!" they shouted. "You'll seethe for all eternity in Sheol!"

Manean consulted the standing officer. "What did they do?"

"Turned over a stage in the public court."

"And tore down some banners," added the deputy.

With Herod now on premises, Naaman had lost his juridisction. It fell to Manean, as Herod's legal proxy, to decide. "Take them to the cages until after the feast is done." He told this to the head jailer, the Samaritan, who was also there. "We'll decide then."

As the guards led the prisoners away, Manean made the mistake of looking at one, a younger one, whose head was bleeding.

"You cannot keep him," the young man growled. "You cannot imprison the word of the Lord!"

"What even makes you think he's here?" replied Manean, contemptuously.

The answer gave pause, to the youth, to his comrades, and to several of the guards, who took it as further proof of the whispers they'd been hearing.

The strange part was that even as the words came from his own mouth, Manean was half persuaded. Maybe it was true, he thought. Maybe someone had shown that extra ounce of initiative and actually done as he'd pretended to do (and clearly wished he had).

⊰65⊱

The Seventh Hour

I F SALOME'S CUPOLA ENJOYED THE BEST SOUTHERLY VANTAGE AT
Machaerus, the balcony of Herodias's room gave clearest view of
the northern road, the King's Road, winding its way back up toward
civilization.

She and the eunuchs had been checking it all morning, though not
too nervously. Much of Vitellius's retinue had already arrived; there
was no doubt he would be following. For the queen, all suspense
rested on the question of whether the proconsul would be bringing
his son, Aulus, along.

"There." She pointed.

All peered. The lances of the posted guard were like little splinters
of light in the low sun.

"Coming out from behind the shoulder. What are those?"

"More priests, I think." There were. On mules.

"No. Beyond."

Faisool craned, and indeed it did appear to be the gold glint of the
Roman standard.

"That's them," she said, already turning to make straight for the
cupola.

———

Salome's nursemaid, Cardea, was as ever sewing by the lamp outside her mistress's bedroom.

"Is she still sleeping?" asked the queen.

"Yes, Your Majesty."

"Enough. Get her up."

She entered in. The room was dark, draped, and thick with the fragrance of unguents, perfumes, and powders wafting from all the gauzes and veils. Cinnamon was burning in a porphyry vase.

Her daughter lay on the bed.

"Salome, you must get up." Herodias swept open the curtain. "Put that on." She tossed the peplum. "They're here."

"Who?"

" 'Who?' Vitellius. Pay attention."

"I don't feel well."

"Of course you don't feel well. All you do is sleep. Now up."

She pointed Cardea to the vanity. "And those are for her hair, which I want up."

"I can dress myself."

"One hour." The queen returned to the door. "And someone should probably tell my husband."

Her husband hardly needed telling. Antipas was already on the palace steps when Herodias and Salome arrived. He had chosen a rather elaborate costume for the occasion, given the heat: a heavily embroidered mantle of black ermine, a scattering of blue powder in his hair, a diadem of sapphire and pearl. His fingers were stiff and splayed with rings.

His aides were there as well: Manean, of course; Chuza; Naaman; Tholmai; Schon. They were all standing between the two marble columns at the entrance of the palace, while the rest of the court was arranged, in descending order, along the steps, the aisle lined on each side by maidens and eunuchs carrying aromatic torches set in silver-gilt sockets.

The terrace beyond enjoyed the shade of an enormous purple

awning, hung for the event and extending all the way from the columns to the gate, beyond which two rows of sycamore provided a more shifting canopy, and also served as natural barrier (they and the soldiers) against the throng of people now cramming in to see: The Romans had finally arrived!

They could hear the boots even now and the cheering of the crowds along the ramparts below, buoyed by a day of free wine and the sight of their protectors in the flesh.

The advance guard came into view. "Hail Caesar!" the people called, as the soldiers stomped impassively by, like the weapons they bore, only showing life as they passed through the Palace gate and, line by line, removed the covers from the shields. The suddenly glancing light roused the crowd to an even louder ovation.

The various lieutenants and officers followed, then the publicans, all carrying wooden tablets beneath their arms, for show. The proconsul's lieutenant, Marcellus, came next, then finally the royal litter—three in a row, decorated with plumes and mirrors, and surrounded by lectors two rows deep, all with their ceremonial axes, symbol of the empire's power over the lives and deaths of all its citizens.

As the first litter passed through the gate, Antipas started down the palace steps, followed by his wife, his stepdaughter, then the rest.

The people were ecstatic. Not since Aulus Gabinius had such an eminence come to their town. In the meeting of Antipas and Vitellius, they might have been watching the collision of two planets.

All halted at the foot of the palace steps. First the lectors descended to one knee, then the litter-bearers gently set down the royal carriages. The crowd fell silent as Marcellus, the publican, made way to the door of the first litter and opened it. A hand appeared, and then the boot.

Herodias did not remember his being quite so large or unwieldy. Perhaps it was the journey, perhaps his attire. He wore a toga with laticlave, a broad purple sash, and high buckskin boots, but as the great Lucius Vitellius now descended from his perch, he looked slightly sluggish and off-balance, leaning on the arm of his interpreter.

This was not her first concern, however. She sneaked a peek back inside the carriage, her heart sinking. Was he alone?

Antipas too had taken a knee but now lifted his head and formally welcomed his guest the proconsul, in Latin: something to the effect that on behalf of his family, his court and his people and so on and so forth, he wished to express how honored they all were by his presence, which could be regarded as a kind of homecoming, insofar as it brought him back to the "land of the gods" (and just as well that her husband was speaking in Latin, thought Herodias, as this last bit would not have gone over very well among the people).

Vitellius accepted this, and Herod Antipas's professed loyalty to all Caesars, with a suitable indifference, replying (likewise in Latin) that the great Herod Antipas was, for his constancy and fidelity, for the temples he had built to Augustus, for his patience, his genius, his ferocity, and so on and so forth, the glory and honor of the great nation of Israel.

Antipas then proceeded to introduce the principal members of his court and family, beginning with Herodias, who had chosen a long white gown with train (which had once belonged to her grandmother Mariamne). Salome was surely the most simply dressed of all those present, but she could afford to be. Her tunic and peplum were in the imperial style, with tassels of emeralds. Cardea had dressed her hair with white almond flowers but otherwise let her natural ringlets frame her face. Her eyes were lined, but that was all; the flush in her cheek, nature.

She honored him with a bow, not meant to call attention to her grace, which it therefore did, of course.

"Ah, yes," said the proconsul, now in the less formal Greek, "we have heard of this one. The little dancer."

Just then, in the litter directly behind the proconsul's, a figure sat up from what had been a full recline—a drowsy youth. Still pimply and plump, with a dense mop of curly hair.

Could it be? He was younger than she'd expected, and much odder. As he descended, she couldn't help noting there seemed something awfully arch about the way he moved. He had a cup of wine, which he downed in a gulp and then held out for one of the stewards to take.

So this was Aulus. As the proconsul introduced him, Salome shot a simmering look at her mother. She understood now, why all the interest.

Antipas invited them in—first to show them to their quarters and then, provided they had the energy, to allow him and his family to tour them through the highlights of the palace. Theortes of Media had said he might join them as well.

The proconsul seemed to think that would be very nice—or compulsory, at any rate—then remembered the first of the gifts he'd brought. It was in the casks behind the litter, the same from which young Aulus had apparently been drawing his refreshment.

"Honey wine," said Vitellius. "A favorite, no?"

Antipas offered a bow of profoundest thanks; it was indeed. Then he stole a glance at Manean and smiled. The choice was clear for now, at least: He was pleased.

⋲66⋲

Joanna

IN THE MIDST OF ALL THIS POMP, THE LAST OF THE TERTRACH'S courtiers was able to slip in largely unnoticed: Chuza's wife, Joanna.

She had come from Galilee, where she had spent the last several months following Jesus and his disciples. She first heard him speak in Capernaum. At the Sea of Galilee, he cured her bleeding. She had followed him to Chorazin. She was one of those who had opened her purse to him and to his followers, to see they would be provided for. She did not think twice. In him she saw the coming Kingdom, and she did not want to leave him, least of all to come to Machaerus, which is where they were keeping John. She knew this.

She had never seen John herself. She had been baptized by Andrew's brother, Simon, but she was aware that a great many of Jesus' followers had been followers of John as well, and she had heard the things that Jesus said of him. Jesus spoke of John as a brother. He said that John was a burning, shining lamp and that they had all been fortunate to rejoice in his light. So it sickened her, the thought of what Herod had done, taking him captive. Why? To muffle and to silence, to darken. And it sickened her that her own husband should be accomplice to such wickedness.

Arriving as late as she did, there had been little time to settle in and rest before the evening's festivities, enough to bathe and to dress, but she could not put the thought out of her mind that somewhere in the bowels of this monstrosity was a holy man, huddling in the dark. She asked her maidservant several times as they made their way up to their quarters, "Do you not hear?"

They stopped. They listened.

Tha-dum, tha-dum . . .

The maidservant shook her head. She heard nothing.

Chuza was nowhere to be found. Attending to Herod, no doubt, but he had left a jeweled necklace out for her to wear and a basket of rockrose to cast before the royals. Joanna let that be her purpose then: to bring the flowers, make sure that she was seen, greet whom she should greet, the wives of court and gentlemen, who could report that she was there.

She did nap briefly. She dreamed that she was out above the wilderness, and high. It was night. There was a hand in hers, his. She could still hear his heart beating.

The land below was nearly black. She barely saw the marls and cuts, the hills and ravines. The sky was pitch, but in the distance there was a tent on a hillside, lit from within. The sun and stars were there inside, she thought, and she would see them too if she could go inside, if she could make it there . . .

Just then, a warm, foul wind began to buffet them from below. Something was burning.

She could see now. The land was all char and ash and smoldering coals, and she could hear the voices, screaming out and gnashing as the fire consumed their flesh.

The wind was much too strong now, and the tent too far. The hand of her companion was slipping. She could feel his last ecstatic heartbeats galloping; then, with a sudden shudder and a crack, she felt the gust of his departing wing. He was gone, and she began to fall toward the screaming voices.

By the time she finally dressed and made her way down, the great banquet hall was already packed with guests. It was by far the largest space inside the palace, comprised of three separate naves, divided by sandal-wood columns, and lit for this occasion by enormous, hanging candelabra. There were large galleries on each side of the hall, meant for spectators, but this evening everyone was out on the main floor, milling.

She heard Greek and Persian tongues, German sailors telling stories of a storm and a new route they'd found to the Caspian. Priests from Jerusalem were standing beside Pharisees, standing beside high-ranking publicans, while servants moved through noiselessly in felt sandals, carrying dishes, drinks, bowls of pistachio nuts.

But how did they all smile and greet? How did they shut their ears, for even here, standing on the checkered marble of the banquet hall, all Joanna had to do was close her eyes.

Tha-dum tha-dum, like a giant drum, and they were all inside.

She thought it best to look for food. Long mahogany tables had been stationed throughout the hall; it was just a matter of getting to one or the right one. Each was heaped with a slightly different array of delicacies. The fruit was most appealing. She spied a table not far away, offering up a pyramid of pomegranates, surrounded by melons, dates, and figs.

Unfortunately, it was being scavenged by Livia and Priopy, and they had seen her.

"Oh, look." Their glances spoke. "She did make it down." "And where has she been again?" "With whom?" "Doing what?"

Joanna opted for the next table over, which featured a more savory fare: plates of dormice and kidney, stuffed grape leaves, and olives. A circle of soldiers was gathered around the far end.

"Oh, don't worry," said the tallest, taking up a spiced lamb's tail. "One has been set aside, a special one." His teeth snapped happily through the cartilage.

"But how do we know which one?" asked another.

"It'll be the one tied to a tree," said a third.

They all laughed, lips slick with grease; they wiped their fingers on the bread.

Joanna did not understand. Were they speaking of the Baptist?

She turned away, and her eye fell on a priest helping himself to another fistful of nuts. How could they stand by? Were they not only blind but deaf as well?

Just then there was a hall-wide swoon. The guests all turned and began to drift like minnows. Herod had arrived. He was up on the gallery that banded the front half of the hall. The queen was there as well, and the usual retinue. Manean. Naaman. She looked for Chuza, and there he was out front.

They had apparently finished touring their most esteemed guests. Joanna could tell the Roman Vitellius by his purple sash, but there was an aged man as well, who must have been the Parthian. There was a boy trailing behind, and then Salome, looking beautiful as usual, if sullen.

None of them seemed to pay much mind to the crowd below. They were making their way around to the great balcony, where Chuza and the guard were already standing, already directing them to the outside porch first.

The crowd in the courtyard gave a welcome roar as soon as they appeared. No speeches followed. Just a wave, another roar, and then the party stepped back in and repeated the gesture for the higher-ups below. Herod's right hand was in the Roman's, his left in the Parthian's. He raised them both. The people cheered.

Long live Caesar!

Long live Herod!

They drowned each other out.

Herod smiled, already pink.

Finally, the two guests let down their hands, but he kept his high. He swirled them in little circles as he descended the stairs. *Continue. As you were.*

But that was just for show, of course. The throng was too excited. They swarmed in upon the descending party, who were like crumbs tossed to a flock of pigeons.

Joanna hadn't the strength to follow, and in fact the royal party was only passing through. Already she'd noticed the servants had been spiriting away the members of court, she wasn't sure where. Priopy and Livia were gone, and Herod himself stayed in the main hall just long enough to let the people have a glimpse; then he too was guided through to wherever it was the rest were going.

Joanna wondered if she absolutely had to. Her stomach was getting worse. Couldn't she simply claim illness and return to her room? But then a servant found her. He said her husband had asked for her, so she took his arm and he led her back, behind a great hanging veil and through a maze of papyrus screens to a part of the palace she had actually never seen before. They passed by several lavers, which had been provided mostly for the sake of the priests and Pharisees, though one unfortunate attendant was having politely to inform the boy from the balcony, the one with all the hair, he was not to pee in the water. He didn't seem to hear.

From there the servant led her down into what appeared to be an emptied pool, filled with more guests. She was met by gentle sprays of galbanum and frankincense, flung from leaves of hyssop; then another servant came and crowned her with a floral wreath, the same as all the guests were wearing, save for the Pharisees.

It turned out to be a great complex of pools, in fact, drained dry and of all different depths and lengths. She quickly lost any sense of where she was, but followed the servant past the High Priest Caius, several sultans, and other members of the court. She could feel the sneer and smear of every sidelong glance: "Oh, there she is. I'd heard she wasn't coming." "Yes, but did you know why?" Joanna lowered her eyes and followed around another corner, up a few steps and into what appeared to be largest and deepest of the tanks.

From the stairs she could see that Herod and his most honored guests were all at the far end, receiving. Three separate divans had been set out beside a long cushioned shelf, piled high with other pillows, framed against a crimson veil embroidered with flowers. Various aides and deputies and bodyguards were there as well, but Joanna's eye once again fell upon Salome, looking mortified and bored—but still lovely—sitting near the satrap, who kept smiling agedly at the awkward silence that hung between them.

Joanna was handed a cup of wine. She had no intention of drinking it. The queasiness in her stomach had turned into a much sharper pang now. She wanted to complete her mission and go, and so, although women were expected to remain on the periphery—at least at this early hour—she let go of her escort's hand and cut directly through the crowd.

It was not as easy here to avoid the familiar faces. She fixed her attention on the sounds instead, the snatches of conversation: A physician was admitting to his ignorance of the stars; a priest from Aphaka regaling a group of high publicans with his description of the temple at Hierapolis.

"How much would such a pilgrimage cost?" he was asked.

She did not hear the answer. A blind German was singing a hymn about a mountaintop in Scandinavia.

Then she heard someone say his name.

"John."

It was a group up ahead, standing not so far from Herod.

"Trust me, he won't be getting past that detail," said one, the youngest in the circle, with much too loud a voice and a ghastly harelip that for whatever reason put her in mind of a satyr.

"How can you be certain?" asked a small Phoenician with a waxed and pointed beard.

"I went and saw."

"How?" chimed in one of the eunuchs. "They won't let me past the kitchen."

"I have my ways," said the satyr. "I can assure you, the prophet will not be attending."

"Ah, so you say." The Phoenician raised his finger directly to the satyr's face. "But these holy men, they are shape-shifters, you know. They can take on any form they please—fire, cloud."

Just then, Joanna's nose detected the sickly sweet of her mistress's perfume. The queen was about—right behind her in fact. She swept up, sails aloft, greeting Joanna (but barely) with a nod. *Late.*

"Did you hear, Your Highness?" said the satyr. "You are keeping a shape-shifter."

"Is that so?" said the queen.

"But it is true," the Phoenician insisted, unaware that he was being ridiculed. "The same as when you or I think of something and it comes to mind, a picture, when these men think of it, so they become . . . it!"

"Hmm." The queen plucked a grape from its stem. "Then he might be this grape, you mean?"

"He might well."

"Interesting." She plunked it in her mouth and crushed it between her teeth.

The others laughed, the eunuch and the satyr—again far too eagerly, shoulders to his ears. Behind, Herod and the proconsul both noticed, which of course the satyr noticed.

"The Baptizer," he explained.

Herod nodded. The topic seemed to be of only mild interest to him, but the proconsul asked what was to become of him.

Herod shrugged. "I frankly haven't given it much thought."

"And that may be the wisest course," said the satyr. "In any case, they say all his followers have switched to another?"

The queen took another grape. "These people are sheep, aren't they?" Her eye slid slyly over at Joanna, who still was not quite part of the circle. "Did you see your husband?"

She gestured upward. Chuza was standing up above the tank, looking down at her directly. He lifted his bowl of wine in greeting and took a sip.

Joanna could feel her cheeks burning. The queen was still looking at her, merely to observe. Without thinking, but simply for the momentary mask, Joanna lifted her bowl up to her face. The wine slid past her lips, warm and thick and bitter. It tasted like blood. Her stomach heaved.

Only the satyr's feet were splattered, thankfully, but Joanna nearly fainted. A servant came and caught her and helped take her away before she made an even greater mess.

Again she barely heard the sounds as she was carried away, a strange mix of nervous laughter and revulsion, and one voice—Livia's, she thought—whispering, "Yes, and she has apparently given him *all* her money."

≋67≋

The Former King

JOHN HAD TOLD AZHARAN MANY TIMES THAT WHEN THE LIGHT
revealed itself, it was not like a lantern on a prow. It was more like
the swallow's song: To hear it upon waking was to wonder how long
the swallow had been singing, and to realize that everything that had
come before—all the faces and the words and the fears and yearning
—had been nothing but a dream.

John found himself beside the river again. Not at Bethabara. Not at
Aenon, but at the other place, the stream beside the Thadi tree. The
sun was just descending but still strong. He was sitting in the shade of
the leaves and blossoms. He had been there all day, and he was tired.
He had been baptizing, but everyone was gone now: the disciples, his
family. Not even Annhar was there.

But in the distance there was a man coming. John sat and watched
him. He had a beard and a smile, and a bag and a bowl.

When he saw John, he hailed him: "John! You are John!"

"I am."

The man said, "I have come to be baptized! Baptize me in the
name of Life."

John welcomed him. He was tired, but the stranger was a friend. "What have you to confess?"

"What have I to confess?" The man sat beside him. He set down his bowl, which was empty, and told him his story.

"I confess I was once a king. Do you believe me? I had beneath me an entire nation of men and countless treasures and armies at my disposal.

"But one day I was traveling with a band of my bravest and most fearsome soldiers, high in the hills of Harran, when we came upon a brotherhood of holy men. A dozen, if that. They lived a simple life. They tilled. They prayed. They had no wives. They had no books. But my priest told me these men could hear the heavens sing. So it was said.

"I wanted this too. I told my captain to find out how they did this, so he went to them and said, 'Share with us what you know. Tell us your secrets.'

"The brothers said they had no secret they could share. My captain asked again, 'Tell us what you know,' and this time when the brothers refused, my captain ordered his men take to hold of them and bind them. The soliders laid kindling all around them in a circle.

" 'Tell us, or we shall burn you,' the captain said, but the holy men were not bothered. Again they said there was no secret they could share, so the captain did as he had warned. He set fire to the kindling.

"The holy men showed no fear. They stood. They walked about freely within the flames. With my own eyes I saw, it was as if an unseen cloak were protecting them, and there was one who looked at me directly, smiling, and I heard his voice: 'You rule these men, and yet you know nothing.'

"I was afraid. My soldiers were afraid. They fled. They said, 'Let us never speak of this again!' But I remained. I went to my priest. I said, 'I need to know what these men know. How is it they do not burn? How is it they hear the heavens sing?'

"My priest warned me. He said, 'My powers are of darkness; theirs, of light. Theirs will prevail.'

"Still, I made him try. While the brothers prayed, he scattered sand around them, then he cast a spell beneath the moonlight, so that the sand turned into an army of wild demons with talons and fangs.

"Again my priest said to the brothers, 'Teach us what you know, or these demons will have at you!'

"The brothers paid no mind. They prayed. The demons closed in, but every time they came near enough to hear the brothers' prayer, they flew apart like dust. More came, larger demons with sharper claws and axes and lances in their hands, but they also turned back to sand and blew away at the sound of the brother's prayer.

"Seeing this, my priest turned and fled as well. These men were much too powerful for him. Only I remained. I threw myself down before them. I said, 'I supplicate myself to you and to your wisdom. How is it that you do these things? Teach me your secrets.'

"They answered me, 'All we know we know from prayer. All our power comes from God!'

" 'But why do you not take this power and make yourselves kings?' I asked. 'You could rule the world.'

"They said, 'Why should we be kings? God is king. What need have we for servants? We do our own work. We make our bread with our own hands. Otherwise we worship and we pray.'

"Finally I heard them. I said, 'And if I worship and pray, will I hear the heavens sing?'

"They said, 'If you pray and you are just, you will become a good man.'

"So I left them there, but I did not return to my palace or to my riches. I gave them up. I gave up my armies. I gave up my wealth. I prayed as they said, and I journeyed, and my prayer and my journey have brought me here to you, that I might be cleansed by the hand of John."

Hearing all this, John smiled. "I know these men," he said. "I once was one of them. They are holy indeed, for they know the name of God."

"Then speak the name upon me, John, and baptize me."

John said, "What is in your purse there?"

And the man showed him a handful of jewels. "The last to my name," he said, "in case I should be in dire need."

"Then let us cast them in the water," said John, "and I will baptize you in the name of Life."

The man did not hesitate. He flung the jewels into the river, and John took his hand, and he baptized him there. He asked that there be mercy and forgiveness for this man who once was king, that he be sealed in heavenly light and clothed in glory.

And when the man had risen the final time, John saw that standing on the shore beside them was a child—a beautiful child, no more than three years old, smiling up at them, yet no one else was near.

"Yahya!" cried the boy. "Now come and baptize me!"

The former king laughed. "Look at this one, asking to be baptized at his age!"

John laughed as well, but as he looked at the child, he suddenly grew very tired. All at once the day's work overcame him.

"I have to rest," he said. "Come tomorrow, and I will baptize you then."

The child did not object. He said, "Come out of the water and sleep, Yahya."

John came out, and while the child looked on, he lay down on the shore and fell into a deep, deep sleep.

≋68≋

Midnight

TEMICULUS UNDERSTOOD THE RHYTHM OF A GOOD FEAST. BY
midnight all the meat had been served and devoured; all the carcasses had been taken away. The flesh was comfortably digesting in
the bellies of the guests or had been vomited into pots and tossed
down the western walls.

The public had been excused from the palace. They were back in
the village, drinking from their own stores. The Pharisees and their
phylacteries had retired to their chambers as well, signal to let the
games begin.

The pools were opened, those that still had water in them. The
baths and springs as well. Brave souls led expeditions out onto the
rocks, while back inside, all the favored concubines and courtesans
were summoned to come and play. The eunuchs, dusted blue and gold
but otherwise unclothed, entered down into the drowsy aromatic air
and began blending the guests, who up until then had observed a
stricter separation between the men and women.

All wines flowed—the tamarisk, the palm, and the honey as well.
The servants were on orders to let no cup go dry. Many of the musicians who had been performing outside in the courtyards and public
halls now entered as well and were moving through with drums and
flutes, hand-held harps and sistrums; the dancers too, in their slippers

and veils, the little cymbals on the fingers, their jangling bracelets, bells, and undulating bellies.

Even Herodias, who liked to keep a sober eye, was succumbing to the atmosphere. She stood at her usual remove, above the sanctum, on what would have been the edge of the pool had it been filled with water instead of bodies. She could see the moon and the southern hills through the open arches facing south, then, without even turning her head, glance down at the churning revelry below. To a more jaundiced eye, a bowl of maggots, no?

The guests did look pleased, though. The lectors and bodyguards were enjoying themselves with the hired help. Antipas had the ear of Odayan, the sultan of Palmyra. Both Pithon and Flebus were surrounded by eunuchs, having stolen Jacob ben Dama's prize, Faisool. Even Temiculus seemed to have let down his guard. He had a drink in his hand, and one of the servants was rubbing his feet. Theortes (or Theortes's father) looked to be asleep again, but he was smiling, and refusing to be taken to his room anytime he was awakened. Vitellius, the other most honored guest, was more than justifying his reputation: at least five trips to the pisspots, by her count, and just as many (with just many partners) to the amber room, southernmost of the empty pools, which, by design of all pillows and a gossamer canopy flung overtop, seemed to have turned into the banquet's unofficial orgy space. A steady offering of grunts, shrieks, and cries had been gurgling up since midnight, perfectly punctuating the steadier effluence of music and laughter flowing out from the other sancta. A very gratifying concert; she only wished these breezes had the arms to lift it up and bear it out across those distant hills and down into the ears of Aretas and his sullen, sneering daughter.

One particularly ecstatic howl vaulted from the amber room, and it occurred to her she had lost track of Salome.

She scanned below. So many limbs and heads, but none seemed to be her daughter's. Then over on the far side, up on the main floor, she did see a bare arm coming out from behind a pillar, gently stroking the sanded wood. She knew it was Salome's from the half-time rhythm it kept, but also because there was Aulus standing in front of her. That inane frazzle of hair was hard to miss.

They certainly seemed to have taken to each other, those two, a fact that Herodias might have found more encouraging if she could understand the reason why. As silly as he'd seemed out on the terrace, she had concluded by the time they'd all finished their tour of the palace that there was something distinctly *wrong* with him, something broken or damaged. There was a disconcerting drift of his eye, an apparent need to touch all the molding, to leave his smeary finger-prints, and then there was that ponylike prance. And the laugh. The fact that Salome—purely sensual Salome—should have found some-thing in there worth paying attention to, Herodias couldn't decide if it spoke well of her or ill. His lone appeal, so far as she could tell—all the power that lay in store—was of a kind that Salome had never seemed all that interested in. But was she taking pity then? Had she sensed a kindred spirit? Or was her attraction based on something much sim-pler, the fact that her mother had clearly lost all interest in him?

It must have been something, though, for as Salome now stepped out from behind the pillar, Herodias could see she was in her *third* dress of the evening, an even simpler and more gossamer shift than before, down to the knee, with shawl. And she had let her hair down. She looked divine.

But there was a reason she'd stepped out. Something was stirring below. One of the proconsul's lectors was making a quick exit up the steps, tailed by one of Antipas's spearmen. Something was amiss.

Antipas saw as well. All that faux jocularity—that pink-faced insou-ciance—drained from his face like pig's blood. His eyes were wide, his mouth puckered. Already he was sending his lapdog, Manean, to go find out what it was, and she knew what he was thinking—that this was it finally. Aretas was here with his army. Somehow they'd duped the lookouts and come to ruin his party.

She glanced over at Temiculus to see if he had any idea what was really going on. He shook his head, but likewise sensing His Majesty's concern, he signaled one of the musicians to proceed.

A mere three strums upon his lyre, that and several loud taps upon his partner's tambourine, summoned the attention of all. One of the female dancers slid over. Time for another gift.

Another? thought Herodias. They'd given out how many already?

So many perfumes and unguents and lapis backscratchers, she'd lost track. This one seemed to be important, though. They were awakening Theortes. It might actually be from him, in fact, which was somewhat important. The guests were all parting in front of Antipas, to make way for the dancer. She had the gift in hand, set upon a purple pillow, beneath a golden scarf. He was doing his best to look appreciative, but he was clearly still distracted by whatever was going on below.

It wasn't until the woman started weaving her way toward him, however, that Herodias recognized this was Salome's dance, no? She realized it the same moment Antipas did. She could see his face alight and grimace slightly. This was the maiden's dance, the one about Ishtar. She recognized that gesture there, the backside of the hand sweeping across her eyes. This was the dance the courtiers had taught Salome back at Ascalon and that she liked to perform so much for guests.

But was Temiculus aware? Herodias looked back over at him. He was pretending to ignore her, but of course he knew. He must. He was smiling.

She could see that Salome had recognized it too. She was looking down at the dancer and swaying slightly, smirking, not intentionally, not to be mean, but who could blame her? Even her silly little romp versions, with all the girlish mugging and giggling, still possessed an elegance about them, glimmers of an inner stillness that could rivet the most distracted room of drunken toadies and ambassadors. This dancer here, poor thing—it wasn't her fault, of course—but by comparison to Salome she might as well have been a bucket of piss, swishing and splishing and splashing all over the floor.

Antipas clearly felt the same, but he was still trying to be polite. He nodded gamely, grinning, wishing for the spectacle to end—*just bring the gift here. Yes, dear, come along.*

At one point he shot a glance up in Herodias's direction, but only because Manean had just returned. He was standing right beside her.

"That was quick," she said.

Below, Antipas queried with his eyes: *Anything to worry about?*

Manean shook his head no. All was well.

And that quickly the blood returned to His Majesty's cheek. No attack. They were safe. He turned and gave full attention to the dancer and the gift, which were mercifully now only two or three swishes away.

"So what was it?" Herodias whispered.

"Just the soldiers gambling," said Manean.

"Tsk." She feigned disappointment.

And now the music stopped. The dancer had handed off the gift, still on its pillow, still covered. The people offered polite applause and waited.

Antipas played along, much more relaxed now. Furtively he peeked beneath the veil. He touched his heart, he was so moved. He looked to the satrap (if it was the satrap), who acknowledged his thanks with a sleepy grin.

"What is it?" someone cried. "Show us!"

"Yes, let us see!"

Antipas took the edge of the veil between his fingertips and slowly slid it off:

Oooooh, the guests intoned. A crown . . .

. . . of gold no less.

(It really did appear to be.)

Even Salome was impressed. Her head tilted slightly as if it felt the weight already.

Antipas noticed this, needless to say. He lifted it up to her. Would she like to try it on?

(But of course, thought Herodias. What was the point of having anything, if you cannot instantly give it to Salome?)

Still standing at the top of the steps, Salome shook her head, but Antipas insisted. He turned to the satrap. Did he mind?

Of course not.

Then someone called out, "Dance!" and it wasn't clear if the person had been very loud or the sanctum had for some reason gone very silent just before he said it, but the word seemed to hang for a moment and resound.

Antipas looked at Salome. Might she?

The lyre thrummed in with an encouraging strum, followed by several jingle-jangles from the tambourine.

"Dance!" called out another of the guests. This time the queen did see: It was that cloven-faced lawyer, grinning hideously as a flurry of snaps and cackles seconded the motion, and thirded and fourthed. Even Vitellius was among those in favor. Yes, indeed, the proconsul *had* heard about this one, "the little dancer."

"Come," the people said. "Do. Grace us."

Herodias looked over at Temiculus, who sipped from his cup, grinning as Salome continued to demur. She had to, and yet her body had given her away. And look at the dress she was wearing. She already was Ishtar's little maiden.

The players prodded her with another measure, the flutist piping in. Antipas was still looking up at her, almost coquettishly. He tapped the golden wreath again. *Please?*

"But it is his birthday," the guests all urged. Yes, his jubilee. "Don't make a man beg on his birthday."

(Or do, thought Herodias, if that's his pleasure.)

Now the dancers were ascending the steps to fetch her. They took her hands, which she did not like. She did not like being touched, but the music and the begging of those below were doing their work. For the first time she glanced across at her mother.

Herodias nodded, why not? You have the boy's attention. Don't waste it.

The dancer was starting to show her now, to demonstrate. Salome shucked her hands away; she did not need to be shown. She cinched her brow, and that was what let the people know she had consented. She let the shawl drop.

They applauded, yes.

And Aulus smiled.

Temiculus smiled, the little devil.

And it began. The dulcimer chimed in. The dancers withdrew as the whole sanctum sat back to welcome her descent.

Of all those present, only Manean was excluded from the guests' enthusiasm. This might have been because he was still standing above, for he could plainly see the girl was drunk. She had been drinking all evening, because of the boy. She had spirits in her that had never been in her before.

He knew that Antipas was drunk as well, which might not have been so worrisome except that this evening's culprit was honey wine, which always seemed to bring out the worst of his demons.

Indeed here the demon was, wearing the very nubile flesh of his stepdaughter. Looking at her, Manean finally had to admit the extent to which he had been turning a blind eye to this, the blossoming of Salome, trusting his friend to negotiate this pass on his own. Only now, as he watched her gliding down the steps, did he appreciate what a treacherous pass it was.

Had it only been a year since they'd last been treated to this vision? Or no, a year and a half; the banquet at Sebaste had been in the summer. However many it had been, the intervening months had ushered her several crucial strides toward womanhood. Her hair, in its abundant length, still emphasized how petite she was, how narrow in the hips. Still, there was a far greater maturity to her carriage, and a curvature. She was hardly dancing at all as yet. She was using the steps to find the rhythm, but this alone was enough to cast a spell. With every movement she seemed to be creating a kind of invisible perimeter around herself, inside of which to move, to sway and swing, to rouse the serpent from its slumber.

When she reached the foot and the smooth flat floor, the players knew enough to increase their volume and tempo. The music took hold of her, inviting her to widen her scope. She turned for them. She gyred, her hips a half time faster than her feet, but all somehow in sync. Three times she spun this way, while the snake within her seemed to spawn two more. They danced within her arms and wrists. They rose above her head so as not to obscure the impossible fluidity of her torso.

She could clearly feel her power, in the gazes and glassy smiles of all the guests. There was indeed something mesmerizing about it, a kind of affirmation in seeing royalty possessed of such natural grace.

The dancers handed her their scarves—seven, yes? One for each gate the goddess had to pass through, to enter the underworld in search of her fallen love—the shepherd or a fisherman, Manean couldn't quite recall—only that in order to descend, she had to leave behind all earthly vestments, seven veils. She had to be stripped naked.

And yet it occurred to Manean that there must be two versions of the dance. There was the one that Salome had performed the year before (and the year before that too; it had become a tradition, he supposed): the maiden's dance, a dance of spring, of welcoming the goddess back to earth and, with her, all fertility. In that version the dancer was a girl, stealing a moment to play with each veil before returning it to Ishtar in thanks and praise—the breechcloth, the girdle, the breastplate, and so forth, until finally she returned the crown.

But this was not that. Not nearly.

Perhaps it was those eighteen months, or something in Salome's eye. Perhaps it was only the order of the veils, but right away Manean understood that this was not the little maiden's dance. This was the dance of the goddess herself. This was Ishtar's descent and her unveiling, which was quite a different matter.

It *began* with the crown—the invisible one on her head, that is—and in this instance, the first gatekeeper turned out to be the prince of Cappadocia, who had imposed himself upon the royal couch some three hours ago and not yet left. Here was the reward for his persistence, an unseen diadem, but more: the fleeting, floating gossamer attention of this rhythmic little beast, this fairy, this goddess in the flesh.

Next to him, and there somewhat by chance, one of the centurions from the army of Antipas's father. He received her scepter. But had she stroked it? No. For a moment maybe, but then the arms floated away again, all innocence, like ribbons above her head, and it was on to the next gate, the next jewel to be surrendered, the next planet to spin away.

Her movements were growing more and more dynamic now, more violent. With each discarded veil, her gyres widened, the crook of her ankle was more acute as she hooked it around the other calf and spun, but she did not ever lose her axis. It was like a rod within her, balancing her head so still, even now as she removed her invisible earrings for the sultan (the one who'd brought the horse), now as she laid her invisible necklace upon the shoulder of the proconsul's lector, Yamin. She did not distinguish high from low. To a goddess, what was the difference between a governor and his guard? Surely neither of them was about to object.

But could they not see the anger in her? It seemed so clear to Manean, and palpable, the closer she came to Antipas, that a darkness had entered the room through her and was subsuming her. Were they too close to see? Would Manean himself have been so taken in, he wondered, so beguiled by her skin, the sheen of her shoulder, the fine hair of her slender arms, that he too would have ignored her purpose?

Perhaps.

She had come upon Theortes now, who was wide awake and sitting up. To him went Ishtar's breastplate. And though it was not real, the pantomime of its removal did focus the room on her two recent blooms, still barely there, but there enough. Enough to be seen beneath her dress. She knew this. She brought them near him. Did she let them graze his cheek? Did he? The nearest guests stole glances at one another, brows high, cups raised. Just as well the hour. Just as well these bottomless cups, and we can say come morning, "We forget." Or "it cannot have been as we remember."

The players too were consulting one another. Should they not tame the serpent? They could have. But no, the woman with all the jangling bracelets let her eyes roll up beneath her lids as she continued with her tambourine. Their alibi, not wine then, but music. That and the fact that Lucius Vitellius was next, sitting there with his hands on his knees, waiting his turn like a good little boy. They could hardly deny the proconsul his spoil.

And the goddess showed her appreciation, giving him the nearest view yet. To him the girdle. As she removed it, he could hardly breathe, she let him gape so openly at those barely spreading hips, at how that fine linen danced against the even finer skin of her midriff. How many women had the proconsul been inside tonight? How many boys? All forgotten. He was agog. He was agape. His nostrils flared, as he drank her in, so flushed and helpless that someone actually did laugh out loud. Someone high above let free with a burst, meant to be heard.

A few of the spectators turned around to see who: the only one who could have gotten away with it. Young Aulus, delighted, as delighted as if he'd seen a servant slip on camel shit. What a quivering lump Salome had made of his father. He laughed again, and his high, obnoxious cackle broke his father's spell. The proconsul remembered where he was and who this was in front of him. He laughed as well. He held up his bowl for more and directed the girl to his host, the tetrarch, who was right there beside him, as he had been all along, slumped in his chair, his belly like a bowl of aspic.

At least to judge by his appearance—and Manean was an old hand at that—Antipas's reaction to all of this was mixed. On the one hand, the girl's display had stoked a jealousy in him (but was "jealousy" the word?) to see others enjoying in public that for which he so privately yearned. But he was clearly feeling pride as well, at their being given this glimpse of his greatest treasure. No golden crown, no kingdom, or anything that anyone could give him would compare to her, his beloved Salome.

All of which is to say that Antipas, too, seemed completely oblivious to the furies that were firing his stepdaughter's dance. His senses were too busy, his eyes too wild, darting back and forth between her face, her body, her hands. She held them out like sconces. She folded them over her womb. She held her hips that way, her wrists crossed in the middle. And for him, of course, all that remained was the goddess's loincloth; she had counted correctly, and she let there be no mistake. This was what he wanted, no? The final scarf hung down, the merest imaginable veil between him and her purest, tenderest, and most inviolable folds.

But even as she offered it to him, her brow above was like an arrow, like a falcon glaring down at him and daring him. He simply did not see, no more clever than a moth trapped inside a lantern.

And yet it wasn't his helplessness that finally gave him away, or even the lascivious curl at the edge of his lips as he watched the last of the veils dance so tantalizingly before him. That was all to be expected; that was nothing but her puppetry. It was the furtive glances upward, trying to meet her eyes. They were what let Manean know (and every other person there, he had to guess). For these were not lascivious at all. Quite the opposite. Antipas's counteriance was much more searching, more frantic and ecstatic. In fact, Manean could have sworn he'd seen that look somewhere before, and recently: the lifted, almost fearful brow, the helplessness of the mouth. But where? Even the hands. His hands were down on the cushions beside him, slack and slightly upturned.

Then it came to him: It had been at Bethabara, hadn't it? Among the penitents along the bank, when they had watched John making his way down and stepping across the little stream there. That was the expression on Antipas's face, distinctly.

And all at once Manean understood, or he conceded finally what he had known—the truth of what these two had been up to. But his first reaction was not of horror or contempt, or even disgust. It was of pity.

What a fool, he thought. *Is that what Antipas believes is happening here? That he is being forgiven?*

The scarf was still there, still dancing like a pony's tail, but the musicians were in the final measures of their crescendo, thrashing at their instruments. The end was near, and it happened very simply. Salome drew the scarf between her legs, front to back. It did not touch her flesh. Her dress was still there, but she pulled the scarf slowly through and around and then dropped it in front of him. She even flung it slightly. It floated. He snatched. He missed. The people laughed as the veil descended, its gentle landing timed precisely to the final strum of the lyre, the final thump of the drummer on his drum. Salome stood before him, naked, as it were, but unbowed, her hands turned out, ready now to enter in the unlit cave of the netherworld.

The sanctum answered quickly and eagerly. Their loud appreciation was the swiftest way past the scandal, but Manean was not a part. He turned and for the first time looked directly at the queen.

Her eyes were like two black stones in her skull.

For she had seen as well—the truth that she had been denying— so even as the people cheered below, whistling and stamping their feet, it was her brother's words that echoed in her ears, as clearly as if he'd been standing there beside her, whispering close: "He's much too keen."

How she had scoffed back then. She had said her husband didn't have it in him. But look at him now. She knew that expression all too well, the vague smile, the glazed eyes. She knew the posture, of pitiful gratitude. Even the angle of his tunic. She thought of the blood on Salome's bedclothes, and it was like a lightning bolt inside her. What had he been doing? *What had he been doing here?*

And she?

Herodias felt nothing like the same fury for Salome, strangely, or maybe not so. Salome she felt sorry for. Salome she half admired. Again, she wouldn't have thought her daughter was capable of this— what she had just seen—exposing her stepfather in public, revealing him to be the cur he truly was. An act of such contempt the queen had rarely seen—for him and all of them.

She did not even blame her daughter for whatever she had done. Salome clearly despised the man, but what choice did she have? The beast would slink into her room, the beast they had brought her here to serve, would stagger in and fall and whisper in her ear with that rancid, wine-soaked breath of his—sweet nothings, and thanks, and succors, about their little secret. Was she to resist that, and face the wrath, and face the retribution? Or merely turn away? That was all he asked, Herodias knew all too well, just for Salome to roll on her side, focus on a crack in the wall and let him have his momentary way; a thrust, a shudder, and he was usually done. It even slightly broke the mother's heart, the tenderness, the innocence behind her daughter's submission—of course, of course, embroidered here and there by threads of vanity and rivalry and retribution—but was it not ultimately an act of loyalty that she received him? After all, if she was this to him, the temporary vessel of his vile and worthless seed, then she remained her father's daughter, no?

And Salome did love Philip.

It was for her husband, then, that all of Herodias's fires were now raging—the bastard; the ruinous infection; the wretched taint, pre-suming to claim her daughter's purity for his filthy little self. It was a conflagration in her, and she would have spewed it out at him if she could have. She would have burned the palace to a crisp. She would have razed the mountain and everything in it. But failing that, she was moving very coolly, very evenly and quietly. No one saw but Manean (and Temiculus, of course), but even as the guests continued with their thumping and calling, she was already making her way around to the far side of the pool. She knew already what was to follow, right down to the word.

Salome had yet to move, other than to have gone slightly limp. The musicians all were bowing to her, the ideal to which they aspired. And yet as there was no music or rhythm in the people's ovation, the snake that had been animating her seemed to have withdrawn again, leaving Salome suddenly sobered in their midst and slack, like a puppet whose strings had been dropped.

The crown was still with Antipas: the real crown, Theortes's gift. He took it up in both hands and offered it to her, daintily.

It wasn't clear she even saw at first. He tried again. She shook her head.

"But you must let me thank you," he said. "Let me show my appreciation." He opened his arms. He did not see, or care apparently, that she had gone cold before him. He was still too thrilled.

"Anything. Just say, and it shall be yours."

The tongue clucks among the guests, intended mostly to express a mawkish appreciation of his offer, he took as expression of doubt.

"But it's true," he said, looking around. "She knows it's true. She has but to ask, and it is hers." He turned his doggish, oblong eyes on her. "Even unto half my kingdom, I would give you, Salome."

She still did not answer, and in the silence, someone's aside could be heard: "I know which half I'd take." A flutter of guffaws followed, but Antipas stayed focused on the girl.

"What?" he said to her. "Just say."

As he waited, his nervousness began to show. Manean could only marvel at how quickly this simplest of gestures, of giving thanks, had somehow turned into a kind of challenge, a chance for Antipas to prove himself; she *must* provide it. And Manean knew why he was so eager: because if she would simply name her price, any price, then he would pay it, and he would have exactly what he'd wanted all along. Her consent. His sin and absolution all at once.

Alas, Salome's mind was not nearly as nimble as her body. She could have simply turned away, Manean thought. Just bow and grant the man his birthday. Go. And everyone would say, well done, and they would speak of it in the weeks to come—or years—of how she'd toyed with them, how she had given the great Lucius Vitellius his seventh rise of the evening, and that would be the end of it.

But she was frozen in their midst, locked in place by the sudden silence of the space, and all those eyes and ears—including his, the one who'd spoiled her—waiting, and with every passing moment, growing more desperate.

Please.

Anything . . .

Finally. "Daughter!"

The voice rang out as clear as a trumpet. All turned.

Herodias had made her way around. She was halfway down the steps now, chin high, one shoulder forward. "Come." She motioned.

The eunuchs sitting on the lower steps made way. Salome had no choice but to comply. She padded over and raised up on her toes so that her mother could whisper in her ear. The people smiled. Even Antipas pretended to be amused, but underneath that nervous grin was a very yellow glare: Careful, woman. This is no business of yours.

Herodias whispered nonetheless, but Salome did not seem to understand at first. She shook her head, *again?* Her mother repeated her suggestion, but more emphatically this time. Ears turned. Eyes squinted. Still no one could tell, except that Salome's face had seemed to light. Yes. She agreed. The crowd agreed as well—anything. The girl returned, skipping back through them, her strings now taut and dancing again. She took her place in front of Antipas. And he, the dupe, was looking hopeful.

He opened his arms. "Only ask, my jewel, and it shall be yours."

She was all girl again, but nervous. Her voice was barely there, and she was smiling as she spoke, making the words more difficult to understand.

Antipas leaned forward, touching his ear.

"Can't hear," a voice agreed from above.

"What did she say?" The guests consulted one another. No one knew.

"I would like the head of John the Baptist," she said, more clearly now.

All fell quiet. They still weren't sure they'd heard correctly, Antipas included. He leaned in further, so she repeated.

"I would like the head of John the Baptist," she said, "on a silver charger."

Antipas looked over at Herodias, assuming this was some kind of joke. He grinned. "I think this is what your mother wants. I want to know what *you* want, my dear."

"That is what I want," she said firmly. "I want the head of John the Baptist on a silver charger. Now."

Again, the sanctum was silent for a moment, long enough to let the realization set in: she was deadly serious. To punctuate the point, that high cackle sounded from above, young Aulus, still standing beside the column.

No one turned. They all were looking at Antipas and waiting—the queen, and Theortes, Vitellius, the eunuchs, all of them, their expressions reading much the same:

He *had said* anything.

Manean knew already the decision had been made. Not by Antipas but by the fates and by the setting. Antipas could not possibly rescind his offer, not here in front of all the guests. And yet his verdict, when it came, was a function of more than mere capitulation, more than the need to prove himself a man of his word. Manean actually watched it happen—it only took a moment—for the sense of horror to fade from his old friend's eyes, and be replaced not merely by acceptance, not by resignation or consent, but by agreement. Perhaps this was as it should be. Perhaps his wife was right. The prophet had had his chance, but he had refused to take it, to be of any help. So be it.

His hand was still extended. All he had to do was lift it slightly, and open it, and the guests let out a howl so sudden and so loud, Manean actually jolted back. They stamped their feet again. They brayed in triumph. Herodias descended the last two steps and went to join her husband on the divan. Salome kept her place. Her focus remained on Antipas, to see if he would look back at her just once. He didn't. His eyes were like a gnat, flicking nervously about the space, from gleaming face to gleaming face. He shifted to make space for his wife, whose countenance could not have been more pleased.

No, this, it seemed to say, amid the roar and the delight of the guests, *this* was the sound that she'd have liked the breezes to carry all the way to Petra.

⋙69⋘

Execution

THERE HAD BEEN NO BEHEADINGS IN EITHER GALILEE OR PERAEA during the reign of Antipas. Even his father's executions, when he ruled, had taken a different form: Jonathan was drowned; Alexander and Aristobulus were hanged; Judas and Matthias, burned alive.

The taking of the head was more of a Roman custom and judged to be a relatively honorable means. That is why, even as the guests inside the sanctum were still celebrating Antipas's decision, Manean made straight for Iuventius, captain of the lectors.

"Have you a man?"

He did. He signaled a Syrian named Arman. "But we will need a good blade."

Temiculus was at their side as well now, with his assistants. "And obviously the deed should be done there in the northern hall," he said.

Manean agreed. He took the lector, Arman, with him, and Pithon, while Temiculus and Flebus hurried off to find a suitable platter.

Word spread quickly, from the sanctum out to the baths, the kitchens, and the terraces where the servants and freedmen had been enjoying these moments of relative irresponsibility. Manean and his party had detoured briefly to the arsenal to let Arman select an ax, but by the time they reached the northern hall, several dozen gawkers were already there, crammed up against the crossed spears of the two guards stationed at the entrance.

Not that they believed it would really happen. Many were insisting it was a ruse. It made no sense that the king would do this tonight (unless of course this was the night he'd been waiting for). And what of the rumor that John was not there? What of the claim he was impervious? They took bets: that his neck would split the blade; that the guards would be unable to find him—either because he had been taken away before the banquet or because he had escaped, shifted shape and slipped away as a mouse.

Grim and purposeful, Manean and his party cut through the lot of them. Manean had hoped to find the head jailer there, the Samaritan Jacim. He had been sent for, but as yet no one had been able to find him, which came as a great disappointment to the posted guards. Until they saw Jacim, they weren't sure what to believe, only that if it was true—if the Baptist's head was to be taken tonight—it was unthinkable that the task should fall to someone from outside the palace.

Still, they offered no objection when Manean asked which cistern the Baptist was being kept in. They showed him to the one.

The lid was wedged open to its usual height at night, an arm's length, but no sound could be heard from within, just the distant swells of revelry coming from the second level. The music had started up again, new vats of honey wine had been tapped, and more dishes served. Sweets.

Manean motioned to the guards. "Bring him out then." He watched as they took up the winch and the lid groaned wider and wider open. Back at the entrance, the slaves and guests all rose up on their toes, craning to see as the guards then descended with the torches, the light spiraling slowly down.

Manean thought of the morning's protesters, the bloodied one he'd told that John might not even be here. He thought of the cart headed north with Salome's horse, and of the Baptist's disciples just a mile upstream, even now counting the moments until they could see him again, as they'd been promised. He thought of the Essene, of his eyes, and of the faith this man had placed in him, and his soul shuddered. Again Manean looked to the black mouth of the cistern and for a moment imagined the guards emerging, confused, saying the prisoner was gone, vanished, they didn't know where. Even as he heard their boots ascending, he nursed his hope. That didn't sound like three pairs of feet, did it?

It wasn't. The guards were carrying him. His feet were dragging.

Manean would not have guessed it was the same man he had seen at Bethabara. That one had seemed so large. He had filled the valley with his magnificence. He had seemed to beam. This one here was bent, and gaunt, and pale. The hair and beard were shorn and patchy. His eyes were rolled; the lids spasmed in the light. The mouth was open slightly, but the tongue inside was languid, speechless.

"Is he asleep?"

They shrugged. As much.

He turned to the lector. "Does that matter?"

He had thought it might, that a sleeping neck might be too lissome, might not yield as easily.

The lector seemed unconcerned. He directed the guards to move the prisoner over to a space within the cloister, beneath the sconce where he could see. They dragged him by the arms. They knelt him on the marble and bound his hands behind him.

At the far end of the hall, the guards had turned to look as well. The gawkers had given up trying to push past. They stayed where they were, silent and passive—in disbelief.

The lector began rolling his shoulder, feeling the heft of the ax he'd chosen. Manean had the sense this was for show; only it took him a moment to realize why.

"Oh."

He handed over the purse he'd brought for this very purpose. The lector gave it a shake to make sure.

Just then a loud hiss sounded back at the far end of the hall. A lone figure was cutting through the onlookers, not running but moving swiftly and intently. Manean could see his outline against the light of the archway: the narrow waist, the billowing pants, and that curious plume of hair on top. It was the Samaritan, and he had a weapon in his hand—a spear, was it?

He was coming at them with such speed that for a moment Manean thought he might be there to challenge them, or challenge the lector. Sensing the same, the lector took firm hold of his ax, but the Samaritan stopped just short of them, heaving like a bull. He had a sheepskin flung over his shoulder.

"My prisoner. My charge." His eyes were simmering.

Manean took note of the weapon in his hand, a scimitar. The shaft was four feet long, the blade another three. As the Samaritan turned it over, the muscles in his arms shifted like iron cords beneath his flesh.

Manean turned back to Arman, who shrugged. It made no difference to him. He tucked the purse safely beneath his belt.

"I can see that you're properly compensated for—"

sssSSS! The Samaritan hissed again. He didn't want money.

With that, the guards, now much relieved, moved to clear the space. Manean and the lector stepped aside, but purposefully stood where they blocked the view of those at the far end, most of whom had turned away in any case.

The Samaritan went to John, who was still kneeling in the cloister. Gently, he wrapped his arm around his waist to move him—not far. A step farther out from the wall. He laid the sheepskin down a stride away.

Never having witnessed such a thing, Manean had thought they might lean the prisoner down against the stone to use the floor as a brace, but the Samaritan left him kneeling upright. He whispered something in his ear the rest could barely hear.

"Peace be to you, John. None here will see you again."

The two nearest guards seemed to agree with this, but even as they stood, nodding, the final blow had already begun. Swiftly and without warning, the Samaritan gave John a firm nudge below the nape with the tip of his weapon. By reflex the head turned up a notch, as if he might be fed a crust of bread, while in the same motion, the Samaritan now swept the scimitar in a full circle, sliding his right hand down to meet his left, letting the weapon swing on its weight, so fast and savage Manean could see only the sharp edge flashing in the torchlight, like a fiery thread headed for the neck.

It split clean through the matted hair, the muscles, and the vertebrae. The head flew like a gourd, tumbling once in the air before landing softly on the sheepskin, which had been laid there for that purpose.

The body, still upright, barely geysered from the neck. Still, the guards moved in with rags and bowls and tipped it forward gently, so as not to stain the marble.

⋛70⋚

Ascent

WHEN JOHN AWOKE, HE WAS STILL BESIDE THE RIVER. THE CHILD was standing above him, smiling as his shadow slid past John's face.

The sun was high; the sky, an azure dome, dangling wispy white clouds. John looked around and saw that no one else was there, other than the former king, who was upstream, kneeling by the water, washing his bowl.

John asked the child, "Where is your family?"

"My family is everywhere. Come baptize me, and I will show you."

John stood, and as they walked to the river's edge together, all the birds came around. They flew above their heads, singing, and the surface of the water began to sparkle and shine from all the fish now swimming up. And yet as the boy's little foot came near the water, the surface drew back. It pulled away and rose up.

John said, "I cannot baptize you if the water will not let me. What is your name?"

The child replied, "Did you not hear the birds? Did you not speak it yourself? My name is the name that you proclaim, Yahya. I am the Truth, and I have come to take your soul above."

He held out his hand. Up the river the former king stood to watch as John took the child's hand, and together they began to rise from where they were. The former king shielded his eyes. John and the child ascended above the river and the land, above the tallest of the cypress trees, but John could still see his body in the water. Already the vultures were circling.

"Why gaze on that?" said the child. He waved his hand, and the body was covered over in earth. John was glad, for he had loved his body. The grave was a mound beside the river.

They rose higher to where the land rolled soft and green beneath them and all the sheep grazing along the hillsides looked like white flowers. John understood as he looked down that these were not all the sheep. Some had fallen prey—to pestilence and to wolves. Some had been led astray, but these were here, and they would multiply and feed by the meadows of the kingdom, for the kingdom was here. It was not roiling at the veil. The veil had been torn down and burned away, and the light was pouring through and radiating all around them. The truth was being revealed even now, to those who would receive it.

"Praise be to thee, Yahya," the child said. "Well for thee and all who follow thee, and let them be.

"Be at peace, Yahya-Yuhana. Your page is written and shall be read, for they will speak of a man who was pure. They will speak of a man who was not afraid. They will speak of one who went into the desert and saw the truth, that all might be redeemed, and who bore witness to that truth, that it might be fulfilled. They shall speak of a voice that spoke the name of God to men and the names of men to God, and they shall praise thee, Yahya, and all who follow thee."

And they were ascending even higher now, above the clouds. John could only see the world around the edges, but he could hear the song of the Uthras, calling out to one another across the heavens, and he heard the voices of all things below, praying as one. He heard their song, stirring in his heart and in his voice. So he lifted his eyes and finally beheld in all its fullness the light which he had seen from the first, the light from which all light draws, and from which all life is born. He did not look back. He let go of the child's hand and ascended to that realm where only the purest of souls can go. He was baptized in its glory, and its radiance filled his heart and magnified it, and there within his heart he received all who had come before him and all who were to follow: all the fathers going back to Adam, and all the prophets and the sages; and all those whom he had loved and who loved him, his guardians and his keepers, who taught him and walked with him and showed him what was hidden, he received; those who found him and raised him, and taught their songs and ways to him and who instructed him by the river, he received; those who prayed that he might live, and ransomed him, and planted him, she who carried him and bore him twice, and he who gave his life that he might live, John received; and all those who were still living in the world, his brothers and his sisters and all his kin, and the one who kissed his infant feet and nursed him, he received; and all whom he had taught and all whom he baptized, and all those who wept for him; she who grieved by giving bread, and he who grieved by remembering him to others, John received; and all who worship life by bearing witness to its triumph, by giving all that they've been given until their arms are empy, John remembers and receives and will receive for as long as life prevails.

Epilogues

HEROD ANTIPAS RULED FOR THREE MORE YEARS BEFORE HIS fears were finally realized. Not surprisingly, it was the unresolved border dispute near Gadara that served as pretext. Antipas and Aretas had been amassing armies on both sides for a while beforehand. Antipas's new friend Lucius Vitellius proved less supportive than might have been hoped, while Herod Philip turned out to be surprisingly generous. However, it was a renegade brigade from Philip's ranks that apparently informed the Nabataeans of the strategies and deployments on the Jewish side, resulting in the complete decimation of Antipas's army almost as soon as the battle was joined. The rout was so quick, so thorough, and so humiliating that more than a few onlookers took it that the Lord was finally punishing Antipas for how he had treated John the Baptist.

Forces were aligning against him back in Rome as well. His ally Tiberias had died and was succeeded, as expected, by Caius Caligula, a close friend of Agrippa, Herodias's ne'er-do-well brother. The proof of the friendship was put in evidence soon enough when Caligula made Agrippa governor of the territories formerly ruled by Philip, Varus, and Lysanias.

Soon after the devastation of Antipas's army, Damascus fell as well, and this proved to be his real undoing. Rome had lost all patience with him. At Agrippa's urging, Caligula stripped Antipas of his title and territories and then sent him to live out his days in exile, just as his brother Archelaus had, first in Lyon, Gaul, and then in Spain. Herodias went with him.

Agrippa was put in charge of Galilee and Peraea, and he served well enough that even after the assassination of Caligula in A.D. 41, the new emperor, Claudius, turned over Samaria and Judaea to him as well, making Agrippa, in both name and deed, the first king over all of Palestine since the death of his grandfather Herod the Great.

He was also the last. Following his death in A.D. 46 (to worms), Judaea reverted to the governance of Roman procurators, who ruled for one more generation before the Zealots, still thriving in anger, stoked the rebellion of A.D. 73. Rome replied decisively, destroying Jerusalem and reducing the Holy Temple to rubble. It was never rebuilt.

Salome had met her end by then as well. She married an uncle (yet another Philip). According to legend, the Sepphoris river had frozen over during one unusually cold winter. While she was inadvisably crossing in her litter, the ice gave way. Salome fell in, was stunned by the freezing water, floundered, and was decapitated by the jagged drifts. Her body sank to the bottom of the river, never to be found. Her head was delivered to her mother and stepfather in Gaul.

Only Manean appears to have escaped fate's retribution, and only by acts of extreme contrition. Jesus survived John by a year, but his ministry continued thanks to the efforts of his most devoted disciples. On the road to Ptolemais, Manean heard them speaking and converted soon after. He was baptized and followed them to Antioch, where he helped found the first Christian church and became one of the earliest and most influential teachers of the gospel of Jesus.

According to that gospel, Jesus spoke one final time of John. He had journeyed into the wilderness with three of his disciples, Peter,

James, and another named John, none of whom had been with Jesus at Dalmanutha. While descending Mount Hermon, the disciples had asked him: If he was the Chosen One (as their experience that day had seemed to confirm), then where was Elijah? Why hadn't Elijah come first, as had been foretold?

"And so he has," Jesus replied, "only they did not know him, but did with him as they pleased. Just as they will do with the Son of Man."

Hearing his answer, the disciples had no doubt that Jesus was referring to John the Baptist.

As for John's disciples, they endured much grief and disbelief and anger, together and in solitude, but nothing in what had taken place at Machaerus—or before—caused them to abandon their faith in him or the practices and the truths that he had taught them. They buried him in a secret place and directly in the ground. They said the prayer to the dead for him, and they gave bread to the hungry.

Some, like Andrew, became followers and disciples of Jesus. Others did not, but took on students, who took on students of their own, who continued to expound John's teachings and his example. When Jesus' disciple Paul traveled to Corinth and to Ephesus, he encountered there many followers of John, none of whom had yet heard of Jesus.

However, the Johannites did not ultimately flourish as the Christians did, perhaps because they never claimed John to be their savior or redeemer. They honored him as one who spoke the truth, a "bringer of light" whose words, whose example, and whose purity of spirit served for them as both an inspiration and aspiration, but they did not ever worship John. For them, the way was his, not him.

So they carried on in pockets and sects, particularly in the basin of the Tigris and the Euphrates, where they have been known by many names and in many variations—as Sabaean, Nazoraean, Mughtasilah, and Elkasaite.

Today only one of these sects still remains, the Mandaeans of Iraq—though their survival is more a function of constancy and stubbornness than profusion. They never have accepted converts. Their way of life is essentially ascetic. Their beliefs are both arcane and, in certain instances, hostile to those of their Christian, Jewish, and Muslim neighbors. Jesus is judged by many of them to have been a deceiver, as was Moses. According to their tradition, John died peacefully beside a river and was buried there.

Still, because of their devotion to him and to the line of patriarchs leading back through Noah to Adam, the Mandaeans have long been considered "people of the book." That is, they are seen as recognizing the same supreme God of Abraham as do the Jews, Christians, and Muslims, and to subscribe to the same basic narrative that traces from the Old Testament to the New and on into the Koran.

Under this basic protection, they lived more or less peacefully in the southern regions of Iraq until very recently, paying the same extra tithe as the Jews and Christians who live there, and acknowledging the legal subservience of their faith to Islam.

Immediately following the fall of Saddam Hussein, however, all power and influence reverted back to the traditional leaders and arbiters of Muslim law, the mullahs. One of these, the prominent Shiite leader and jurist Ayatollah al-Hakeem, only months before he was assassinated in August 2003, used his restored authority to declare that the Mandaeans were not in fact "people of the book." They were, as such, deemed unclean and therefore subject to various forms of legal persecution, including forced conversion, stoning, rape, and even burning.

Prior to the American-led invasion, sixty thousand Mandaeans lived in Iraq. As of this writing, fewer than five thousand remain, most having fled to Jordan and Syria to live as refugees.

If their current plight elicits any shame or anger, that the last surviving truly Gnostic faith on earth may die off on our watch and by the hand of our neglect, the reader is encouraged to petition his or her own government and ask that safe and legal haven be provided for the Mandaeans as soon as possible. The reader may also take heart that however scattered their members, however dire their situation, this is not the first time the Mandaeans have faced extinction, and that as traditional dwellers of the desert, and as a people avowed against the trappings of all worldliness, they are more accustomed than others might be to the various deprivations that come with living under persecution, in poverty, and as strangers in exile.

By all accounts, their faith remains intact, the same in practice as it has been since the time of John and long before that. Provided they can find water that is clean and flowing, they still purify themselves according to the laws of the sect. They dress and eat according to the same laws. They continue to look to Adam as the first man to awake, to hear the truth, and to ascend. They continue to look to John as the greatest of exemplars. The names of his fathers and forefathers are the names of theirs. They pray the prayers he taught and that he himself was taught. Their sacred language is the same. And despite the hostility of the world which holds them captive, and always has, the abiding purpose of their worship—to be pure and to be ready—remains unchanged, as does its abiding object: the eternal triumph of light over dark and of life over death.

Dramatis Personae

Part One: The Forerunners

Abijah—given name of the order of the Jewish priesthood assigned by King David to serve the eighth turn of service at the Temple. There were twenty-four orders, or courses, in all.

Achiabus—a cousin of Herod.

Alaric—captain of a Gallic brigade under Herod.

Alexander—eldest son of Herod the Great by Mariamne.

Alexandra—Mariamne's mother.

Alexis—second husband of Salome (I).

Anne—mother of Mary.

Antipater—son of Herod the Great by the commoner Doris.

Archelaus—eldest surviving son of Herod the Great, by Malthace; older brother of Antipas; ethnarch of Judaea during John's boyhood.

Aristobulus (II)—second eldest son of Herod the Great by Mariamne.

Ashabel—one of the brethren of the course of Abijah.

Cleopatra—queen of Egypt, lover of Mark Antony.

Eleazer—High Priest of the Temple at the time of John's birth.

Eli ben Kozar—student of Judas and Matthias.

Elizabeth—mother of John, wife of Zechariah.

Elohim—counselor to Eleazar.

Gamla—one of the brethren of the course of Abijah.

Herod the Great—King of Judaea at the time of John's birth.

Jaozar—one of the brethren of the course of Abijah.

Joachim—father of Mary.

John (Yohannan, Yahya, Yahya-Yuhana)—a prophet, birth son of Elizabeth and Zecharia, adopted son of the tribe of Subba living to the east of the Jordan River.

John Hyrcanus—the last lawful king of the Hasmonaean line.

Jonathan—High Priest, brother of Mariamne, drowned by Herod's order at Jericho.

Joseph—first husband of Salome (I).

Judas and **Matthias**—influential rabbis in Jerusalem.

Lilyukh—hermit and seer in Judea.

Mark Antony—Roman general and close adviser to Caesar.

Mary—cousin of Elizabeth, foster child of Elizabeth and Zechariah.

Mariamne—most beloved wife of Herod the Great, of the Hasmonaean line.

Menahem—an Essene seer and adviser to Herod the Great; also father of Manean.

Pannaeus—chief steward to Herod the Great.

Ruben—an elder priest in the course of Abijah, from Hebron.

Salome (I)—sister of Herod the Great.

Simeon—chief priest from the course of Abijah.

Sufnai the Lilith (Zahara'il)—spiritual midwife to Elizabeth, bride of Hibil-Ziwa.

Tab-Yumin—a younger priest from the course of Abijah.

Zecharia (Old Father)—father of John, priest from the course of Abijah.

Zerai—one of the brethren of the course of Abijah.

Part Two: Youth

Ahura—chieftain of the Subba.

Antipas (the tetrarch, Herod Antipas, Herod, the king)—son of Herod the Great by Malthace; younger brother of Archelaus;

tetrarch of Galilee and Peraea at the time of John's mission; husband to Phassaelis, husband to Herodias; stepfather to Salome.

Anush (the Uthra, aka Enoch)—an early prophet of the third generation after Adam, spiritual guardian and teacher of John.

Aretas—king of Nabataea, the nation bordering Peraea to the east, site of Petra.

Azharan (Azha)—brother and most loyal disciple of John.

Darawish—a brotherhood of ascetics living in Harran.

Elijah—early Jewish prophet of the wilderness who denounced the marriage of Ahab and Jezebel, and who challenged and defeated Jezebel's pagan priesthood before ascending into heaven east of the Jordan; promised by the prophet Malachi to return before the great and dreadful day of the Lord.

Herodias—granddaughter of Herod the Great; granddaughter of Salome; granddaughter of Mariamne; sister of Agrippa; wife of Philip (II); wife of Herod Antipas; mother of Salome (II).

Herod Philip—second eldest surviving son of Herod the Great, tetrarch of Trachonitis.

Hibil-Ziwa—a light being, creator of heaven and earth; savior spirit of mankind.

Kharsand—a Nasurai and eldest disciple of John.

Manean—stepbrother, childhood friend of Herod Antipas; son of Menahem.

Nazarite—any given Jewish male avowed, either permanently or for a set time, to live separate and wholly unto the Lord, to drink no ferment, not to come into contact with death, to let no blade upon the hair of his head.

Par'am (the Perfect)—a Nasurai of the tribe of Subba, east of the Jordan; earthly guardian and teacher of John.

Perida—a fellow Essene at Qumram and eventual elder disciple of John's.

Pharisees—the most popular party in the Holy Land, comprised of teachers, merchants, scribes; the self-proclaimed party of the people and foremost protectors of the law.

Phasaelis—daughter of Aretas, first wife of Herod Antipas.

Philip (II)—son of Herod the Great, grandson of the High Priest Simon, first husband of Herodias.

Sabinus—Roman procurator of Syria.

Sadducees—the wealthiest and most powerful party in Judaea, comprised of judges, high counselors, landowners, and priests.

Subba—a small tribe of potters living east of the Jordan, distant descendants of Zoroastrian and Babylonian worship.

Taraneh—wife of Ahura.

Zealots (Sacaari)—most radical and seditious party in Israel; avowed enemies of Rome and all who did business with them.

Part Three: The Mission

Andrew—a fisherman, brother of Simon, disciple of John; disciple of Jesus.

Annhar—the twenty-ninth disciple and only female disciple of John; a former maiden of the temple in Zoan.

Benyamin—a disciple of John, formerly a priest at the Temple.

Galgula—a leading Zealot.

Ismael—a disciple of John, formerly a priest at the Temple.

Jaquif—a disciple of John, formerly a priest.

Joshua ben Sekar—a Pharisee and former student of Judas and Matthias.

Kanufar—a disciple of John from Nabalaea.

Lazarus—a Pharisee, living in Bethany.

Nathaniel—a fisherman from Bethsaida.

Neri (the Swift)—a disciple of John, the smallest and swiftest.

Nidba—a disciple of John, formerly a Darawish.

Pontius Pilate—Roman procurator of Judaea after Coponius.

Samuel—a disciple of John.

Shurbel—a disciple of John, formerly a Darawish.

Simon—head of Andrew's family, brother of Andrew, disciple of Jesus.

Temiculus—renowned Roman caterer.

Yaquif—a disciple of John and former Darawish.

Part Four: The Messiah

Faisool—a eunuch in the court of Herodias.

Jacob ben Dama—a Herodian and Sadducee, procurator for the Temple.

Jesus (the Nazarene, the Messiah, Yeshu Messiah)—the Messiah from Galilee; son of Mary.

Livia—a courtier to Herodias, twin sister of Priopy.

Priopy—courtier to Herodias, twin sister of Livia.

Simon-Matthew—a former Essene and current priest at the Temple; adviser to Manean.

Part Five: Prison

Aulus—the as-yet unmarried son of Lucius Vitellius.

Chuza—chief financial minister to Herod Antipas; husband of Joanna.

Jacim—warden of Macheras; a Samaritan.

Naaman—governor at Macheras.

Tholmai—captain of the brigade of spearmen who arrest John.

Part Six: The Banquet

Arman—a lector to Vitellius.

Aulus—son of Vitellius.

Flebus—assistant to Temiculus.

Joanna—wife of Chuza, follower of Jesus.

Lucius Vitellius—Roman proconsul.

Marcellus—chief publican under Lucius Vitellius.

Pithon—assistant to Temiculus.

Theortes—satrap (or father of the satrap) of Media.

Author's Note

Raised as I was in the Roman Catholic faith, my acquaintance with John the Baptist began when I was very young, most likely with gospel readings in church and the homilies that followed. Those early encounters can't have been too impressive, though, since up until the writing of this book, my sense of John was curiously vague, especially when one considers the vivid imagery with which all the evangelists describe him and the equally vivid language that colors much of his speech. It's possible that I was already smitten, experiencing the typical aversion that foretells a future preoccupation, but I can't say I really understood John back then or the need for John. I didn't see why Jesus, or anyone, should need a precursor, and the behavior of this one in particular didn't make sense to me. He seemed more like a caricature than a real person, too extreme, too belligerent, but at the same time much too compliant; too willing to play such a subsidiary role. I just don't think I ever really bought him.

Three decades later the confluence of two separate streams in my life brought me back to the Jordan. For several years my wife and I struggled to start a family. It was, for the time it lasted, an unremitting hardship that reacquainted me with the pew and eventually opened my ears to the plight of Zechariah and Elizabeth, another childless couple who late in life became parents to John.

The second current was music, which has been leading me by the ear for most of my life. Bach and whole slew of others kept referring me to the Magnificat, the name given Mary's joyful prayer of pregnant thanksgiving on reuniting with her older cousin Elizabeth, who also had been mysteriously visited with child. Certain traditions place the prayer in Elizabeth's mouth as well, though again, I can't say that I was ever so moved by the words, which devolve into the boilerplate "God hath defended Israel" rhetoric that the two silent characters in the scene eventually gave their lives to dispel.

It was the moment immediately preceding the famous prayer that finally caught my eye—the "quickening"—where upon Mary's entrance to her home, Elizabeth exclaims:

For behold, when the voice of your greeting came to my ears, the babe in my womb leapt for joy [Luke 1:44].

That kick—the simple beauty of that alluded detail, implying a moment of unspoken communication between the unborn John and Jesus—is what first truly sparked my interest.

I have a close lifelong friend who is a composer. For years coming on decades we had wanted to collaborate. John's story occurred to me as a possibility. The musical spirit of the Magnificat (also known as Mary's Canticle) is a given; no passage in history has been set to music more often. But as I looked at the several incidents surrounding it—John's kick, Zechariah's encounter with the angel Gabriel, John's reappearance at the Jordan—I was struck time and again not only by the beauty of the scenes but by the specifically musical invitation that they all offered. Around this time I'd been listening to Heinrich Schütz's *The Last Seven Words of Christ* and *The Story of the Ascension*, the texts of which also served as inspiration to me, insofar as both represent what might be called composite renderings of incidents mentioned in all four Gospels. My initial idea was, for the purpose of providing my friend and collaborator a libretto, to attempt a similar sort of composite rendering, but that the incident at question would be the life of John the Baptist.

Simple enough. I got out my Bible and searched the four Gospels for any and all mentions of John, snipped them out, and started arranging them, ordering and editing and reordering them, fitting them together just to see if something like a story, or at the very least a serviceable libretto, might emerge.

More than a story, a world emerged, all surrounding a character far different from the one who'd been struggling so unsuccessfully for my attention in church. Even there in the Gospels, a closer and more sustained look at John revealed previously unseen wrinkles and incongruities that all cast doubt on the portrait that Christian orthodoxy had been painting for me. My questions quickly drew me beyond the bounds of church canon—to histories, to ancient commentaries, and then into the shadowy world of apocryphal and Gnostic Gospels— and it has been my great good fortune to live in the present time, on the crest of the ecumenical explosion wrought by technology, scholarship, and the discovery of the Nag Hammadi library, all of which has helped broaden our view not only of the early Christian era but of what constitutes the sacred. The wider I cast my net, the more questions I encountered, and the more I was drawn to the charisma and the mystery of John, whose features only seemed to deepen the longer I looked at him.

Sadly for the listeners of the world, as my own interest was luring me further into John's story, my musical collaborator was pulled away to other more immediate obligations. Happily, by then I had before me a glittering heap of incident, commentary, legend, and scripture, all of a woven complexity and length that not even the most sadistic kapellmeister could ask a choir to sing or a congregation to sit through. So was born in earnest this more comprehensive effort to approach history's most fathomless story once again, but by turning an unwavering eye on the life of the man who sets it all in motion.

At no point did I have anything like a traditional biography in mind or some "search for the historical John." As potentially fascinating as such an undertaking might be, I recognized early on that too much sand, too much wind, and frankly too many different agendas have treated themselves to John's name and legend for us to pretend now that we could ever reconstruct with any degree of certainty the paths he walked, the precise mechanisms of his influence, or the absolute nature of his relationship with his followers, his disciples, and Jesus.

Moreover, the deeper I delved into the material at hand—all the different scriptures and anecdotes, images, pericopes, art, artifacts, and histories—the clearer it became that to confine myself to the province of what really happened would be to deprive myself, and the reader, of far too much beauty, too much possibility, too much of what had drawn me to John in the first place. Worse, it risked missing the point of such an exploration by obscuring and ignoring the larger truths that might be revealed to us by John if only we set aside the fetish for literal truth and allowed his story to come down to us through the centuries, to recognize how it has grown and evolved and survived in the disparate prayers and imaginations of so many distant, different, and far-flung seekers.

I tried to cast my net as wide as I could, then, across a variety of different disciplines and creeds and media. Among the academicians, I relied most heavily on the research and scholarship of Alfred Edersheim (*The Temple*), E. S. Drower (*The Mandaeans of Iraq and Iran*), G. R. S. Mead (*Gnostic John the Baptizer*), Harold Hoehner (*Herod Antipas*), Ron Cameron (*The Other Gospels*), Stefano Zuffi (*Gospel Figures in Art*), and Elaine Pagels (*The Gnostic Gospels*), each of whom in his or her way helped provide insight and perspective on the wide array of "primary" material to which I turned. This included the Koran, the Protoevangelium of James, the Gospel of Thomas, the Prolog of Ohrid, the writing of the Ebionites, the Nazarenes, the Pseudo-Clementines; also Ephraem, Serapion, *The Golden Legend*, and even the Akasha (as read by Levi Dowling). I availed myself just as liberally of the works of many more patently literary writers—including Ernst Renan (*The Life of Jesus*), Stéphane Mallarmé (*Hérodiade*), Gustave Flaubert (*Hérodias*), Khalil Gibran (*The Prophet* and *John the Baptist*), and Oscar Wilde (*Salome*)—as well as countless painters, sculptors, and composers, whose meditations can only have been completely imagined. Among these were Caravaggio, Leonardo da Vinci, Jacques Stella, Poussin, Rembrandt, Philippe de Champagne, Juan Martinez Montañez, J. S. Bach, Orlando Gibson, and Arvo Pärt, but there were many more, of course, and none of these lists is nearly exhaustive. Basically, I sought out anyone who might have anything to offer about John or any of the characters surrounding him. I looked, I listened, I read, and in those instances where I found the insight to be of particular value or beauty, I used it, quite often shamelessly. I openly and happily admit this.

Yet indebted as I am to all these artists, scholars, witnesses, and scribes, and as grateful as I am for the light each shed, the truth is that the vast majority of the material in this book was drawn from just three main sources: the canonical Gospels, the histories of Josephus, and the sacred scriptures and oral traditions of the Mandaeans.

The seminal role of the Gospels I have already mentioned, not only in introducing me to John but in providing the basic sequence of the scenes with which most churchgoers should be somewhat familiar: the infancy story; the incidents of John's mission prior to his meeting Jesus; the baptism of Jesus; the conferral of authority to Jesus; and finally John's arrest, imprisonment, and execution. Taken together, these constitute what might be called the orthodox take on John, though even they contain much that should trouble the conscience, and pique the curiosity, of even the most devout Christian believer.

Josephus, a near contemporary of John, provides further fodder inasmuch as his accounts portray the missions of John and Jesus as being completely independent, and in fact accord a slightly greater significance to John.* Of even greater value—to this project, at least— is the generously detailed and dramatic portrait Josephus paints of the cultural and political climate that gave rise to John: the state of Judaism at this time; the character of its various sects; the nature and influence of the Roman occupation; and most important, the Herodian dynasty that presided throughout. Indeed, among the more gratuitous and unexpected pleasures of telling John's story was the attendant responsibility of providing the reader some sense of who the Herods were, which meant including a tale of dynastic intrigue, treachery, murder, vengeance, and lust that need bow to none in all recorded history. Specifically at issue, and worthy of the most Technicolor of treat-

---

* This assumes the scholarly consensus that the references to Jesus having been "the Christ" and having risen from the dead are obvious interpolations, added hundreds of years after Josephus's death.

ments, was the deeply conflicted relationship that existed between the various Herods and their adopted faith of Judaism, wherein they time and again found themselves drawn to, and intoxicated by, the "purest" of Jews (the High Priest Hyrcanus, the Essenes, Mariamne, Herodias, and John), only to end up slaughtering them almost every time, no better example than the infamous, and still jarringly capricious, incident that was said to have ended the Baptist's earthly life.

But even if one grants the extraordinary power and appeal of both the Gospels and Josephus, it was the third and final constituent of the present account, the Mandaean material, that ultimately committed me to the task. The Mandaean relationship to John has been touched upon elsewhere, though, given the arcane nature of the faith, is surely of a kind that discourages any brief description. (I would urge anyone with an interest in John or in Gnosticism to go read firsthand the Mandaean material, most of which is readily accessible online.) The most tangible and apprehensible elements of that relationship, however, are to be found in the various Mandaean prayer books, in their traditional stories, but especially in The Book of John (Sidra d Yahya), a compendium of meditations that address many of chapters and aspects of John's life that the Gospels do not: the broader circumstances of John's birth and infancy, for instance; his upbringing, his early revelations, his assumptions of the prophet's mantle, his teaching, his family, and his relationship with Jesus.

Such material was obviously to be approached with great caution, seeing as much of it is highly esoteric in nature, employing unfamiliar conventions and often impenetrable symbolism derived from a kind of second sight that regards most of what we would call real as false and most of what we might call metaphysical or allegorical as true. For the Mandaeans, as for all Gnostics, the truth is ultimately to be derived from a deepened understanding of the Self. As such, the primary function of prophets like John, and the personal sagas of prophets like John, are to serve that understanding, to stand as emblems and reflections of the aspirant's own spiritual progress. The Mandaean contribution to my understanding of John's biography was not negligible then—I used every scrap I could, in fact—but its greater value to me was in portraying John as something other than a functionary within a Judeo-Christian narrative of sin and redemption. Rather, he is presented as a vessel of pure insight, an incursion of eternity into history, a window into a higher world of truth and light. He is not a harbinger or a forerunner. He is a teacher, a bringer of light, and an example.

If the Gospels and much of the orthodox literature that followed may be seen as providing a kind of John thesis, the Book of John offered a clear antithesis, a glimpse of the prophet from the other side of the Jordan. In so doing, it helped serve as a reminder that the evangelical mission of prophecy is only the public face of what is an essentially private and basically inexpressible experience, one that is therefore liable to radical misinterpretation and abuse. Still, much the same as with the Christian Gnostic documents I'd been reading, I found that if I squinted at them long enough and listened hard enough, the Mandaean books and prayers did begin to fit in with the rest, striking notes that often sounded dissonant in context of the larger harmony, but that by the same token served to deepen it as well and to breathe life into a character and into a story that, for me, had previously lacked human dimension.

This, then, was the task I set myself: not to invent, not to hypothesize or imagine what *else* might have been, but to try to combine and distill what was already there; to take what we know, take what we have found, what we have been told and what we have imagined to be so and try to give it some coherence; to ascribe privilege to no one source over another, but to assume that all contain elements of truth, all contain elements of fiction, and that all could be used to serve the same end: of informing a single, comprehensive account of a story that remarkably no one had yet tried to tell, at least not in its entirety, and never for its own purpose, this despite the fact that its protagonist is the first real character mentioned in all four Gospels, the one who sets in motion what is, at least by measure of influence, the most significant drama in the history of the Western world.

Given the diversity, and in certain cases, the mutual antagonism, of source material, one of the persistent challenges of trying to write that single account was finding ways to reconcile all the conflicts that arose between them, not just matters of chronology and incident, but of philosophy, dogma, and style—to forge a single, unified story, that is, but to present it in a way that still managed to reflect the unique perspectives, the voice, and music of its various inspirations. Equally important was recognizing that *certain* of the conflicts at question, such as whether Jesus was the Messiah or what is even meant by that word, weren't ultimately for the story to resolve but rather to incorporate as part of its inherent drama. It was, after all, these very conflicts and the troubling questions they posed that helped sustain me through the years it took to tame (if barely) all the material at question:

- If John's appointed purpose was to testify to Christ, and if he accepted this role as willingly as we are led to believe, why did he continue to have followers after Jesus' ministry began?
- Did he consider his mission finished at the time of his arrest?
- Was John simply used by the Christian evangelists and shoehorned into the role of Elijah in order to justify Jesus' messianic claim? Or is John—John's anger, John's austerity, and his stubbornness—the natural and necessary precursor to the gospel of love and forgiveness that his "cousin" was subsequently to offer?
- What exactly prompted his doubts in prison? Were those doubts ever answered?
- Finally, and as always, how are we to assess the fact that so many of John's, as well as Jesus', admonitions are offered in expectation of a kingdom that has yet ostensibly to arrive?

As essential as these questions may be, I was under no illusion that I, in the course of telling John's story, would be offering any definitive answers. That happy burden should probably fall on the reader. Moreover, it seemed to me that this book would never have been worth the effort of writing if the problems it posed, and the solutions it provided, were of only historical or theological or interest.

Our old friends the Swedenborgians do well in reminding us that "sacred" texts acquire their authority not so much from their origins as from the ongoing pertinence of their every part to some aspect of the reader's own interior journey. The question was, What aspect of my own experience did the story of John the Baptist instruct? Sin, surely. Repentance, yes. Death, as always. But there was one more theme that, for me, functioned as a kind of prism through which John could be viewed and that held out the promise of transforming his story from mere argument into something more universally—that is to say, more personally—relevant: doubt.

John's vision, the gift he possessed that set him apart from his fellowmen and from us, was his apprehension of a clear and imminent heavenly light, a light we may deduce he first glimpsed inside his mother's womb. Ironically, though his was a vision that few others can claim to share—that none, according to Jesus, had so far attained in his day—it is in John's *relationship* to the Light that we may have the best chance of understanding him, insofar as we all experience the same glimmering of our own purpose. Few men in history have ever had their roles laid out for them as explicitly and as persistently as John the Baptist (at least according to the sources). Foretold in the Books of Malachi and Isaiah, assigned by the angel Gabriel to both his parents, shown him briefly in his mother's womb, predicted in his father's benediction, instilled in him during his upbringing, suggested to him again by lawyerly Pharisees and Sadducees, and then fulfilled in his encounter with Jesus, John was, from the moment of his conception, a prophet and a prophecy fulfilled. But as such, Jehovah's warning to Moses can never have been far from John's mind:

> But the prophet who presumes to speak in my name words which
> I have not commanded him, or who speaks in the name of other
> gods, that prophet shall die [Deut. 18:20].

As insistent as John's calling may have been, he must *by that same token* have encountered grave doubts about whether he was answering it properly, whether he could, whether he wanted to, whether he should. Indeed, even the Gospels, which would otherwise seem to gain nothing by informing us of John's doubts, do. "Go and ask him," he tells his followers while he himself is in prison, "is he [Jesus] the one, or should we wait for another?"

Explicit in that moment of uncertainty are questions that lie at the heart of Christianity. Implicit are questions that lie at the hearts of all men and women everywhere: Who am I that this should be my life? Have I done right? Is my purpose fulfilled? Christian orthodoxy would have us think of John as the first happy martyr of his own self, who would without qualm step aside, accept his own diminishment, be content merely to point and then recede. But a closer look at history and scripture, canonical and non-, reveal a character of extraordinary independence, who rightly grappled with his purpose every step in his outstanding path, and who therefore might serve to remind us that acceptance means nothing without resistance. Likewise, faith—a faith of any kind, whether placed in something as exalted as a kingdom come or something as commonplace as one's own identity—is born from a constant bed of mystery and doubt.

So it was that John's story should rightly—or rightly to me, at least—find its conclusion in the shadow of the cistern cell. If all begins with that kick in Elizabeth's womb—the spontaneous dance at an unborn, inborn vision of grace—all leads ultimately to Machaerus, to John alone, awaiting his answer as he awaits his almost certain death. These were the two poles of my concern and of my focus. The book in hand is a meditation born from each. It is the path I've managed to find between them and the horrible, strange, and beautiful landscape surrounding.

Finally, and as always, I could never have found that path without the ongoing and generous support of friends, family, and foundations, whose various expressions of faith have been so crucial to this effort.

In particular let me thank my father and mother, my brother and my sister, my wife, my son, and my daughter. You are all, in a word, why. Thanks also to my agent, Sarah Chalfant, for her commitment and patience, and to all the people at the Wylie Agency, but especially Edward Orloff; to Alane Mason, whose eye for the diamond in the rough remains a godsend, and to all the people who work with her at W. W. Norton, but especially Denise Scarfi, Alexandra Heifetz, Francine Kass, and Anna Oler. My thanks to the New York Society Library, for haven; to John Ziegler; to Kate Philips for the extraordinary generosity of her reading attention, as well as her meticulous taste, and eye; to the John Simon Guggenheim Memorial Foundation, for the tremendous help and service it provides; Chang-rae Lee; Claire Messud; Adam Guettel (on three separate counts); and finally Marvin Barrett, whose passing has injected into these efforts a note of regret, that I was not able to finish this book before he could read it. I can think of no one whose opinion I would have been keener to hear or whose confidence I could more have hoped to justify.